THE
HOUSE
OF PAIN

THE
HOUSE
OF PAIN

FRANKLIN ALLEN LEIB

A TOM DOHERTY ASSOCIATES BOOK
NEW YORK

This book is dedicated to my dear sister Marian,
who fought a harder fight than I ever did, and won it.

This is a work of fiction. All the characters and events portrayed
in this novel are either fictitious or are used fictitiously.

A Forge Book
Published by Tom Doherty Associates, Inc.
175 Fifth Avenue
New York, NY 10010

Forge® is a registered trademark of Tom Doherty Associates, Inc.

Library of Congress Cataloging-in-Publication Data
Leib, Franklin Allen, date
    The house of pain / Franklin Allen Leib. —1st ed.
        p.   cm.
    "A Tom Doherty Associates book."
    ISBN 0–312–86616–X
    I. Title.
PS3562.E447H78   1999
813'.54—dc21   98–44609

First Edition: January 1999

Printed in the United States of America

0 9 8 7 6 5 4 3 2 1

Acknowledgments

I am not an attorney but have read extensively in Connecticut law and procedure, which are somewhat unique in the United States. I was greatly assisted by three distinguished members of the Connecticut bar, Bernard Green, Peter Penczer, and Mark Stern. Thank you, gentlemen. None of these lawyers reviewed the manuscript, so all errors are mine.

I

CRAZY JOHNNY

1

AT THREE-FIFTEEN in the afternoon cars began arriving at Westport Country Day School to collect pupils. Most were Volvos and Mercedes and BMWs; WCDS was exclusive and expensive. In the middle of the line of cars that snaked back from the front of the Norman-style stone mansion to the modern classroom blocks nearer the gate was a tan Chrysler minivan, dented and dirty. Many of the mothers behind the wheels of their European cars would later remark that it seemed out of place, but not one picked up her cell phone to alert the school's considerable security force.

It was sunny and crisp; early fall in New England at its finest. Boys and girls in blue and white uniforms played soccer and field hockey on the spacious lawns. Students with no athletic or other after-school commitments drifted out of the school singly or in small groups, craning their necks around looking for the right ride among so many similar-looking automobiles.

Sally Collins rushed out just at three-thirty. Dark-haired and blue-eyed, very pretty at fifteen years old, Sally wore a uniform of blue pleated skirt, white blouse and a blue blazer with the WCDS arms on the pocket. She pushed her long hair impatiently over her shoulder as the wind lifted it. She walked down the line of cars toward the van that was inching forward with the other vehicles as cars in front took kids aboard and pulled away. Sally saw her mother, Jane, standing beside their gray Volvo wagon and waved.

The van halted as Sally approached. The side door slid open

and two men dropped to the ground, grabbed Sally by either arm and boosted her into the vehicle. Her single loud shriek was cut off by the slamming door as the van pulled out and sped away, side-swiping a Mercedes 560 SEL as it went.

Jane Collins ran forward to stand where the van had been. She gripped her long blond hair and keened softly, struck dumb by what she had seen. When the realization finally hit she screamed a single word, her daughter's name, over and over until a large woman she didn't know put her arms around her and made her sit on a bench near the gap in the line left by the van.

The driver of the car behind Jane's Volvo picked up her car phone and called 911.

2

EDWARD COLLINS WAS in a room full of lawyers at his office in Westport, trying to close a deal to sell an office building. They had been at it for hours but the damn deal wouldn't close. There was a knock on the door and Edward's secretary entered. Edward looked up with annoyance; the last thing he needed was any interruption that might give the increasingly reluctant purchaser an excuse to walk away. "What?" he said sharply.

"Your wife," Shirley whispered.

"I'll call her as soon as we finish in here."

"She seemed very upset," Shirley insisted.

He sighed as he stood up. "Please continue with the agreement, gentlemen. This will only take a moment, I'm sure." He followed Shirley out of the conference room and went into his own office. He snatched up the phone and hit the light. "Jane, I'm in the middle of a very tricky negotiation—"

"Well, *fuck* your negotiation," Jane screamed. "Your daughter's just been kidnapped."

Edward fell into his chair, nearly upsetting it. "Tell me what happened," he said gently. "I'm sorry, baby."

Edward apologized to the lawyers and his purchaser with a brief explanation and drove straight home to the large house on Long Island Sound he had bought for his family in the middle of the booming eighties. Edward sat with his distraught wife on a couch before the fireplace, holding her hands as she told the story yet again. There was so little to tell. The minivan was tan, or maybe yellow. The two men were white and appeared young. Sally screamed as they pushed her inside, then there was the terrible finality of the door slamming shut and the van speeding away, leaving the damaged Mercedes rocking in its wake.

Edward made himself a drink, a dark scotch, and insisted Jane take a little herself. He placed the drink in her hand as the phone rang. They looked at each other, startled by the commonplace sound. Edward crossed the room and picked up the instrument on the second ring. "Hello."

"Mr. Collins?" The voice was young and scared.

"This is Edward Collins."

"We have your daughter. We want a half million in cash. We'll give you three days to arrange that, then call you with instructions."

"Half a million? What makes you think I have half a million in cash—"

"We know you have it. Fuck with us and the bitch dies."

Edward heard the phone on the other end rattle as if it had been dropped on a table. "Listen, you—"

"Daddy?" Sally's tiny voice, sounding like she had at five years old. "Daddy, I'm *scared.*"

Edward felt his wind knocked out as if he'd been kicked in the chest. "Sweetheart, we'll do whatever we have to. We'll get you home."

The male voice returned, but it was no longer tinged with fear. "Three days, asshole. No cops, no bullshit, just half a million in cash, old bills. We'll call again."

Edward put the phone back into its cradle, gently as if it was the daughter he had once placed in her crib. He walked slowly back to sit next to his wife, who stared at him wide-eyed, her pretty face twisted in terror. Edward sat and dropped his big head in his hands. "They want half a million dollars," he said, his voice breaking, "in three days, or they say they'll kill her."

"My God, what can we do? Can you raise the money?"

Edward Collins thought back over the last few years, the go-go eighties—when any damn fool with more balls than brains could make millions buying and selling real estate as Fairfield County and much of Connecticut boomed. But the bubble had burst years ago; the stock market collapse of 1987 had cost bankers and brokers their bonuses and often their jobs. Few residents of comfortable southern Connecticut realized how many jobs very near to their elegant homes were dependent on the defense industry until those jobs began to disappear and the local economies declined. GE and rival Pratt and Whitney had fewer jet engines to build, Avco-Lycoming fewer tanks, Electric Boat fewer submarines. Edward Collins had been a wealthy man but had watched the money slip away as office buildings and shopping centers he owned emptied out. He raised his head as his wife hugged him. "Ten years ago I could have written the bastards a check," he said angrily.

"But not now?" she asked. Jane took little interest in his business as long as money was always available. "Not *now?*"

"Now I'm having trouble servicing my debt."

"What'll we do?" Jane said, her voice breaking at last and the tears starting.

"I'll have to find someone to lend it to me. Someone I don't already owe; someone I didn't wipe out in my partnerships while I was wiping out myself."

"I didn't know it was that bad."

"It is. We've been getting by and the economy is making a comeback. But we don't have five hundred thousand in cash or anything like it."

"Can you get it from the bank?"

Edward chuckled despite himself. "They're in worse shape than I am." The bank was a small Fairfield institution Edward had helped set up, and given a lot of business. Unfortunately the business was no longer good as one of Edward's properties after another stopped paying.

"What about your sailing buddies?"

Edward had two boats, a J-24 he raced and a Swan 57 he cruised. He sailed both out of the Black Rock Yacht Club in nearby Bridgeport. There were many nice boats in the fleet, but Black Rock was not a rich man's club. Edward doubted he could raise more than a few tens of thousands if he put the arm on everybody. He saw his friends in his mind's eye, and then he saw a man who had sailed with him for years, usually on deliveries because he mostly sailed his own boat alone. He was a member of the yacht club but took no interest in its affairs or facilities, rarely even taking a post-race drink in the bar. Every year he ended up writing a check for his two-hundred-dollar minimum restaurant charge; he never took a meal. Edward had known him for years without knowing him at all, and if the truth were told, he was a little afraid of the man people called, if only behind his back, Crazy Johnny.

3

JOHN DIETRICH LIVED in a small house, actually once a guest house, on a large estate in Greenfield Hill, one of Fairfield's prettiest neighborhoods. He considered himself retired from a life that had never been easy. He had grown up in Fairfield, become a promising wide receiver if an indifferent student. In 1966 he received his draft notice to the army and decided to join the marines instead. In less than six months he was in Vietnam. Since he was small and wiry, the platoon sergeant made him be the tunnel rat, the first marine to enter a bunker when one was discovered, the one with the pistol and grenades and a flashlight in his teeth, the one to spot the booby traps or announce their presence by being blown up. Johnny never admitted it but he was terribly claustrophobic and he hated the tunnels.

Johnny grew up in Vietnam. He hated the fighting, especially the tunnels, especially at night, but he loved the flower-choked jungle and the gentle, suffering people. He was especially drawn to the children, so pretty, so doll-like, so silent. Johnny knew that everything in Vietnam was dangerous; any object seen on the ground could be wired to a land mine, any pretty "boom-boom" girl could have a razor in the hem of her floating *ao-dai,* even the children might have a grenade or offer him a poisoned Coke. Nonetheless he loved them, wished he could help them, wished he could make the war that would only hurt him a little while longer go away before it scarred their lives forever.

Johnny was within two months of going home when the Vietcong and the North Vietnamese Army launched the Tet Offensive, penetrating American and South Vietnamese positions all over the country. Johnny was in Da Nang at the time, in the hospital recovering from burns suffered in a helicopter crash that had killed three of his squad mates. He was swept up, still in burn dressings, along with any other marine, soldier, sailor, or airman not seriously wounded, and rushed north to support the assault to recapture the old imperial capital of Hue, a battle known to all who fought in it, but none who claimed to report it, as the Battle of the Twenty-six Days.

Johnny found his own unit—Echo Company of the Second Battalion, Twenty-Sixth Marines—south of the Perfume River. Many marines from the hospital never did find their own people and had to be put together in pickup units to support the assault. Johnny was back with the squad, and back doing tunnels, except the tunnels were houses with basements that had to be fought over one at a time. At first the marines tried to use artillery and naval gunfire sparingly, to avoid inflicting casualties on civilians, but as they forced more and more houses they found most of the occupants had been slaughtered by the retreating Vietcong.

Even the children. Johnny wept for their tiny broken bodies, beaten to death, not even shot; the VC were short on ammunition. The marines began to use more heavy weapons and air strikes, hoping to save some of the civilians before the VC killed them all.

Johnny led the squad through the houses, especially at night. He carried a short-barreled Swedish K submachine gun, easier to push through confined spaces than the standard M16. He shot his way through the VC—any armed adult was assumed to be VC—and he saved some terrified abandoned children. His platoon sergeant told the company commander that nobody shot out a house better, took more risks to save kids, than Corporal Johnny Dietrich. The weary captain said there would be a medal after the battle was won.

The unit took casualties, every day, and every day new meat was brought up from Da Nang, green kids new in the country or house marines who had always been in the rear. Johnny felt the stink of death that lay on him, and the new men seemed to shy away from the tunnel rat. He kept going. He couldn't sleep even when the unit was pulled back for rest, and he cried a lot. But he kept going until he picked his way through the rubble of an abandoned and destroyed Catholic church and found a basement full of children.

Johnny thought at first they might be sleeping, all laid out in rows on straw mats, but as he knelt and touched one, then another, he knew they were dead. He touched every one; there were hundreds. Each had been bayoneted in the stomach; many were no more than babies. Some of the girls—they could have been teenagers or younger; Vietnamese women were all tiny—had been stripped of their clothing and had blood on their legs and bellies, bite marks on their tiny breasts, fear and horror in their staring eyes.

Johnny broke down, lost all the courage he'd used to hold himself together. He picked up one tiny girl and rocked her in his arms.

The lieutenant came up, then the captain. "We have to keep going, Corporal," the captain said. "This building, this street, are still dangerous."

"We have to help these kids," Johnny said, trying to pull himself together. "We have to help these kids."

"Son," the captain said. "You can see they're past help. They're all dead."

"No, no," Johnny crooned, still holding the lifeless baby girl. "I'll stay here. I'll wait for the medics."

The captain drew the lieutenant and the sergeant aside. "How long has this man been walking point?"

The sergeant shrugged. "Days. Weeks, I guess. He's the best we have."

"Get him back to the rear. He's done more than enough."

Johnny was flown back to the hospital in Da Nang the next day, after waiting in a tent with the non-emergency medevacs as the serious ones were put in the helos first. He was cleaned up, his filthy burn dressings replaced, and given a strong injection of tranquilizers.

The nightmares began the same night.

4

AFTER THIRTEEN MONTHS in Vietnam, Johnny flew home on the Freedom Bird, a chartered Braniff airliner from Saigon's Tan Sanh Hut airport to San Francisco via Guam and Honolulu. He wore his tropical khaki uniform with his ribbons: a Silver Star, a "hard bronze"—a Bronze Star with Combat V—and a Purple Heart with two gold stars indicating he had been wounded three times, plus the usual show-up shit everybody got. In San Francisco a woman, well-dressed and attractive, ran up to him and kissed him, saying welcome home. A hundred yards farther into the terminal another woman, similarly attractive and dressed, cursed him for a baby killer and spat at him.

Baby killer, Johnny thought. I tried to save them.

A day later Johnny got home to Fairfield. His mother embraced him, his father praised him. His old girlfriend, Linda, came over and cried over him, then dragged him outside and fucked him in the backseat of her father's Cadillac.

I'll be fine, Johnny thought, though he hurt terribly inside. The doctors in Da Nang told him he should report to a navy hospital for counseling; that he had seen too much and needed to get it out, but Johnny told them he was fine. He was after all a marine and marines don't whine.

Within days of reaching home, Johnny received his discharge from the marines in the mail. With thanks from a grateful nation.

So it goes, Johnny thought. The Marine Corps good-bye: thank you, and fuck you from The Crotch.

Linda stayed around a week, then went back to Boston and college. She wrote that she no longer knew him and that he frightened her. She begged him not to call, or write, or try to see her. Johnny

felt strangely relieved; he wasn't the same man who had left her behind, and the idea of a marriage, kids of his own and a normal life
no longer made any sense to him.

Because of the kids. How could he bring kids into the world he
now knew?

Johnny had money saved up from his back pay as well as forty-
five days of leave he had been entitled to but had never taken. He
decided to relax; work on forgetting. His parents wanted him to
stay at home, but he could see in their eyes and hear in their si-
lences that they wished he'd go. There was a friend of his, an army
vet, who had a house with a couple of other guys. His friend, Jim
Holiday, was a bartender at Breakaway Restaurant, and the other
guys, who Johnny never bothered to put names to, worked in the
restaurant business throughout the area. Jim offered to get Johnny
on at Breakaway; Johnny said no.

But he began to go there at night, hoping to meet a girl to replace
Linda, to fill up the hurt inside him.

And he began to drink.

5

EDWARD COLLINS DROVE his leased Mercedes up to Greenfield
Hill. Crazy Johnny had a telephone, but it was always connected to
his computer, and he never returned e-mail messages. There was a
black Ford Explorer, meticulously maintained, parked beside the
house. Edward's hands were shaking as he reached for Johnny's
doorbell. How do I ask this? he wondered. A man like Johnny, who
had sailed with Edward but always kept his distance. Edward had
tried to interest Johnny in his real estate limited partnerships, but
Johnny always said no; he had enough money. Edward at least convinced him to take his cash out of bank CDs; he was far too exposed

to local banks beyond their FDIC insurance. Johnny bought government bonds; never anything else.

But Johnny was Sally's godfather; Edward had talked him into that. Johnny had no time for churches. Edward admitted to himself he had used the device to get closer to Johnny; to Johnny's money.

Johnny's money built no shopping centers or office buildings, but now Edward needed it more than ever.

Johnny Dietrich pulled his door open three inches. He held a large semiautomatic pistol in his hand. "Edward," he said. "You should have called." He lowered the gun.

"You never answer the phone," Edward said, his heart in his throat.

"Nonetheless, you should know better than to enter a man's camp without hailing. But come in; you look troubled."

6

JOHNNY DRANK AND smoked his way through his back pay in much less time than he would have believed, but time had no meaning at all. His roommates threw him out of the house because he never made his share of the rent and he stank, rarely washing himself or his clothes. He drifted to New York and slept on grates and in doorways. Wherever he slept he had the nightmares full of dead and dying children. He lost weight and grew old and haggard. He was sleeping next to a fence one cold night in Washington Square Park when he was awakened by a rough hand gripping his shoulder. Johnny came awake quickly, his razor-sharp boxcutter in his hand, ready to slash. The stranger, a bearded bear of a black man in a Marine Corps warm jacket like Johnny's own, though cleaner and pressed, slapped the cutter away with no evident fear of its sharp edge. "You be a marine? Was a marine?" the bear said.

"Yes. Fuck off," Johnny said, getting to his feet. "Fuck you and fuck The Crotch,"

"What outfit?" The man pressed Johnny back against the fence.

"Two-Twenty-Six."

"Name and rank?"

"John Dietrich, Corporal," Johnny said, not knowing why he was answering this guy at all.

"Staff Sergeant Willy Tolliver." The man took Johnny's bicep in an iron grip. "I run the veterans' project over at St. Anne's. Come with me, Corporal."

"Leave me alone, man." Johnny tried to edge away but the bear tightened his grip past the point of pain. Johnny felt his legs tremble as he struggled weakly. "Leggo, damn you."

"No. You're mine. The Crotch takes care of its own forever. I'm taking you to the shelter, clean your smelly ass up and unfuck your mind."

"What if—"

Sergeant Tolliver spun Johnny around and frisked him for more weapons, then dragged him toward the gate of the park. "Unfuck your mind, Marine," Tolliver grated. "Or kill you trying."

7

JOHNNY STAYED IN the shelter at St. Anne's for a while, he couldn't be sure how long, and got better. He slipped out one night and got drunk using cash he'd stolen from the steel box with the broken lock in Tolliver's desk. Tolliver found him passed out in an alley only four blocks from the church, facedown in his own vomit. Tolliver let him sober up for four hours handcuffed to a radiator, then fed him some tough love by beating the shit out of him.

Johnny got back into the rhythm of the shelter, worked out,

gained weight and had no more relapses. He went to the counseling sessions because they were compulsory, but he rarely spoke. I don't want to talk about the 'Nam, he said, I want to forget it. He found the other men's stories of their experiences strangely unaffecting. Whatever horrors they had seen, whatever ghosts pursued them, they hadn't been in that basement with the children.

After a month, or several months—Johnny still had no sense of time passing—Tolliver called him into the office and, as always, called him to attention. " 'Bout time you moved on, boy," he said gently.

Johnny grinned. "You'd really let me go?"

"You ain't doing yourself no good. You taking up a rack another heartsick marine might need."

Johnny felt chilled. He understood for the first time that he needed these guys and their stories. He needed Staff Sergeant Tolliver. "I don't want to go," he whispered.

"Then you got to do something, boy."

"What? I—I'll pay more attention at meetings. I'll try to talk—"

Tolliver spun his chair. Behind him on another desk stood a computer, a Compaq portable with a tiny screen and two disk drives. "You use that, Corporal?" Tolliver said, pointing to the machine.

Johnny shrugged. "I learned to type in high school."

"Then write it down. The part you can't bring yourself to talk about, even here among your brother marines."

Johnny felt filled with despair. "I don't think I can do that."

"Try, and maybe I'll let you stay in my sorry-ass Marine Corps." Tolliver stood. "Or pack your shit and go." The sergeant marched from the office, slamming the door behind him.

Johnny sat down in front of the computer. The screen displayed a word-processing menu, and Johnny typed "Edit." The machine asked him to name the document and Johnny typed "Horror." The machine gave him a blank screen, and Johnny began to type, making it a story, a story of the war through the eyes of the children who would all die in the basement because the Vietcong considered even the most innocent as threats to their totalitarian dream. Johnny typed all day and into the night, and every day thereafter for nearly four months.

He titled the finished novel *The House of Pain.*

Sergeant Tolliver had a friend and benefactor at Williams and Roth, Publishers, an ex-marine captain. Johnny hand-delivered the manuscript and fled, embarrassed that a former marine officer, a guy living his life with all his shit together, would read about Johnny's fear and his failure to help the children.

Williams and Roth bought the book for an advance of $25,000. The book sold over three hundred thousand copies in hardcover, millions in paperback, and rode the *Times* bestseller list for nine months. It was made into a film that grossed over three hundred million in the U.S. and more overseas.

Johnny was suddenly a very rich man, and the nightmares receded. They didn't go away, but they became less frightening because he had shared them with the world.

But he never forgot the children.

8

EDWARD COLLINS SAT in Johnny's tiny shabby living room. His hands were shaking badly. "I don't suppose you have any whiskey?"

"You know I don't, Edward. I can barely be alone in a room with the stuff." Johnny sat in a peacock chair opposite Edward on the couch. "You didn't drive all the way up here to ask an alcoholic to pour you a drink."

"I need your help," Edward blurted. "It's Sally; she's been kidnapped. I need you to lend me money; a million dollars." Edward wondered why he had doubled the amount, but hell, Johnny wouldn't miss it or care. "I'm broke; up to my ears in debt. There isn't anyone else I can ask."

Johnny's eyes turned as gray as a cold sea, then he closed them against a burst of pain. His mind threw images of mutilated children rioting around his skull. He opened his eyes and Edward saw they were hard as stone. "Tell me what happened," Johnny said in a voice so full of cold fury that it frightened Edward. "Everything."

JOHNNY WAS UP, pacing the small room like a caged cat, his fists balled and banging at his thighs. Edward smelled a rank odor in the air: fear? No, anger. Edward wished he'd never come up to Johnny's house, never provoked the monster that lived within his tortured mind, but Edward didn't know anyone else with twenty million dollars in liquid assets. "Johnny?" Edward whispered as Johnny turned. "Will you help me? Help Sally? I'll repay you as soon as I can, though you know I owe everybody."

Johnny stopped, looked down at Edward, and abruptly sat back in his ratty peacock chair. He picked up the heavy pistol off the table where he'd left it and ejected the magazine. Edward could see it was full of copper-jacketed bullets. Edward was uneasy around weapons. Johnny slid the magazine back into the grip and rammed it home with the heel of his hand. The click was loud in the still, stuffy room, and Edward started. He fought down an urge to bolt from the place, but Sally's frightened little-girl's voice on the phone held him steady. "Johnny, will you lend me a—a million dollars?"

Johnny looked at Edward, his eyes harder than ever. He held his gun loosely in his left hand. "No."

"Johnny, for God's sake, you've told me before you have more money than you can ever spend."

"That isn't the problem," Johnny said carefully. "If I thought a million dollars would bring Sally safely home, or even get her out of her terror a single hour earlier, I wouldn't lend it to you"—he shook his shaggy head and toyed with the gun. "I'd give it to you."

"But—" Edward stood. "But Johnny, Jesus!"

"From what you told me, the snatch took place in broad daylight. The kidnappers, according to your wife, were two young white males, neither masked. Jane says she can't remember their faces, but there's no question Sally saw them. She can identify them."

"Isn't that something we can worry about after we get her freed?"

"Edward, the moment you pay the money, they'll kill her. She's proof of their guilt."

"Jesus," Edward whispered. "What can I do?"

Johnny threw the pistol on the table with a loud crash. "We have to get her back ourselves."

Edward found he was walking in tight circles. "I'd better call the police. Jane doesn't want me to."

"By now they'll know what happened at the school. They'll call you, but they'll be worthless."

"What do we do?"

Johnny stood and took an old leather jacket from the back of a chair. He picked up the big pistol and slid it into an inside pocket. "We start with Jane. She may have seen more than she knows. We'll go in your car because I have to make a few calls."

When they reached the house on Beachside Avenue, there was a battered Chevrolet Cavalier parked behind Jane's Volvo. Abby Grieg, the first person Johnny called from the car, got out as Edward parked behind her. She was a pretty black woman in a smart red suit who looked thirty but was probably older. She shook hands with Johnny, then Edward as she was introduced. "Abby's a therapist," Johnny explained. "She's going to hypnotize Jane, try to get her to remember more of what she saw. I could do it myself, but I suspect your wife finds me a bit frightening."

Edward followed them into his house. He was amazed at how

quickly Johnny had taken control; Edward was a man who did his own controlling. Now he was surrendering the most important decision of his life to a man haunted by Post Traumatic Stress Disorder, a man of violence, a man with a loaded pistol in his coat pocket.

If he's right, they'll kill my little girl as soon as I pay. But I can't pay. Maybe I need a violent, even a crazy man.

Jane led them into the spacious living room with its flickering fireplace and its broad view of Long Island Sound. She shook hands with Abby but wouldn't look Crazy Johnny in the eye. Her face was red and wrinkled and she clutched a soaked handkerchief in her hand. Abby's eyes went from Jane to the men. She said, "You boys go someplace and leave us alone. I need to explain to Jane how this works."

Edward took Johnny into his office and closed the door. He poured himself a large scotch and Johnny a club soda. "Don't worry, man," Johnny said. "Abby's good people. She's the widow of a marine."

Edward nodded dully and sat down.

"I WANT YOU to trust me to help you," Abby said. "It's painless and safe, and we may be able to walk you back through the kidnapping, get you to remember details you would have had no reason to focus on at the time."

"I thought my husband was just going to ask Cr— ask Johnny for money."

"Johnny thinks paying the ransom without an exchange deal will greatly jeopardize your daughter. He also thinks the kidnappers lack the sophistication to set up such an exchange."

"You mean you think they'll kill her." Tears streamed from Jane's cheeks.

"Johnny believes it. Johnny knows this shit."

"Please tell me who you are," Jane said. "And how you know, ah, Johnny."

"Let me tell you a little about the man you call Crazy Johnny,"

Abby said softly. "He served with my husband in Vietnam. They both came back wounded, body and soul. Johnny sank to the bottom and beyond, whereas my Raymond fought it out alone, never even telling me his pain."

"But you're a therapist. You could have helped."

"I wasn't a therapist then. I was a secretary in a psychiatrist's office. Johnny made it back from being a drunk and a thief in a program run for marines by marines. He tried to get my Raymond to go into it, just to meetings, but Raymond was too proud, too hurt. Then he died."

"My God, I'm so sorry," Jane said. "What happened?"

"Three years ago on a cold November evening he drove down to the beach in Southport, put a pistol in his mouth, and ended his pain." Abby was now crying too, but soundlessly. "Crazy Johnny put me through school, paid my rent, counseled my son, helps me in any way he can. He never asks for anything; he says the Marine Corps takes care of its own, forever."

"Tell me what I have to do," Jane whispered, wiping away her tears.

9

ABBY KNOCKED ON the door of Edward's study and entered. Johnny looked alert, focused, and angry. Edward seemed somnolent, perhaps drunk. Poor bastard, she thought. "She's ready, under," Abby said. She handed each man a yellow pad and a broad-tipped marker. "Don't speak, either of you. The only voice she should hear is mine."

They followed her into the living room, where Jane lay on a couch, her eyes closed, her breathing slow and deep. Abby had moved a chair close to the couch; Johnny and Edward took seats on another couch that was at a right angle to Jane. "Jane, you're in your car. You're waiting for Sally."

"Yes," Jane said in distant voice.

Johnny scribbled on his pad, "The van."

"Jane, do you see a minivan in front of you?" Abby asked, her voice soft and level.

"Yes."

"Can you describe it for me?"

"Tan. More yellow. Dusty, dented."

"Can you see the license plate?"

"There's, there's other cars between me and it."

"Did you get out of your car? To look for Sally?"

"No. Yes, I got out to have a cigarette. I saw Sally coming, and I waved."

"Look at the van, Jane."

Jane's eyelids fluttered. "All right. Yes."

"Look at the license plate."

"Yes. I see it." She smiled. "The first three letters spelled SEX."

Abby looked at Johnny who simply nodded. "Before the letters are numbers. Can you see them?"

Jane was silent for a long minute. "No, after the letters. I think one two four. Yes, I see that."

Johnny wrote furiously. "Letters before the numbers is not Connecticut. She's an artist and a photographer. Work *colors.*"

Abby nodded. "What color is the plate, Jane?"

"White," Jane said without hesitation.

"Connecticut plates are blue, Jane."

"White."

Johnny tore off a page and wrote again. Abby nodded.

"Was there anything between the numbers and the letters?"

"A figure. Red, I think."

"What figure?" Johnny wrote some more but Abby shook her head. "Was it the Statue of Liberty, Jane?"

"I don't—yes, it was."

"New York plate," Johnny whispered. "Ask about the men."

Abby shushed him and pointed to his pad. "Jane, let's see the men."

"All too fast."

"Slow it down. Run the camera of your mind slowly."

Jane stirred and cried out. "They're taking her!"

"Slowly."

"Two men. One facing me, short, maybe five-six. Jeans, a black sweater, dark eyes, short hair."

"Have you ever seen him?"

"No. No."

"The other?"

"Only his back. Taller, but only a little. Stocky, muscular." Jane writhed on the couch as though burning. "I think I've seen him, but I don't know him." She began to cry. "They hurt my baby."

Abby wrote on her own pad. "Not much more."

Johnny wrote. "Enough, for now."

Abby signaled for the men to leave the room.

10

"TOLLIVER." THE SERGEANT answered on the first ring.

"It's Johnny Dietrich, Staff Sergeant."

"Johnny. You still clean and sober?"

"Yes, Staff Sergeant."

"Hey, boy, I don't own you anymore. Call me Willy."

"Willy, I got a problem. A girl I know's been kidnapped and I need a little help and some shit."

Tolliver gripped the phone tighter and leaned forward. He knew Johnny had pulled back from the edge, from the horror, but how far? "Anything my little band of banged-up irregulars can do we will."

"Can you get me an ID on a New York plate?"

"Sure. We got lots of brothers on the cops."

Johnny read him the number. "I might need a guy to help me. Ride shotgun."

"We got people. In fact, I think I'll come on out there and pay you a visit."

"You're too busy, Staff Sergeant. They need you at the shelter."

"Hell, Johnny, I got lots of help here now, since you gave us all that money. Besides, you said you needed some shit and somebody's got to get it to you." Before Johnny could refuse Tolliver went on. "What you need?"

Johnny read a list. Camouflage clothing, a ski mask, tight leather driving gloves, canvas boot covers that would make footprint identification difficult. Two short-range UHF hand-held radios.

"Not a problem. Got most of that shit in the basement."

"Willy, I'm going to need a weapon. Something cold, preferably silenced."

"This be very serious shit, Johnny." Tolliver knew that by "cold" Johnny meant unregistered, untraceable.

"I know. There's no alternative."

Tolliver didn't ask Johnny to explain. "You ever handle a Swedish K?"

"For two years in 'Nam," Johnny replied sadly. "Almost every night since in my dreams."

EDWARD DROVE JOHNNY home and Johnny hooked up his telephone. Tolliver called back less than an hour later. It was the first time Johnny had used the phone in his house in years, and it felt strange. "I got the plate," Tolliver said. "The van was stolen, of

course, but maybe this'll help anyway. The van is owned by a re-
frigeration guy in Harrison, New York, who was working that day on
a job in Bridgeport. He came out from lunch and his van was gone;
he reported it immediately. Six hours later the police found it in
front of a house in Black Rock."

Johnny's breathing picked up. "Address?"

Tolliver read it off. "I got a guy I know, a Connecticut state police lieutenant, talking to the Bridgeport police. They impounded
the vehicle. They haven't touched it other than to tow it, and hadn't
even checked for prints or anything."

Figures, Johnny thought. The Bridgeport cops were so notoriously
inept it was amazing they even found it. "You can get something?"

"Yeah, as a favor to my guy they're going to run prints, hair and
fiber, that shit. Maybe you'll get lucky."

Not likely, Johnny thought. Most likely kids, but maybe kids
with records. "How about my stuff?"

"I'll be on my way with that van you gave the shelter within an
hour or so. Give me directions."

Johnny did so, then went to lie down. It was nearly midnight.
Johnny wondered if he dared close his eyes, then he did.

THE JUNGLE FLOODED his mind immediately, and the tunnels.
It hadn't been this vivid in years, but Johnny had learned to let it
flow. They say the sense of smell shuts off during sleep, which is why
they make smoke detectors to change odor into sound. But Johnny
smelled the jungle, and the feces and urine reek of the VC tunnels
that often guided tunnel rats to them before anyone saw them.

The tunnels became the warrens of streets in Hue, then the basements, and finally the basement full of slaughtered innocents. Sally
turned to look at him as he entered the room. She was pretty and
smiling, but there was a bayonet protruding from—

From between her legs. Johnny couldn't use the word. He shivered in bed and thrashed, but he let the dream run because he needed the anger, he needed strength. Sally walked up to him and kissed him on the lips, but said nothing, and the dream suddenly disappeared.

JOHNNY AWAKENED THREE hours later when he heard a pounding on his door. He folded a bathrobe around his naked body and held his pistol in the fold.

Something in the dream was wrong. What was it?

He opened the door to admit Staff Sergeant Tolliver.

11

EDWARD LAY IN bed next to his wife all night, sleepless. He sensed she was not sleeping either, though she made no sound. He wondered what Johnny would do, could do. He wondered whether Johnny was even right, that the kidnappers would simply kill Sally if he paid, or didn't pay. What would he tell them when they called again? Bargain? Work out an exchange? He felt Johnny would let him have the money if he could indeed arrange an exchange of Sally alive for the cash; why was Johnny so sure that couldn't be done?

He got out of bed at his usual hour of 6:00. He shaved, showered, dressed and walked down the lawn to the seawall. The tide was out and seagulls were catching crabs and picking up hard-shelled clams, wheeling above, and dropping them on the rocks to break their shells. The tidal flat had a strong odor of marine life transiting between life and death. Edward thought it beautiful and peaceful, but this morning it gave no comfort. He turned and walked back to the house.

He found Jane in the kitchen cooking breakfast. She rarely rose before eight, just in time to drive Sally to school, and she never made breakfast. He accepted a cup of coffee and sat at the counter that separated the kitchen from the formal dining room two steps below. After a moment she handed him a plate of bacon and scrambled eggs. He had no appetite. She sat next to him with only a cup of coffee. "Honey, what are we going to do?"

"I'm going into the office. I'll try to raise some money; maybe we can reason with these guys."

"Johnny won't help?"

"He might, if he thinks we can do a real exchange, not one of those deals were we dump the money someplace and leave and they call us later and tell us where she is."

"I've been wondering. I didn't know we were so broke; I guess I've never thought much about money or business. Do you think Sally knows?"

"Why would she? I should have talked to both of you about it, we should have discussed it as a family, but I've always been sure I could make it back." He leaned over and kissed his wife. "Actually, I am making it back, albeit slowly, but I'm in no shape to meet these guys' demands. Why did you ask about Sally?"

"I guess if she knew you had no money she could tell the kidnappers."

Edward shook his head. "I'd better get going. What are you going to do?"

"I don't know. Hang on, I guess. Try to paint, yearn for the phone to ring, perhaps go to church."

Edward felt sudden tears slide down his cheeks and spill into his cold eggs. "You know, Johnny once told me the story, the one that was the basis of his novel about the murdered Vietnamese kids. He told me one night far out at sea on the way to Bermuda when we shared a watch. I wasn't moved very much, and wondered how such an experience in the middle of a terrible war would be enough to take a hardened marine into this Post Traumatic Stress Disorder that almost killed him and plagues him still."

Jane dabbed at his tears with her napkin, then hugged his shaking shoulders. "Take it easy, honey. You have to be strong for Sally and for me."

"I'll try, babe. It's just that now I think I finally know the man we derided as Crazy Johnny. I feel what he felt, and I'm afraid if we don't get our little girl back, I'll be like he is, or worse, how he was before he got help."

"We can't give up." Jane sobbed, dabbing her own tears.

"No." Edward rose, kissed his wife's fine blond hair. "Of course not."

II

THE HOUSE OF PAIN

12

SERGEANT TOLLIVER DROVE the shelter's blue Ford van slowly past the address he'd gotten from the Bridgeport police, the place where the stolen minivan had been found. Johnny sat beside him, low in the seat. "Right there, by that telephone pole," Tolliver said.

"Black pickup there now," Johnny said. "Plenty of empty space along the street. Do you suppose?"

"Hard to believe they be *that* dumb, but we'll run the plate. What do you think about the houses?"

"I better get another car and watch them."

"Why don't I do that?" Tolliver said as he dialed the police on his car phone.

"It's a white, blue-collar neighborhood, Willy."

"I *see.*" Willy laughed. "Nigger in a truck attract attention. But you don't want to be seen here before you operate."

"I have a better idea. Let's go get a bite to eat and talk about it."

Tolliver pulled slowly away from the parked pickup and around a corner. "Where you want to eat?"

"Just drive around. Look for a Bridgeport Gas truck; they're all over, putting in new mains."

"Oh, Johnny, not that old chestnut."

"Yeah, it'll save time. And we ought to disguise this vehicle."

"New York plates be a bit of a giveaway, but I ain't stealing no car."

Johnny spotted a Bridgeport Gas truck by an open manhole. "Pull in behind and stop. We got no reason to steal a car, Willy; we'll just hit a big parking lot and pick us up a nice set of commercial license plates."

13

EDWARD CALLED JANE at midday. "How you holding up, honey?"

"I'm okay. A police detective was by to get a statement; I told him what I could. He said he'd stay behind the scenes. He said he knows Johnny through a third party, he's another ex-marine."

"What else? No word from the kidnappers?"

"Nothing. Jeff, Sally's boyfriend, called. He's very upset and asked if there was anything he could do."

"You ask him if he had a half a million cash?" Edward said, not meaning it. Jeff came from a solid Italian family only two generations up from manual labor; people Edward tended to treat with contempt because they had no money he could steal.

"Edward," Jane said, starting to sniffle.

"Sorry, honey. Anything else?"

"Johnny came by right after you left. He attached some gadget to the phone that will trace and record a local call. Johnny said not to mention it to the police because it's illegal."

"I guess we have to go along. Honey, are you completely with me on letting Johnny run with this?"

"I thought we had no choice."

"These men, all these ex-marines, they must be planning to take her back by force. What if the kidnappers really don't plan to harm her?"

"We still can't pay."

"No, but maybe we can deal. I think we should slow Johnny down until we get the next call from the kidnappers."

Jane pondered. The sight of her daughter and her solitary scream ran behind her eyelids like a slow-motion movie. "Edward, if Johnny's right and they are planning to kill Sally whether we pay or not, and if we agree to let him go after her, are you prepared for the fact that we may be causing the deaths of others? Even if they're guilty of an unspeakable crime?"

Edward was surprised by the coldness in his voice. "If it saves our daughter, I can accept that."

"What will we do after? If that's how it turns out?"

What would Johnny do? Edward thought fleetingly. "We'll live with it," he said gently to his wife.

14

JOHNNY WENT TO the back of the blue Bridgeport Gas van and pounded on it. When he got no response, he pulled the double doors open and slipped inside. In a moment he emerged with a coverall and a plastic toolkit marked "Testing." When he jumped back in beside Tolliver the big man was sweating. "You must love this girl a lot, boy. That's a felony for sure."

"Let's go get some plates," Johnny said, his breathing slowing. "Then you get to go door-to-door looking for a gas leak."

"What I be looking for?"

"I have notes from Jane's debrief under hypnosis. You won't likely see the girl, but get a good look at whoever you do see." He paused and looked at the man who had saved him from the abyss. "We only have tonight, Willy, then they'll demand payment."

"You thinking of going already? *Tonight*, for Christ's sake?"

"If we find the right house, yes."

Tolliver shook his big head. "They right to call you Crazy Johnny."

Johnny smiled, but without a hint of mirth. " 'Mad Marine Killing Machine.' "

JOHNNY AND TOLLIVER ate their lunch at the diner across from the parked gas truck. Two gas company pipe layers sat in a corner booth, eating with the leisurely pace of public utility employees. When they left, Johnny and Tolliver followed, watched long enough to be sure they had apparently noticed nothing missing and weren't planning to go anywhere, then got back into their van with its newly acquired Connecticut commercial license plates. Tolliver dropped Johnny off in the parking lot of the Fayerweather Yacht Club, a few blocks from the spot where the minivan was found, where he had left his black Ford Explorer. "Take your time, Willy. See as many rooms in each house as you can, especially basements. Two or three young guys. Watch for attitude. As I recall, you're quite an expert on attitude."

"Not to mention its adjustment." Tolliver grinned. "What you do now?"

"Go back to my place, look to my equipment. Meet me back there as soon as you're done."

"What if I don't find nothing?"

Johnny shrugged. "I don't know."

EDWARD WENT HOME immediately after lunch. The Kings East Building deal had finally closed. Jane was calm, Edward suspected sedated. The therapist, Abby, was with her. He went over and kissed his wife tenderly. She smiled sadly and hugged him fiercely, a long minute. "Hello, Abby," he said.

"Edward. Jane and I are trying to work up a psychological profile of the kidnappers."

"But we know so little."

Abby gave him a look that said maybe it was just a way to keep Jane engaged in the rescue effort, to keep her from falling into total despair.

"Good idea," Edward said woodenly. He sat beside his wife and took her hand. "How's it going?"

Abby looked at her notes. "They're amateurs; I agree with Johnny on that. They must know Sally but probably not well. They know enough about her family to know you have a lot of money."

"*Had* a lot of money," Edward said grimly.

"Clearly, they don't know that, or don't believe it."

This is getting us nowhere, Edward thought, looking at his watch. He wondered when Johnny would show up, or call. He considered having a drink but thought better of it; it was only three in the afternoon. "Okay with you if I take a walk, honey?"

"What if someone calls?" Jane said anxiously.

"I'll just go down to the seawall. I need some air."

"Okay." Jane smiled bravely. "I'll shout if I need you."

He kissed her again and nodded to Abby. "Keep working on it; it may be really helpful." Abby smiled slightly and Edward went out.

15

TOLLIVER WAS NERVOUS as he approached the houses near the spot the van had been recovered. In the first he found an elderly white woman who invited him in without question when she heard his quick tale of a drop in main pressure and the possibility of a leak in one of the houses in the area. He flashed his laminated photo ID from the Department of Veterans' Affairs, and gave a quick and courteous inspection of the house and basement, sweeping around with something from the Bridgeport Gas toolkit that looked like a portable vacuum cleaner. Mrs. Perrone, the householder, let him roam freely but followed him around, ensuring, he supposed, that he didn't pocket any of her possessions. He left her greatly relieved; no leak detected.

At the second house, no one responded to his loud knock and cry of "Gas Company." He walked around back, looking through windows as he went, and knocked again. He wondered how long he could keep this up before someone called the police, but he had squared it with his contact in the state police barracks at Bridgeport who had promised to tell the Bridgeport police dispatcher that the staties had an undercover surveillance operating in the area.

As he regained the sidewalk, a short, dark young man, very similar to Johnny's notes of Jane's description under hypnosis, emerged from the next house, crossed the lawn and climbed into the pickup truck. Tolliver waited until he pulled away, then approached the front door cautiously. He knocked, and another young man appeared, fitting the profile of the second kidnapper. He told his story, now smoother from the first practice. "You the man of this house?" Willy asked, proffering his ID.

"Uh, yeah. My dad's not home." The man seemed very nervous, but he let Tolliver in and led him right to the kitchen. Tolliver got out his sniffer, or whatever it was, and began to search around the range. He got up quickly and grinned at the man; the stove was electric. The man took no notice of Tolliver's mistake and that made hairs on the back of his neck bristle.

Willy heard voices from another room. The young man stayed right behind him, his breathing loud and rapid. Hope the son of a bitch doesn't take it in mind to shoot me, Tolliver thought as he stood up. "Okay here," he said cheerfully. "I need to see the basement. Furnace, water heater?" Without waiting for the watchful young man to say anything, Tolliver picked up his toolkit and marched down a hall toward the muffled argument.

The youth scuttled around him, pushed past him. "Not that way, man," the boy rasped. He held his hand behind him in the small of his back.

Pistol, Tolliver thought, his heart racing. He smiled. "Sorry. Where's the basement, then?"

"Uh, the stairs are on the other side of the kitchen." Tolliver walked back through the kitchen and opened a door. It was a broom closet. He looked back at the youth who still held his hand behind his back. His face was shiny with sweat. Tolliver opened the only other door and saw stairs leading down into darkness. Don't make this kid any more jumpy than he is, Tolliver thought. "Right you are," he said cheerily. He found the light and switched on. "Coming down?"

"I'll wait here," the boy said.

Tolliver quickly found the furnace and attached water heater. The boiler was an old Peerless with a new-looking Beckett burner on the front.

Tolliver got out of the house as quickly as he could, thanking the lad who managed a relieved smile. As Tolliver reached Post Road two police cars turned into his street in the opposite direction. Neither paid him any mind. Tolliver pulled into the lot of a huge discount store, replaced the stolen plates with his New York plates, took off the Bridgeport Gas coverall and threw it, the plates and the toolkit into a high Dumpster.

He drove to Johnny's house, observing speed limits and getting his heartbeat back into high normal.

Johnny inspected the equipment Tolliver had brought out from New York. The one-piece black camouflage jumpsuit fit well enough. The ski mask covered his face completely, leaving only eye holes.

It was midnight blue with a red accent stripe that Johnny blacked with Magic Marker.

Johnny tore down the Swedish K, an ugly submachine gun with some very good features for work in the tunnels and some bad ones. It was short: only twenty-two inches long with its wire stock folded in; barely three inches longer with the bulbous sound suppressor on the end of the barrel. It fired a special high-velocity nine-millimeter round with a heavy jacket that had great penetrating power against wood or earthen barricades. Johnny had used this ammo in the tunnels and basements, but it was supersonic and would leave a sonic boom after the suppressor silenced the sound of the discharge. Johnny had asked Tolliver to get him some lower-velocity rounds the New York cops were supposed to use in their pistols so as not to kill someone two miles away if they missed the bad guy.

The K-gun's major flaw was that it only fired on full automatic. Not the best when a tunnel rat had to enter a room of VC and hostages and separate the righteous from the ungodly.

The gun was reasonably clean but Johnny made it much cleaner. He reassembled it carefully and cycled the action. He put on rubber gloves and wiped down each cartridge from the box of fifty with gun oil, then inserted thirty-six into the box magazine. He slung the weapon and took five Coke cans and a soup can from his recycling bin and walked outside. He set the cans in a row on a fallen tree trunk as he watched Tolliver skid to a stop in his driveway. "What you doin' boy? We got to talk."

"In a minute, Staff Sergeant," Johnny said. "Go over and place those cans a meter apart on the log. The soup can is the hostage; the others are bad guys."

Tolliver shook his head but complied as Johnny turned away. He'd seen the glow in Johnny's eyes, the scary glow. He moved the soup can from the right end to the second from left. "Clear," he said once he had stepped ten yards away.

Johnny wheeled immediately. It was a rapid movement but seemed almost balletic since it was so smooth. He fired a burst of six rounds, loud coughs through the sound suppressor. The five Coke cans spun away, torn nearly in half. The soup can sat on the log unharmed. "Just wanted to check the gun," Johnny said conversationally.

"Whadn't the gun you be checking. You and me gotta talk."

Johnny safed the weapon and slung it. "Let's go inside and get a cold drink."

Tolliver gathered up the six cans. Each Coke can had been hit dead-center. He followed Johnny inside.

16

THE YOUTH WHO had escorted Tolliver around the house locked the door as soon as he saw him drive away. He pounded on the bedroom door and finally the loud argument stopped. Another youth emerged and closed the door behind him. "What?" he said, his tone annoyed.

"Inspector from the gas company. Real scary nigger, Jeff. We should turn her loose or at least move her."

"No. We're nearly there. I'll up the ante; call her father tonight. What's some nigger from the gas company got to do with Edward Collins anyway?"

"He made me nervous, man. He had eyes of, like, stone."

"Everybody makes you nervous, Tom," Jeff said. "Do you have the pistol?"

"Right here," Tom said, taking the long-barreled Colt revolver from the small of his back. His hand shook badly.

"Go dump it in the river. You don't have the guts to use it and you're scaring yourself and the rest of us."

Tom looked at the gun and tried to steady it. "But what if her dad calls in his connections?"

"Like you're gonna shoot them with that rusty piece? Get rid of it." Jeff went back into the bedroom and the argument resumed.

TOLLIVER RUBBED THE frosty can of club soda against his hot forehead. "I'm getting too old for this shit, man." He'd told his story of the three houses as sparingly as possible. Johnny had held him with his scary eyes throughout.

Johnny stood up and went to a window. "You think the third house."

"If not there, then not on that block. You listen to what I told you?"

"Say it again. The evidence."

"Okay. Number one, the kid is nervous, very nervous, borderline afraid. Number two, I hear two people arguing behind a closed door, a man and a woman, both sounded young and white. Number three, when I go toward that door, the kid reaches around behind himself, like he's got a piece in his waistband, small of his back. Number four, he don't exactly know where the basement door is, and number five, when I get down there I find a furnace with a Beckett burner. That's an *oil* burner, man, and in the kitchen an electric stove. That house has no gas service at all. That boy do *not* live in that house!"

Johnny nodded slowly. "And another young white man took the black pickup and drove away before you went in. It fits, but I'm troubled."

"*Why*, man? Both men I saw fit the notes you gave me from the interview with the mother. There's a young female and another male in the house."

"But why are the victim and one of the kidnappers arguing?"

Tolliver looked at the man he had dragged back from his demons. "People argue all the time, boy."

Johnny turned to face him. "Can you make me a sketch of the internal layout of the house?"

"Do it right now."

"That's it, then. I'd better go see Edward and Jane."

Tolliver took a yellow pad, a pencil and a ruler from Johnny's messy desk and began carefully drawing. Johnny watched in silence. Tolliver put an "X" on the room at the end of the hall from which he had heard the man and woman arguing. "My best guess she be held here."

"Have another soda," Johnny said. "I'll clean this weapon, pack the equipment and put it in your van."

"Tonight, then. You're sure?"

"If I'm wrong and that house is full of sleeping innocents I'll be in and out of there without anyone ever knowing."

17

EDWARD AND JANE sat side by side on the sofa before the fireplace, holding hands. Abby sat across the room by herself, and Johnny sat on the couch at a right angle to Edward and Jane. Edward and Jane were drinking dark whiskey, Johnny had a Coke. "Johnny, I'm scared of this," Edward said. "Isn't there any way we can do this without violence?"

"Violence," Johnny said coldly, "has already commenced. They snatched Sally off the street; they've threatened to kill her."

Edward hung his head. "When they call tomorrow, shouldn't I try to reason? Offer them the money if they'll agree to exchange her for it, say in a public place?" Edward couldn't help thinking of the extra half million he'd asked Johnny for, and what it could do for his hurting businesses.

"Sure, try," Johnny said. "She's seen them and she's proof of their crime. But try."

The phone rang. It was a soft sound but they all jumped. Johnny crossed the room and looked at the tracing/recording device and saw its light come on, then motioned for Edward to take it. Edward's legs were rubbery as he crossed to the antique escritoire and picked it up. "Hello?"

"Mr. Collins?" a voice said rapidly. "Got my money?"

Jane gave a little yelp as the sound came through the speaker on the recorder. Edward immediately recognized the voice of the man who had called within hours of Sally's abduction. "You said three days. We spoke only yesterday."

"So? Yesterday was day one, today is day two, and I want my money tomorrow, day three."

"I'm getting it together, but I'll need a full three days." He looked across at Johnny, who nodded. "How will we exchange my daughter for the money?"

"No exchange. We'll tell you where to put the money and when. If you do that, alone, no cops, no followers, no bullshit, we'll pick up the money, count it, then call you to tell you where you can pick up your daughter."

"How will I know she's safe? There has to be an exchange."

The voice went away from the telephone and became soft. "Get the bitch over here." A loud slap blasted from the speaker, and a scream.

Edward gripped the phone as Jane jumped out of the sofa. Sally's voice cut through her like a knife. "Daddy? Mummy?" There was another hard slap and wail. "They're hurting me, please get me out of here."

The male voice returned. His breathing was labored. "I'll give you another day. Tomorrow night I'll tell you where to drop the money. If you don't, or if you fuck with me in any way, we'll call and tell you where to find the bitch's body."

The phone went dead and Edward dropped it in the cradle. His wife ran to him and flung herself into his arms, sobbing. Edward held her and tried to soothe her, and looked over her shoulder at Johnny. "Do it," he said, his voice tight.

Johnny stood up, went to the recorder and noted the incoming phone number. He'd get Tolliver to check it, but he would bet a pay phone somewhere close to the house in Black Rock. "You did good," he said soothingly. "You bought us some time; they'll be relaxed tonight."

"You're going *tonight?* You know where she is?"

Johnny hesitated. He felt it; he did know. "Yes."

"I don't even know the plan. What do I do?"

"You won't be going," Johnny said as he got up.

"She's my daughter!" Edward shouted, releasing his sobbing wife. "I have a right—"

"You won't be going."

"WHAT AN ASSHOLE," Tom said, grinning at Jeff and Gil after returning from the pay phone at a minimart called Wawa a half mile from the house in Black Rock. "He wants us to agree to an exchange. How stupid does he think we are?"

"Yeah," Gil said. "We'd get to hold the cash for maybe a minute before the cops grabbed our asses. You play that tape we made?"

Tom laughed. At seventeen he was the oldest of the kidnappers, and he thought of the scheme as his own. "The slaps, the screams? It was perfect. He'll pay tomorrow and we're out of this shithole of a town forever."

"Shit, I'm hungry," Jeff said. "Let's get some pizza." He went to the bedroom door and opened it. "Hey Sally? What do you want on your pizza?"

JOHNNY DROVE BACK to the cottage in Greenfield Hill. He felt himself slipping, sliding back in time to 'Nam, the fear, the horror, the rage.

The children.

He tried to compress his mind, to get it right. He knew how far down he had gone before he regained control, and he knew as well if he ever went all the way back, there might be no escape. He parked his truck and went inside, where he found Tolliver asleep on the sofa. Johnny loved the big black bear of a man, remembering how his tough love and hard fists had helped him face his demons, and face himself. Now the demons were creeping back from the cage in his brain where he had imprisoned them. Let us in, they whispered. We can help. We'll make you sharp.

Maybe just a little, Johnny thought. Just enough to get my edge back, my nightcrawler sense, my tunnel rat instincts.

We're your friends, the demons whispered. Your friends.

Tolliver awakened to find Johnny staring out into the woods. "You gone awfully quiet, bro."

Johnny turned and faced the old sergeant. "Just getting ready, Willy. Shall we go over it one more time?"

"Right. Then we best get some sack time. Be a long night ahead."

18

JOHNNY DREAMED AND dreamed. He visited many old friends from Vietnam, men he knew were dead even in his dream. They were all glad to see him, shook his hand. You're going in again, bro. Going to save the kids this time. We'll be right outside if you need us, but you know that.

Vietnam was at its most gorgeous after the first rains of the spring monsoon, a riot of flowers in the chinar trees, the gold and blue of orchids and the red of the flamboyant. Parrots, red, yellow and bright indigo, screeched and shouted, insects clicked and whirred. There were no sounds of war, no gunfire, no crump of mortars, no scream of jets or grinding threatening of tanks.

Helicopters had given the skies back to the birds.

Johnny visited villages he had patrolled. The children watched the marines pass by, perfectly silent, perfectly beautiful. Did they ever laugh? he wondered. Would they ever?

A glow rose in the northern sky and raced toward him. Night fell like a shroud that was quickly rent by loud demands of war. He was huddled in the foundation of a burned-out house with the rest of the company. Across a broad plaza was a temple the lieutenant said was the Palace of Harmony, a place where the emperor presided over important religious rites in the imperial city of Hue. The marines were waiting for a cold-eyed navy lieutenant to call in gunfire from ships far at sea to blast away rubble barricades on either side of the temple and eliminate the mortar- and rocket-fire that was falling all around them, sending shrapnel and stone splinters over their meager shelter. This was day three of what they would come to call the Battle of the Twenty-six Days.

The dream raced forward into night and Johnny was in the alleys, going house-to-house with his platoon, listening to other platoons on parallel streets. In and out, firing the K-gun, magazine after magazine, stepping over twitching bodies of VC he had just killed and finding cold corpses of civilians piled in corners. Finally he was in the church where he knew he was destined to go, so quiet, so dignified in its blasted state.

Johnny heard the cries of frightened children and raced down the stairs to the basement. Hundreds of children, all turning to stare at him, the long-nosed barbarian they had been told to hate. But they loved him and his eyes brimmed. He swept away his tears with a hand blackened by gunsmoke and dirt, and when he looked again all the children were lying down in rows, and all were dead. A great cry of pain burst from his body and he surged awake. Staff Sergeant Tolliver laid a gentle hand on his shoulder. "Two A.M., Marine. Best we prepare."

19

JOHNNY DRESSED IN the black cammie uniform, his own jungle boots and the canvas boot-covers. He put on the web harness that would support extra ammo, canteens and other equipment if he were going into the tunnels, even though this morning he would take only the full magazine in the K-gun, a small black flashlight, a pouch of small tools and the radio Tolliver had brought from New York. He tied his diving knife to his thigh and taped it. He took the magazine out of the submachine gun and checked it, and cycled the action. He'd taken a little tension off the recoil spring to compensate for the lower energy of the police cartridges he had loaded. He wiped the magazine clean of fingerprints and reinserted it with a handkerchief. He would wipe down the entire weapon just before he went in, after he put on his gloves. He stuffed the handkerchief, gloves and ski mask in a leg pocket and walked into the living room. Tolliver was dressed in dark slacks, shirt and a blue windbreaker. He had a pot of strong coffee made and two cups on the table along with his sketch of the house on Prescott Street.

"Good morning, Staff Sergeant," Johnny said cheerfully.

"You sleep?"

"Yep."

"How's your mind, boy?"

"It's right, Staff Sergeant."

"Remember there's an edge out there, one you fell over and climbed back to. Remember how hard that climb was, and stay the hell away from the edge. Keep your mind right."

Johnny nodded. "I know what's out there, or"—he pointed to his head—"in here."

"I think maybe I should go in with you."

Johnny smiled. "Willy, you weigh two hundred fifty easy, and you were never a tunnel rat. This's a one-man op."

"I confess I'm worried about you, boy. You ain't cut out for this kind of stress no more."

Johnny stood up and downed his coffee, hot as it was. "Let's go get that scared little girl, Willy."

Tolliver shook his big head, then stood up and followed.

TOLLIVER DROVE THE van to the nearly deserted parking lot of the Fayerweather Yacht Club. He turned on the dome light above their heads. "Sweet Jesus, what happened to your eyes?"

Johnny's eyes glowed yellow like a devil's. "Contacts. Improves night vision."

"Scary as shit. I see you come into my bedroom at night, I wet my pants before I shoot you."

Johnny smiled. He felt very relaxed. He twisted the rear-view mirror toward himself and blackened the skin below his eyes with greasepaint to help absorb glare if he went rapidly from darkness to bright light. He pulled on the tight leather gloves, sprayed the weapon with gun oil, and wiped it down carefully from the silencer on the muzzle to the end of the folded wire stock. He dropped the handkerchief into the black plastic garbage bag they had brought along for the purpose. He donned the ski mask and tucked in the collar of his cammies, then zipped the one-piece garment to the neck. His watch read three-fifteen. "Let's do it, Willy."

"I don't like the idea of just leaving you there."

"We went over this. Someone might notice the truck with a man in it and call the police."

"I don't like it."

"You drop me off, come back here. We have the radios; you're minutes away."

"Say again the signals."

"One click, I'm in. Two, all's well, come quickly. Three, I'm in trouble. Four, I'm fucked, get out of here."

"I'm not sure I'd accept a four, Corporal."

"It's not your battle, Staff Sergeant. But expect a one and then a two."

Tolliver put the van in gear.

TOLLIVER DROPPED JOHNNY at the corner of Ellsworth and Prescott Streets and reluctantly drove away. I should stay with him, Tolliver thought. He's come so far back, but the hell he went through is still inside him, waiting to emerge if he gets stressed. Johnny knew that; it was why he chose to live such a lonely life.

Tolliver made a U-turn and started back toward the Fayerweather Yacht Club parking lot, where there were at least a few cars as members played pool into the early-morning hours. He didn't want to leave Johnny, but he didn't want to get stopped by a curious cop. He parked and shut off the engine, then lay down across the front seats to make the van look empty. He took out the handheld radio and checked it was on for about the tenth time. He also checked the heavy semiautomatic pistol he carried in his jacket pocket.

JOHNNY CROSSED BEHIND the first house on Prescott Street and slipped into the backyard of the second. There was a half-moon, partially obscured by passing clouds. Tolliver had reported seeing no dogs. Johnny edged along the back fence and pulled himself up and over it into the backyard of the third, his target. The house was as pitch-dark as the first two, although there was a bright porch light burning. Johnny sank to the ground and lizard-crawled from shadow to shadow. He had memorized Tolliver's sketch; the back door was nearer the bedrooms, but he had to anticipate announcing himself prematurely if he made any noise getting in, although he didn't intend to do so.

Johnny circled the house, slowly. The front door was solid wood and had a good-quality lock. There were no open windows; it was quite cold for October. Johnny kept moving, slowly, carefully, the way one moved before cutting wire and ambushing the VC in their sleep. On the side of the house he found a casement window closed but not locked; probably sprung from age. He completed his circle then returned to the window. He took a scalpel from his tool pouch and cut the wire screen inside the window, then curled his fingers over the edge of the metal window and pulled. He couldn't budge it. He took a roll of duct tape from the pouch and made an "X" on the glass near where the crank had to be. He took a glass cutter and made a circle through the "X" with a single smooth stroke. He tapped the circle once, heard it break free with a tiny click. He peeled off the tape and the circle of glass came with it. He reached inside, found the crank and turned it cautiously. It made a tiny sound. He took his small can of gun oil spray and squirted the mechanism beneath the handle liberally, then looked at his watch for an entire minute. The smell of the jungle rose in his nostrils. *"Toi la con ran,"* he whispered to himself. He felt a sudden heat, realizing he had spoken in Vietnamese: I was the snake, the motto of the tunnel rats. He reached in again and turned the handle. The window opened silently and Johnny slid over the sill, like the snake. His canvas-covered boot slipped on the narrow window sill and he fell into a tunnel twenty feet deep and nearly thirty years old.

20

EDWARD PACED HIS living room, going from the flickering fire-place to the dark window. Intermittent moonlight appearing and disappearing behind low wind-driven clouds flashed on whitecaps on the Sound. Edward had a drink in his hand, mostly melting ice cubes. He desperately wanted another, but he knew he would be up all night, waiting for Crazy Johnny to tell him where to find his daughter.

Or something far worse.

Jane sat quietly, staring into the fire. Abby sat next to her, talking softly. For some reason he did not know, a thought popped into his mind, a scene from his favorite of Shakespeare's plays, *Henry V,* from just before the Battle of Agincourt, where the French prince and the Marshal of France are arming themselves and predicting a crushing victory against the outnumbered English in the valley below their camp. The French prince, the Dauphin, cries, "Will it never be day?"

Edward desperately wanted the light of day, the light of deliverance.

But the day the Dauphin sought had ended in disaster, Edward thought. Be careful what you wish for.

"Go to bed, honey," Jane said. "Try to rest a bit."

"How can I?" Edward moaned. He returned to the bar and made another dark drink.

Will it never be day?

JOHNNY WAS OVERCOME with the smell at the bottom of the tunnel. It was pitch-black, and he reached for the L-shaped GI flashlight that should have been on his web harness. Lost, gone. He heard the distant gabble of Vietnamese voices, and smelled the urine and feces of poorly drained latrines. He also smelled the pungent odor of unwashed flesh, and rice and fish being cooked in rancid oil. And *nouk-mam,* the fish paste the Vietnamese smeared on everything. Johnny fought back waves of nausea. He felt around him for his weapon, and found it, his trusted Swedish K. He checked the magazine and reinserted it, and took the safety off.

Faint light streamed into the tunnel, and Johnny saw framed windows. Instead of lying on damp leaf-litter as he had thought, he was kneeling on a carpet. He shook his head to clear it; he wasn't in Vietnam at all but in a house in Black Rock, Connecticut. He was here to rescue a girl, who?

Sally Collins, Edward and Jane's daughter.

Let us run this, said his demons. We've not lost our edge.

No, Johnny commanded them, inside his burning skull. He got up and began walking toward the bedrooms, using Tolliver's memorized sketch to guide him.

The first VC came suddenly out of deep shadow, his AK held across his body. The smells and sounds returned immediately but were drowned by the K-gun's firing three times, three soft coughs. The VC crashed backwards into the wall, making far more noise than the gun.

Up, the demons said. Run! Clear the tunnel before they can trap you!

Johnny ran to the first bedroom and through the open door. A VC sat up suddenly and gasped. *"Im lang di,"* Johnny rasped, Vietnamese for silence.

"What the fuck!" the man shouted. "Jeff!"

Johnny shot him three times and was running for the last bedroom as a light came on and streamed out from beneath the door. Johnny took the door with a single thrust of his boot. A woman with long dark hair was sitting up in bed, her pert breasts exposed. She was struggling in the grasp of a Vietnamese of above-average height. He let her go and reached over the side of the bed toward the floor. The K-gun went off by itself; Johnny had no sense of pulling the trigger. The man tumbled out of the bed. The woman screamed and recoiled from the twitching corpse, then looked up at Johnny.

Johnny's mind cleared with a bang. The smells receded; Vietnam receded, he was in a house in Black Rock. The woman was Edward and Jane's daughter, Sally.

Holy shit, Johnny thought. What have I done?

"Jeff, Jeff," the girl keened, but she wouldn't look at the body. Johnny found her school uniform on a chair; blue skirt and blazer, white shirt and underwear. He picked them up and threw them onto the bed. "Get dressed," he rasped. "Immediately." He took the radio from his web gear and pressed the transmit button three times: come at once.

The girl dressed. Johnny took a pillowcase and tore it in three strips. He tied her hands behind her and wrapped a blindfold around her eyes and ears, turned out the bedroom light and hustled her out of the house and into deep shadows. Tolliver's blue van appeared in less than two minutes, and Johnny bundled her into the back. Tolliver turned from the front seat and opened his mouth. Johnny touched a finger to his lips, and Tolliver drove off.

"Who are you, you *murderer?*" Sally cried. Johnny answered in a harsh Spanish accent; it was the only thing he could think of and he spoke the language well. "*Tranquilate.* Be calm and quiet. We're taking you home."

"You—you killed my Jeff, you bastard." She struggled against her bonds.

"Be silent," he said again, and squeezed a pressure point at her elbow that made her gasp.

Tolliver drove carefully through darkened streets to the house on

Beachside Avenue. Johnny led the girl out of the van and seated her on the lawn next to the gatehouse. "Your father will come soon," he said, still disguising his voice. "We will watch until he comes."

"Oh God, oh God," the girl wailed.

Johnny went back to the van and dialed Edward's number on the cell phone. "What the fuck happened?" Tolliver whispered.

Johnny held up his hand. "Edward. Sally is safe, sitting down by your gatehouse. The whole thing went very wrong; the kidnapper was Sally's boyfriend, Jeff."

"Jesus, the bastard."

"Edward, Sally was clearly a willing participant. You must tell her nothing of me, or your recruitment of me. We'll talk soon, but come pick her up."

"On my way. And thanks, man."

"Not a word."

"Understood."

21

TOLLIVER DROVE AWAY as soon as Edward appeared in his doorway carrying a large flashlight. "Now tell me what happened, Corporal."

Johnny was in the back of the van, stripping off his gloves, ski mask, boot covers, and camouflage uniform and putting them in the black plastic garbage bag. He put the K-gun, flashlight and tools in the bottom for weight.

"I got in easily enough."

"You didn't signal."

"Sergeant, suddenly I was back in 'Nam, in a tunnel. It was fantastically real; I could hear them deeper in the tunnel and smell their cooking food."

"Jesus, you flashed-back. I was afraid of that."

"But I knew it was an hallucination. You know, how when you're dreaming, and you know you're in a dream? I knew I was in Black Rock and why. Until the first one came at me."

"The *first one?*"

"He held an AKS assault rifle across his chest. He was VC, for an instant."

"Oh, Jesus."

"I shot him. I knew he couldn't be VC, but I would have anyway, Staff Sergeant, it's what we agreed. Any armed man."

"Then what happened?"

"I entered the bedroom, the first on your sketch. Another man rose up and I told him to be quiet. He yelled something, I'm not sure what, so I killed him as well."

"Then?"

"I kicked the door in to the last bedroom, where you heard the argument. Again I saw a Vietnamese woman, long black hair, struggling with a man. He reached for something on the floor, and I shot him. Then I just came out of it, and I realized what had bothered me about your story of a man and woman arguing. I recognized Sally, of course, but then I recognized the man in bed with her; kid named Jeff, hangs around the yacht club."

"So it was a setup. The girl was in on it, but why?"

"God knows, Willy. But I killed three people tonight."

They were driving through Saugatuck, the other end of Westport from the Collins's shoreside home. The streets were totally deserted at four-thirty in the morning, but Tolliver drove at the speed limit. He drove onto an old ironwork swing bridge over the Saugatuck River. "This the place?"

"Yeah. Stop at the center; I'm ready." Johnny tied the top of the garbage bag then punched holes in it with his thumb. Now he slashed the upper side. He dropped from the van onto the bridge and tossed the bag into the swift outgoing tide. The weapons and tools should drop out as the bag rolled in the current and sink deep into soft mud within days. The uniform, mask, gloves and bootcovers would drift with the tide and disperse, but all were weighted to sink.

"Okay," he said as he climbed into the front passenger seat. "Let's go call the Bridgeport police."

"You're sure we have to do that?"

"Kids deserve burial, whatever they were." Or perhaps were not, a thought began to plague him. "There's a pay phone by that gas station." Johnny started to get out. "Maybe you should do it. They record those calls and if they come after me they might be able to do a voiceprint or something."

Tolliver frowned. "You aren't trying to lay this off on a brother, are you?"

"No. I'll make the call."

Tolliver grasped Johnny's forearm. "No, you're right. I'll do it; no way they're ever going to hear my voice again." He dropped out of the truck, made his call, and returned. "Okay, now what?"

"Drop me off at home and go home yourself. Forget this ever happened."

"How do you feel?"

Johnny shrugged. "I don't really feel anything, at least not yet." He looked at his old friend, his savior. "It was a righteous shoot. They snatched the girl, demanded ransom, threatened to kill her. We both believed they were armed, and I saw one for sure with an AK."

"An *AK?* Wasn't that part of your hallucination?"

"I recognized the curved magazine. No marine will ever forget that shape." He looked at Tolliver again. "All the street gangs have them, Willy."

"Those kids I saw didn't look like gang bangers, Johnny."

"What're you saying?"

"Maybe it *was* part of your dream."

"No, I was in control. It was a righteous shoot and I had every right to take her the way I did."

"Do you think the police can put it together? They might not agree."

"How can they ever find me?"

AS SOON AS Edward untied Sally and removed her blindfold, she ran from him screaming. He had to chase her across the lawn and drag her into the house. She raked his face with her nails and spat at him. "You killed Jeff, you son of a bitch."

"What?" Edward said. He'd heard what Johnny had told him, but it hadn't sunk in.

Jane rushed forward and tried to embrace her daughter. Sally hit her hard on her breasts, and Jane staggered and fell back into a chair. Sally fell to the floor in front of the fireplace and curled into a fetal position, wailing and crying.

"Call the doctor," Edward said urgently, standing over his daughter.

The doctor, a near neighbor, came at once and administered a powerful sedative. Edward carried Sally upstairs and put her to bed, and Jane watched her until her crying ceased and her breathing became regular.

When her mother came in to check on her at noon, Sally pretended to be asleep, although she wasn't. When Jane closed the door softly behind her, Sally picked up the Princess phone beside her bed and telephoned the Bridgeport police.

III

A SERPENT'S TOOTH

How sharper than a serpent's tooth it is
To have a thankless child.   *King Lear*

22

DETECTIVES MIKE KOLSLOVSKY and Jamal Jones finished with the crime scene at 11 Prescott Street at 6:00 A.M., October 18. They stopped for coffee at the Wawa convenience store on Fairfield Avenue then returned to the detective bureau on Congress Street and prepared to go off shift. Jamal rolled a form into his IBM Selectric, typed in the address and the details of what had been discovered. "What do you think, man?" Jamal felt a rare tremor in his hands. He'd seen death many times before, but the three young men shot up stuck in his mind and made him angry.

Kolslovsky shrugged. "Drugs, I guess. We recovered some marijuana."

"An ounce, maybe two. Not exactly enough to assume these guys were dealing. I don't think drugs."

"So? Let's finish the report and go home."

"Shit, man, if this happened in the P.T. Barnum Housing Projects and the vics were black, I could see you filing this and forgetting it. But three white kids? In Black Rock?"

Kolslovsky yawned. "When'd you get so interested in white kids?"

"Come on, Mike. I know you're tired, and I'm tired. But that crime scene was eerie. Three men dead by gunshots, multiple gunshots, and little or no physical evidence that anyone was even there."

Mike got out his notes. "Okay, a window was cut to open it. No footprints around the house, but it hasn't rained for over a week. Footprints inside no pattern, could be any of the occupants. These people weren't into housekeeping. We recovered fourteen nine-millimeter shell casings; the crime lab has those. Print guys got nothing."

"The sheets from the bed had stains."

"So somebody got laid. You know the lab; if they don't lose the stuff, it'll be days before we get anything back."

"A little bell is tinkling in my brain, Mike."

"What?" Mike said crossly. "I gotta get home, man; my wife's sick and I'm supposed to take my kid to school."

"Remember the lieutenant from the state police here a few days ago, rattling O'Hara's cage?" O'Hara was Bridgeport's Chief of Detectives. "The guy asking about a stolen van that got squealed by some contractor from Westchester County? I think it was recovered in the same neighborhood."

Mike sat up straight. "Wait. Westport police had a bell out a couple of days ago; watch out for a tan van used in a kidnapping. Watch only; don't intervene at the request of the parents. You think this could be tied in?"

Jamal began to type rapidly. "Go home; take care of your boy. I'm going to make a few calls."

Mike got up and took his jacket from the back of his chair. "Call me, partner, if you find anything."

Jamal got a cup of coffee and cranked up the department's antiquated computer. He brought up the notice from the Westport police, and got a detective's name. He checked the report on the recovery of the stolen minivan: right in front of the house where the three bodies were found after an anonymous tip over the phone. Jamal went down to Communications and listened to the tape of the call-in. The voice was that of a black man.

Why *do* I care about this one? He asked himself. In a city as racist as Bridgeport, why should a black detective want to find out who killed three white boys at least somewhat involved in drugs? He and Mike had canvassed the neighboring houses to the crime scene, waking people up and interviewing them in their bathrobes; nobody had seen anything or heard someone fire fourteen gunshots.

A professional did this, but why?

Jamal returned to his desk and called the Westport detective.

JANE TOOK SOME scrambled eggs, toast and a glass of orange juice up to Sally's room at one o'clock. She found her daughter dressed in jeans and a sweater, sitting on the edge of her bed staring out at the Sound. Jane set the tray on Sally's desk and was surprised but pleased when Sally went to her chair and devoured the meal quickly. "Thanks, Mom," Sally said listlessly.

"Can you tell me what happened?" Jane said. Abby, who was downstairs, had emphatically warned Jane against being accusatory or judgmental.

"Jeff's dead. Daddy killed him."

Jane felt a great hurt in her womb and sat on the bed. "What Daddy did was only to try to get you home. I saw you kidnapped outside the school; I heard the kidnappers say terrifying things to Daddy."

"Why didn't he just fucking *pay!*" Sally screamed, sweeping the tray to the floor. "A half million is nothing to Daddy, or to you."

Jane found she didn't want to tell Sally that Edward was broke, or nearly so. At this moment she felt more loyal to her husband than to this angry, spiteful daughter. "Why did you go along with Jeff's idea? Why did you want us to pay him?"

Sally stood and began pacing. "Because I want a life. I want to be free of all your petty bullshit rules. I'm grown up and you treat me like a child."

"You're fifteen," Jane said gently. "You are a child."

"See? That's it. I'll be sixteen in two months; I've had sex with Jeff for over a year, and I'm much older than you were at my age, but you just won't see it."

"What would you have done with the money?" Jane asked softly.

"We had to give some to Gill and Tom; I suppose Daddy had them killed as well. Then Jeff and I were going to Mexico; Jeff knows a place called Bahia de Navidad on the west coast where you never would have found us."

"Do you truly hate us so much?"

"Christ! You had the man I love killed. For years you've treated me like shit, making me go to that awful school, telling me I shouldn't see so much of Jeff, criticizing my friends." Sally began to cry. Her mother tried to hold her but Sally pushed her away. "Yes, Mother, I hate you both."

Jane burst into tears and ran from the room. Sally picked up her phone and called the Bridgeport police again.

Jane sat on the stairs outside Sally's room and wept. How sharper than a serpent's tooth, she thought, it is to have a thankless child.

THOMAS JACKSON, ESQUIRE, had hired the small private dining room at Ralph and Ritchie's Restaurant in downtown Bridgeport to celebrate a verdict he had confidently predicted two weeks before the trial began, and had received just this morning from Judge Grogan only minutes before the noon recess. The case was an arson, the burning of a lumberyard on the east side of Bridgeport. The jury had deliberated overnight; they could have taken days, but Thomas Jackson was confident enough to book the room.

The victory was sweet because the case and its evidence were complicated, the judge difficult and obtuse, and the prosecutor better than usual.

The win was especially sweet because Thomas Jackson knew his client was guilty as hell.

Seated around the table were his associate, pretty, talented Angela Hughes, two other associates, the two clerks he employed in his office in Westport, and the investigator he had used to destroy the prosecution's theory of arson. The warehouse where the fire had started contained paint and solvents, and the investigator swore the "accelerant" that spread the fire throughout the property had been solvent and paint, not gasoline as the police had concluded. Thomas Jackson had taken advantage, as he often had, of the sloppy record-keeping and crime-scene preservation of the Bridgeport police.

Jackson was not loved by the Bridgeport police. Few defense lawyers were, if they were any good. So he was surprised to be interrupted amid the champagne, smoked Scottish salmon and caviar that constituted the first course (billable of course to his grateful client, Jimmy Nagy, who sat at the head of the table) by a waiter who whispered that there was an urgent call for him, a call from Police Headquarters. The waiter invited him to use the restaurant's tiny office for a bit of privacy.

The caller was a detective Thomas Jackson had worked with before; one of the few on the Bridgeport PD Thomas Jackson thought could be expected to find his own ass in the shower with both hands. His name was Jamal Jones, and he had never made any secret of the fact that he thought Thomas Jackson was devious, deceitful, dishonest and a threat to civil order. But in a strange way, the two men trusted each other. "Detective Jones," Thomas Jackson said heartily. "How can I help you?"

"As I recall you were in the marines, Attorney Jackson. In 'Nam."

"True," Jackson said cautiously.

"We have a crime scene. Triple homicide, in Black Rock. Has an eerie feeling about it, like 'Nam. Somebody or somebodies, we don't even know that, got in and out of this house like silk. No sounds, nothing to wake the neighbors."

"Okay," Thomas Jackson said. "Why tell me?"

"Off the record?"

"Sure," Thomas Jackson said, wondering if he would keep the promise.

"Chief O'Hara wants this buried. Written off to drugs; there was a tiny amount of grass at the scene, so who cares? I don't think that's it and I want someone with drag to get interested."

"Why me?"

"You know I don't love defense lawyers, especially ones as slick as you. But you're ex-military and so am I. I think this was a professional hit."

"Who were the victims?"

"Three white teenagers, middle-class."

"Why would they be hit? Unless, as the esteemed O'Hara believes, drugs?"

"There may be an angle. A kidnapping a few days ago in Westport nobody wants to talk about. A cover-up a mile deep."

"What are you thinking, Detective?"

"Maybe a vigilante. I don't know but I have been told to write it off."

"Again, why me?"

"You could ask around; make sure the case is investigated. I have an uneasy feeling the shooter—and I think only one—was military, or ex. Scene is too clean, each vic three in the chest, one in the head, except one who was apparently moving when he got shot. He took six.

"It looks like the way the special ops boys did business, Attorney Jackson. SEALs, your Force Recon, our Delta Force. Only thing scarier than a loose killer is a loose killer who knows how to do it and scoot."

"Scarier than a wildass defense lawyer?"

"Is why I called."

Thomas Jackson considered it. "You want me to rattle some military cages?"

"Might could."

"And?"

"When I catch the perp, you could defend him. Or them."

Thomas Jackson considered it. "Do you know my associate, Angela Hughes?"

"Met her. Good."

"Should I send her over to see you? This afternoon?"

"Yeah. She's in this building a lot; nobody notice."

Thomas Jackson hung up and returned to his party.

MIKE KOLSLOVSKY RETURNED to the detective squadroom in downtown Bridgeport just after two in the afternoon. He found a yawning Jamal Jones sitting in front of the computer terminal surrounded by printouts. "How come you still here?" he asked his partner.

"How come you're back? We don't begin our watch again until midnight."

Mike sat at his desk that faced Jamal. "Couldn't sleep. Got the kid squared-away, and began to think. You're right, Jamal, there's something odd in all this."

"Be right. A disturbance in my natural rhythm."

"I stopped at the front desk on the way up." He laid two message slips in front of Jamal. "As usual, they just threw them in 'circulation' without trying to trace them to any case in progress."

Jamal picked them up. Two calls, from the same number in Westport, no name attached. The first said simply, "The man killed at Eleven Prescott Street is Jeff Paglia." The second said "Edward Collins killed Jeff."

Jamal tapped the messages. He'd go to Communications and listen to the tapes later. "What's the trace on the number?"

"Fifty-six Beachside Avenue, Westport. Residence of Edward and Jane Collins; this number is registered to their daughter Sally."

"The kidnap victim?" Jamal asked.

"Yes," Mike said. "I checked."

Jamal handed two printouts across to his partner. "Forensics. Read 'em and weep."

Kolslovsky read. They were reports from the crime lab. "How'd you get those fat butts to move so fast?"

"Wasn't easy. Read."

Koslovsky read. No prints in the house other than the victims' plus an unidentified set the criminologist speculated belonged to a young female. The fourteen brass shell casings had been carefully wiped clean and had nothing on them at all. Hair and fiber: nothing unconnected to the victims except some very long dark brown hairs. The description of the kidnapped girl from Westport described long dark hair. The sheets on the only made bed had semen stains, also vaginal fluid. The semen matched the blood type of the victim in the bedroom, identified as Jeff Paglia of Lake Avenue in Black Rock. "Almost looks like a professional hit."

"Doesn't it just," Jamal said. "Go see O'Hara, see if he'll get us a John Doe warrant in this matter; Judge Rogers is in his chambers."

Mike got up. "O'Hara wants this written off. A dispute over drugs."

"I don't think so. Neither do you, Mike. Try him again, please."

Mike shrugged, got up, yawned. "I'm on it." He went down the corridor to the Chief of Detectives' office.

Jamal picked up the phone and dialed Detective Russo in Westport, told the tale and hung up. Mike came back. "Boss says get going. Strange; total change in attitude. He'll get the warrant and have a patrol unit bring it to Westport. All of a sudden, O'Hara's hot on this one, Jamal."

Jackson made the call, Jamal thought, disgusted; disgusted with himself, but knowing it had to be done. Black kids in the projects got shot every day, and while politicians, black and white, deplored it, nothing was done. Jamal agonized about the voice on the tape tipping the police to the crime scene, the black man's voice. I hope a brother didn't do this, he thought. "Detective Russo will meet us at the gate of the Collins home as soon as we get there."

J OHNNY SLEP T SEVEN hours after Tolliver dropped him off; slept with no dreams. He cooked himself a substantial lunch, then went back to his computer. He brought up a book he was working on, had been writing very slowly, and looked at the screen for an hour. It was a book about a Vietnam vet with Post Traumatic Stress Disorder, and how he suffered not only from the horror of Vietnam but also from the rejection he faced when he returned to the World, as vets called the United States. A man very much like himself.

I should feel remorse about those dead men, Johnny said to himself. Pain. But I don't, I wonder why? The girl must have designed the thing to extort money from her father, money she didn't know he didn't have.

What would those boys have done if Edward had paid, or if he hadn't? Had the girl thought that out? After all, they had made a threat of extortion to the parents; that has to be some kind of crime by itself.

Johnny was blocked on the book, right as the vet first entered treatment in a program modeled after Staff Sergeant Tolliver's. He couldn't continue, and then suddenly he was typing at the speed of heat. The book was boiling out of him uncontrolled, unbidden.

23

Jane Collins met the three detectives at her front door. She had seen the blue and white Westport patrol car roll up the long driveway followed by a dirty unmarked Chevrolet sedan. She glanced at the badges and identity cards the officers showed her, then invited them into the living room. She offered coffee that all three declined. Abby, who had spent a fruitless hour talking to Sally, sat in a chair near the broad window overlooking the Sound. She was introduced to the two big white men and one even larger African-American. Once the formalities were completed, Detective Russo spoke. "Mrs. Collins, how's Sally?"

"Very upset. She only got home last night, or rather near dawn this morning. I called the police to report she'd come home."

"These detectives from Bridgeport need to speak with her, Mrs. Collins. It seems she called their switchboard twice earlier this afternoon."

"Sally did?"

"May we speak with her, please?" Detective Russo asked gently.

"I guess. I don't know. May I call my husband?"

Russo looked at the Bridgeport cops. They were expressionless. "Of course, Mrs. Collins."

The detectives watched as Jane left the room, went into the kitchen to call even though there was a phone plainly visible on an antique desk across the room. They turned as one when they heard a footstep on the hardwood floor at the base of the staircase.

This must be Sally, Detective Kolslovsky thought, looking at the girl with long dark hair, pale skin and blue eyes, large like a frightened doe's.

How pretty she is, Detective Jones thought.

Detective Russo went over and shook the girl's hand, introduced the Bridgeport men. "We need to ask you some questions, Sally, but we should wait until your mom comes back."

Abby had risen from her chair, but now she nodded to Jamal and sat back down.

"How did you know it was me?" Sally asked.

J ANE'S CALL GOT Edward out of a meeting. "Don't let them talk to her until I get home," he said. "I'll be there in ten minutes. Peter Bates is here with me and I'll bring him." He hung up abruptly. Peter Bates was the family lawyer who also represented Edward in most of his business deals.

"W E TRACED THE calls," Jamal said, as the girl came forward into the room and sat on a couch. She seemed calm and poised but her eyes were red and swollen.

"I only said a few words, then hung up," she said.

"Technology," Mike Kolslovsky offered. "It's not like the movies where you need three or five minutes to trace. You probably have it here in your own home; it's called Caller ID."

Sally nodded slowly. "We do have it. How stupid of me. What do you want?"

Abby got up and crossed the room, stood between the girl and the policemen. "Wait for your mother, Sally," she said sharply, glaring at the police.

Jane came back. "My husband wants to be here before you talk to our daughter. He said ten minutes. I hope that's all right."

"Perfectly all right," Detective Russo said.

"You have a beautiful home and grounds," Jamal Jones said.

"Might we take a walk down to the Sound while we wait for your husband?"

Jane looked at her daughter. Abby had sat beside her and taken her hand. "Of course," Jane said. "Thank you."

Edward arrived nine minutes after receiving Jane's call. Peter Bates parked his Lexus behind Edward's Mercedes and they strode together into the house. Edward took in the scene: Abby and Jane seated on the couch on either side of Sally, who was once again crying silently. She greeted her father with a look of such hostility that he stopped in his tracks. Outside on the lawn he saw three large men looking out at the water. Peter Bates sat opposite the three women. "Did they ask you anything?" he asked Sally.

"No," Abby answered for her. "They waited for both parents as Jane requested."

"I *want* to talk to them. I want to tell them what you *did,*" Sally shouted, glaring at her father.

"Give us a minute," Peter said, drawing Edward toward his study. "Then we'll talk to them."

"WHAT DO YOU think?" Jamal asked Mike.

"I think Westport cops handle these things a little too soft for us. This is a capital felony, Russo; three counts of murder with intent."

"Relax," Russo said, stiffening. "We all get to the same place. Westport isn't Bridgeport and these are people of flawless reputation. My guess is they'll have their attorney present when we go back in and he'd tear you a new asshole if you'd gone after that minor without the parents' informed consent."

EDWARD SAT BEHIND his desk and told the story. His lawyer listened in silence. "Did you know Johnny intended to go in shooting?"

"Truthfully, no, but I certainly didn't know he wouldn't."

"Sally's told you the kidnapping was a fake, but you couldn't have known that."

"Hell, no. The guy who called me and threatened to kill Sally scared the hell out of me. I was absolutely sure he meant business."

Peter Blake was silent for a moment. "This isn't going to be good for Johnny."

"Jesus, Peter, he did it for me, for Sally. We have to protect him."

"Help him, yes, where we can. But you can't tell all to the cops; at best that makes you an accessory to murder before and after, at worst, a co-conspirator. My job is to protect your ass, not Crazy Johnny's."

"But those bastards kidnapped my daughter and said they'd kill her! Johnny said that in cases like this where the victim sees her attackers and where they refuse to make a direct exchange, the victims are nearly always killed."

"He's right, and the cops know it. Why'd Sally call the cops? What's she want to tell them?"

Edward hung his head. "That I caused her lover's death. That I had him killed."

Peter saw no reason to pursue that. "Can Sally have recognized Crazy Johnny? Or have you or Jane told her?"

"I certainly haven't told her. I hope Jane hasn't but I doubt she would. Johnny did a lot of covert shit in his time in the Marine Corps, and maybe afterwards. I doubt he'd do this without his face blackened, or some form of disguise. When he dropped Sally off at four in the morning, she was bound and blindfolded. I naturally assumed that's the way he took her from the kidnappers."

Peter thought about it; it wasn't good. "We better not keep these guys waiting any longer; they'll assume we're getting our stories straight. You go in and tell Jane, and if possible, Sally, to say as little as possible without lying. I'll go outside and talk to the cops."

Edward nodded. "I really had no idea her boyfriend was involved."

"Or that *she* was. Don't forget that." He stood up. "We have to prevent her from talking to the cops. She could incriminate you and Jane, and worse, all three of you. We have to get her counsel of her own. She may not understand it, but she participated in extortion."

"Can't you just make them go away?"

"Maybe. I doubt it. Westport cops defer to residents and their attorneys; Bridgeport cops are used to having their way. But I'll try. In the meantime, call Marvin Levin, the best criminal guy I know." He took a notebook from his pocket and wrote down a number. "Retain him. Then call Eben Shaw, the second best, and have him prepare to represent Sally."

"What about Johnny? He should have counsel; I doubt he does."

"Stay the hell away from that crazy bastard. He is nothing but trouble for you. Poison."

"But he—he brought her back. I owe—"

"Stay the hell away from him, that's an order."

PETER WALKED DOWN to the seawall. He extended his hand, first to the black man; a white lawyer's trick with cops. "I'm Peter Bates. I represent the family. They thank you for your patience; please come inside."

Detectives Russo, Kolslovsky and Jones filed back into the living room, followed by Peter Bates. The girl, her mother and the black woman, Abby, were seated by the window, in deep conversation. Edward had a drink in his hand.

"Gentlemen," Peter began, addressing the detectives, "As attorney for the family, I am advising her parents to direct her not to speak, on the grounds she may incriminate herself. I'll arrange counsel for her as quickly as possible, but if you insist on interviewing her, a minor, against her parents' wishes, you'll have to get a court order."

Detective Russo turned to his Bridgeport colleagues and shrugged. "I guess that's all for today—"

"Wait," Jamal Jones said. "We have two calls from this house, Sally's phone. They were automatically traced and recorded. If she doesn't wish to speak with us until represented, fine, but we have a capital felony here, three counts of murder with intent. We'll have to take her into custody as a material witness with the possibility of charges being lodged. She'll be confined at the Women's Correctional Facility in Niantic until such time as she is represented and will answer questions."

"Niantic!" Peter Bates leaped from his chair. "You can't put this child in Niantic overnight! I can't imagine a worse horror for a girl already traumatized—"

"There's no other place in Connecticut we can hold a female overnight," Kolslovsky said evenly.

"What's Niantic?" Jane said in a weak voice.

"A hellhole," Peter bellowed. "It's a confinement center for the hardest female prisoners in the state. Murderers, child abusers, *rapists* for Christ's sake. You can't do this."

"We can," Jamal said. "We will." In a classic cop gesture of intimidation, he eased handcuffs from a holster on his belt. "Come along, Sally."

"No, no, *no!"* Jane screamed, clutching her daughter to her breast. "Peter, stop this!"

"I—I, at least let me get counsel for her."

"Then she'll talk?" Jamal said, swinging the handcuffs. "Here, today?"

Peter turned to Jane and Edward, who stood open mouthed. "Take the deal," Peter mouthed.

"Okay. Get the lawyer," Jane keened. "Just don't let my baby be taken away again."

Peter went into the office to call. Edward said weakly, "Like another walk in the garden?"

"We'll keep the subject in sight, thank you," Jamal said. The doorbell rang and Abby went to answer it. She returned leading a uniformed Bridgeport policeman. "Those the arrest warrants?" Jamal said in a carrying voice. The cop produced the paperwork, turned and left.

Jamal pretended to study the warrant, although it was all boilerplate. He still held the handcuffs in plain view. Twenty minutes later Eben Shaw, the second-best criminal lawyer in the state of Connecticut arrived in his Jaguar. He talked to the parents and the daughter for thirty minutes in the kitchen, then led them back to the living room to face the three stone-faced cops there. "Ground rules," Eben Shaw said. "Is my client a target of investigation, or a suspect?"

"Depends on what she has to say," Jamal said. "She called us."

"Neither the girl nor her parents are to be targets, or there will be no interrogation until they are charged."

Mike leaned forward and pinned the fat attorney with his hard eyes. "Niantic," he said. Jane gasped. "There is, counselor," Mike rasped, "as you well know, a fine line between representation and obstruction of justice."

"Take it easy, Mike," Jamal said. "We want the shooter or shooters. We'll work with the State's Attorney on the rest of it, but we can't give guarantees."

"No Niantic."

"Not tonight, if she answers truthfully."

"Begin," Attorney Shaw said simply, seating himself next to the girl. Her parents and the therapist, Abby, took the couch at right angles.

Jamal put his handcuffs back in their holster and leaned forward. "Tell us why you called us, Sally," he said.

24

"Jeff and the others, Gil and Tom, picked me up at school. I was surprised; I wasn't expecting them, and they just grabbed me. We were all laughing; Jeff knows my mother doesn't like him, and she was waiting right there by her car. We drove around for a while, had a few beers, then went over to Gil's house in Black Rock. His parents are on a cruise."

"Gil would be Gilbert Herrero?" Jamal said, consulting his notes. The boy found in the living room clutching a field hockey stick.

"Yes," Sally said in her steady monotone. "Later one of the guys, I forget who, suggested we call Mom and tell her it was a kidnapping, maybe get Daddy to give us some money. I said that was dumb, but Tom called."

She says her lines beautifully, Eben Shaw thought. She's just taken herself out of extortion and conspiracy to commit extortion. He watched with satisfaction as the black cop, who didn't look terribly bright, dutifully wrote all the claptrap down.

Little bitch be lying through her expensively straightened teeth, Jamal thought. "Did you hear what Tom, Thomas O'Connor?"— the boy in the smaller bedroom. Sally nodded—"what Tom said to your mother?"

"I think he said he spoke to Daddy. But no, I didn't hear what he said."

Jamal nodded gravely. They had found only one phone in the tiny house and it was in the living room, next to a tiny kitchen. Almost surely another lie; the fat butt lawyer had coached her to lay all the evil on the voiceless dead. "How much money was asked for?"

"I'm not sure," Sally said. Jamal saw her mother look up sharply.

Sally caught the look and for the first time lost her chilling composure. "I think maybe he said a half-million dollars."

Jamal turned to his partner and smiled. Mike nodded; his turn. "Tell us what happened last night."

Sally's face screwed up with pain that seemed genuine. "We were all asleep. I heard Tom, in the other bedroom, cry out, call Jeff's name. Then there was a crash like he'd fallen out of bed. I turned on the light. This man kicked the door right off the hinges and burst through. I threw my arms around Jeff but he pushed me away, tried to get in front of me to protect me. The man shot Jeff three or four times; the gun made hardly any sound."

"Then?" Mike prompted.

"The man threw my clothes at me and told me to dress. He tore up a pillowcase and bound my arms, then he blindfolded me, took me outside and pushed me into a truck or something." Sally relaxed; Jamal sensed she was back on truth.

"A minivan?"

"It seemed bigger, higher."

"Describe the man. The shooter."

"He was dressed in one of those uniforms soldiers wear, black and green all mixed up. He had a black ski mask with only eyeholes."

"Could you see the skin around his eyes?" Mike asked. She shook her head. "I'm asking you if he was black or white, Sally."

"I really didn't see, but I think black. But his eyes were weird, like, yellow."

Yellow eyes, Mike thought. Great. "Height, weight?"

"Maybe six feet, or a bit less. His clothing was loose but he didn't look fat."

Super, Jamal thought. A guy of average height and build who might be black and was wearing colored contacts. Be a snap picking him up. "Sally, you still haven't said why you called us."

Her face changed completely, reddened and became mottled and twisted with rage. In an instant the pretty girl was rendered ugly. "Because Daddy must have sent him, and he killed my Jeff!" she shrieked.

Attorney Shaw was on his feet. "Sally, be silent!" He turned to the detectives. "She can't possibly know that."

"Why do you think your father sent the shooter?" Mike demanded, an edge on his voice.

Eben Shaw was still standing. "Sally, don't answer. This interview is over."

"It's *over?*" Mike asked softly. "Cooperation is *ended?*"

"Unless you are prepared to charge my client—"

"We can do that," Jamal said with a smile. "The girl, with conspiracy to commit extortion, the father with three capital felony murders."

"The girl told you she had no foreknowledge of the extortion—"

"She was lying," Jamal said pleasantly. "Shall we go?"

"But Daddy didn't actually commit the murders," Sally blurted.

"We don't even know that," Mike said. "He fits your description." As do half the men on the planet, he said to himself.

Sally looked around wildly. Detective Kolslovsky got out his plastic laminated Miranda card and began to read Edward his rights. Edward was blubbering like a child; the thought of spending even one night in the Bridgeport jail terrified him even more than the thought of Sally in the women's prison in Niantic. Jamal produced the handcuffs he had displayed earlier. Sally felt close to panic. "Wait, wait!" she wailed. "I know who must have done it! The only man Daddy knows who would. Mr. Dietrich, the sick Vietnam vet, the one everyone calls Crazy Johnny."

Mike finished reading the Miranda warning and sat down. He took a small tape recorder from his jacket pocket and turned it on. A red light glowed as he set it on the table between the couches.

"Perhaps, with counsel's permission, we may begin again, without the bullshit."

Edward spoke for nearly two hours. His lawyer cautioned him a couple of times but was met with baleful stares from Detective Kolslovsky. He told of the threats the caller had made, and of how he'd gone to see Johnny to borrow the money. He looked at his daughter when he told the cops how short of cash he was, and she looked away. He told the cops Johnny's view that since the kidnappers hadn't even masked themselves that they would surely kill Sally, the proof of their crime, if he paid without a direct exchange, and that the kidnappers had refused any direct exchange and again threatened to kill her.

Jamal began to feel for this tormented man, this Crazy Johnny. He was the man he had felt in the crime scene; the man he had called Jackson about. Jamal knew the statistics and Johnny was right, the girl was dead meat once the payment was made.

If this had been a real kidnapping. What a clusterfuck.

Jamal found sympathy for Edward, too. He'd tried to protect his family, his only child. "What did Johnny say to do?"

"He said he'd rescue her the same evening of the second demand. Christ, that was yesterday; it seems weeks ago. He wouldn't let me go with him."

"Did he say he would go in shooting?"

"No. I had no idea what his plan was."

"So to your knowledge he acted alone."

"So far as I know. Johnny is an ex-marine, he was what they called a tunnel rat in Vietnam. I guess he'd know how to do something like this."

Mike was an ex-marine. Jamal had been an army Airborne Ranger. "Before Johnny went in, did he ask your permission?" Jamal asked.

"No, he kind of assumed it from the very beginning. I didn't tell him not to go. I was afraid for my daughter's life and I didn't know what to do."

Mike stood up and rubbed his back above the waist. "Let's take a little break," he said. "Jamal? A word outside?"

Edward smiled with relief. Jane held his hand tightly. Jamal followed Mike out onto the driveway, where they both lit their first cigarettes in hours. "You're the senior, man," Mike said. "What do you want to do?"

"Let's not charge him for now, or the girl. Their lawyers'd have her out in a few minutes anyway; him too if the judge didn't buy the capital charge. If he's telling the truth that this Johnny never told him he was planning an armed assault, we probably couldn't make conspiracy stick, and the state would plead out the accessory shit."

"Yeah. Better just leave them scared. We better go bust this crazy guy."

"Yeah. You know, I think in his shoes, I might have done the same thing." Jamal saw the blasted faces of the dead men, and remembered others.

"Me, too," Mike said. "It's that damn girl who really should be wearing these." He nodded at the handcuffs.

"Call the Fairfield cops, ask them to back us up while we take the guy. I'll go back in and give them the 'Don't leave town' speech, and thank them for their 'cooperation,' so graciously volunteered. Fairfield's got a mini-SWAT team if the guy resists."

"Okay, but I'm betting he doesn't. I'm also betting I'm going to like the fucker."

"Yeah. This job's a bitch."

Mike made the arrangements over his cell phone. No sense using the radio; if the guy was a nut he might have a police radio scanner. Jamal returned with Detective Russo in tow. "You guys are something else," Russo said angrily as he climbed into his blue and white.

"Yeah," Mike said to Jamal as the Westport car pulled away. "We're cops."

"Let's go find this Crazy Johnny."

25

JAMAL AND MIKE met the Fairfield police at the foot of John Dietrich's long driveway, two radio cars each with four uniforms in it, and a truck that contained the SWAT team. "Sergeant Dunleavy," said the senior man of the detail.

Mike and Jamal introduced themselves and gave Dunleavy a thumbnail sketch of the facts. "You know anything about this guy?" Jamal asked.

"Yeah, I know him. Real quiet, hardly ever comes into town. He has a woman who cleans for him and she does his routine shopping. Good marine, fine jacket, serious decorations; we got it from the FBI when he applied for a pistol permit."

"He has a carry permit?" Jamal asked. "We were told there's a history of mental instability."

"Nothing solid. He has that post-traumatic stress shit that half the 'Nam vets have. Lotta our cops have it too; I'm sure yours do, those old enough to have served."

Mike was old enough, and had served. "So he's a recluse" he said. "Any local history of violent behavior?"

"None. In fact I was in one of our local bars where he was meeting his sailing friends—he sails, it seems to be his only interest other than his novels—and some asshole who'd read one of his books insisted on buying him a drink. Johnny's a recovered alcoholic; he said no thanks. The guy pushed, called him a fake marine, a pussy who wouldn't drink with a real veteran. Johnny just got up and walked out without a word."

"Shit," Mike said. "I knew I was going to like this guy."

"You will. I brought my Special Weapons and Tactics guys because you asked, but I'd like to leave them in the truck."

"Your call," Jamal said. "We'll follow you."

The two radio cars led the dirty Bridgeport sedan slowly up to the house. They all got out warily, but no weapons were drawn. Dunleavy knocked at the door. "Johnny? Its Sean Dunleavy of the police."

The door opened almost immediately, and Johnny came out onto the porch. He was dressed in jeans and a T-shirt. He looked at the eight uniforms and two plainclothes men he didn't recognize. "Sean, what's all this?"

"I'm truly sorry, Johnny," Dunleavy said.

Jamal stepped forward. "John Dietrich?"

"Yes."

"Detective Jamal Jones, Bridgeport PD. You're under arrest for the capital felony of murder with intent of three human beings: Jeffrey Paglia, Thomas O'Connor and Gilbert Herrero. Mike?"

Mike produced his Miranda card and began to read. "You have the right to remain silent. If you give up that right, anything you say may be used against you in a court of law . . ." He got to the end. "Do you understand your rights?"

"Yes."

"Do you have an attorney or do you want the court to appoint one for you?"

"I don't have one, but I have the means to pay for one."

"Do you wish to say anything at this time?" Mike asked gently, hoping to hell the guy wouldn't.

"No. I'll remain silent."

A black Mercedes 560 SEL glided to a silent stop behind the police vehicles. A man about sixty, handsome and silver-haired in a suit that must have cost a month's pay for a cop, got out and stepped forward. "Thomas Jonathan Jackson the Sixth," he said with a little bow. "I'm an attorney, and I understand you have need of representation."

"Who sent you?" Johnny asked.

Jackson looked at Jamal Jones, then quickly away. "Peter Bates. He represents Edward Collins."

Mike said quickly, "Maybe you want a guy that has nothing to do with Collins."

"Shut up, Mike," Jamal said.

"I have never met Mr. Collins. I am a very fine attorney, Mr. Dietrich." Jackson had a soft Southern accent.

Johnny was good with languages and accents and guessed northern Virginia. "I want to call a guy, a friend," Johnny said. "Everybody I really trust was a marine; he'll get me a lawyer who served."

"Twenty-seven years ago I was Captain Thomas Jonathan Jackson, Echo Company, Second of the Ninth Marines, at Khe Sanh and later Da Nang."

"You guys were next to us at Hue in the battle after Tet."

"Yes, the Battle of the Twenty-six Days."

"Okay, we'll talk. But I was only a corporal."

"I've read your books, Mr. Dietrich. And in the Marine Corps we served in, there is no such thing as 'only a corporal.' "

"We have to get downtown," Mike said gently. "Sorry, man, I have to cuff you; please turn around." Johnny turned and placed his wrists behind him. Mike fastened the cuffs, but not tightly. He whispered, "Kolslovsky, Buck Sergeant, First of the Sixth. Keep cool, man. Semper Fi."

"I'll follow right behind, Mr. Dietrich," Thomas Jackson said. "Detectives, I'd like to interview my client as soon as he's booked."

"N-no problem," Mike stammered. For no reason he could think of, his eyes were brimming with tears. He looked at Jamal and his eyes were shining also. Mike gently turned Johnny around to lead him to the police car.

Johnny's face was a mask of stone.

IV

MURDER WITH INTENT

26

KOLSLOVSKY TOOK JOHNNY to the booking area and turned him over to a uniformed officer for processing. "Treat this guy right, Pilsudski," Mike said to the uniform. "Get him a clean cell, by himself if possible."

Pilsudski read the charge sheet. "Jesus, a triple homicide and you want this guy privileged?"

"That's right, Pilsudski," Mike Kolslovsky growled.

"Anything you say, Mike."

Kolslovsky went into the detective bureau and found the lawyer Thomas Jackson sitting next to his desk. Jamal was already typing up the Q and A session with the Collinses. He had headphones on, connected to the tape recorder, and he had his notes. "Do the arrest report, okay, Mike?" he said without looking up.

"Sure." Mike sat down and looked at the lawyer. I hope this guy's a miracle worker, he thought. "As soon as they get through with the fingerprinting, photos, uniform issue and all that, I'll get you an interview room. Be about half an hour."

"Thanks. How soon will I get copies of your report and the crime-scene and lab reports?"

"Crime-scene and lab stuff are all here," Mike said. "I'll make copies." He nodded toward Jamal who was typing at his usual incredible speed. "Jamal'll be done by the time Johnny's ready."

The lawyer smiled. "Usually I have to ask several times and wait days."

Mike leaned close. "This guy may have done what that slickster in Westport says, but even if he did I think he's getting a raw deal."

"You probably shouldn't say anything further, Detective. But thanks."

"Semper Fi, sir."

Johnny looked very unhappy in his orange uniform. He managed a smile as he shook Jackson's hand. The police officer left and closed the door behind him. Johnny and Jackson sat on opposite sides of a plain wooden table. "Let's just chat a moment," Jackson said. "Get to know each other."

Johnny nodded, staring at Jackson's engraved card. " 'Thomas Jonathan Jackson the *Sixth.*' Sounds like an English king."

"You don't recognize the name? You're not a Southern man."

"No—hey, not Thomas *Stonewall* Jackson, the Confederate general?"

"Exactly. I'm not a direct descendant, but from a collateral branch of the family that decided to perpetuate the name. In the legal fraternity, I have been accorded the same nickname, Stonewall, but you must never call me that when anyone might hear."

"Because you stonewall people?"

"Not in the sense Nixon's men used the word. Because it's the way I build a defense, a stone at a time. Big stones and little stones, Mr. Dietrich, until it's a wall."

"What should I call you? Please call me Johnny."

"Tom will do nicely, Johnny."

"Okay, Tom. How do we start?"

"First, I'll need to have you sign powers of attorney so I can begin to draw funds from your accounts—a retainer for me, expenses for my investigator, et cetera." Johnny started to speak but

Jackson held up his hand. "If you can't pay, I'll do this *pro bono*. I owe my life to marines like you."

"Thank you for offering, but I made a lot of money on the books and films. What next?"

"Maybe you'd better tell me what happened."

"First let me ask a question. A hypothetical question. Suppose you have a client who's accused of a crime, and he admits to you he did it. You couldn't let him testify, could you?"

"Not quite true. If I thought this hypothetical client was going to *lie* in his testimony, then I couldn't let him on the stand because I'd be suborning perjury. If he were intending to tell the truth, perhaps in the form of an explanation, there would be no problem."

"I see."

"Do you? If I were to put you on the witness stand, a decision we are a long, long way from even considering, were you planning on lying to me or the court?"

"No, sir," Johnny said, looking Jackson hard in the eyes.

"I believe you." Jackson found Johnny's eyes profoundly unnerving. "Let's begin at the very beginning." He opened up his huge lawyer's briefcase, took out a cassette recorder and a lined legal pad, and took a gold pen from his jacket pocket.

"Three days ago I had a visit from Edward Collins," Johnny said, watching the glowing red light on the little recorder. "He told me his daughter had been kidnapped and he needed to borrow a million dollars for ransom or they'd kill her . . ."

G EORGE CARELLI, THE state's attorney for the city of Bridgeport, was leaving his office at Lyon Terrace at a quarter past six when the phone rang. It was Paul O'Hara, the Chief of Detectives. "Glad I caught you, sir," O'Hara said.

"Well, I'm not. I have a political fund-raiser tonight." The Democratic Party Convention was only months away, and Carelli thought he had a good shot at being nominated for lieutenant governor. "What is it, Paul?"

"We got a guy for the shoot-up on Prescott Street. It's a little odd; I'd like to send my detectives over to brief you before the press gets it."

"Which detectives?" Carelli didn't think much of the quality of the Bridgeport PD's detective squad.

"Jamal Jones and Mike Kolslovsky."

At least they're competent, actually better than competent, Carelli thought. He took off his raincoat and threw it on a chair. "Send them right over."

"They're on their way."

Jamal and Mike walked around the corner to the State's Attorney's office, and were there in two minutes. Jamal carried a copy of all the documentation to date. He put the Q and A of Edward Collins on the top. Carelli speed-read through the report and the top sheets of the arrest report, the crime-scene report and the lab report. "Jesus, this sucks."

"Chief O'Hara thought you'd want time to think about this before the press gets it at the arraignment."

"So. We got a guy, a deranged Vietnam vet—"

"Not deranged," Mike said firmly. "Stressed-out, but never been a problem to anyone."

"I'm thinking for the press, Mike," Carelli said. "If we land on this guy with both feet, we're persecuting a war hero—was he a hero?"

"Silver star, Bronze with V, three Purples."

"Okay, a hero, who goes on a mission to rescue a girl kidnap victim who turns out not to be a victim at all, and shoots three unarmed teenagers."

"That's all we have so far."

"Of course, we could go easy on him, plead him down to

manslaughter, maybe get him psychiatric treatment instead of hard time, and the parents of the dead kids will go apeshit."

"That could happen too," Jamal said. "That's why Chief O'Hara sent us over."

Carelli leafed through the reports again. "No witnesses?"

"No," Jamal said.

"No weapon? No prints? Nothing to place this guy at the scene?"

"Nothing," Mike said, "except what this guy Collins says."

"How do you read him?"

"He may be telling the truth, but maybe not all of it," Jamal said. "He says he didn't know Johnny planned an armed assault, but we don't think he's telling us the whole truth."

"He's slick, sir," Mike said. "I checked his business reputation—not good; most of his deals, and his investors, lost money."

Carelli got up. "Okay, I'm going to take this home. You guys get relieved and take the night off; be back here before eight-thirty in the morning."

"Yes, sir," they chorused.

"Oh, does he have counsel? Public Defender?"

"He's a successful novelist," Jamal said. He took the card the lawyer had handed him from his shirt pocket and handed it to the State's Attorney. "Pressure."

"Oh, shit," Carelli said, shaking his head sadly. "Not Stonewall Fucking Jackson."

JOHNNY FINISHED HIS description of the rescue—in his mind he still saw it as a rescue. Jackson stared at him in amazement. "You actually thought you were back in 'Nam? In a tunnel?"

"I didn't think it, I felt it and heard it and smelled it. It was like being in a dream and knowing you're dreaming. I knew I was in Black Rock and what I was there for."

"But you lost it. You started shooting."

"I started shooting when the first armed man rose up out of the shadows."

"The man you say had an AK 47."

"Well, actually the AK variant with a folding wire stock; the one they call the AKS."

"Why were you sure?"

"In a flash of moonlight I saw the curved shape of the magazine. You don't forget that shape, sir, not if you've been as close to them as I was in the tunnels."

That's certainly true, Tom thought. "Did you see the weapon again on the way out?"

"No, but I'd turned out the bedroom light and was pushing the girl. But surely the cops—"

"Johnny, according to the crime-scene report, no weapons of any kind were found in the house."

"But sir—"

Tom stood up. "Try to get some sleep. Arraignment is at eleven; I'll see you before then."

Johnny hung his head as the policemen led him to his small cell in the holding area. No *weapons?*

If Johnny's cell was a clean one, he would hate to see a dirty one. He'd missed the evening meal by several hours, and his stomach growled. He made his bed with the thin gray sheets and darker blanket, relieved himself in the one-piece stainless steel commode and brushed his teeth with the toilet kit supplied with the uniform. The kit contained no razor. He sat on the bed and stared at the opposite wall. How could the police have failed to find the kid's AKS?

Detective Kolslovsky came by about eight and had himself let into the cell by the jail guard. He stood across the tiny cell, seven feet by eight, and waited for the guard to take the hint and move out of earshot. "How's it going, Marine?" Kolslovsky said softly. "Need anything?"

"I guess I missed chow, and I didn't get a shower."

"I can fix a shower and some kind of sandwich from the deli across the street. Only thing good is Polish ham."

"Thanks."

"Anything else? Books?"

"Am I gonna get bailed out?"

Kolslovsky shook his head slowly. "Your lawyer will apply, but bail's unlikely in a capital felony case."

"So I'm going to be here for a while."

"Yeah, I'm sorry."

"Could you get me the computer from my house? At least the little laptop? Writing's the only thing that'll keep me sane in this cage."

"I'll see what I can do. My partner, Jamal, will probably want to search your files; see if there's anything about this matter, but I'll ask him."

"Thanks."

"Dubini!" Kolslovsky shouted. The guard returned and unlocked the cell. "Try to go with this thing, Johnny. Don't forget you were a marine and always will be a marine. You've dealt with far worse shit than this. Dubini, take this man to the shower."

"Shower's secured, Detective,"

"Well, *unsecure* it, you got the key." He turned back to Johnny. "I'll leave the sandwich; I gotta get home or my wife will kill me again. Hang tough."

"Thanks."

JOHNNY FOUND A thick ham sandwich and a lukewarm Coke when he got back from the shower. He ate slowly, making it last. Lights began going off soon after he finished; it seemed very early but they'd taken his watch. Johnny stretched out on top of the blanket; the cell was warm. He tried to sleep, but his eyes wouldn't stay closed for more than a few seconds at a time. The dimly lit corridor began to resound with snores, whimpers and moans. Johnny lay awake for what seemed like hours, then fell asleep abruptly, right into a dream. It was a mixture of the old dream about the tunnels and the houses of Hue, but there were new elements; Johnny chasing children through dark passages, children who made no sound, children he ran down and killed even though they had no weapons.

When the guard came at 6:00 A.M. to take him to shave and shower, Johnny was sitting bolt upright on the bunk, shaking and drenched in sweat.

27

JOHNNY WAS DRESSED in the jeans and T-shirt he had been arrested in as he was led from his cell to an interview room in the holding area. Tom Jackson thought he looked gray and very shaky. "Bad first night, Johnny?" he asked gently.

"They got the death penalty in this state?" Johnny asked, his voice as flat as sand.

"Yes," Tom said carefully, "but I don't think there's been an execution in more than twenty years." He took off his half-glasses and looked at his client. "Not giving up, are you?"

"What do I have to hold on to?"

"Justice, Johnny," Tom said. "And me."

Tom put his glasses back on and read the transcript that had been made from the interview of last evening. He had spent hours comparing it to the police reports. "There seems to have been nothing recovered at the crime scene except fourteen shell casings. No prints, nothing else."

Johnny said nothing. The only thing he had left out was the involvement of Staff Sergeant Tolliver, and he was wondering about that.

"The girl said the assailant wore a mask and gloves, a camouflage uniform, and carried a weapon she described as a submachine gun." He looked up at Johnny. "Any of that stuff going to turn up?"

"No, sir."

"They'll search your house tomorrow, also your truck, and any storage facilities in your name. Is there anyplace else they'll search?"

"I have a boat."

"They'll search that too. Will they find anything?"

"Nothing to do with this."

"Any weapons at all?"

"My pistol, at the house. A Smith and Wesson nine-millimeter automatic."

"They'll test it against whatever slugs they recover from the bodies or dig out of walls and furniture. Any chance of a match?"

"Zero. Not even the same twist."

Tom made a note. The Smith, like most American pistols, had rifling grooves that twisted left. Johnny must have used a European weapon; typically they had right-hand twist barrels.

Most likely a Swedish K if he could get one, Tom thought. The tunnel rats' favorite. "You've left nothing out? It seems hard to believe you could have organized all this and carried it out in such a short time all by yourself."

Johnny squirmed. "A friend helped me a little, but had nothing to do with the rescue itself. I'd like to keep him out of it."

"I'd better know before the detectives find him."

"There's no way he goes down."

"Johnny, it's privileged. If I can keep him out, I will."

"Okay," Johnny said, surprised at how quickly he had come to trust the attorney. "His name is Willy Tolliver; he was a staff sergeant in the Corps. He runs a recovery program for ex-marines in trouble from drugs or booze or stress. He rescued me from the gutter; saved my life, and started me writing. I owe him no grief."

"What part did he play?"

"He got the uniform and equipment. He drove that morning."

"Leave you at the house?"

"End of the block."

"Picked you up after?"

"Yes."

"Bad, very bad," Tom said. "He can place you at the scene, he knew the plan and saw you together with the girl."

"Yes."

"Did he ever meet the girl's family?"

"No; he waited at my place when I saw them."

"The girl was blindfolded the whole time the three of you were together?"

"Yes, and we didn't speak."

"He's in this up to his neck."

"He's—gone."

"Not in the area?"

"No. How hard are the Bridgeport cops going to look for a man they have no reason to believe exists?"

"Normally you'd be right; they're a lazy bunch. Unfortunately the lead on your case is Jamal Jones, the only first-rate detective on the force."

JOHNNY WAS BROUGHT before a judge in Bridgeport Superior Court at 11:00 A.M. in his civilian clothes but handcuffed. When the time came, he pled not guilty to three counts of capital felony: murder with intent. Because of the room full of press people, the judge agreed to hold a bail hearing immediately after binding Johnny over to a grand jury. Jackson argued eloquently that Johnny was a man with no record of criminal activity of any kind, and with strong ties to the community. The State's Attorney, Carelli, appearing in person, said the defendant was charged with three capital crimes. Bail was denied and Johnny was returned to his cell.

He found a brown-paper police evidence envelope on his bunk. In it was his laptop computer. He opened a new file; the novel he was working on was only on the desktop at home, and began to work. If I have to live this, he thought, I'll write it.

STONEWALL JACKSON HAD three associates and four paralegals, but no partners. He knew his senior associate, Angela Hughes, would have to become the first soon or she would leave him. Angela was, like himself, a graduate of the University of Virginia and Yale Law School. She was thirty-five, divorced with no children, and achingly beautiful. Angela was tall and slender with full, shapely breasts, pale, luminescent skin, regular features unremarkable except for Caribbean-blue eyes, and long dark brown hair shot with red. She had been with him three years. He knew she was thinking of politics, and had offers from every firm in Connecticut and many in New York and even Washington. Soon he would have to decide. Jackson and Hughes? "Angela, come in. I'll want your help on this one."

She took the file. "Johnny Dietrich. I'm up to speed."

"Start back with the cops. Jamal, and the crime scene. Find some mistake."

"The AKS?"

"Would be a godsend."

———

MIKE KOLSLOVSKY DROVE Angela out to the crime scene himself. She'd been waiting to see him when he returned from lunch. Normally he would have stalled the lawyer to give the techs one more go since this was going to be a high-profile case, but the more he thought about it, the more he thought Johnny deserved help.

He lifted the yellow crime-scene tape as she stooped under. Unbelievable body, he thought. He broke the seal on the door and let her into the modest dwelling. The parents of the dead boy who had lived there had returned from their cruise and were staying at a local hotel.

Angela walked through the house, trying to see it as Johnny said he had seen it, in the dark. She went to the window that had been cut, then followed the route he had described to Tom. She moved very slowly, noting the chalk marks in the living room and two bedrooms where three bodies had fallen. The house was black with fingerprint powder and yellow tags were pasted to bullet holes on walls and one bed. The blood had not been cleaned up and there was a lot of it, black, spattered in patterns she knew to be consistent with bullets fired at close range.

She reread the crime-scene and lab reports as she went, again, to the places each victim had been found. Two in bed, one next to a fallen chair—perhaps supposed to be on guard.

Subject nr one, a white male identified from wallet contents as Gilbert Herrero of 11 Prescott Street, Bridgeport. Found next to an upset chair clutching a street hockey stick.

"What's a street hockey stick, Mike?"
"Well, it's like an ice hockey stick, but smaller."

"Where is it?"

"I'm sure it's in Property; the lab guys'll have checked it."

"I'd like to see it when we get back downtown."

"No problem." If they haven't lost it, he thought grimly.

Angela walked through the house, and around it. "How was the crime discovered?"

"An anonymous call from a pay phone in Westport. Uniforms responded, then called us."

"Any way anyone could have got in and removed a weapon or weapons before the scene was secured?"

Mike looked at his own notes. "The uniforms found house dark and the door ajar. I guess it's possible, but it was after four A.M."

Angela shook her head. She'd seen a lot of crime scenes, but this one was such a blank. "Any thought given to any other suspect than my client? This seems to have the look of a professional hit." She bit her lip. "Drugs?"

Mike shrugged. "My first guess. We found a little grass, but very little."

"Could the father have hired someone else and just laid it off on Johnny because he's afraid of his own shooter?"

Mike grinned broadly. "Works for me."

"You like Johnny, don't you? He told my boss about your getting him a shower and a sandwich."

"I don't know him, but he was a marine; so was I. If he did this, I think he was trying to save the girl from almost certain death. You know what happens to kidnap victims once they've seen their abductors."

She nodded. "Have you worked kidnappings?"

"Jamal and me had one two years ago, and assisted the Milford PD on another. Same deal; both girls, one only five years old, the other twelve. The five-year-old was found alive; the twelve-year-old was never found."

"After ransom was paid."

"In both cases."

Angela made a note to save that for trial. "Let's go back downtown and look at the evidence."

MIKE DROVE BACK to Congress Street and took Angela up to Property. Miraculously, all the listed items were there, bagged and tagged. Angela looked at everything, then concentrated on the child's street hockey stick. She took a steel measuring tape and measured it: thirty-four inches long with a sharply curved black plastic blade. The blade bore evidence of scorching, plainly visible through the clear plastic wrap she couldn't remove. "Any guess how this got scorched?"

"Yeah, my kid did that too. They heat the blades up and make them more curved; thinks it gives them more action on the puck or ball."

The blade had been distorted upward at the end like a Persian slipper, and curved sharply inward on itself. Odd, and why was the boy clutching it, unless he was supposed to be on guard? The thing was much too light to be an adequate weapon. She put it back. "Thanks, Mike. I'll get out of your hair."

"Hey, any time, Angela." God, she was pretty, he thought.

Angela drove back to Westport, where Jackson's law office was located. She stopped at Herman's World of Sports on the Post Road, found a street hockey stick as near to the measurements as she could, bought it and took it home. In the basement were a few old tools her ex-husband hadn't taken when he'd moved out two years ago. She put the stick's aluminum shaft in a rusty vise, then lit off an old propane torch. She set the torch a foot away from the plastic blade and put on leather work gloves. She tested the plastic; in a minute or so it softened and she began to bend it, first upward at the end, then increasing the curvature. About right, she thought. When the blade cooled it retained its new shape. She threw it in the back of her BMW and drove to the office.

Angela was deeply disturbed by the case of John Dietrich. She knew her law well enough to see his position was grave, yet at the same time she couldn't shake the idea that somehow he was drawn into the situation, and that his motives had been just—more than just, in fact, he was risking his life to rescue the girl. Angela felt a stirring of doubt inside her, doubt about the law and the power of the law to condemn. The law was the instrument of the sovereign, but the sovereign retained his right to judge only to the extent that he was just himself.

Angela had grown up in comfort if not affluence along the banks of the James River in the Virginia Tidewater. Her mother had died when Angela was six, a fall from a horse while hunting had broken her neck. Her father was a judge and a minor politician, and he had raised her in the indulgent but absentminded ways of busy men. She doted on John Jefferson Hughes and from him learned to love the law. She was an honors student at the University of Virginia at Charlottesville, and a law-review student at Yale. She spent two years as an assistant prosecuting attorney in Richmond, then married a Yale Law classmate who had courted her in New Haven and pursued her in Virginia every time he could get away from his New York law firm. She insisted they find a house in the suburbs; she found northeastern cities threatening and unlivable after the broad lands of the James and the genteel charm of Richmond.

F. Langley Fitzwilliam III, Fitz to his friends, did well at the Wall Street firm of Danger Close, and was made a partner in under seven years. The marriage drifted, cooled slowly like a dying star, lost its sense of purpose if indeed it had ever had one. Fitz wanted to sire children—his word; it infuriated Angela—she wanted her career. She landed a job with the State's Attorney in Stamford, Connecticut, after they moved to Westport, then was hired by Thomas Jackson at twice her state salary. She became learned in the law,

Jackson said "wise beyond her years," and she was even better at defense than she had been at prosecution. It was all a grand game, an intricate mosaic. She loved it and she never had Fitz's children. When he left her suddenly to live with his pregnant paralegal, she let him go without demur and without any of his money, though she kept the fine old Colonial in the Green's Farms section of Westport.

She didn't miss him; she had the law and the firm of Thomas Jackson. She had the law and her guilty clients with their intricate lies. She liked the lies, they made the game more interesting. Then John Dietrich's case file hit her desk and she was no longer sure she trusted the law.

Jackson wasn't back from his lunch when she reached the office. She set the hockey stick on her desk and went into the library, returning with a paper-bound volume called *Military Small Arms of the Twentieth Century*, and found a picture and description of an AKS.

28

JOHNNY BEGAN WORK on a new novel, to which he gave a working title of *Prometheus*, in his cell immediately after the arraignment. Jackson had told him the process: the State's Attorney would have to bring his charges before a sitting grand jury, and Johnny would have to speak there without his attorney. If the grand jury indicted, which, Tom said, it almost always did, Johnny would be bound over for trial.

Tom also told him that his case had taken on political ramifications. Connecticut had an election for governor in the next year, and State's Attorney Carelli was the likely choice of the Democratic Party to run for lieutenant governor. The father of one of the dead boys, Mario Paglia, was a power in Democratic Party matters in

Fairfield County, which includes Bridgeport, and had once been Bridgeport's City Attorney. The father of Tom O'Connor was the ranking Republican member of the Bridgeport City Council. Both were pressing for a swift trial and talking to the media, and the media had latched on to the client's unfortunate nickname, Crazy Johnny.

The media also reported statements in support of Johnny from the American Legion, Veterans of Foreign Wars, AMVETS, and the Navy League. All these respected and conservative institutions urged no rush to judgment on a decorated marine veteran. If he had done what the State's Attorney charged him with, they said to all who would print or broadcast, he'd had cause, the desire to save an innocent life.

Mike left Johnny the *Connecticut Post* when he stopped by after lunch. Johnny read the stories, mostly wildly speculative. It was clear that even his well-wishers assumed he had fired the fatal shots.

Well, he had. And the police had found no weapons in the house. Could he have imagined the AKS in the man's hands? Was he hallucinating more than he thought? No, the memories were mixed with where he knew he was and when, but he was in control and in Black Rock in 1996, not Hue in 1968. Damn it, the kid had a weapon and was moving toward him. Johnny had seen the curved magazine in silhouette and then not seen it as the man trained the gun around.

Tolliver had told him he thought the man he spoke to had a pistol in his waistband. Tolliver had believed that enough to be afraid for his own life, and Tolliver was a man who had seen more and done far too much to jump at shadows.

Tom explained the course the State's case might take, if they went for indictment on the murder charges. Johnny was shocked to find out that he, as a private citizen, had no right to enter a house to rescue a kidnap victim. If he had simply snatched her and taken her away, *he* could have been charged with kidnapping or wrongful imprisonment. Johnny had no option but to take his suspicions—Johnny had no *proof* that the girl was being held at that house—to the Westport police, who would have had to obtain the cooperation of the Bridgeport police, get a search warrant, and then in all likelihood fuck the whole thing up.

Except, of course, if the cops had simply walked up to the door and knocked, and if the men really had no weapons, the girl would be just as safe and three kids would be in some trouble, but not dead.

Three dead kids.

Johnny began to write a story of evil done in the service of good. He described a man sitting in a jail cell wondering if he indeed deserved a defense, or whether a just society might not be compelled to cast him out. The ghosts of all his dead buddies, guys who'd been shot through the face and had the bullet travel down through their hearts and lungs into their guts as they crept through tunnels on their bellies, cried out to him, admonishing him not to be his own enemy, to keep faith with himself and his fellow marines.

This is no different from 'Nam, they said. They tell you to fight a dirty war but not to win it, then bring you home to a nation ready and willing to greet you with accusation, scorn, contempt and isolation.

Johnny wrote on. His sentences broke and he knew he'd be rewriting for a long time if he ever finished the project, but now he needed to get words on paper, to analyze what he had done, to understand it, and to see if he deserved salvation.

TOM JACKSON RETURNED to his office after a long lunch and meeting with a client. He stuck his head into Angela's office. "Any insights from the crime scene?" he asked.

Angela stood up. "One, although I'm not sure if it's good news or bad. Let me give you a demonstration."

Tom raised his eyebrows. "Okay."

"I'll set up in the conference room. When I call you, come in. The blinds will be closed so it will be dark, but don't turn on the lights. Come in fast and close the door behind you; I want your eyes to be unadjusted to the dark when I show you."

Tom was a bit mystified. Games weren't like Angela. "All right, I'll wait in my office. Give a shout when you're ready." He went into his office and checked his e-mail. A minute later, Angela called and he got up and went to the conference room. He opened the door, stepped in and closed the door behind him. The room was quite dark with only dim sunlight filtering through the closed blinds. He saw movement from the deeper shadow in the corner where there was no light from the window at all: a human form, Angela certainly, although he couldn't see her. A shape, curved, beside her body as she moved in front of the window. A straight shape with a sharply curving magazine below—

"Jesus, you found the weapon!"

"Hit the lights, Tom."

He did and saw his associate holding a street hockey stick in her hands. "No."

"Yes. I bought this and reshaped the blade as nearly as I could like the one the police found in the hands of Gilbert Herrero."

"That's what Johnny saw."

"I think so. Does it help?"

Tom pondered. "I don't know. Johnny still had no right to enter that house. But at least we know what set him off."

Angela wiped away angry tears. "Does this case have a happy ending, Tom?"

"I don't see one yet. I have to see Carelli tomorrow morning, see which way he wants to go. It's a hot potato for him especially since someone—I suspect someone in the police—leaked the kidnap part of the story to the media. The *Post* had it on the front page this morning and there'll be a special on channel 8 news tonight."

"That may help."

"In the court of public opinion, sure. But if all the facts that we know become known, Johnny's a dead duck."

"Do you think Carelli wants to deal? All he has is the father, and he may be seen as self-serving."

"What can we do with the father? Suppose we get him to admit he induced Johnny to undertake the rescue, and knew the plan included violence. Maybe that lands Edward Collins in the shit, but it doesn't get Johnny out. It may even make Johnny's situation worse."

"How's the wall coming, boss?"

"I need stones." Tom got up and picked up his hat. "Find me some stones; I'd better go see our client."

"Take me with you? I'd like to meet him."

"Of course, how discourteous of me. You should meet the man, it will help you think this thing through."

Mike took Jamal out for a beer at 4:00 P.M. The Prescott Street case had them back on day shift a week earlier than scheduled, but none of the other detectives whose schedules had been disrupted bitched. "Everybody's pulling for this guy, Jamal."

"We're still cops, Mike. The fact we like him doesn't make three dead boys go away."

"Partner, we been together almost five years. We know each other pretty well, but there's things we never talk about."

"Things most cops don't talk about, like race. Race doesn't have a piece of this, Mike."

"Not race, man. Vietnam."

"Ah, yes, 'you few, you happy few, you band of brothers,' " Jamal paraphrased.

Mike didn't recognize the line, but Jamal often quoted. Jamal was far better educated than Mike, and Mike respected him for it, and never resented being junior to the younger man. "Vietnam made all of us different from those who didn't serve, and somehow the same among ourselves. You'd been ten years older, you'd have been there. I know you served honorably as an Airborne Ranger, and I know you got shot at in Grenada and Panama, but those operations didn't go on long enough to create the kind of brotherhood we 'Nam vets share." Mike paused, and his eyes misted. "Besides, you won those two, and were welcomed home heroes."

"Okay, Mike, we respect each other. I know I don't know what you saw and did over there, and I feel for you."

"And Johnny."

"Sure. But we're still cops, and we're still investigating this thing."

"Jamal, suppose this hump, Collins, hired some other guy, a mob guy, to rescue his daughter. Suppose he's afraid of his own hitter, so he gives us Johnny, knowing his record in the war and afterward."

"How does Edward Collins find a mob shooter?"

"Shit, Jamal, he's in big-time real estate. Those guys run across the mob all the time: cleaning contractors, builders, providers to his restaurant holdings. He says a word, a price, it's done. Now Collins is afraid to expose himself or the connection."

"How does this hypothetical mob guy find the place where the girl is happily screwing her boyfriend while Collins is thinking she's kidnapped?"

"How did Johnny find her, if he did?"

Jamal thought about it, and a little buzz in the back of his brain began nagging him. Who was the black man whose voice he'd heard on the tape that called in the crime scene? "I gotta go,

Mike," Jamal said. "You keep thinking about it and we'll talk to-morrow."

Mike frowned. "Okay, man."

Jamal pulled on his raincoat and went out into the cold, damp night. He hated this case and wished he could chuck it. *Had* chucked it; it would have been easy enough, just show the drugs to the state's attorney and it was another senseless tragedy. But he hadn't dumped it and he wouldn't. The faces of the three dead teenagers kept after him, and he kept thinking of the older brother who had raised him in his mother's apartment in Father Panik Village, a shabby Bridgeport public housing project only recently torn down.

Jamal's brother Chris had a different father from Jamal and his younger brother, Raquib. Jamal's father had been a Muslim ranter; he'd beat all three boys until the day he disappeared. Jamal's mother tried very hard to protect the boys and raise them right. She was always a heavy woman no matter how little the family had to eat, and Jamal remembered holding her hand as she struggled to the bus stop, sending him on to school while she took the intercity bus to Westport where she worked cleaning houses. Chris, five years older than Jamal, was a promising basketball player and earned a scholarship to the University of Connecticut. The gangs in the pro-ject ridiculed the *future* college boy and hassled the younger kids, Raquib especially, because he was soft and, the gangbangers said, queer-bait.

Jamal remembered an afternoon when his older brother had come home, so badly beaten he'd collapsed in the doorway. Jamal and Raquib pulled him inside and got him onto a sofa. Jamal was scared and wanted to dial 911 but Chris wouldn't let him. "No cops," he'd choked.

"Who did this?" Jamal asked.

"The Bloods. They say I got to join; sell drugs. They say they want you and Raquib to be apprentices. You know what that means?"

"No."

"They want you to steal, and to kill. Because you're underage, you do juvie, then nothing, no record. I said no and they beat the shit out of me. Say they'll do it again, every day till I change my mind, and yours, too."

"Why don't we do it?" twelve-year-old Raquib asked. "The gangs have everything here in the projects; it's just a matter of choosing one gang or another."

"No," Chris gasped as Jamal taped his kicked-in ribs. "Not us."

Chris didn't get beat up again, not for a week, but then Jamal and his mother came home together to find both his brothers dead. Raquib had been stripped naked and sodomized while Chris had struggled to free himself from two rolls of duct tape that held him. Then the boys had been shot.

Stitched. That was Jamal had learned to call it in the army; three shots from an automatic weapon, the first one low and right, the other two rising to the left of the victim as the gun kicked up and right in the shooter's hand.

Stitched, just like the boys at 11 Prescott Street. The murders of Jamal Jones's brothers had never been solved, or, as near as Jamal could tell, even investigated. Chris and Raquib had been taken out of the blood-soaked apartment in black plastic bags like so much garbage.

Just like the white boys on Prescott Street.

Jamal had never given up on a homicide since he'd been a cop. The killings in Prescott Street would be investigated, Jamal promised himself, and solved.

29

"NO," JOHNNY SAID. His voice was quiet but hard as iron. "No, I won't consider a plea of insanity. I'm not insane; I fought so hard to bring myself back from the brink of what might have become insanity, and I had so much help." Johnny choked and tears started streaming down his cheeks. "I won't dishonor myself or the friends that helped me put my life back together."

"Johnny," Tom said with genuine sympathy. "I'm not talking about asking the court to find you not guilty by reason of insanity. There is no such defense in Connecticut. What we can plead, if we have to, is that you lacked the ability, at the time of the shootings, to know you were doing wrong, or to conform your conduct to the law because you were in an hallucinatory state—you thought you were in a tunnel in Vietnam menaced by an armed Vietcong soldier." Tom got up and began to pace, waving his arms in the air. "Look, Johnny, I'm willing to try this case, do everything I can to get you acquitted, but neither the facts as we know them nor the law are going to make that easy."

Johnny shook his head. "I did what I did. I'm not insane."

"Johnny," Tom said softly. "Let us think about it. We don't know what the prosecution has, or may find out, but it may be our only shot at keeping you out of prison."

Johnny turned to look at the pretty woman who sat next to Tom. She hadn't spoken since being introduced; she took notes. How sad she looks, Johnny thought. "I won't do it. Hell, Tom, you were in 'Nam, you know what it was like in the jungle. On the best days you were bored and hot and stank from the rotting of your own living flesh. On the best nights you froze your ass and prayed for daylight to drive out the fear. The worst was the tunnels, the guys getting shot in the face if some asshole lieutenant—sorry, sir—insisted on having the tunnels searched instead of just blowing them. The next worst were the night ambushes, a sudden burst of machine-gun fire from a concealed position or trip wires that snagged some marine's boot or a radio antenna and blew away five or six guys you knew even though you also knew you shouldn't ever know anyone too well."

"I know. I remember."

"Maybe you were stronger than me, or maybe officers got better training. But I came back a mess and didn't even know it until my country, this country, fell in on me and told me what it thought of the value of what I considered service to the nation. That drove me into the gutters as much as the tunnels. What do you do when you're hurting and no one wants to touch you, much less give you a hug, say well done, help you heal?"

"I can't argue with what you say, Johnny, and believe me, I have a little of the stress disorder myself. I wouldn't diminish your suffering or your heroism by comparing it my own little problems."

"What do you feel, sir?"

"Tears, when the National Anthem is played at a football game, at an emotional point in a bad movie, when I wake up at two A.M. and remember dead and mutilated friends. When I see or read something that really takes me back to that implacable killing ground, I double up with pain and cry like a widow over her husband's corpse."

"I'm sorry I asked that, sir."

"I cried a lot when I read your books, Johnny. I didn't dare confront your movies until I could rent videos and see them at home with just my wife."

"Thank you, sir."

"But Johnny, we have this thing you did. I'll fight like hell to make your actions seem reasonable, even righteous, but if the State's Attorney figures out how to place you inside that house, all the nobility of your intent will make little difference."

"But not insanity."

"Even if it's the only way to keep you out of jail?"

"Maybe I deserve to go to jail. Not insanity; there has to be another way."

Tom got up and mopped his face with a fine linen handkerchief. He took a deep breath and fought to compose himself. "I'd better hit the books, Johnny. I'll sit with the State's Attorney tomorrow."

"Sir?"

"Yes, Johnny."

"Thank you for saying what you said, about my books."

Tom shook Johnny's hand and gave him a dry handkerchief. Tom found he was too choked to speak, so he just nodded and went to the door of the interview room and waited for the guard to let him out. Angela followed, her eyes stinging. She had never seen her boss so emotional, so racked with his old suffering. It made him seem less the reserved legal scholar, the master of the stone wall. It made him seem human and vulnerable.

It made him seem very much like their client, with his soft scared eyes.

Another guard went in and handcuffed Johnny when he stood and turned around. Tom hurried away, needing air, needing to see the sky Johnny wouldn't see for months, if ever again.

Poor *bastard*, Tom thought. Poor, suffering bastard.

30

WILLY TOLLIVER READ of Johnny's arrest, a tiny story in the *New York Times*. Arrested and charged with three counts of murder. Tolliver felt a surge of rage, a feeling he hadn't experienced for years, since he made his own peace with the past. How could I let him go in there? Tolliver asked himself. I knew how fragile he was; hell, *he* knew it. He was so sure of his right to save the girl, of his right to treat her attackers as hostile.

There was no mention of kidnapping in the first story he read.

The next day there was. Tolliver wondered if that made it better for Johnny. He doubted it; Johnny had no right to storm a house even if they'd known what they really only suspected.

But Johnny knew the Bridgeport police, and thought them incompetent to organize a rescue. Tolliver's Connecticut State Police buddy had told him the same thing, even hinting that Bridgeport cops wouldn't get too worked up about something that happened in Westport, a far more affluent community.

Johnny knew he was committing a crime entering that house, especially armed. He thought he was justified and he thought he would never get caught.

How had the cops found him, and so fast?

The girl and her family must have given him up. No one else knew Johnny's mind.

Except Tolliver. He knew.

The question was what was he going to do about it.

ANGELA FOUND TOM already at his desk when she reached the office at eight-thirty in the morning. The usual drill at Thomas Jackson Law Offices was for the associates, paralegals and staff to be in by eight to get things organized, and for Angela as Senior Associate to be in a half hour later to see the great man's day was planned with no waste and ready to commence when he arrived at nine-thirty. Tom looked up and waved her into the room.

Angela sat in a leather club chair in front of an antique brass-bound campaign desk—the kind general officers carried in the field and set up on matching folding saw horses—that was said ironically to have belonged to Union General McClellan. The room was paneled in light oak and had a chandelier glowing above and a Persian rug in light colors accented by purple patterns below. The boss's room had an opulent, nineteenth-century air in contrast to the bright pastels and open layout of the rest of the office.

Tom was gazing at his computer. "There's fresh coffee in the thermos, Angela," Tom said softly. He turned to face her. "I must confess I'm at a loss."

"Johnny?"

"Who else?"

"Do you think he'll eventually see the wisdom of a diminished capacity defense?"

"Maybe, maybe not. Last night he all but had me convinced he wanted to die."

"I think he'll see it through," she said, for no other reason than to rally her mentor. Johnny had seemed very sad indeed. "What do we do now?"

"I want you to find this Staff Sergeant Willy Tolliver. We have to get to him before Jamal Jones does."

She frowned. "Okay."

"Jamal may have a leg up. The cops got an anonymous phone tip about the crime scene. I'm betting Tolliver made the call, and they have a recording of it."

"Why not just ask Johnny where to find him?"

"Johnny might not want to cooperate. He sees his situation as hopeless and doesn't want to drag down a friend. Besides, I want to know how hard it is to find this guy, starting with only a name and Johnny's story. Jamal doesn't have either, but he may have another card."

"What's that?"

"Tolliver is an old name in the South, and many black people have it as do many whites. I'm guessing, but an adult called Willy is likely black. Jamal has access to the black police underground."

"What do I do when I find him?"

"Find out what he knows. Tell him to be careful when Jamal finds him; he ties Johnny to the crime much more firmly than Edward Collins's half-truths. Evaluate him as a witness presuming the prosecution calls him—what does he know of Johnny's motivation, mental state, ability to deal with high stress."

"The hockey stick."

"That's part of it. We need to be able to interpret Johnny's testimony before he gives it."

"Backdoor the diminished capacity?"

"Maybe. Right now I don't know what else to do, except go see Carelli and see how strongly he feels."

Angela got up. "When do you want me to start looking?"

"Now, please."

JOHNNY WAS ESCORTED from his cell to a small gymnasium. A half-court basketball game was in progress at either end of the floor, and a few men in orange prison uniforms sat and watched. The air was poisonous with cigarette smoke.

Johnny laced up the running shoes in which he had been arrested and began to jog around the running track, joining several others, all younger and working harder. A black man with a shaved head and a small beard slowed his pace to match Johnny's, and spoke softly. "You be that crazy dude wasted them kidnappers, freed the girl?"

"I'm charged with it," Johnny said carefully.

"Right, cool, don't admit nothin' to no one." The runner grinned. "But be aware, talk in the blocks here is if you did, you did right."

"Thanks for your support."

"Don' mean nothin', sad to say. But you'll be all right in the joint here, if you're like worried." The runner increased his pace, leaving Johnny behind.

Johnny wasn't sure what the man meant. As he completed his circle, he realized his face was the only white one in the gym.

Glad they're on my side, Johnny thought. Glad someone believes I did right.

If I did right. Johnny kicked up the pace as his muscles warmed up.

ANGELA REVIEWED JOHNNY'S statement, especially the part about Staff Sergeant Willy Tolliver. He ran a veterans' outreach program; he'd been a marine. She'd start with the Veterans Administration and the Marine Corps. Then the IRS; the guy would have to have a tax-exempt ID number to accept donations. Johnny had said that Tolliver was "gone"—out of the area. Where had Johnny been when he met Tolliver, went into his rehab? Where did stressed-out Vietnam vets go?

She was inclined to believe New York. That didn't make it any easier.

Angela called the VA and drew a blank. The IRS needed a program name to search for an ID number, and had no match to William or Willy Tolliver.

There was a Marine Corps recruiting station on Main Street in Bridgeport. Angela decided to pay them a visit.

Angela was ushered to a chair in front of the marine recruiter's desk with exaggerated ceremony by an army staff sergeant. The recruiting office was shared with Army, Air Force and Navy, and Angela felt eyes in uniforms of all the services caressing away her clothes—even those of a tough-looking female navy first-class petty officer.

The chief of the Marine Corps office was a grizzled master gunnery sergeant with his hair cut as short as a two-day beard. He harrumped and scowled, and the gawkers fled. He closed the door of his glass-walled office and poured coffee into two thick white china cups with the Marine Corps Globe and Anchor emblem on them without asking Angela if she wanted any. She sipped; the coffee was strong but good.

"Tanner, ma'am," he said, extending a huge, horny paw. "Why do I suspect you're not here today, ma'am, to join my Marine Corps?"

"I'm an attorney, Master Gunnery Sergeant," she said. His eyebrows rose imperceptibly; perhaps he didn't expect a civilian *woman* to read his insignia correctly, but Angela's father had been a reserve navy captain and she learned her etiquette early. "I need to locate a former marine and I don't know how to do that."

Master Gunnery Sergeant Tanner smiled a tiny smile. "Not the case of the guy—"

"I can't say what case. I just need to find an ex-marine who runs or ran an outreach program that helps other marines that have drug or alcohol problems, and stressed-out vets."

"In Bridgeport? I don't know of any other than the American Legion–sponsored Alcoholics Anonymous."

"Probably not in Bridgeport," she offered with no conviction. "Perhaps New York."

"Well," Tanner said. "The right thing for me to tell you is to write to the Reserve and Retired Records Office of the Naval Personnel Department. I can give you their address in St. Louis."

"That," Angela said slowly, "sounds like a matter of some weeks."

"Many weeks, and without a serial or social security number, or a date and place of birth, likely no good result."

"What other way is there? My client can't wait weeks."

"I'll ask you only one question, because I know you can't discuss your work. If I help you, will it help this ex-marine or hurt him?"

What was the honest answer to that? Jamal would find him anyway. "Help him, and help another."

Tanner turned to his computer. "What's the ex-marine's name, and if you know it, his rank on separation from the corps?"

Angela's breath came out in a whoosh, leaving her nearly unable to speak. "Staff Sergeant Willy Tolliver," she said softly.

Tanner was already typing. "The corps is a small family, Ms. Hughes. Let's see what we can do to help a brother."

Tom Jackson met State's Attorney George Carelli at the Algonquin Club in downtown Bridgeport. The club was perched atop one of the highest buildings in the city and provided a panoramic view of the town, the river, and Long Island Sound beyond. From this high up, the city doesn't show its wear, its despair, Tom thought as he shook hands with Carelli at the bar. Heads all over the room turned to the two men, and conversation virtually ceased. "I've arranged a private room," Carelli whispered. He placed a hand on Tom's shoulder and guided him out of the bar and across the lobby.

"Good idea," Tom said.

Carelli was a handsome man, big at six foot four and over two hundred fifty pounds. He always wore carefully tailored blue wool suits, snowy starched white shirts and a red tie with a fine figure. He always had a blue handkerchief flowing from the breast pocket of his jacket. He used his imposing figure well, especially in court. Tom thought him a thorough lawyer if not brilliant, a politician at heart who would one day run for governor. A case as high-profile as Johnny's could bring that race up years earlier, or it could put an end to Carelli's political hopes once and for all.

They took chairs at a small table in the middle of a room spacious enough for twenty-four. The setting was somewhat barren, almost unsettling, and Tom could see the damaged walls and dirty corners that would have been concealed had the room contained its normal furniture. "Drink?" Carelli asked, moving to a small trolley in the corner.

"Perhaps a dry sherry if there is any," Tom said, mentally preparing himself for the exchange that Carelli would begin abruptly as soon as he felt he had been polite enough to a distinguished member of the defense bar. The two men had opposed each other only once before, and Tom had won, a complicated assault case. Carelli loathed all defense lawyers, especially the expensive ones. "Or a glass of white wine."

George poured himself a vodka on the rocks and for Tom a small glass of La Ina, a dry sherry. Pansy drink, he sniffed as he brought it over to the lawyer. He noted with envy that Tom wore even better clothes than he did, today a soft gray double-breasted suit that fit his compact frame perfectly. "Shall we sit? They'll be along in a moment to take lunch orders."

Tom sipped the sherry and sat down, folded his napkin into his lap. "How's the election shaping up?"

George frowned. "Fine. We'd better get to the business at hand."

Tom smiled. As subtle as a thrown brick. "Yours to open."

"This case could divide the community. It might be best if it were dealt with swiftly."

"At least there's no racial issue."

"No, but class. Westport and Fairfield having their way with Bridgeport as usual. Rich people with rich lawyers beating down the working class, in this case murdering them, to enforce social control."

"Sounds like *Romeo and Juliet.*"

"In Bridgeport, more like *West Side Story.* All three of those boys were well-liked, as are their families. The *Post* is out to make the lads folk heroes."

"Pity they decided to dabble in kidnapping."

George spread his long arms. "A teenage prank. Certainly no justification for sending in an assassin, a deranged vet with terrible experiences in Vietnam to guide his mind."

"If that's what happened," Tom said carefully.

George leaned forward. "He did it, Tom. I don't expect you to say so, now or ever, but he did it."

"When do you go before the grand jury?"

"Next Thursday."

Tom sipped his sherry, careful not to spill it. George had overfilled the glass on purpose. "Quick."

"Want to get this behind me. You should too."

"I'll take such time as I need to develop my defense, George."

" 'Not criminally responsible,' obviously. It won't work."

Tom was getting angry and trying not to let it show. "Do you have a witness of whom I'm unaware? Physical evidence? A weapon? Has your discovery been incomplete?"

"You know what I have," George said grimly.

"Could be a difficult case to prove, with *all* you have."

George glowered as a waitress came in and took lunch orders. Tom made a point of smiling at the homely woman, and engaging her in extended conversation about the specials.

JOHNNY SPENT A long afternoon in his cell, trying to write, remembering the therapeutic effect of writing when he had been in

Tolliver's care. He had to come to terms with a new horror, that unlike in the tunnels where he risked his life to save children, he had lost his head and killed three teenagers who the police said were unarmed.

Is that what really happened? Would he ever know? He'd been completely sure he'd seen the AKS with its long, severely curved magazine in the first one's hands, and if one was armed, why not all three? The second boy had reached toward a bedside table, the last toward the floor.

Why had Edward Collins rolled over on him? But Edward was not a standup guy, never had been, the police may have threatened to lay the crime on him. How had the police made the connection?

It probably made no difference. He'd thought about the risks to himself before he went in, but more in terms of getting shot in the face than of being arrested and charged with murder. He wondered whether he *might* have been temporarily insane, but he rejected the thought as an excuse. He'd read some books on mental states while at the outreach center; Tolliver encouraged all the PTSD patients— virtually all the vets at the center—to do so, to understand why they felt the way they did. He thought he was in what the shrinks called a fugue state—in the past, the tunnels, and the present, Black Rock, at the same time.

He wrote all this as he thought it. He kept it abstract; he didn't know if the police could read his computer and use it against him.

Do I deserve to be defended? he asked himself for the hundredth time. If the kidnapping had been real, if the men had been armed—

I had every reason to believe it was real. I heard the voice on the phone, the savage menace in the man's voice, the fear in the girl's. Tolliver thought the man he saw had a pistol and was about to draw it, and I saw the damned AKS. Keep faith with yourself, he thought.

How many times can a man be fucked over for fighting a war his nation gave him?

Not once more, Johnny swore to himself. Not even once more.

Make a fight of it, he raged at himself, pounding the wall. For the good of your soul.

Tom, his new lawyer, had told him that the sovereign has no right except as he is just; the state can't take my life if I acted to save an innocent.

Even if she wasn't.

He felt better but far from sure. He resolved to raise the matter with Tom again when next he saw him.

He stored his work, shut off the computer, and lay down on his bunk. He slept, and he did not dream.

V

THE BODY OF EVIDENCE

31

ANGELA WAITED AS Master Gunnery Sergeant Tanner tapped away at his computer, two-finger style. "Tolliver," he said. "Separated as staff sergeants. Many. Six Williams, one Wilson. Got any idea of his age?"

"Vietnam."

"Hm. Say twenty to thirty, 1965 to 1975. Birthdate between 1935 and 1955. That eliminates three; one younger and two older. Two are partially disabled, but that could mean anything from a limp to a wheelchair."

"The marine I'm looking for," Angela said carefully, "runs or ran an outreach center for marines suffering from Post Traumatic Stress Disorder, alcohol, drugs—"

Tanner slapped himself on the temple with the heel of his hand. "You said that when you first sat down. Here's a guy, runs a program at St. Anne's Church in Manhattan called Marines Helping Marines."

Angela took a shallow breath. "That could be it." Tanner marked the address on his computer and hit the print command. A single sheet of paper flopped out and he picked it up. "Tolliver, Wilson Robert. The church is on West Ninth Street."

Angela took the address from the gruff old marine. "Thank you," she whispered.

Tanner looked her hard in the eyes. "Be sure you be helping marines with that information." She got up to leave. "One last thing,

Ms. Hughes." His voice had an edge to it. "You're a real pretty lady and a visit from you might cheer these good folks up, but if you ever again come through that door, it will be for the very first time. Understood?"

"Understood." She put out her hand and he shook it. "Thank you."

He turned back to his computer and she walked out through the crowded bay, followed right out into the street by probing eyes.

JAMAL WATCHED JACKSON'S senior associate get into her BMW and pull away from the curb in front of the Armed Forces Recruiting Center. He logged the date and time and wondered, but decided not to go in and ask what she was doing. Like many businesses in downtown Bridgeport, the Armed Forces guys didn't think much of the job the cops did protecting their lives and property.

As the woman pulled into the dense traffic, he followed, leaving two cars between them.

Angela hit the I-95 onramp and drove swiftly south. Heading for her office, Jamal thought, knowing he should leave off the pursuit, thinking but not being exactly sure whether he had any right to be following a member of the defense attorney's staff. But she had to be following up on a lead, and the lead might be the black man on the police phone tape Jamal believed could be Johnny's accomplice.

Or maybe Mike was right. Maybe the black man was the shooter that Edward Collins really hired.

Jamal didn't want that to be true, but he liked Johnny too.

THE BMW SPED south through Fairfield into Westport, where it left the highway. Jamal's wheezy Dodge K was barely keeping up.

He caught her at the light at the bottom of the ramp and turned right behind her. She ran a yellow at the next light and Jamal took the red. She turned left at the train station, into the parking lot and parked illegally in a striped zone. She was out of the car running before Jamal could pull into a spot reserved for taxis and flip the Police Vehicle sign on the sunshade down into view. A cabby yelled at him as he hurried after Angela into the tunnel that led under the tracks to the southbound platform. He heard a train rumble overhead, its brakes squealing as it stopped. He ran up the stairs just in time to see the doors close. There was no one on the platform as the train departed. Damn, Jamal said to himself, out of breath. So this story goes to New York.

Why can't I just leave this alone?

JAMAL WALKED SLOWLY back to his car, catching his breath. At least I know she's looking for someone in the Armed Forces, most probably a marine like Johnny, he thought. Shouldn't I give that to the DA and let him worry about hassling the guys in the recruiting station?

Jesus, why can't I leave this alone?

ANGELA CAUGHT A cab on Vanderbilt Avenue outside Grand Central Station and gave the driver the address on West Ninth Street. The Catholic church was small, built of red brick with decades of soot discoloring it. There was a square building of the same soiled brick beside the church, both enclosed by a waist-high black iron railing. Angela walked up the steps of the building. The green wooden door had a fresh coat of paint and a carved sign with letters picked out in gold, St. Anne's Rectory. Angela pushed the door open and went in. The building was musty and strangely silent, as if it hadn't been occupied in years. There was a bulletin board in the tiny lobby that listed various activities from catechism classes to counseling to building committee meetings. There were marriage banns posted in a section by themselves. Marines Helping Marines was listed in room B101, in the basement. An arrow directed Angela to the stairs and she started down. Inside the stairwell the smells of despair were powerful: old sweat, disinfectant, bad cooking. She found room B101 and went in. Inside, behind a glass barrier, was a kind of small gymnasium with bunks lined up in rows. Each bunk was made up precisely and the room looked spotlessly clean. The linoleum floor beneath Angela's feet was polished and buffed to a high shine, and the walls and the windows were clean. Angela heard voices, a loud discussion, from farther down the hall. She found a room marked Office—Off Limits, and knocked. A young man wearing green utilities opened the door. There was a single metal desk, clean and free of papers, and a small table in the corner where a computer glowed. "Yes, ma'am?" the man said courteously. He was painfully thin and had a tic in his cheek.

"I'm looking for Staff Sergeant Tolliver," Angela said breathlessly. She felt as though she had run here all the way from Bridgeport.

"He's leading a meeting," the man inclined his head in the direction of the voices. "I guess you can wait here."

"Thank you," Angela said, putting her heavy briefcase on the floor. She looked around; there was no place to sit other than at the sergeant's desk, and she thought that would be a bad idea. The man had returned to the computer. "Excuse me," she said. "Is there someplace I could get a glass of cold water?"

The young man jumped up. "The galley. I'll get it; would you rather have a soda?"

"No, thank you. Just plain water." As soon as the man left the room she sat down in his chair and tried to catch her breath.

Three minutes later the conversation in the adjoining room ceased with a scraping of chairs. A minute after that a huge black man entered carrying a tray with a pitcher of ice water and two glasses. He set the tray in the center of his desk and closed the door behind him, then took his chair and motioned Angela to pull her chair closer.

The man wore marine utility trousers, polished jump boots, and a green T-shirt with dark sweat stains under the arms and down the center of his powerful chest. His arms and neck looked thicker than Angela's thighs. His face and scalp were closely shaved. He had intelligent, curious eyes, broad features and very dark skin.

He poured two glasses full of ice water and nodded to her. He had not spoken. She drank greedily and he refilled the glass. "I'm Willy Tolliver, the director of this program. I hope you're who I think you are and not who I fear you may be."

"Angela Hughes," she said, extending her hand. Tolliver enveloped it in a huge paw and held it gently as if he feared crushing her bones. "I'm a lawyer in the firm of Thomas Jackson. We represent Johnny Dietrich in his upcoming trial for murder in Bridgeport, Connecticut."

"Do I have to talk to you?"

"No," Angela said sheepishly. "But it might help."

"Is my conversation with you, if we have one, confidential?" His tone was even, firm but not hostile.

"My notes will be confidential, but this conference isn't privileged because I don't represent you."

"Let's take a walk," he said, getting to his feet. "I need a little air."

She followed him up the stairs and out into the street.

T HE AFTERNOON WAS overcast and chilly, but Tolliver didn't seem to notice it as he walked beside Angela. She pulled her raincoat tightly around her and shielded her eyes against the blown grit and litter swirling in the streets in a biting north wind. Tolliver led her into Washington Square Park and to a corner of the iron fence shaded by a sickly maple tree. "Right here is where I first met your client, Ms. Hughes."

"Angela, please."

"Okay, Angela, I'm Willy. Here he was, passed-out drunk, smelling worse than a goat. He had a marine jacket like this one," he said, touching his light utility jacket that he had slipped over his T-shirt but not zipped. "I dragged his sorry ass back over there to the shelter, had some of the guys in the program take him in the shower and scrub the shit and dirt and stink off him, then we began to work on him, to bring back to him what he'd lost somewhere inside his half-dead soul. He was difficult, Angela; he wouldn't talk, wouldn't try. I reckon I hadn't found him when I did he'd been dead in a few months."

"How'd you bring him around?"

Tolliver shrugged. "Our program is tough. We don't take excuses any more than the drill instructors that make marines out of soft, asshole civilians take excuses. We allow no backtalk, no attitudes. We do whatever it takes to bring the proud marine back out of the tub of shit these men have made of themselves and their lives. Sorry for my language, Angela; it's the language of the program and no woman has ever asked me to explain."

"That's all right; it's easier to imagine your program in its own tongue. How do you deal with violent ones?"

"Violently, when necessary," Tolliver said sadly. "Failure is not an option in my program, although we've had a few failures."

"How was Johnny?"

"In the end, a success, though I almost sent him away because even though his body became clean and sober, his soul was still hollowed out and full of pain. I got him started writing down what he couldn't speak of, never suspecting he would write a bestselling novel."

Angela stared at the filthy corner where Johnny's long journey back from hell had begun, and thought about the bars of his cell. Tolliver sat on a bench. "Why did Johnny send you to see me?"

Angela looked up. Tolliver's face was expressive, and now sad. She said, "He didn't. He told me how you helped him. My boss sent me to find you, number one to see how difficult it was."

"Wasn't, hey?"

"No, but I started with your name and rank. We have no reason to believe the police have any inkling of your existence, much less identity."

"You think the police might find me?"

"If they know to look. Suppose they find a witness that saw you the night of the rescue." Tom had decreed all his staff to refer to the incident on Prescott Street as "the rescue."

"What the police do to me?"

"They'd want you to testify. You can place Johnny at the scene, and you know he was armed. You saw him bring the girl out."

"I won't roll over on Johnny."

"They'll charge you as an accessory to murder."

"I'll plead the Fifth Amendment."

"The prosecution will get you a grant of immunity. You would then be compelled to testify."

I reckon they can make me sit there, Tolliver thought angrily. Can't make me say anything I don't want long's Johnny keeps his head. "What can you do for me?"

"Prepare you. Find out what you know that might help Johnny."

"Let's walk back to the center. You getting chilled."

ANGELA RODE THE train back to Westport in darkness. She had worked with Tolliver for more than three hours, and believed the staff sergeant understood what the prosecution would ask. She warned him of the consequences of being untruthful, and he smiled. She had him tell her why he entered the houses on Prescott Street in stolen disguise and what he had seen. She asked him about the boy he had seen at the rescue site, and how he thought the kid was reaching for a pistol. "Did you tell Johnny this?" she asked.

"Damn right. Boy had to know what he was up against."

"Did you demonstrate what the man did? How he reached around behind himself?"

Tolliver stood up and slipped his hand behind him, just as the man had. "Showed him just like this."

Angela made a note. "Okay. Let me know if the prosecution or the police contact you. If they charge you, I'll arrange counsel for you in Connecticut."

Tolliver waved away the thought as though it actually was of no importance to him. "Look around you, Angela. See how nice we keep this place? See we got computers, new furniture, exercise gear, workshops? Shrinks and lawyers retained and on call?"

"It must be a lot of work."

"Work, yes, but we got plenty of recovering marines to do work. Also takes money."

Was he asking her for money? she wondered.

He shook his head, seeming to read her thoughts. "Johnny gives this center anything it needs. Johnny cares about us and we care about him. Tell him Willy says hang tough, be a marine, and keep his mouth shut. Just 'cause that smooth-talking bastard in Westport told the police he done something don't mean he did."

"I'll . . . tell him."

"I'm right, ain't I? State has to prove Johnny done what they said; Johnny don't have to prove nothing."

"Of course you're right." Angela began to think of the case in new ways.

GEORGE CARELLI SUMMONED Detectives Kolslovsky and Jones to his office. He was still fuming about Jackson's inflexible attitude and taunting manner expressed at lunch the previous day, and he was a bit concerned. There was no question the grand jury would indict based on the deposition of Edward Collins as corroborated by his wife, especially if, as seemed inevitable, Johnny pleaded the Fifth Amendment. But the state had no hard evidence and Jackson was a snake. "How have you two been getting on to finding me a witness?" he asked the detectives.

Mike Kolslovsky looked at Jamal. Carelli's nickname, which Mike knew he rather liked, was Knifefighter. The ever-so-tough crusading prosecutor, the protector of the people.

Mike began to read from his notes. "We interviewed all the neighbors on Prescott Street and on the adjoining streets. No one saw anything or heard anything. No suspicious vehicles, no vehicles at all. We've subpoenaed Johnny's phone records and should have them later today. We had the criminologists out to the scene for a full day yesterday, then had to turn the house back to the Herrero family or risk a lawsuit. They found nothing new; all the recent prints, hair, fluids, et cetera, are traced to the victims, the Collins girl or Herrero's parents."

"Weren't there some stray fibers on the carpet?" George rummaged through his notes.

"The polyester blend, threads in black and two shades of green," Jamal said. "Stuff's woven into fabric then dyed to make Battle Dress Utilities for the entire United States Army and Marine Corps, plus many foreign nations. The only utilities we found at Johnny's house were Vietnam-era, a completely different fabric."

"So the guy was a pro." George brooded.

"Johnny was a marine, George," Mike said. "Why would he know shit about evidence?"

"How would he get hold of a silenced weapon?" George asked. "He had to have help."

"I still think we should consider the hit might have been truly professional," Mike said strongly, "and this Collins asshole just dumped it on Johnny because he's afraid of what his hitter might do."

Carelli looked at Mike with cold eyes. "Find me another suspect, Mike, or I'm going to fry this one."

"Whether he did it or not?" Mike said with some heat. Knife-fighter George would jail his mother to keep up his conviction rate.

The State's Attorney ignored the detective's question. "Stonewall Jackson knows something," he said. "He won't deal."

"Jeez, George, maybe he knows the man is innocent," Mike said sharply.

"There's a lead we haven't been able to develop," Jamal said, breaking in to save his partner from further insubordination. "After the crime went down, the switchboard got a phone call from a pay phone in Westport tipping the crime scene. I have the tape of that very short conversation, and I'm quite sure the voice isn't Johnny's, unless he's a master of mimicry."

"Can you voiceprint it? That should penetrate any effort to disguise a voice."

"I don't have a tape of Johnny to compare. He's never agreed to make a statement." Jamal looked at Mike, who looked disgusted. "I did run it against Edward Collins's taped statement; no chance of a match."

"What Jamal don't want to say," Mike said angrily, "is that the voice on the tape sounds like a black man."

George looked at Jamal. "It does," Jamal said evenly.

"So how many black friends and associates this Johnny have?" George asked, perking up.

"He doesn't have any known close friends, as near as we can find out," Jamal said. "Of any race."

The State's Attorney's face darkened. "Keep looking."

32

ANGELA VISITED JOHNNY in the interview room near his cell. It was eight o'clock at night, nearly lockdown time. She found Johnny trying to be cheerful, even laughing at her lame jokes. Angela had worked with a lot of defendants in major crimes, and she recognized the signs of severe depression.

He's beginning to imagine what it will be like to spend the rest of his life in a cell, she thought. "Johnny, I went to see your friend Tolliver today."

Johnny was suddenly alert, and looked hurt as well as angry. "I don't want him dragged into this. He only tried to help."

"If the prosecution finds him, his testimony will be devastating to you."

"I guess I'm going down anyway. Tolliver won't talk."

"The prosecution could charge him with accessory to murder and misprision of a felony. Those are serious crimes; major jail time. The State's Attorney can grant immunity from those charges and force Tolliver to testify."

"Maybe I should change my plea. The grand jury is tomorrow."

"Johnny, don't give up. The State hasn't begun to prove its case."

"Do you think they'll find Tolliver?"

"I did. Of course, I knew of his existence, and perhaps they don't. How often were you two in contact?"

"I don't know; once or twice a month, usually by e-mail. Sometimes the center needs a little help, or a specific graduate does. I don't guess I've actually seen Willy face-to-face for years, until the day before the rescue."

A tiny warning bell tolled deep in Angela's brain. She shook her head, but it would neither enlighten her nor go away.

"Angela?" Johnny said. "You look upset."

"I'm trying to figure out how the police might know enough about Tolliver to begin looking for him."

"If anyone out here saw him, or saw us, the police would have found them by now."

"I need to think that through." She shoved papers in her brief-case and got up to leave. "Johnny, Tolliver said hang tough, be a marine, and keep your mouth shut. He's pulling for you."

"He saved my life, and now I have to hope I'll never see him again."

"You'll see him after the trial," Angela said carefully. "When you're out of here."

Johnny smiled. Angela thought he had a beautiful smile. "Angela," he asked shyly, "are you married?"

She was taken aback. "I was. No more; my life didn't take to it."

Johnny fairly grinned. "Mine neither. Thanks for coming down to see me."

Angela felt another warning tingle in her brain, this one pleasant. "Good night, Johnny. You *will* walk out of here."

He smiled at her again, warming her spirit. "Good night."

TOM JACKSON ESCORTED Johnny over to Superior Court where the grand jury was sitting. Johnny wore a suit Tom had managed to get out of his house. The suit hung on him loosely; never fat, Johnny had lost weight in jail, but it was the best they could do. "Sit here," Tom said. "They'll call you when they get to you."

"Aren't you coming in with me?"

"I can't; lawyers don't go before grand juries. But remember, anything happens we haven't discussed, you can request a recess to come out and talk to me."

"We don't present any defense?"

"No. The grand jury almost always indicts, no matter how flimsy the State's case, and anything we try to present will only help the State prepare."

"So I just stand there and plead the Fifth. It seems dishonest, sneaky."

"It's neither." Tom said. "The State has to prove its case and right now I don't think it can. As soon as you're indicted I'm going to request the earliest trial date, give the State the least possible time to get lucky and find new evidence."

"Tom, answer me one question."

"Sure."

"Does it bother you, defending me, knowing I did it?"

"It would, Marine, if I didn't know why. This is a terrible tragedy, Johnny, but not one for which you should be held solely responsible."

"Who should?" Johnny pressed.

"That girl, for one, the boys who snatched her and threatened the terrified parents, for others. Perhaps the entire society bears blame, Johnny, for exchanging a mosaic of lies and excuses for the fabric of honor you and I once knew and believed in."

The clerk opened the door to the grand jury room. "The grand jury is ready to hear John Dietrich."

Johnny went in and the clerk closed the door behind him. He was asked about twenty questions by a pretty blond assistant state's attorney. He answered each the same way: "Upon advice of counsel, I decline to answer on the grounds that it may tend to incriminate me."

The grand jury handed up its indictment, three counts of capital felony murder with intent, after deliberating less than ten minutes.

SARA STEVENS, ONE of Tom Jackson's paralegals, entered Angela's cramped office and placed a single large envelope on her desk. "Here's the State's evidence in the John Dietrich case."

Angela undid the string fastener and slid the papers out onto her blotter. "This's all of it?" Discovery in capital felony cases usually arrived in multiple boxes.

"Yes." Sara perched on the edge of a chair in front of Angela's desk. She was a very pretty black woman, a recent graduate of Yale Law School now studying for the bar exam. "Do you want me to inventory the contents?"

"Let's do it together. It can't take long."

The State's case contained all the crime-scene and lab reports Angela had already read, plus Edward Collins's deposition and his wife's, and a deposition from the daughter, Sally, that Angela hadn't seen. The only witness the State would call other than the Collinses and certain unspecified experts was one Abigail Grieg. "Find out who she is," Angela said.

Sara made a note. "There's also a subpoena. The state wants to have Johnny examined by a psychiatrist."

Angela frowned. "We'll have to get one of our own. Leave a note on Tom's e-mail."

"He's in his office."

Angela got up and picked up the thin case file. "I'll go in to see him."

"Okay, I'll check out this—Abigail."

TOM WAS IN shirtsleeves, pecking away at his computer. "Good morning, Angela," he said, removing his reading glasses and rubbing at red spots on the bridge of his nose.

"Here's the prosecution's discovery," she said, placing the envelope before him. "It's basically just Collins's statement. The State demands a psychiatric exam."

"Really? Well, I guess I'm not surprised. I didn't say anything about a plea of 'not criminally responsible' but Carelli has a right to anticipate it and be prepared. Arrange for Dr. Lewes to examine Johnny after the State's man, and you see Johnny before either of them. It's important that he answer truthfully but not say anything whatever about the rescue."

"I'll see to both. What are you doing?"

"Knocking out the pretrial motions."

Angela's eyebrows rose. "I could do that." Tom never worried about the boilerplate motions that were always filed in a criminal case, the most important of which were motions for bill of particulars and discovery and inspection that required the prosecution to disclose all its information, including any fact or testimony that might help the defendant. The prosecution had already complied by handing over its evidence and witness list, but the motions had to be filed anyway.

Tom looked at his associate quizzically. "I'm using your standard motions, Angela, but I want to think a bit on the motion to dismiss."

"Do you think there's a chance?"

"A very good chance, if this case hadn't had so much publicity, but as it is, there will probably be a trial. It's critical we get to trial as quickly as possible."

"When's the rearraignment?"

"Tomorrow morning. I got Judge Levine to make a space in his schedule."

Angela got up. "I'd better go talk to Johnny about this psychiatrist thing. Let me know if you need any help with the motions."

"I'll want you to read them before they're filed."

Angela nodded and left. She found herself looking forward to seeing her client again.

JAMAL JONES FOUND his partner doing what he hated the most, clearing up paperwork. "Morning, Mike."

"Hey, Jamal. Johnny's phone records came in. They're on your desk."

Jamal took off his jacket and hung it over the back of his chair. "You look at them?"

"Yeah. Mostly local calls to two numbers. I dialed them up and they both screeched at me."

"Computer access lines," Jamal said, picking up the record. "I recognize them; Microsoft Network and a pay-by-computer bank line." He leafed through the muddy copies. "Here's long-distance. One number in 212; Manhattan. Guy's not a big fan of AT&T."

"I didn't check that one out yet."

"I'll do it." Jamal picked up his phone, dialed his accounting code so the long-distance bill could be properly charged, then dialed the New York number. A voice answered immediately, "Marines Helping Marines, may I help you?"

Jamal's heart rose up in his chest. The voice was that of a black man of the northeastern cities. He reached for the recorder that was slaved to his phone, but hesitated. The voice was younger, higher in pitch, than he remembered. He was sure the voice wouldn't match the voice on the tape. "May I help you, sir?" the voice repeated.

"Just tell me where you at, man," Jamal said, laying on a street accent he had abandoned years ago.

"You in trouble?"

"Some."

"What's your name? You don't have to say, but I gotta know what outfit."

Jamal put his hand over the phone. "Mike, what was your outfit in the marines?"

"First of the Sixth. Why?"

Jamal shushed him and spoke into the receiver. "First of the Sixth."

"Okay, brother, come on in. We're in the basement of St. Anne's Church on West Ninth. You know the neighborhood?"

"I'll get there." Jamal broke the connection.

A marine outreach program! Jamal recalled Stonewall Jackson's assistant at the Armed Forces Recruiting Station, then high-tailing it for New York. It fell together in his mind with a solid click. "Damn."

"What?" Mike said.

"It's a veterans' program. That could be Johnny's connection with the black man who called in the crime scene. That could be our witness."

"It could be anybody, Jamal," Mike said, an edge to his voice.

"It's a lead, Mike. It has to be checked."

"Then get the New York cops to check it. You know how they love outside cops coming into their bailiwick."

Jamal thought about it. New York cops were notorious all over the country for granting neither assistance nor courtesy to out-of-town cops. He and Mike had bumped heads with them on a fugitive warrant a few years ago and had been all but thrown out of the Big Apple. "I'm going to check it out, that's all."

"You better get some paper from Carelli, cover our ass."

"He's out of town until tomorrow, when the arraignment on the indictment goes down."

"Talk to him then."

No, Jamal thought. If my hunch is right, Johnny's attorney's assistant has already reached this guy. If I go through the State's Attorney, and he goes through channels, Connecticut court order, request for service through a New York court, it could take forever. Right now the SA was sweating bullets; the defense was pressing for an immediate trial and Carelli had nothing for this high-profile case except the statement of the father and mother and some therapist who might shed some light on Johnny's state of mind or might not.

"I guess you're right, partner," Jamal said, placing the phone records aside. "I'll mention it tomorrow at the arraignment."

"Who was that?" Tolliver asked the young volunteer seated at his desk.

"Guy, says he was with Sixth Marines. I told him to come over."

"Fine. Remember my standing order. Anyone wants to talk to me, get a call-back number. I'm taking a week off."

"Where you be, Staff Sergeant?"

"Upstate. Fishing. I'll call in."

"Understood, Staff Sergeant."

Angela watched as Johnny was led into the interview room. His eyes were large and his cheeks hollow. He was still losing weight and he looked haunted. She wondered if he was sleeping.

Johnny sat down as the guard left, closing the door behind him. "Angela, it's nice to see you again," he said listlessly.

"Your rearraignment is tomorrow. I'm here to prepare you."

"I just plead not guilty again, no?"

"Yes. Tom will be filing certain motions, the most important of which is a motion to dismiss the charges. We don't think the State has enough evidence to proceed."

Johnny shook his head. "There'll be a trial. The public and the press demand it."

"Probably so, but we'll be on record, and go on record again at the beginning of the trial. The judge will be very careful in what he allows the State."

"Okay." A small smile.

"Johnny, the State wants to have you examined by a psychiatrist."

"Why? We're agreed that we aren't going to plead guilty but not criminally responsible."

"The State doesn't know we may not raise that in future."

"But we won't," Johnny said firmly. "Do I have to talk to their guy?"

"Yes, it's nontestimonial, so not covered by the Fifth Amendment. It's the same as giving fingerprints or a blood sample."

"What do I say?"

"Be truthful. The doctor can't ask you about the rescue, since you've made no statement. Don't volunteer anything. Tom will have our own expert examine you after the State's does, for rebuttal of anything the State might want to bring in. Just be circumspect."

"Okay." Johnny said with no expression. It was almost as if he hadn't heard or didn't care.

Angela reached out and stroked his hand. He rolled his hand over and gripped hers, first tightly then gently. She felt his anxiety surge through her like an electric charge. "Johnny," she said, her voice catching in her throat. "Be strong. Tom is very, very good."

He squeezed her hand again. "I'm sure he is, and you too. I'm not yet sure I don't deserve to be punished for what I did."

Angela fought back a sob. "Johnny, we know what you saw in the house. We found an object that might have looked like the AKS carbine you thought you saw."

"You did?" He brightened. "What was it?"

"A street hockey stick with a blade curved down like a magazine. The first man to be shot was holding it."

Johnny slumped, seemed to shrink into his chair. "Not a real weapon?"

"No. But it lets us know what set you off, what your motivation was. Because you believed the kidnapping was real, you had reason to see that man as armed."

"Then why is the State trying to fry my ass? Sorry, Angela."

"The State sees the crime from a different perspective. They weren't there in the dark, pumped up, attempting to rescue a young girl in deadly peril. They see only the bodies and a girl prepared to say the whole kidnap was a harmless prank." Angela gave Johnny's hot, dry hand a little squeeze. "Don't forget, Johnny, justice in this country is based on the principle of accused and adversary. The State has to make its case and only if they do, do we have to make ours."

"Angela." He lifted his soft blue eyes to hers and she once again felt his emotions surge through her. "Advocacy aside, do you think I was justified to treat the scene as hostile? Shouldn't I have called the police?"

"You believed the kidnappers' deadline. So did the parents. The police might have taken days to get organized, even then they don't have the resources. The FBI hostage rescue teams are hard to get and the nearest one is in New York and very busy trying bombing conspiracy cases." She paused. "Johnny, if Sally had been my daughter, I'd have wanted you to get her free and safe. Those men lost all rights given by God or the Constitution when they committed their crime upon the person of the girl."

"Is that the law?"

"No. That's a woman talking, a woman sometimes scared of muggers and rapists and carjackers. I believe in you."

He sat up straight and gave her a little smile. "That means a lot, more than you can know."

She got up quickly, kissed him on the lips and ran to the door. Her loud hammering brought the guard immediately and she fled, not looking back at Johnny, not wanting him to see her sobs, her tears, her fears and her weaknesses.

33

BEN LEVINE, THE Chief Judge of the State Superior Court sitting in Bridgeport, summoned Johnny, his lawyer, and the Assistant State's Attorney to the front of his elevated bench. Levine was a small man with slicked-back iron gray hair and a prominent beak of a nose. Johnny thought he looked like a bird of prey, but his pursed mouth suggested the strictness of an old-fashioned elementary school teacher.

The Chief Judge read out the case number and asked the lawyers to identify themselves for the record. The Assistant State's Attorney, a pretty blond woman in a blue suit with a very short skirt, gave her name, Evelyn Pulaski, and that of George Carelli as appearing for the State. Tom Jackson identified himself and Angela for the defendant.

Judge Levine noted the appearances for the record. Tom took a step forward. "Your honor, the defendant being present before you, I ask that a plea be entered of not guilty to the charges in the indictment. The charges against the defendant are false, and we request that trial be set for the earliest possible date."

Johnny had been briefed for this, and stood silently. Time was on the side of the State, Tom had explained, because the State was still searching for a tie between the events surrounding the rescue and Johnny. A witness might be developed, a weapon found.

Judge Levine consulted a court schedule. "Judge Kerry has an opening; an assault case scheduled for trial in two weeks has been pled. Would that suit you, Mr. Jackson?"

Johnny's heart came up into his throat. Two weeks! The nightmare over in two weeks? It didn't seem possible; Angela had told him they hoped for trial in early spring.

"The defense will be ready, Your Honor," Tom intoned gravely.

"Ms. Pulaski?" The judge smiled at the pretty deputy SA.

Ms. Pulaski was visibly taken aback. "Your Honor, this is a complex case, and still in development—"

The judge interrupted. "Mr. Jackson, how long has your client been incarcerated?"

"Forty-one days, Your Honor," Tom responded with no hesitation.

Judge Levine peered down over his half-glasses. "Ms. Pulaski, the State arrested this man, charged him, incarcerated him and indicted him. Does the State now argue that it acted precipitously? That it is unable to try the case? If so, I may entertain a motion for immediate dismissal."

"We'll be ready, Your Honor," Evelyn Pulaski said, trying to build conviction into her voice.

"Good. I'll send this matter to Judge Kerry's clerk, and if he agrees, you may begin in his court in two weeks. Please file your pretrial motions with him as soon as possible."

Tom and Angela placed hands on Johnny's elbows. They made it out of the court before succumbing to happy grins.

Johnny found that he was uneasy. Of course I want this over, he thought. Don't I?

"THAT WAS A good result indeed," Tom said as Johnny was led into the interview room in the city jail. Johnny was once again dressed in his orange prison uniform, and until he entered the room, handcuffed. Tom thought he looked upset. "We expected to wait months to try this thing, Johnny," Tom said soothingly. "Judge Kerry is a good judge for us; a stickler for proper police and prosecutorial behavior. He started out his legal career as a public defender, then private practice with one of the best firms in New Haven. He's a black man, intensely proud, a product of the old Father Panik Village housing projects; a rotten ghetto. He believes in victims' rights and has a healthy suspicion of the police and the way the State proceeds against victims."

"How does he feel about rich white guys from Fairfield who shoot unarmed kids in Black Rock?" Johnny tried to make it a joke, but it fell flat, dampening the mood in the tiny room.

"He's fair," Angela said softly. "He'll make the State prove its case."

"I'll move for dismissal as soon as he summons us for a pretrial hearing," Tom said. "The State doesn't have enough to try you, John."

"I got indicted real quick," Johnny said sadly. "Doesn't that mean they think I'm guilty?"

"The role of the grand jury is to determine whether there is sufficient reason to believe a crime was committed, and that the accused may be responsible. No defense was offered for the reasons I've already explained. The judge at trial may still determine that the prosecution's case, even if not contested—of course we will contest it—is insufficient for a reasonable jury to convict. The judge may make such a determination at the beginning of the trial, after the state rests, or after our defense rests."

Johnny looked at Angela. "What if they find Tolliver?"

Angela shifted in her seat. "They haven't, and now they have only two weeks."

Johnny turned back to Tom. "The grand jury found that a crime was committed. Hell, those boys are dead, and I killed them. I still haven't come to peace with that, and I wonder if I'm worthy of your defense."

Tom looked at his client a long time. Defense lawyers—in fact, prosecutors, judges, investigators, cops, everyone associated with criminal justice—operated by the rule that defendants always lie. Johnny seemed unable to reach for the life preserver of self-serving half-truth. "Johnny," he said very softly. "I can go back to the State's Attorney, plead you down to some lesser included offense, probably get you treatment in lieu of jail time, or a reduced sentence, if that's what you want."

"No!" Angela said, rising out of her seat. "Johnny, you want to be free." Johnny lowered his head and she touched his shoulder. "You deserve to be vindicated."

"I guess what I want," Johnny said, his silent tears starting, "is to be heard, to be judged. I don't want to be let go because of a legal trick."

Tom stood up and took Angela by the elbow. Stubborn bastard, he thought, looking at his client. "We'll talk in the morning, Johnny. We'll talk it all out."

"Thank you, sir," Johnny said miserably as the guard entered and put the handcuffs back on.

JAMAL DRESSED IN his old army utilities for his trip to New York to visit the marine outreach center. The uniform was the same as marines wore except for the cap, but he wasn't going to wear the cap. He considered razoring off the patches that marked him for a soldier, the black Airborne and Ranger shoulder patches, his jump wings, his combat infantryman badge, but decided against it. He was going to say he was trying to locate a marine buddy and there was no point getting tripped up on some trivial item of nomenclature that would unmask him if he posed as a marine.

He had worked with marines in Grenada, and he remembered how differently they talked. To a marine, he recalled, a bathroom was a head; to a soldier it was a latrine.

The loose-fitting uniform had lots of pockets, and Jamal stowed his nine-millimeter Beretta service automatic in a right leg pocket. He put his mini tape recorder in a high shirt pocket. He looked in the mirror and marveled at how much older his face looked than when he had last seen it above the uniform.

Mike is right, he thought. I'm going way out on a limb. I have no right to ask these guys any questions, even to be in New York on official business. I certainly have no right to tape any conversation. I'll just go in, ask around, see what the machine picks up. If I get a match to the voice on the police tape, I'll tell the State's Attorney and he can get the court orders, maybe even an arrest warrant if I get a good match on the voice and some connection between Marines Helping Marines and Crazy Johnny.

What could go wrong? he said to himself as he locked his apartment and drove his car to the Bridgeport train station.

34

JOHNNY WAS WARY when the psychiatrist who did work for the state welcomed him effusively into the interview room. "I'm Doctor Merrill," the trim middle-aged black woman said. "Please sit down."

"John Dietrich," Johnny said superfluously. He sat on the edge of a wooden chair.

"Try to relax," the doctor said with a pleasant smile. "This isn't meant to be unpleasant; I just need to know a bit about you."

"To find out if I'm crazy," Johnny blurted, then bit his lip.

The doctor's kindly smile slipped. "Do you think you are?"

"No." Johnny forced himself to relax a little. "Although being locked up here for a month and a half is beginning to get to me."

"How does it get to you?"

"I don't sleep well. I have no appetite and I have stomach pains. I feel listless, drifting."

The doctor made a note on a yellow pad. "Is anything else bothering you, besides the confinement?"

"Not knowing where this is all going to end up."

"You've pled not guilty."

Careful, Johnny thought. "Yes, twice now." He looked up at the doctor and tried to keep the doubt out of his eyes. "I'm *not* guilty."

"Good, I hope you're out of here soon. I'm sure your counsel has told you we can't discuss the crime for which you've been charged, because you've declined to make any statement and have indeed pled not guilty. Let's discuss your life, your life experiences, starting very early. Anything you say is privileged between doctor and patient; only my conclusions, if any, will ever be heard at trial."

Johnny nodded. Angela had told him that in her briefing just before Dr. Merrill came in. "Dr. Merrill will look for signs of stress," Angela had coached him. "She'll find them but that's fine. No normal human being in your situation would not feel stress, and if you tried to hide it, she'd know."

"The doctor gonna ask about Vietnam?"

"Almost certainly. If she leads you into areas where you don't want to go, say so."

"What if I break down? Start crying, like you've seen me do."

"Don't worry; she's studied people with Post Traumatic Stress Disorder, from Vietnam to grieving widows to survivors of the bombing of the Murrah Federal Building in Oklahoma City. She's written about that event and is considered an expert in the field.

"Just let yourself relax; she can't ask you about the rescue. Johnny, she works a lot of cases for the State, but she's fair."

Johnny told the shrink about his aimless and lonely childhood, his lack of direction and the effect the Marine Corps had on him. He told her The Crotch broke guys down to get rid of selfish attitudes and instill loyalty and pride among marines. For him training had been less a matter of tearing him down than of filling him up; he'd arrived at Parris Island with no plan for his life, and left with a whole new set of values, and a new family.

"You were a marine in Vietnam," Dr. Merrill said. It wasn't a question; Johnny knew the State had his service records. "Were you much in combat?"

"Saw a little of everything, ma'am." Johnny said softly.

"When you came home, did you have trouble talking about it?"

"When I came home." Johnny felt the tears welling, and he let them go without wiping them away. "No one wanted to talk about it."

"Friends? Loved ones?"

"People who were never there treated me like someone with a disease, something I should take a pill for, get well and forget about. Loved ones couldn't understand why I didn't hang the whole experience away in the attic with the uniforms."

"What about other veterans? There must have been many."

"Most of the guys tried to fade into the woodwork. I guess we figured if the whole country wanted to walk away from the war, we were entitled, too. So no, nobody really wanted to talk."

"But later you entered a rehab program."

Johnny looked at the woman, who maintained a bland, unreadable expression. How much did she know about the program?

About Tolliver?

"A lot of guys went very badly adrift, while trying to handle the hurt of it all alone." Johnny didn't want to tell her what a drunk he'd been, or that he stole to feed his need for booze. "I was lucky I got taken into a program at the right time. I think it's like quitting a bad habit, like maybe smoking. You have to wait until you really feel the need to quit, then you can get help."

"The group therapy helped."

"The therapy, yes. Just being around other guys who needed to get their shit back together—sorry, ma'am." Her bland expression didn't change. "Needed to get a grip on themselves, all helped. Mostly I was helped by a tough counselor who got me to write."

"Bestselling novels."

"Yes. The success was invigorating, but the first step was accepting what I had seen and done, facing it, getting on with living."

"Writing helped, then. Good, so many have great difficulty in getting the hurt out in front of them. You've learned that is the first step in healing yourself."

Johnny nodded. His tears had stopped and he blew his nose on a tissue he carried in his prison uniform's only small pocket.

"Do you still think about Vietnam?" she asked.

"It seems long ago," he said, the first lie he had told the doctor. "It was long ago." He thought her eyebrows moved a millimeter.

"Dreams?"

"Sometimes. I've gotten used to them."

"They don't frighten you anymore?"

"It's like I know I'm dreaming. I have to take the pain, but pain is just pain." The doctor made another note and Johnny felt uneasy for the first time in the interview.

"You feel you've adjusted?"

"Yes."

"No violent moods? Sudden rages?"

"I lead a very quiet life."

She made another note. "Why so quiet? A successful man like you usually has many friends."

"I feel better by myself. People rarely come to me unless they want something, and I'm a pretty easy touch."

"What's your strongest memory of Vietnam?"

Johnny flinched. He'd thought they were past Vietnam, but of course, he never would be. The doctor must have picked that up. "I'd rather not go into detail about 'Nam. My lawyer said I didn't have to."

"It's still a central influence on your life," she said gently.

Johnny couldn't help liking her and trusting her, but he reminded himself she was the State's witness. "I really don't want to go back to it."

She leaned forward and touched his hand. Her skin was dry and cool. "I wish you would, just a little. If you answer that question, we can finish this interview early."

Johnny sat silently, shaking his head slowly, waiting for the doctor to move on, to tell him it was all right. She continued to regard him with the bland, gentle expression, undisturbed by his silence. Johnny felt tension rising within him; he had to speak. I'll tell her just a little, he thought. He began to speak about the Battle of the Twenty-six Days, the streets and shattered houses of Hue. I'll just say a little and then stop, he told himself.

He talked for nearly an hour. He told it all, all the way to the basement of the church with the neat rows of dead and violated children.

Dr. Merrill lost her bland expression in the end, and cried with him. She put her notes into her briefcase, gave Johnny a fresh tissue, and tiptoed out of the room.

Johnny was taken back to his cell. He sat, too drained to write, even to read. He knew he'd blown it; Dr. Merrill would surely conclude he was crazy. Angela came down an hour later and he was returned to the interview room.

"You're upset," she said.

"I—I told the shrink everything about 'Nam. I couldn't stand the silence when she asked."

Angela sat opposite him and took his trembling hand. His skin was hot, almost feverish. "That may not be bad, Johnny. It will certainly demonstrate your honesty. You didn't say anything about the rescue, did you?" God, say you didn't, she thought as she watched him fight for control.

"No. We just talked about me, my life, how I felt about coming home. Then she asked me what was my worst time in the war, and

I told her about Hue, and the basement full of dead children." His hand relaxed its grip on hers. "If she has the usual mental picture of the bedeviled Vietnam vet, she'll conclude the rescue fits me like a glove."

"The State still has to place you at the scene, Johnny."

"Yeah." He released her hand and knuckled his red eyes.

"Dr. Lewes, our psychiatric expert, is waiting. Are you up to going through all this again?"

"I guess. I'd like to get this over with."

"Since this is our guy, I think you should tell him what you saw and felt when you went into the house."

"The hockey stick." Johnny balled his fists on the table top.

"No, what *you* saw and felt, just as you've told Tom and me."

"That's wise?"

"Yes. If the State somehow places you at the scene, we'll need to know how to portray your motivation, your sense of danger to you and to the girl."

Johnny nodded. "Angela, I'm scared. Really scared. Will you sit with me for a few minutes while I pull myself together?"

"Of course." She covered his fists with her hands and once again felt tension crackle from his body into hers.

JAMAL FOUND ST. Anne's Church without difficulty, and entered the rectory next door. The building bustled with activity at 6:00 P.M.; Jamal could hear children laughing and others singing. He followed an arrow pointing downstairs and found the door to Marines Helping Marines. He saw about twenty men sitting around in a large room of neatly made-up bunks. Some talked in small groups, some read, some slept. All wore battle dress utility trousers and olive-drab T-shirts. A television was on in the far corner of the room, a basketball game. Jamal couldn't hear the sound through the glass panel that separated the bunk room from the narrow hall. He found the door with "Office—Off Limits" stenciled on it. Jamal took a deep breath, turned on the tape recorder in his pocket, then knocked. The door was opened immediately by a young Hispanic-looking man in the program's uniform. Jamal went in and saw another man, older and black, sitting behind a metal desk. "May I help you?" the black man said as the other man resumed his seat in front of a computer.

The voice was a definite maybe. Jamal hoped the recording would be sharp enough for voice-printing, made through the fabric of his pocket. "I'm looking for a marine buddy of mine I haven't seen for years," Jamal said, moving closer to the desk. "He lived in New York years ago and he wrote to me from this program."

"You are?" the man leaned forward and read the name tag sewn above the right shirt pocket and the metal rank devices on the collar points, "Sergeant Jones?"

"Yes, Oscar Jones, originally from LA."

"You don't hardly seem old enough for 'Nam."

"Just at the end," Jamal said smoothly.

"We can't give out any information about our graduates except with their prior permission, and then only if the director says so."

"You're not the director?"

"No. He's away. I'm Gunny Miller, one of the counselors. What's your buddy's name?"

"John Dietrich. Was a corporal."

Miller wrote it down. A light winked on his telephone and he punched a button. "Yes?"

"Gunny, Staff Sergeant Tolliver is on line three."

Miller looked up at the soldier standing before him. "I have to take this call, Oscar. Ramirez, why not take this soldier to the galley and get him a cup of coffee."

Ramirez got up and gestured for Jamal to follow him. Miller

waited until the door was closed behind him, then punched up Tolliver's call. "Boss, I'm glad you called. We got a guy walked in from the street, looking for Johnny Dietrich."

"Shit. Who is he?"

"Says he's Oscar Jones. He's wearing utilities with Eighty-Second Airborne and Ranger patches. Looks too young for 'Nam; he says he was in at the end."

"Johnny wasn't in at the end; he came out after Tet in sixty-eight. Is Ismael in the building?"

"Yes."

"Bring him into the discussion. See if he recognizes the voice of the guy who called in a few days ago and never showed up."

"You think cop?"

"Good chance."

"What do you want us to do with him?"

"Give him the usual runaround. He writes a letter to his buddy care of the shelter, we forward it if we have an address, the guy will get back to him directly if he wants to."

"Okay."

"If he presses, tell him to come back tomorrow, the director'll be back. Don't give him my name."

"Right—hold on, Willy." Ramirez had rushed back into the office and closed the door behind him. "What did you do with that dogface, Juan?"

"He's drinking coffee with Ahmed Ismael. Ahmed's got an odd look on his face. Reason I came back, I bumped into the guy in the hall and I think he has a gun in his leg pocket."

"You hear that, Willy," Miller said into the phone.

"I heard. Get rid of him but say he can come back tomorrow."

"I wonder if Ismael recognized the voice."

"So do I. Find out, and I'll call you back in a little while." Tolliver hung up the phone; he wasn't Upstate fishing, he was staying with his sister in Queens, and he was tempted to go right to the shelter and confront the guy. If Ismael recognized the voice—

It hit Tolliver like a thunderbolt. The cops in Bridgeport must have a tape of him calling in the crime scene, and this geek Oscar Jones who was *not* in 'Nam with Johnny was wearing a wire, looking to record Tolliver's voice for a match.

I'm gonna put a stop to this shit, Tolliver thought, and dialed the shelter again.

35

DOCTOR MERRILL HANDED her report to Assistant State's Attorney Pulaski the morning after her interview with John Dietrich. Evelyn Pulaski had worked with Merrill before, and had never seen her as upset as she was when she described the interview. "That man thinks he's adjusted, but his head is full of horrible scenes."

"Could he have done it?"

"Sure."

"What about a plea of not criminally responsible?"

"Probably be sustained. The man needs treatment whether or not he did this thing you say. He's stressed, profoundly sad, depressed and perhaps suicidal."

"Jesus, we'd better alert the jail."

"One thing. I doubt he's normally violent. If he killed those men, he had to believe the girl was in danger."

"Okay. Thanks, Ida. I'll read this and talk to George. I'm sure he'll want to talk to you very soon."

Dr. Lewes delivered his report of the interview to Angela Hughes. He was visibly shaken. "He was in a fugue state inside the house; in two places at once."

"Was he sane when he shot those men?"

"Definitely not. Too bad there's no insanity defense in this state."

"Is he sane now?" Angela asked, and not just because of the case.

"Yes, but his head is full of snakes. You have to get him away from that cell, all this scary courtroom stuff."

"Will he make it through a trial?"

"Jesus, I don't know. I'm not sure he even wants to live."

Angela winced. "I'll go over this with Tom and we'll call you."

VI

OPENING ARGUMENTS

36

ANGELA SAT GRAINY-EYED in the firm's library, running the computer looking for precedents that might allow the defense to invoke a finding of guilty but not criminally responsible, whether Johnny agreed to it or not. Tom trained his staff to be pessimistic in their research; assume the worst, the incredible luck that sometimes turned the weakest prosecution into conviction.

Surely Johnny would be better off in a mental institution than in jail.

But not much, she thought bleakly.

Johnny wasn't crazy. He just needed support. Maybe he would need to spend some more time with Tolliver when he got out, or maybe with her.

Angela felt her attraction for Johnny growing. He had a wonderful untamed intensity, forged by his experiences in Vietnam and after, compounded by his chosen life of isolation. He had a rugged, unflinching sense of right and wrong. Angela had read his books, staying up even later than the case demanded. She hadn't expected to like them, and on some levels, she didn't. But the books had power, and passion, and a clear sense of what could be made right and what could not. Angela found to her dismay that right and wrong had left her in the study of the law and the often strained concept of justice.

Justice often had little to do with right and wrong, she realized, and that scared her. Tom might get Johnny off, but was that what he wanted? In her years of trying cases with Tom, they had got many guilty people off, and that was all they had wanted, just slide out and walk away. Johnny wanted absolution, a quantity of great rarity. If Tom got the case dismissed, as he would try in the status hearing before Judge Kerry in the morning, where would Johnny go to retrieve his soul, his sense of himself as a good person?

The phone rang and was answered out in the bay. The paralegals and staff were working late too; it was nearly 8:00 P.M. The phone in the library buzzed and Angela picked it up. Sara Stevens said, "For you. Didn't give his name."

Angela felt her heart race. She hated anonymous calls; they were nearly always bad news. She hit the only light on the console. "Hughes."

"Ms. Hughes, this line be secure?" said the deep voice of a black man.

"Yes, on this end."

"Tolliver."

"I recognized your voice, Willy."

"That's why I'm calling. There's a man over at the shelter asking about Johnny. I just figured out how they might pin me to the deal and screw Johnny. When we got done rescuing the girl, I called the Bridgeport cops from a pay phone and gave them the scene. Johnny insisted those kids not be left undiscovered, after he figured out what the girl done."

Angela started. "They have you on tape. The police tape all incoming calls."

"That's what I just figured out. This guy at the shelter must be recording voices, looking for a match."

"Have you talked to him?" Angela's heart beat even harder.

"No, I'm off-post, at my sister's house. If this guy's a cop, he'd have to show us something, wouldn't he?"

Angela's mind raced. "Maybe not. Maybe Bridgeport's got NYPD to send an undercover man in with a wire. If you ask him straight out if he's a cop and he doesn't say, they risk entrapment—but if he's legal, a voiceprint might tie you in even if they couldn't use the contents of whatever you said."

"I made a few calls before you. I got friends in the cops, and they say there has been no inquiry from Bridgeport on anything."

Could a Bridgeport cop be freelancing? she wondered. "What does the guy look like?"

"My guy says black, mid-thirties, clean-cut, wearing a set of army utilities that look like they ain't been off the hanger in years. Say he from LA but talks like a Northeast city street nigger."

Jamal? Angela wondered. Jamal had no accent, but maybe he remembered one.

"My guys also think he's carrying a gun in his pocket."

Jamal's a better cop than that, Angela thought. But the State is desperate, with no time to go through channels and nothing to show a judge if there was time. The trial would begin in less than two weeks. "Stay away from him, Willy."

"Can't have some rogue inside my program. I have to promise my guys confidentiality to get them to open up."

"Just send them away."

"Program can't work, my guys think the cops can come in here. I got me a deal with the city, Angela, no cops in the basement of St. Anne's Rectory lessen I say so."

"Jesus, Willy, just get rid of him."

"Not without I give him a message." Tolliver hung up and Angela was left staring at the phone. God, this is coming apart, she thought. What is *right* for Johnny?

JOHNNY LAY SLEEPLESS in his bunk, surrounded by snores and moans and the stink of sleeping men. Why can't I make peace with myself? he wondered. Killing the boys was wrong, but saving the girl was righteous.

If only the kid *had* had an AKS, and the cops had found it. Angela had told him that made little difference under the law; he had no right to enter the house no matter what he thought, and in fact the legal tenants of the house had the right to shoot *him*.

If only the kidnapping hadn't been a sham to extract money from a father estranged from a daughter in the throes of the most difficult emotional transition of her life.

If only, if only. Johnny shook his head. If wishes were horses then beggars would ride.

I don't deserve to die for this. I don't deserve to stay forever in this tiny cell without the press of wind on my face to drive out the dry demons of solitude. Perhaps I owe a penance for my sin of haste in the darkened house, but not my life.

My grandfather used to say "no good deed goes unpunished." I was punished for trying to do right in Vietnam, for trying to save little kids.

For trying, for failing.

Now Johnny Dietrich will fight, he said to himself, fighting tears. Johnny will not be fucked again.

He thought of Angela and felt better, less alone. At last he slept and did not dream.

"You in luck," Miller said, joining Jamal and Ahmed Ismael in the Spartan mess deck where they sat drinking coffee. "The director's on his way in; says he'll talk to you. He's been here since the first days; in fact, he ran this program all by himself, the early years."

"I'd like to meet him," Jamal said guardedly. "What's he called?"

Ismael started to answer but Miller cut him off with a look. " 'Round here he's called Boss, or Staff Sergeant," Miller said. "He said you could wait an hour, or come back tomorrow, either way."

Jamal didn't like the way it felt. He knew he should go. He knew the marines hadn't bought his act for the simple reason they had asked him *nothing,* not what do you do, where do you live, why are you wearing an old uniform, nothing. But he wanted his answer. "I reckon I'll stay, I not be in the way. But I need to get something to eat."

"We messed early," Ismael said apologetically. "We got anything left, Gunny?"

Jamal took some crumpled bills from his left leg pocket. "Maybe I stand you leathernecks a pizza? Six-pack of beer?"

Miller frowned. "Pizza be all right," he said. "Never no alcohol in this program."

"Of course," Jamal said. He saw that both marines were watching with the alertness of guard dogs. He decided to leave. "I'll go get a pizza, y'all tell me where."

"Stay here, relax," Miller said with a crooked smile. "I'll call it in. A medium with everything?"

Jamal forced a smile. "A large."

Tom Jackson joined two men in the dimly lit cocktail lounge of the Algonquin Club in downtown Bridgeport. He wondered if Attorney Marvin Levin had chosen the location because the darkness would make it difficult for any of them to take notes. It didn't matter to Tom; he had an excellent memory, especially for the spoken word. "Good evening, Marvin," Tom said, greeting the lawyer. "And Mr. Collins, I presume?"

"Edward Collins," the other man said. He was flushed and sweating despite the chill of the lounge. His voice had a slight slur and Jackson wondered if he was drunk.

"I'm Thomas Jackson, representing your *friend* Johnny Dietrich, Mr. Collins."

"He knows who you are and what you're doing, Tom," said Levin in a gravelly voice that spoke of years of acquaintance with alcohol and tobacco. "Let's get to it."

Tom smiled. He and Levin loathed each other, and despised each other's methods. Jackson was silk while Levin was sandpaper. "Mr. Collins, your testimony is central to the State's case. I've read your deposition, but I'd like to know more of what you'll say."

Collins looked quickly at Marvin Levin, whose face gave no signal. "Johnny tried to help. I wish he weren't in this jam."

This *jam*, Tom thought. Three capital felony murders is a *jam?* "I'm glad you want to be helpful," Tom said, swallowing his anger. "What will you say beyond your deposition?"

Edward once again looked at his counsel, who sat as still and expressionless as a stone Buddha. "I, uh, think I pretty much said it all."

"You went to Johnny for money, ransom money," Tom said softly.

Edward drew himself up, pressed against the back of the banquette, steadied himself. He is drunk, Tom thought. "I asked him to lend me money," Edward said.

"What else?"

"Well, Johnny said if he gave me the money—he offered to *give* it to me, not lend it—and I paid the ransom, the kidnappers would kill my girl."

"A conclusion borne out by crime statistics," Tom said dryly.

"My client has no personal knowledge of crime statistics," Levin entered.

"But I *believed* him," Edward blurted. Tom glanced at Levin, who shook his head in weary disgust. "I did."

"What did Johnny say, after you discussed ransom?" Tom asked.

"He said we had to get my Sally back ourselves," Edward replied, with another pleading look at his stone-faced lawyer. "I didn't know what he meant by that."

This man is going to make a shitty witness, Tom thought. He

clearly think Sally's guilty as sin, but that doesn't help Johnny. "Did Johnny suggest any use of violence in rescuing your daughter?"

"No. He didn't suggest anything."

"What did you think he meant?"

"I really had no idea. He was with Jane—Mrs. Collins—and me when the second call came in from the kidnappers. He heard it as we did. Then he said he was going to go after Sally that same evening, and I asked what was the plan, what was I to do? He said I wouldn't be going—his exact words. I protested, and he repeated it, I wouldn't be going."

So you weren't there, Tom thought. Who'd have wanted the likes of you? "What happened next?"

"I don't know. I waited with my wife; we tried to talk. She went up to lie down; I doubt she slept. I had a couple of drinks, to pass the time. Then Johnny called and told me that Sally was safe, sitting by the driveway, and that I should come and get her."

Tom started, leaned forward. "Johnny *called* you? From where?"

"I don't know. But I ran out of the house and found Sally, bound and blindfolded."

"That wasn't in your deposition."

Once again Collins looked at his impassive lawyer. "I may have forgotten to tell the police that," Collins said.

Tom looked at Levin, who smiled for less than a second. That's the deal, then. Edward Collins forgets about the phone call, and I don't press him toward his own criminality.

Tom forced his expression to be grim, but inside he was more than pleased. Works for me, you lying coward, he thought as he rose and shook the two men's hands.

37

WILLY TOLLIVER ENTERED St. Anne's Rectory through a back entrance and went into the space leased by Marines Helping Marines by an unmarked door to which he had the only key. The door gave onto a well-lighted exercise room equipped with free weights, Soloflex machines and Stairmasters. He picked up an internal phone and buzzed his office. "Ramirez," a voice said.

"Juan, this is Tolliver. Where's the soldier?"

"With Miller and Ismael in the galley."

"Good. You go get him and take him back to the office. Don't let him out of your sight, and send Ismael and Miller to me in the weight room."

"Right away, Staff Sergeant."

Tolliver paced the empty room for the minute it took Ismael and Miller to arrive. He turned to them as the door closed behind them. Tolliver was wearing a blue Cardin blazer, starched white shirt, red silk tie and gray slacks.

"You look sharp, Bro," Miller said with evident amusement.

"I took my sister and her husband out to dinner. I suppose I should change back into utilities for the next act, but you men will do the heavy lifting."

"Ready when you are," Miller said, still grinning.

"Ahmed, what do you make of the voice? Same as called a couple of days ago?"

"I think so, Boss. Who do you think this guy is?"

"I'm guessing he's a Connecticut cop on a fishing trip," Tolliver said carefully. He had never related his role in Johnny's rescue mission to anyone and didn't intend to, but they had all seen press accounts of the incident and knew Johnny was not only a graduate of the program but its biggest benefactor. "I don't like that a bit."

Miller shifted and flexed his muscles. "We could just show him the door."

"No. I want his mind fucked before he leaves. No one comes into my house in search of a marine to hurt."

"Tell us what we gonna do, Boss," Miller said, still pumping himself up.

Tolliver told them, then went down the hall to his office.

JAMAL ASKED TO use the head, and Ramirez escorted him to it, down the hall. Jamal thought the marine was going to follow him inside, but he didn't. Jamal was increasingly uneasy about his position, but he was committed.

He popped the cassette out of his recorder and turned it over. He hoped the batteries held out; he had a good feeling about the director. He restarted the recorder and put it back in his pocket, buttoning the flap. He took a piss and washed his hands, then went back into the hall to find Ramirez waiting. Jamal was once again reminded of guard dogs as Ramirez lead him back to the office of the director. Ramirez opened the door, stepped aside to allow Jamal to go in, then closed the door behind him. Jamal found himself facing a very large black man with a shining shaved head.

The man was in shirtsleeves with his collar unbuttoned and his tie pulled down. He was the first person Jamal had seen in the building not in utility uniform. "Oscar Jones," the man rumbled. Jamal felt a jolt pass through him. The voice matched the one he had heard so often on the police tape. Now all I have to do is get out of here in one piece, he thought. "What do you really want here, Oscar Jones?"

"A guy I know was in this program years ago," Jamal said, his voice dry and raspy. "He wrote me from here, said if I ever come East—"

"Do you like the sound of my voice, *Oscar?*" Tolliver asked sweetly.

"I—"

The door opened behind Jamal and the two counselors, Miller and Ismael, came quickly into the room, slamming the door closed behind them.

"I asked you a question, *Oscar,*" Tolliver said. Jamal turned back to face the big man, who was now standing.

He and Jamal were the same height but the director was much thicker. "I don't need this shit," Jamal said. "I'm leaving."

"Oh? Without what you came for? But then, you already have it, don't you?"

Jamal felt the two burly marines press close behind him. "You can't hold me here." He felt it sounded lame.

"Turn out your pockets, Oscar."

Jamal dropped his street jive. "Look, I'm a police officer." He reached for the pocket on his shirt that contained his badge and ID. He felt a beefy arm slide under his chin, then he was jerked off the floor in a choke hold. His head was forced back and his wind cut off. He went limp and the hold eased slightly, but he was forced to stare at the ceiling while rough hands went through his pockets and dumped his badge, gun and tape recorder on the director's desk. He was lowered to the floor and he staggered. He was dizzy and his vision was blurred and dark. Marines held him tightly by his biceps.

Tolliver picked up the tape recorder and ejected the cassette. He held it out toward Jamal and smiled. Jamal swallowed, couldn't speak. The director made a fist and crushed the plastic cassette to jagged splinters trailing a long crackling tangle of magnetic tape, then hurled it into a wastebasket. "Strip him naked. Most cops carry a backup gun and this clown might have another wire."

Jamal was shoved down into the swivel chair in front of the desk. His boots were unlaced and yanked off, then they stood him up and stripped off every stitch of clothing. They found his hide-out gun, a snubnose five-shot .32 revolver in an ankle holster, and his backup tape recorder, a tiny voice-activated machine taped to his other ankle with a wire microphone that ran up to his belt. The big man examined the recorder, then dropped it on the floor and ground it to bits under his heel. Jamal was forced back into the chair. The vinyl cushion felt cold against his bare ass. The director picked up Jamal's ID and shield wallet. "You want to say anything, *Jamal?*"

"I'm a cop. I'm doing my job."

Tolliver leaned close, his nose an inch from the seated man's. His voice boomed loud enough to be heard across a parade ground, deafening in the small office. "You may be a cop in Bridgeport, Connecticut, but here you are an armed intruder!" Jamal winced and tried to turn away but a tight grip on his neck prevented any movement. "I don't know about your job in Bridgeport, Connecticut, boy, but you got no work, here!" Tolliver backed away and lowered his voice. "Ramirez, call the Sixth Precinct. Sergeant Manelli is there, I spoke to him earlier. Tell him we got us an armed intruder."

"Hey, come on, cut me a little slack," Jamal said angrily.

"You can ask the po-lice for a little slack, boy," Tolliver boomed. "None for you here."

Ramirez held the phone against his shirt and grinned. "Sergeant Manelli wants to know if he should send his tactical team."

Tolliver laughed, then all the marines laughed, hearty and loud. "Tell him just a radio car will do. This puke ain't even New York tough."

Jamal's face felt hot, and humiliation made him angry. "I admit I'm out of line, Staff Sergeant, but don't you think you've made your point?"

Tolliver again leaned close. Jamal braced himself for another blast of the big man's voice, but when he spoke it was barely above a whisper. "Jamal, here's my point. You Bridgeport cops are trying to railroad one of the finest men I've ever known, lock his ass up for-ever, and you coming here and doing what you did shows how des-perate you are and how wrong you are. Am I getting through to you?"

Jamal said nothing. Two policemen in uniform entered the office, and there was barely room for all the bodies. They saw Jamal naked in the chair and snickered. "That the intruder, Willy?" one of them asked.

"Yeah. Claims he's a cop somewhere; wants some courtesy from you guys. Can you help him out?"

"Oh, sure," the second uniform said. He pulled on rubber gloves and swept Jamal's guns, the cassette recorder and his shield into a plastic evidence bag. "NYPD always delighted to have out-of-town cops running around our city. Why, the sergeant said only tonight, they don't even have to tell us they're coming."

"This man come in here naked like this?" the first uniform said.

"No," Miller said, pointing to Jamal's utilities piled up in a cor-ner. "Wore that uniform he musta got from some surplus store."

"It's *my* uniform," Jamal shouted as he was jerked to his feet. "I was an Airborne Ranger; we spit on straight-leg grunts like you."

Miller picked up the uniform, balled it up and fired it into Jamal's belly like a basketball. He curled his hand into a loose fist, his thumb touching the second finger, and waved it up and down in Jamal's face. "Fucking paratroops. Jerkoffs always arriving late, in the wrong place and without they shit."

Jamal dressed with as much dignity as he could muster and was led away by the two cops. At least they didn't handcuff him.

38

ANGELA HUGHES WAITED with Tom Jackson outside Judge Kerry's chambers. Across the small anteroom stood George Carelli and Evelyn Pulaski, his chief deputy, and a nervous-looking Mike Kolslovsky. "I wonder where Jamal is," Angela whispered to Tom. She'd related her conversation with Tolliver to her boss in the car on the way over from Westport. "Mike looks as skittish as a cat."

"No guess," Tom said. "But make it a point to phone the good staff sergeant as soon as we're out of here."

The door opened to the judge's chambers and the clerk, a heavy, dignified black woman, waved them in.

The judge sat behind a big scarred maple desk in shirtsleeves. He was a massive black man with a halo of iron gray hair around a shiny pate. He was short and very round, but his stoutness seemed to confer dignity, like a rock dividing rushing waters of discord. He greeted each player with a word; he prided himself of never forgetting a face or a name once anyone had appeared before him. The seniors took seats before the desk; incongruously, the women were left standing behind them. "I'm prepared to rule on the pretrial motions. They're the usual and you all have copies; does anyone wish to be heard?"

Carelli cleared his throat. "The State vigorously opposes the defense's motion for dismissal, Your Honor."

"Explain your motion, please, Mr. Jackson."

Tom rose to his feet and took a step forward. "Your Honor, the defense's petition is simple and direct: the State does not have sufficient evidence, as set forth in its discovery to the defense, to convict my client before any reasonable jury, even if the State's case were uncontested. My client has been locked up for fifty days, deprived of his comforts and the privacy he craves, deprived of all liberty. I petition in the interest of justice that the charges brought in the indictment be dismissed and my client released."

Judge Kerry nodded slowly. Tom knew Judge Kerry would have studied the motion and the case before him with great care. "Mr. Carelli?"

The State's Attorney stood and stepped up next to Tom. "Your Honor, the State has the burden of proof in a very difficult case. The perpetrator of this crime, the killer of three unarmed and inoffensive young men, committed his crime with great skill. He did it in the dead of night when honest citizens are asleep, he disguised himself and his means, and disposed of evidence. This care and cunning place a great burden on the State that the State accepts, but the perpetrator, tied to the crime by testimony of respected citizens with no motive to dissemble, should not be rewarded for his skill and cunning by being set free before the State is heard in open court."

Judge Kerry allowed himself a little smile. "You planning any surprises, Mr. Carelli? Your case in chief seems a bit thin."

"Your Honor, all we have of evidence points to the defendant and nothing points anywhere else. If the defense can overcome the State's case before a fair-minded judge and jury, then so be it. We hold Mr. Jackson and his firm in the highest regard, as we do Your Honor, and should Mr. Jackson prevail, the State will accept its defeat. We have a case and we want only permission to present it," George finished primly.

Judge Kerry allowed himself another little smile. "Mr. Jackson, I'd like to find for you and dismiss this, I really would. But the State has brought these most serious charges and I think it only fair that you and your client be allowed your say in open court." He sat back and knitted his hands behind his big head. "Especially since this matter has been so heavily tried in the press. The motion is denied, and trial will commence ten days from today."

Tom and George stepped back. The judge dealt swiftly with several procedural matters, and the hearing was over.

"H<small>E</small> *WHAT?*" G<small>EORGE</small> Carelli shouted at Mike Kolslovsky. "He fucking did *what?*"

Mike squirmed. "I only know what Chief O'Hara told me." Chief O'Hara hadn't actually *told* Mike anything; he had shouted at Mike, dressing him down in front of the whole detective squad. "Jamal went into New York on his day off and followed a lead on this guy on the police tape. He wound up at an NYPD precinct at midnight, in the lock-up because there was no one on duty in our detective squad of sufficient rank to talk to a very pissed-off New York police captain."

"Was he charged?" George Carelli turned away from his investigator and looked out the window at nothing.

"No, but Chief O'Hara had to drive into the city to pick Jamal up, sign for his weapons, all that." Mike felt miserable telling the story, and knew he'd feel worse when Jamal told him the rest of it.

"I'll *fry* that nigger's ass!" Carelli thundered.

Mike looked at his shoes. Jamal was in for suspension at the very least; the New York cops would insist as a condition of not charging him. "He was trying to help your case," Mike said doggedly.

Carelli sat behind his desk and covered his face with his hands. "Sweet Jesus," he said. "If Judge Kerry had known of this when he heard us this morning, he'd have booted this case for sure."

"Maybe that would be for the best," Mike said.

Carelli jerked his head up and looked at Mike with fury in his black eyes. "Whose side are you on, Mike?"

"Same's you. Justice."

Carelli shook his head and managed a little ironic smile. "Fuck justice. Go wait for O'Hara; find out as much as you can before the chief rips your ex-partner's lungs out."

"Yes, sir," Mike said angrily as he marched from the room. Loyalty up and loyalty down, he thought, but he knew the SA was right, and the chief was right.

Why couldn't Jamal leave this thing alone?

"He WHAT?" TOM Jackson said as Angela took the chair in front of his desk.

"Jamal went into New York wearing a wire. He found Staff Sergeant Tolliver, I don't know how, and taped him for comparison to the police tapes, but Tolliver figured him out somehow and rousted him. Jamal ended up in New York police custody."

Tom shook his head in bewilderment. "*Jamal?* With no warrant, no cooperation with the NYPD? Why would he do that?"

"This case has made everyone a little crazy."

Tom stood up and paced to the window. "I hope he got all his questions answered, because whatever he learned the State will never be able to use."

"Fruits of the poisonous tree," Angela said. She felt sorry for Jamal. "But if he'd got away with it, matched the tape, then he could have got a proper warrant and gone back."

"You're right, Angela, this case is making everyone close to it crazy. If we'd known about this before Judge Kerry's hearing, we'd have gotten our dismissal."

"We can go back to him."

"No. Judge Kerry made a difficult decision and is unlikely to reverse himself; in effect he said the State had enough to proceed. He'll exact his pain from the State at the trial, however."

"But they'll never be able to charge Tolliver, or subpoena him to testify."

"I can't imagine how they could, unless the man comes forward on his own."

"It's a relief we won't have to deal with Tolliver as a witness, but I can't help feeling sorry for Jamal."

Tom returned and sat down. "What he did was maximum stupid. Why do you think he's being such a bulldog on this case?"

"I asked him that. He says it's because he had to look at the bodies."

JAMAL SAT IN silence next to Chief O'Hara in the back of the unmarked Buick. The chief's driver, a uniformed policeman, pulled into the right lane and prepared to leave I-95 in Bridgeport. Between the chief and Jamal lay the plastic evidence bag containing Jamal's weapons, the empty tape recorder, and his shield. Jamal had made no move to reclaim them. As the car pulled into the police lot, the chief picked up the bag and dropped it into his open briefcase. "Go to your desk, Jamal," the chief said, his voice tight. "You'll see Internal Affairs, then, if you like, the union's lawyer or your own. They'll talk to me and then I'll send for you." The chief strode away without a backward glance.

Jamal nodded. He felt totally humiliated. He had wanted to apologize to the chief but he hadn't. He knew he'd be suspended without pay, maybe demoted and sent back to patrol. Even fired; he knew O'Hara had taken a major ration of shit from the NYPD captain.

The worst thing was Jamal had only the smallest idea why he had hung himself out to dry on this strange, disturbing case. In his mind's eye, he could still see the ruined faces of the dead boys.

He'd seen other dead boys. His brothers, trying to escape from the implacable logic of the gangs in the projects, cut down before they had any life at all. Scared black boys like he had been until he escaped to the United States Army, and the police.

Why?

Because he was sure Crazy Johnny had done it. Damn it, the man *fit*, and no one else did. But he'd seen the girl and her parents, sleek successful people who thought they could do anything, without regard to law or God or decency.

Why?

Jamal climbed the stairs to the detective bureau. The big room was empty, and Jamal began to put his personal effects in boxes. What I would like to do most, he thought, is sit down, one-on-one, and talk to the poor bastard whose soul he had been hunting: Crazy Johnny.

39

JUDGE KERRY'S COURTROOM was crowded on opening day of the trial. Johnny sat between Angela and Tom, and edged his chair closer to Angela. Tom had bought him a new suit that fit better than his somewhat shabby older ones; Johnny felt uncomfortable in the tight collar and tie, but Angela insisted he looked handsome. To their right and nearer the empty jury box sat the prosecutors, George Carelli, Evelyn Pulaski, and the sole investigator assigned to the case, Mike Kolslovsky. Carelli and Pulaski were leaning together, in earnest conversation; Kolslovsky stared ahead at nothing, his face a mask of pain. Angela had told Johnny about Jamal's run at Tolliver and his subsequent suspension; Johnny felt for the detective.

The spectator benches were filled to overflowing. Johnny wondered who the people were and why they wanted to see this. Perhaps the families of the boys I killed are out there, he thought, but he had no idea. There was a section in the front of the spectators for the media, and it, too, was filled. There were reporters and sketch artists; Judge Kerry had banned TV cameras.

Judge Kerry's dignified clerk entered the courtroom from the door that led to the judge's chambers. The room fell silent at once, the loud buzz stilled as a candle flame might be snuffed out. "The State of Connecticut versus John Dietrich," she said in a loud, carrying voice. "Are the State and the Accused present in Court?"

Angela and Tom stood, and Angela's hand on Johnny's elbow brought him to his feet. The State's people got up also, and everybody nodded. Angela had spent several hours yesterday explaining to Johnny what would go on, what the various pieces of the drama meant. She coached him about showing any emotion or reaction to what might be said; he shouldn't under any circumstances. Look at the jury when they were brought in, and look at the witnesses, but show nothing. She offered him a tranquilizer but he said he would be fine. Now he found himself filled with wonder and dread.

"Oyez, oyez," Judge Kerry's clerk intoned in obsolete Norman French in a dingy Bridgeport courtroom. "The Superior Court of the State of Connecticut is now in session, the Honorable Lucius Kerry, Judge, presiding. God bless the United States and this Honorable Court."

Judge Kerry made his entrance even as the clerk recited her lines, took his seat behind the high bench, and struck his gavel once.

Johnny, the lawyers and Kolslovsky approached the bench, and the judge asked if everyone was ready to begin jury selection. Everyone was, and they withdrew. Sixteen citizens were admitted to the courtroom through a side door near the jury box, and the judge began his introductory remarks, stating the nature of the charges, the accused's plea, and the names of counsel on both sides. Judge Kerry reminded the jurors, at times with his finger raised like a plea to heaven, that the prosecution had to prove each element of the offense beyond a reasonable doubt. The judge sat silently for a long moment, watching the prospective jurors, watching as his instructions sank in, then he asked some questions to the panel to determine whether any member was clearly disqualified from sitting because of health, knowledge of the facts, familiarity with the parties, or the like.

Angela had told Johnny that trials were long-winded, even boring. Johnny hadn't believed it could be so; he was on trial for a crime that could send him to the electric chair or to life in prison, but too soon he found she was right and his mind wandered. Tom explained how the process of jury selection would proceed, and Johnny now watched it unfold, slowly, carefully. Each counsel made preliminary statements, talking about themselves, affiliated counsel, names of prospective witnesses, facts considered relevant. Then Tom and George Carelli began the *voir dire*, examining each juror out of the presence of the others, looking for reasons to challenge a juror for cause, and divining the temper and attitudes of each individual to determine whether the prospective member should be struck peremptorily—without stating specific cause. Tom spent much of his time on explicating the principals of reasonable doubt and the presumption of innocence. He was stern but at the same time folksy and amiable. Tom had told Johnny that gaining a rapport with the jury during *voir dire* and selecting a jury favorable to the defense was often the most important aspect of a trial.

Nonetheless, Johnny couldn't concentrate. Prospective jurors who would condemn him or set him free came in waves of bland faces, men, women, well-dressed or in work clothes, all colors, young, old, happy faces and pissed-off faces. Tom and the State's Attorney weeded and pruned, using their peremptory challenges, fifteen each, and fewer challenges for cause. By four in the afternoon, after a lunch recess and several conferences at the bench, a jury of twelve and four alternates was chosen and sworn in. Johnny looked at them without interest as they took their oath, sixteen ordinary citizens who looked at him or did not, citizens representative of Bridgeport's mosaic of the mostly poor and working-class. Five blacks, five whites, two Hispanics. Seven women and five men. The alternates, seated in the back row, were a white man and three black women.

Judge Kerry adjourned the trail until ten the following morning. Then the State would begin its case in chief, its best effort to put Johnny away for the rest of his life. Or put him to death.

40

GEORGE CARELLI APPROACHED the jury box, smiling gratefully. He wore a new blue suit, pale blue shirt (white tended to reflect the glare of TV lights into the face and make the wearer look pale and haggard, and Carelli expected to face cameras every time he left the court), and red tie with a small figure. He wore a VFW pin in his lapel; the message was that he was a thorough professional advocate of the people, the equal of any sharp defense lawyer, but also a regular guy.

Carelli greeted the jury and immediately thanked them for coming forward to do their duty as citizens, then began his opening argument, pacing back and forth in front of the jury, emphasizing his points with chopping motions of his right hand. "On the eighteenth of October, in the middle of a dark, cold night, the defendant entered the dwelling at Eleven Prescott Street, in the Black Rock section of this city. He entered by stealth, by quietly breaking a window. He entered masked, and gloved, and armed. He entered with intent to shoot and to kill, and he did shoot, and kill, three young men, all probably sound asleep, two actually in their beds."

Carelli paused and stopped pacing. Johnny wondered how he was going to deal with the girl, then Carelli started walking again, and resumed in the same measured, assured voice. "The only survivor, the only witness to the shooting, was a young girl, Sally Collins, a friend of the three murdered boys, who will testify before you. The defendant spared her life, but tied and blindfolded her and dragged her away from the scene of carnage. She will testify to the facts of this terrifying slaughter in spite of the fact that she has been under the care of physicians and psychiatrists ever since seeing her friends shot to pieces.

"Sally's father, whose attempt to borrow money from the defendant for ransom in a kidnapping that turned out to be a prank, will testify that he may have inadvertently set this man off on his vicious attack." Carelli turned quickly and pointed at Johnny, and he had to grip his chair to prevent himself from starting. "Edward Collins will testify that this man insisted he would rescue Sally himself.

"Now, that sounds like something a good man might do, ladies and gentlemen, but this is not the Wild West or a war zone, it is Bridgeport, the city where you live. If crimes are suspected and hostage rescues needed, we have a fine police force to call on." Johnny saw a few jurors smile crookedly and wondered if the SA might have made a mistake. Who knew what these citizens might think of Bridgeport's much-maligned police force? "And the police force of this city has available, if it needs it, assistance from the FBI and its hostage-rescue teams in the event of kidnappings, real or imagined. The police and the FBI have the proper training and equipment to resolve situations of that kind usually without violence, especially in an incident such as this where none of the boys participating in a stupid prank had any weapon of any kind." Another pause. Johnny looked at the jury; Carelli had them back with him. "No *private citizen*"—again Carelli turned and pointed to Johnny—"has any cause or right to crawl in a window of *your* house with a gun in the middle of the night, even if he believes *you* may be holding someone in your house. You have the right, we all have the right, to privacy and safety in our own homes."

Johnny's spirits began to sink. Carelli was making the rescue an assault on the persons and homes of the jurors, and he saw several nodding, and some appeared angry when they looked at him.

"The defense is going to say we don't have a lot of evidence of this crime," George boomed, "beyond the shattered bodies of three innocent victims. We admit the defendant, a former combat marine who conducted night infiltrations of buildings in Vietnam, did a skillful job of this bloody business, and left few traces of himself at the scene of the murders. But the State will prove to you, the jury, beyond *any reasonable doubt,* that the defendant had a motive to commit this crime, opportunity and the ability to acquire the means. In a sense, the most important element of the means to commit this crime was the defendant's Marine Corps training and experience. You will decide, and I'm confident you will decide fairly." He approached the box and leaned on the railing, looking at each juror in turn. Johnny couldn't see the State's Attorney's expression, but he guessed it would be friendly and sad at the same time.

Carelli nodded twice to the jury, then walked slowly back to his seat at the prosecution's table. The courtroom was silent, pensive.

The worst of it, Johnny thought, is that it is so nearly all true.

Tom Jackson approached the jury. He was wearing a favorite suit, a silky gray with a fine red stripe. It was so well tailored it seemed never to move on his body, a second skin. Tom looked at each juror in turn, his expression friendly, open. He wanted the working-class jurors to see him as kindly, authoritative. He knew they wouldn't see him as one of them, and he wouldn't patronize them by pretending. He saw a certain amount of suspicion, even hostility. Carelli has succeeded in frightening them, in making the crime seem personal. They all could be predicted to worry about crime, the safety of their children, their property, themselves. Carelli describing Johnny creeping through a window in the dead of night with a gun and intent to kill is a nightmare all too real in Bridgeport, a sharp knife turning in the guts. Tom had to get them to look at Johnny as one of them, not an enemy but a victim. "Ladies and gentlemen, the State has described a crime that was committed in this city, a triple homicide. The State has told you of this crime, of blood and brutality and intent to hurt, even to kill. What the State hasn't told you is that while a crime has been committed, the State has no witness, no weapon, no fingerprints, no physical evidence of any kind that ties my client to this crime in any way.

"Judge Kerry, in his preliminary instructions to you, told you that the defendant must be presumed innocent as we begin, and you must continue to presume him innocent until the prosecution proves not just that a terrible crime occurred, but that the defendant committed it. This the State will not be able to do.

"Judge Kerry also told you in his instructions that the defendant does not have to prove his innocence. The State bears the entire burden of proof. Judge Kerry told you that the defendant may testify in his own behalf, or he may not, and if he does not you may infer nothing from his silence. Johnny Dietrich does not have to say he didn't commit these murders, or prove it. The State must prove he did, and the State will not be able to do that.

"There is another question that the State must answer. Why accuse this man? Johnny is a quiet man, a resident in the community for more than ten years. The State mentions almost in passing that Johnny served in the Marine Corps, and the State would have you believe that service created in him means to commit a terrible crime. But Johnny hasn't committed any crimes in this community, nor in any other. He did not merely serve in the Marine Corps, he was a combat marine with a distinguished record of bravery and compassion for others. He was a noncommissioned officer. He was wounded three times. He was awarded two of the nation's highest medals for bravery, the Silver and Bronze Stars. He saved lives by risking his, saved not only the lives of his men but of civilians in the terrible house-to-house fighting during and after the Tet Offensive in Vietnam in 1968."

Tom granted himself a long pause, his expression that of a man himself wrongly accused. He looked at the faces of the jurors, one by one. He could see no more hostility; one of the black women had tears in her eyes and Tom remembered that Sara, who had done the background checks on the jury pool, had discovered that woman had a son in the army.

Tom had worked to get a jury of Johnny's age or older, people who would remember Vietnam and perhaps had been there. Carelli had gotten rid of the only veterans of any war with his peremptory challenges, but Sara had dug deeper into the potential jurors' background than had the State. In addition to the mother of the soldier, the jury contained a man whose brother had been to Vietnam, and a women whose son had served in the Persian Gulf. "Why does the State bring this decorated veteran, a man hurt in body and soul by violence and war, to you as a criminal? He has no criminal record. Why does the state want you to believe this quiet man should suddenly become a professional killer, able to enter a house at night, shoot three people, kidnap a girl and disappear without trace? *Any* trace?" Tom let that one sink in; it was his alternate theory, the paid killer Edward Collins had hired and was afraid to expose. A few jurors nodded, and for the first time since Carelli finished, looked toward Johnny with sympathy. "The State has a crime to dispose of, and no witnesses, no evidence, nothing. The State should dismiss, or look further, but it does not. It attaches its case to a man the State cannot connect to this tragic affair, other than to counsel the distraught father and mother of a kidnap victim. Having arrested this good man, this man who has suffered and bled for his country, the State has confined him for more than two months in a tiny cell, indicted him and brought him here before you, for a trial in which the State must prove to you, beyond any reasonable doubt." Another pause. *"Beyond any reasonable doubt."* Tom did not raise his voice, but there was an edge on it, an insistence born of his anger at the false accusations. "That this suffering man committed any crime, *this* crime. And *that* the State will not be able to do."

He looked at each juror in turn, and they looked back frankly, saying with their eyes they knew what the State had told them and the State better damn well prove it.

Tom was finished. He took his seat. Judge Kerry called a recess for lunch.

41

JAMAL SAT IN his car, a 1979 Mercedes 380 SE in lustrous silver, perfectly maintained. He was back in the Black Rock neighborhood where the crime had been committed. He had been here in the same spot, across the street from the murder house, from two to five in the morning, to see the crime scene as the perpetrators must have seen it. During the whole time he had sat in the dark, drinking coffee from a thermos to fight off sleep and the sharp cold of mid-December, he had seen nothing and no one, and no one had approached him. There had been very few cars on the adjacent street, Ellsworth, but none had turned into Prescott. Jamal had not seen a single patrol car, although patrol records he had looked at weeks before said the area was regularly watched at night. Jamal figured the uniforms would prefer to protect and serve the white residents of Black Rock; he knew they rarely entered the inner-city projects, where mostly black and Hispanic people lived. Maybe the citizen complaints were true; maybe the patrol cars never left the parking lots of their favorite all-night diners. Anyway, he had seen no police, and as near as he could tell, no one had stirred in any of the houses; no one had turned on a light to get a drink of water or go to the bathroom.

It was now just after noon and Jamal was back with a sandwich and a fresh thermos of coffee. The last thing he had done before he and Mike had carried boxes of his personal stuff out to his car was to get the kid with the Identikit to come up to see him. Working with the artist and his overlays of head shape, hairline, eyes, nose, mouth, ears, chin line and other characteristics of the human face, he had come up with a composite of Staff Sergeant Tolliver, the man he was sure had helped Johnny in the commission of the crime, the man who had humiliated him in front of the ex-marines and the New York cops. He had the Identikit sketch, smoothed and toned and colored dark to reflect Tolliver's dark skin, in a folder beside him on the seat along with copies of Johnny's booking photographs.

Why can't I leave this alone? he wondered for the hundredth time. He was suspended, he had no right to continue this or any other investigation, he didn't have an ID or a shield or a gun. But he could still see the shocked and terrified expressions in the dead eyes of the victims above the bloody holes that had been the rest of their faces. He could still see his brothers, Chris and Raquib.

Jamal got out of the car, carrying the folder. He wanted to reinterview one feisty old lady he had spoken to twice before, the one who seemed to be the neighborhood busybody, the only one who had seen the three young men going in and out and had identified the boy whose family lived there. No one else had seen anything at all they would share with a cop.

JOHNNY WAS ALLOWED to stay in the interview room with his attorneys during the lunch recess, and Angela went to the deli for sandwiches that were a vast improvement over the food in the jail cafeteria. Tom had gone out to call his office. "What did you think of the opening arguments?" Angela asked him, spreading out ham, cheese and turkey sandwiches on paper towels. Johnny opened and poured their soft drinks into plastic cups.

Johnny shrugged. He didn't fully know what to think. "Carelli made it seem impossible that I didn't do it. The jury looked convinced."

"The jury always looks convinced by the State's opening for the same reason the grand jury always indicts. So far, the State's frame of the case is all they've heard."

"Tom seemed to bring them back a bit," he said. "Like maybe they'd have to see the State's case before they made up their minds."

"The State's case will be as Tom suggested; full of supposition and suggestion but with nothing to tie you to the crime. Tom will remind the jury of that with each cross-examination."

"What will you do during the trial?"

"Run down any surprises the State brings out. Do research on points of law should any arise. Tom does the arguing."

Johnny nodded slowly. "I believe you two are doing the right thing by me; you've convinced me I had reason and belief on my side. Somehow I wish I could just tell the people on that jury what happened and let them think about it, then decide."

Angela patted his hand. "We can't do it that way. The law doesn't see what we see."

"I know."

"Johnny, those men you shot did a great wrong, and had they not died, they'd be answering for it in this court."

"I know."

Angela watched Johnny slump, recede into his sadness. She gripped his hand, and at last he responded, squeezing back and raising his brimming eyes. Then he smiled. "I know."

J AMAL KNOCKED ON the screen door of the neat frame house at 14 Prescott Street. The same tired-looking woman answered the door as on his earlier visits with Mike. Jamal already knew she was a widow with two grown sons who had moved away, one to Texas and one to California. She was courteous and alert, and she invited Jamal into her parlor with an elaborate kindness he had come to expect from white people unused to dealing with blacks, especially official blacks.

He wouldn't be telling her he was no longer official. "Hello, again, Mrs. Perrone," he said.

"Detective?"

"Jones, ma'am."

"Of course. How forgetful I've become. Please come in and sit down, Detective Jones." She looked behind him toward the street. "Where's your partner?"

"Detective Kolslovsky is running down other leads," Jamal said evenly. His first open lie; he had no idea what Mike might be doing.

Mrs. Perrone sat in a high-backed armchair covered in yellow chintz. Jamal took the couch opposite and leaned forward to place his face at the same level as the much smaller woman's. "Well, Detective," she said with a little smile. "I wish I had more to tell you about those poor boys and all, but I don't."

Her words said go away, but Jamal suspected the woman was lonely and welcomed any visitor. "We have new evidence, Mrs. Perrone. Evidence of another man involved."

"But you caught the man. He's already on trial."

"Another man, Mrs. Perrone."

"I told you, I never saw anyone except the boys—the victims—near that house."

Jamal withdrew the composite picture of Tolliver from the file he'd brought from his car and held it before Mrs. Perrone. She put on her glasses and looked at it without making any attempt to take it from his hands. "A black fellow?" she asked. "Well, you know—"

"Yes, ma'am, a black man like me."

She reached for the copy reluctantly, and he handed it to her. She shook her head. "My."

"Have you ever seen a man that looked like that?"

"I—don't know. I don't see many black fellows. I mean, I hardly go out, and I do all my shopping in Fairfield." Jamal waited in silence. Mrs. Perrone looked at the composite again. "Is this a big man?"

Jamal gently took the copy from her fingers and turned it over. The description he had given the Identikit man was typed on the back. "Male, black, height six feet to six feet two, weight two hundred fifty, only obvious scars or marks scar on right eyelid, whitish, old. Eyes dark brown, hair none, shaved face and scalp."

She read the description, her lips moving slowly, then turned the composite back toward her face. "I don't know, but there was a black fellow here the day before the boys were killed. A nice man, very polite, but he was from the gas company."

Jamal didn't move, but withdrew a notebook from his pocket. "The gas company?"

"Yes. He had a uniform, you know, a coverall with Southern Connecticut Gas Company on the breast, and one of those little blue flames. He was an inspector looking for a leak. I let him right in, of course; I've always been a little afraid of the gas."

"Did he show you an ID? With a picture?"

"Oh, yes. I wouldn't let anyone come in without an ID. You remember I made you and the other detective show me yours."

Jamal smiled. "Yes, you did. Did you get a real good look at the ID and the photo?"

"Yes. The photo looked like the man."

Like a black fellow, Jamal thought. "What did the man do?"

"He looked around the stove. I seem to remember he had some sort of instrument, like a tank with a horn on the end, kind of like a fire extinguisher. Then he went down into the cellar and looked at the furnace."

"Did he find anything?"

"No, thank God. He thanked me and left."

Jamal knew gas inspectors were supposed to leave a written notice of their inspection, with their findings checked off, and their initials. "Did he leave you a report?"

She frowned. "I don't believe he did. I would have saved it; I save everything. Should he have?"

"Perhaps he forgot. Did you notice where he went when he left?"

"Across the street. He knocked on Mrs. Leary's door, but she works, same's her husband. He walked around the house, then he came back to the sidewalk."

Jamal had a tingle, a cop's nose twitch. "Where did he go next?"

"Why, right into the house over there, number eleven, where the killings happened."

Jamal breathed slowly. "Did you notice his car, or truck?"

She shook her head and looked sad that she couldn't help a little more. Poor, lonely woman, Jamal thought. "No."

"Mrs. Perrone," he said gently. "Take another good look at the picture."

42

THE TRIAL BEGAN with testimony about the crime scene. The first witness for the State was Mike Kolslovsky. Angela knew the prosecutors would rather have Jamal, but he doubted they'd risk bringing him before Judge Kerry.

Mike described the crime scene, economically and unemotionally. There were photographs of the three dead men, to which Tom objected but the court allowed, although in a sidebar conference the judge excluded the closeups of the men's wounds as unnecessary and inflammatory. Carelli lead Mike through the investigation, the taped calls traced back to Sally Collins, and his interview with the Collins family and the subsequent arrest of the defendant. "Are you going to ask him where Jamal is?" Angela wrote on her pad. Tom shook his head.

"Your witness," George Carelli said as he passed the defense table.

Tom stood. "Detective Kolslovsky, you're an experienced investigator?"

"Detective ten years. Me and my partner have the highest rate of closure on the force."

"What most struck you about the crime scene in question?"

"The lack of evidence of the intruder. Other than that a window had been cut out, fourteen untraceable shell casings and the fact of three dead bodies, it was hard to say anyone had been there at all."

"But you looked for evidence."

"Yes, sir. We went over the scene several times. We had the evidence technicians out there three separate times."

"You looked for fingerprints?"

"Fingerprints, footprints inside and outside the house, hair, fiber.

We found nothing that didn't belong to the three victims or the girl except a few threads we determined were consistent with battle dress utilities worn by all the U.S. Armed Forces."

Tom looked up at the jury. They weren't getting it; there was a crime here, their eyes said. Wasn't there? "Detective Kolslovsky, did you search the defendant's residence?"

"Yes, with the same team of evidence technicians."

"His car?"

"His car, his boat. A mini-storage vault he keeps in Fairfield."

"What did you find?"

"Nothing that tied him to the scene."

"No weapon? No military uniform? No mask?"

"Nothing. One weapon, but it didn't match the slugs recovered from the scene and the bodies. An old set of utilities he probably wore in 'Nam, of a completely different fabric."

"The weapon you found; was it a properly registered weapon?"

"Yes."

"Detective Kolslovsky, as an experienced investigator, what did you conclude about this scene? About the perpetrator?"

"Must have been a pro. Hell, even the pros leave some trace of themselves."

"Did you gather any evidence that my client was ever a professional assassin?"

"No."

Tom moved close and smiled at the big policeman. "Detective, did you serve in the armed forces?"

"Yes, sir. Marines."

"As did my client?"

"Yes. We looked at his jacket."

"Did the marines—to your knowledge, Detective—train men to do this kind of traceless killing?"

"I don't know, but from his record, Johnny was a grunt, an infantry corporal. Nothing in the jacket to indicate special training."

Carelli, on redirect, had Kolslovsky read from Jamal's notes of the interview of the Collinses. "They were sure in their statements about the defendant's claim he would rescue the girl, Detective?"

"They sure seemed sure."

"And you were sure enough of their veracity to make an immediate arrest."

"At the time," Mike said acidly.

THE REST OF the afternoon and the following morning was given over to the evidence technicians. Carelli had nothing, but he didn't want the defense to say he had presented no case, or hidden facts favorable to the defense—such as the lack of physical evidence—from the jury. It was boring stuff and Carelli hoped the jury would forget it when the girl took the stand.

I hope she doesn't overact, George thought, as the technical evidence droned up to the lunch recess.

JUDGE KERRY TOOK his seat behind the bench at exactly two-thirty and instructed the State's Attorney to call his next witness. "The State calls Sally Collins, Your Honor."

Johnny looked at Sally. He hadn't seen her since the night of the rescue, and only infrequently in the year before. She looked pretty and composed, perhaps too composed; her eyes were dull and her expression lifeless.

Medicated, Johnny surmised. Angela told him that witnesses, especially emotional ones, were often tranquilized to ensure their behavior in court.

As were defendants, she had also told him, but Johnny continued to refuse her offer of Valium.

Sally was dressed in a blue wool dress with a white linen collar, and her long dark brown hair hung loose to the center of her back.

The effect was to make her look very young and vulnerable. Tom had said during the recess that Sally was a potential minefield for the defense because the State would try to draw the jury into her pain, her terror at being confronted by a man shooting her friends, killing one before her eyes, her boyfriend. Whatever Carelli did, Tom would have to try and counter, but he couldn't risk an attack on the girl.

Johnny asked why Carelli would call Sally before her father and mother, since they had been the only ones to see and speak with him, to hear him say that he would get Sally back from her kidnappers. He should, in logic, Tom said, but Carelli could expect the girl to embroider because she had to lie about parts of her testimony; indeed, had already lied to the police. Carelli would have to have the parents later to smooth over any inconsistencies in Sally's testimony, and that might provide the defense with ways to impeach the girl's testimony without attacking her in open court.

Sally stood in the witness box and was sworn by the Clerk of the Court, then was invited by the judge to be seated. She seemed a little uncertain, but Tom felt sure she had been thoroughly prepared. Carelli stepped forward, an avuncular grin on his face. "Hello, Sally," he said.

"Hello, Mr. Carelli," she replied, her voice tiny.

"Sally, Evelyn—Ms. Pulaski—and I have explained to you the purpose of these proceedings. What I want you to do is explain to the Court"—he inclined his head toward the judge—"and the jury." He turned toward the jury and Sally turned her body to face them.

Well practiced, Tom thought sourly.

"What happened in the early hours of October eighteenth, to you and your friends?"

He's starting with the dramatic stuff, Tom thought, leaving the evasions about whether the kidnapping was real until later. I'd do the same.

Sally immediately began to cry. Tom sneaked a look at the jury, they were hanging on Sally's first words before she even spoke them. "We were all asleep. It was really late, or early morning, I guess. I heard noises from the living room where Gil was sleeping on the couch, a sound like coughing and a thump like someone falling. Then I heard Tom cry out, 'Jeff, Jeff!' and there was another crash. I turned on the light next to my bed and shook Jeff. Then the door burst open—not open, but right off the hinges—and this man"—she paused and looked blackly at Johnny—"masked and dressed in black, rushed in, stomping over the door. Jeff tried to shield me and put up his hands, but the man shot him in the face. His gun made almost no noise, and I thought it might be one of the other boys making a joke, but I felt the heat of the gunfire and then I felt sprayed with Jeff's blood and—and—oh, God." Sally covered her face with her hands, leaned on the rail of the witness box and sobbed.

Carelli placed a hand gently on her head and stroked her hair. "Sally," he said softly, but loud enough for the jury to hear, "do you want to stop for a while?" He looked imploringly at the judge, then at the jury.

The judge cleared his throat. "Certainly, Mr. Carelli, if the State were to request a recess—"

Sally looked up, wiped her eyes and swallowed. "I'd like to finish, Mr. Carelli."

The judge nodded and Carelli took a step back. "Go ahead, then."

Sally sat back, and rubbed her red face with the palms of her hands. "I was covered with Jeff's blood, and, I think, brains. I felt sharp pieces like broken glass on my skin that must have been bone. I pulled my boyfriend to me, held him, tried to make him sit up. Then I saw his face was completely smashed, gone." Again the girl slumped and sobbed.

Angela leaned across Johnny to address Tom. "This is inflammatory," she whispered. "Won't you object?"

"No. If I do, it will merely emphasize the horror."

George Carelli looked away from the girl, and at the jury. By the distraught look on their faces he thought they had had enough. He took a step to the witness box and placed a comforting hand over Sally's, which were now clasped in front of her on the railing, wringing a wet handkerchief. It was a previously agreed signal, and Sally responded by looking up. "I'm sorry." She choked. "It was so horrible."

"I know," Carelli said, looking at the jury. "But tell us what happened next."

"The man—the *murderer*—told me to get dressed. He threw my clothes at me. Then he tore up a pillow case and tied my arms and blindfolded me. He rushed me out of the house and into a truck—"

"A truck?" Carelli interrupted. "Not a car?"

"It was higher than a car. He had to lift me."

"Go on."

"The man was in back, with me. Another man drove. The next thing I knew, I was lifted out of the truck and forced to sit on wet grass. It was cold."

"Then what happened?"

"My daddy came and took me inside. I'd been left on the edge of our driveway."

"How did you feel? Relieved to be home?"

"Relieved? Relieved?" Sally shouted as she leaned forward and her pretty face twisted into an ugly snarl. "My boyfriend and two other friends were *dead!* I was furious and in shock." Her voice became tiny again. "I was afraid."

"Of course," Carelli said. "Of course. You did not, then, feel relieved to be freed from your kidnappers?"

"They weren't kidnappers. That was just a prank the boys thought up so I could stay with them for a couple of days. My parents put me in that awful private school just to keep me from seeing my friends."

"So you never felt in the least danger, while you were with your friends in the house in Black Rock?"

"No, of course not."

"The next day you telephoned the Bridgeport police, is that right?"

"Yes."

"The police came to your house," Carelli said.

"Yes. I guess they traced my call."

"What did you tell the police?"

"What I just said here, I think."

"Did you tell them who you thought had come into the house in Black Rock with a silenced automatic weapon, killed your friends and dragged you into the night, bound and blindfolded?"

Angela leaned over Johnny and whispered urgently. "Jesus, Tom, Carelli is fucking testifying!"

Tom shook his head. The judge was looking at him with raised eyebrows. Tom shook his head again.

"Sally?" Carelli said, with a slight grin at Tom the jury couldn't see.

Sally's face went from sad to hateful in a heartbeat, then she composed herself like an actress. "I told them the only person Daddy knew who could do such a thing was the one they all call Crazy Johnny." Her hand shot out and she pointed right at Johnny at the defense table.

At last Tom Jackson was on his feet. "Objection, Your Honor," he said softly, looking at the girl. "Prosecution has not asked its witness to identify her rescuer, nor, by her testimony that he was masked and clad in black, could she."

"Sustained," Judge Kerry said. "Jury will disregard the witness's gesture toward the defendant."

The damage is done, Tom thought as he looked at Angela, her face mottled with rage. But blunted; the jury has been reminded that the girl could not identify her attacker.

Rescuer, Tom reminded himself as he sat down.

George Carelli turned toward the defense table. "Your witness," he said grimly as he moved toward his own table, sweeping his eyes over the jury as he went as if to tell them the defense was damaged beyond repair.

Tom turned toward the bench and was about to speak when Sally addressed the judge. "Your Honor," she whispered. "Could I have a few minutes? I want to talk to my mother for a little while."

The judge looked at Tom for an objection; there was nearly an hour left before the court's normal recess at 4:00, and the defense wouldn't want the jury to retire with the girl's tale of horror unanswered to ponder it overnight.

Tom felt torn. He knew he should press on, get at the lies while they were fresh in the girl's mind and the jury's, but he couldn't be seen to attack the poor vulnerable child who had shown herself such an accomplished actress. Let her stew overnight, let the jury wonder if maybe it wasn't all too pat. Besides, Tom had an idea that would take time to develop. "The defense has no objection to a recess, Your Honor."

Judge Kerry sighed. He'd seen the State's Attorney's stagecraft before and he neither liked nor approved of it.

"Very well. Given the lateness of the hour, this court stands adjourned until ten o'clock tomorrow morning."

43

JAMAL MET MIKE Kolslovsky in a bar on Fairfield Avenue in Black Rock. It wasn't a usual place for them but Jamal didn't want to go to one of the cop bars near Lyon Terrace, didn't want to talk about his suspension and the Internal Affairs investigation that was just beginning. Jamal related his interview with Mrs. Perrone, consulting his notes.

"That's it, Mike. Tolliver is tied to Johnny and Tolliver is tied to the scene."

Mike chewed ice cubes. "Come on, partner; you got nothing but supposition built on a foundation of slippery shit."

"I went over to the gas company. They had crews all over the area that day replacing old mains."

"So maybe one of the crews sent a black guy around to check for leaks."

"No one in the gas company reported any leaks."

"Maybe they don't report absolutely everything they do, Jamal. We don't."

"We report major events, Mike. In the gas company, a leak is a major event."

"Okay, Okay. Maybe it went down like you say. It could be checked with other neighbors, but your informant says this guy hit her house, couldn't get in the neighbors', then went to the murder scene. But suppose we find someone else who saw this inspector, what are we going to do? We have nothing to say it's this guy Tolliver except your Identikit. We'll never get the State's Attorney to move with that, much less New York, especially since you already rousted the guy and got your dumb ass suspended."

"You're saying we should let this go, let this guy Johnny walk just because it's difficult and I fucked up."

"Come *on*, Jamal. If fucking Tolliver lived in the projects right here in the city, we'd go drag him out of his crib and help him remember, but he's in *New York*, another fucking state, and there's no way he's going to cooperate after what you done. Then there's the small matter of the trial already going on; while you were out looking for ghosts, the State's Attorney is trying his case."

"There's something else on your mind."

"Yeah, there is. Since the day we arrested this guy I been thinking maybe we shouldn't have. All we have is the say-so of that slick bastard from Westport, and the girl who lied to us and lied even more elaborately today in court."

"You remember how those three dead boys looked, Mike?"

"Yeah. Like dead boys. I seen a lot of dead boys in 'Nam, Jamal, Johnny did, too. I seen dead boys I cared about a lot more than I gotta care about three punks from so-called good families who kidnapped a girl for money and told her parents they were gonna kill her. Let the State's Attorney try his case, Jamal, while you and I try to figure out how to get you back on the job."

Jamal ordered another round. "Maybe you're right," he said sadly. "Why can't I let this thing go?"

"Beat's the shit outta me," Mike said, slugging back his 7 and 7 in one gulp. "I gotta get. The wife."

"Call me tomorrow after court."

"Sure."

JOHNNY AND TOM went directly to the interview room after court adjourned. Angela had to go to the clerk's office to pick up some papers on another matter, and would join them. Johnny sat at the table while Tom paced like a caged cat. "I saw you taking notes," Tom said. "What did you hear that perhaps I did not?"

"I just wrote down the lies."

"Tell me." He continued to pace.

"When I entered her bedroom, the man made no effort to shield her. He reached away from her, toward the floor, I assumed for a weapon—"

"Don't think like that, damn it! You can't know that because you were never in that room."

"You're really pissed off, aren't you, Tom? What did she say that you didn't expect?"

"Not much, but she said it beautifully. The jury will have to have vengeance for the terrible wrong done to that girl, and the way the State's Attorney got her to point you out without asking a question he knew would be struck was devastating."

"The judge told the jury to disregard that, when you pointed out she couldn't identify"—he was about to say *"me,"* but said instead, "her rescuer."

"Judges tell juries to disregard things, but strong visual things like that pointing finger stick in their mind. Fucking Carelli!"

Johnny looked at his notes. "You aren't interested in other lies she told about what happened inside the house?"

Tom threw up his hands and sat down heavily. "I'm sorry, Johnny. None of this is your fault. I'm interested in any inconsistencies; they might give me a way to shake her on cross examination."

"Okay. The dramatic speech about her being showered with blood and brains. Not so; his blood and brains ended up on the wall behind him, the only place they could have gone since I fired from in front of him. The crime-scene report should bear that out. She had little or no blood on her."

"Jesus, good point. A lie is a lie."

Angela came in and dropped her heavy briefcase on the floor. "I just saw something curious."

"Any straw," Tom said.

"Remember how Sally ran to her mother when she left the court? The tearful, loving embrace? I stopped in the ladies' room on the way up from the clerk's, and there they were. The mother was crying but the daughter was cold as ice, her face white with fury. Just as I entered Sally struck her mother on the face with her fist and called her a fucking bitch."

"What did you do?" Tom asked.

"Went to the toilet, washed my hands, smiled sweetly and left. Neither of them had moved."

Tom smiled, and pointed at his senior associate. "You, my dear

Angela, are seeing the testimony of that fine young actress far more clearly than I am."

"I'm a woman. That makes a difference."

"So it does, and for that reason you would handle this witness better than I would, don't you agree?"

"You're the best there is, Tom," Angela said sincerely.

Tom shook his head. He was still smiling. "Most days, I believe I am. But you have work to do and Johnny and I are going to help you get ready to do it."

"Tom?"

"I have decided to ask you to do the cross."

VII

TESTIMONY

44

ANGELA APPROACHED THE witness box. Sally sat composed in another new dress, gray silk this time. The jury was attentive, the members' expressions severe. Angela felt they were anxious to see what evil the lawyers defending the savage beast would do to this innocent, traumatized girl. Angela could feel the pressure of their distrust of the defense and their desire to protect the innocent like a heat lamp on the back of her neck. The courtroom, once gaveled to order, was very still.

Angela had tried a number cases by herself during her association with Tom Jackson, but never argued a capital case, or shared argument with Tom. She was delighted that he trusted her to step in and talk to Sally, and she liked the fact that Tom at last appreciated that in this and perhaps other cases they might try together, a woman had certain advantages. Having said all that to herself in the morning as she dressed carefully in a severe black silk suit and dark blue silk blouse, she still felt butterflies. The defense had much ground to make up with the jury, more in their hearts than in their minds. She knew the defense had an advantage because it got to hear the prosecution's case first and then have the jury to itself in the latter part of the trial, but in a case like this it was painful to have her client bombarded by the State while the defense was not yet allowed up to bat.

The case wouldn't be won by her cross of Sally, but it might be lost. "Good morning, Sally."

"Good morning, Ms. Hughes," the girl said, her voice firm, even defiant.

Angela though of the spitting girl in the ladies room yesterday afternoon, striking her mother and calling her a bitch. What manner of person is she? "Sally, you testified yesterday that you never felt the kidnapping was real. Did you know the kidnappers called your parents? Threatened to kill you?"

"It was a joke." Sullen, defensive.

"Did your parents think it was a joke?"

"Objection," Carelli said without rising. "Calls for a conclusion."

"Sustained," Judge Kerry said.

Fine, Angela thought. I'll get that out of the parents anyway. "Sally, how do you get along with your parents?"

"Fine. Well, we have disagreements, but fine."

"What sort of disagreements?"

"Objection," Carelli said. "Relevance?"

The judge looked down at Angela. "Where are you going with this, Counsel?"

"The witness—and the State—insist on portraying this kidnapping as a prank. We are entitled to ask why anyone would frame such a cruel prank, or participate in it, because of the State's argument that my client counseled the parents to rescue the girl rather than pay."

"All right, but let's try to move on."

Angela smiled at the judge and the jury. "Sally, why did you participate in your own kidnapping? You must have known your parents would be terrified."

"I—it was the boys' idea." Sally looked over to Carelli for help. This was going beyond the rehearsed material.

"You went along. You could have asked them to take you home."

"Well, I never thought anyone would get hurt."

"Even though you knew the boys were telling your parents to pay up or collect your body?"

"Objection!" Carelli was on his feet. "Witness has not testified she overheard such threats."

"The telephone conversation was taped, and the witness's voice has been identified," Angela said quickly, knowing she was going to lose this one. "The tape has been made available to the State and the Court."

"Sustained, Ms. Hughes. Move on."

Angela took a step back and looked at the jury. They still focused on Sally, and their urge to protect her seemed intact.

Now for some serious shit, she thought. "Sally, yesterday you told us that you thought my client was the man in black. Would you tell us why you thought so?"

Sally sat back, suddenly relaxed. She was back on script now, and dangerous. "He's a friend of Daddy. He killed people in Vietnam."

"Marines kill people in wartime, Sally. Very few ever hurt anyone outside of war."

"Everybody calls him Crazy Johnny."

"Do they? Does everybody say he kills people?"

"Objection. Argumentative."

"Sustained."

Angela turned to the jury and dismissed the prosecution with a wave of her hand. She turned back to the witness. "Sally, my point is, you have no direct evidence that Johnny was the man in black, do you?"

"No." Calm, well-coached not to go too far.

"Couldn't recognize him?"

"No. He wore a mask."

"What else was he wearing?"

"A military uniform, one of those camouflaged ones."

"Tight-fitting?"

"No, loose."

Angela nodded and walked back to the defense table and pretended to consult a note. Tom gave her the tiniest of winks. "Loose-fitting clothing," Angela said, returning to the witness. "Sally, can you be sure the person in black was even a man?"

Sally looked over at Carelli. Angela stepped into her line of vision. "I don't know," Sally said carefully. "Awful big for a woman."

"How big?"

"What? I don't understand."

"How tall was the person in black?"

"I'm not sure. It all happened very fast."

"Could you see the person's eyes, or his hands?"

"No. I told the police all this. He wore gloves and his eyes were odd, kind of yellow."

"Couldn't see skin around the eyes?"

"Not much. Ah, don't remember."

Angela smiled at Sally, standing at an angle so the jury could see. "Sally, you have no idea who this person was, do you? Male, female, white, black or purple."

"I only said that Crazy Johnny was the only killer my father knew—"

"Do you know everyone your father knows?"

Carelli back on his feet. "Objection. The witness has answered."

Angela looked up at the bench and for the first time showed a flash of anger. "Your Honor, the witness has *not* answered. Yesterday the witness pointed out my client in open court, accusing him, and even though the court instructed the jury to disregard that improper identification, it was a strong signal. I have asked the witness whether or not she could identify the person in black and she has *not* answered."

"Rephrase it," Judge Kerry said wearily. "Ask the question directly, then let's move on."

"Sally, you saw the person in black for several minutes between the time he entered the bedroom and the time he blindfolded you. Can you say with any certainty whether this person was male or female, white or black? Can you *identify* this person?"

Sally hunched down. "No," she said. "But—"

"No." Angela looked at the jury, raised her arms by her sides and set them fall. "No."

There was a silence in the courtroom while Angela stared at Sally and Sally stared back. The judge cleared his throat. "Are we through here, Ms. Hughes?"

"Almost, Your Honor. Sally, you testified yesterday, very graphically, that when your boyfriend was shot you were covered with his blood and tissue."

Sally straightened up. It had been the heart of her performance, and she was proud of it. "Yes. It was horrible."

"Blood sprayed over you." Angela looked at the jury. Remember this detail for later, her look said.

"Yes."

"Brains. Bone."

"Yes. Why?"

"Objection!" Carelli said, but softly. He was quite happy to have the defense revisit the grisly details.

"No further questions, Your Honor," Angela said, and once again turned to the jury. They didn't look as sure of their protective instinct as before.

45

WILLY TOLLIVER WALKED into a travel agency on Broadway, a rather dingy storefront with faded pictures of Greek temples and a dusty broken model of an ocean-liner. Tolliver had never used this particular agency before and wouldn't likely again, but he wanted to make a clean break. Ever since the visit from the Bridgeport cop, Tolliver had been thinking the cop might get lucky and find something to place him at the crime scene, or maybe a witness might remember something. The cop was a bulldog; he might come back. Willy didn't want to make it easy for him, so he decided to wait out the trial in a remote location.

Willy hadn't taken a trip in years. The truth was he hated spending even one night away from the shelter. He was good with damaged marines because he was one of them, and needed their support. But he didn't want to add to Johnny's problems.

Willy bought a discounted ticket to Antigua and got a room in a restored hotel in English Harbour. He paid cash; the plane would leave in three days. He could have paid full fare and left immediately, but why spend an extra $500 he didn't have?

Besides, Willy Tolliver wasn't a man to run. What irked him the most was that he couldn't be out there in Connecticut keeping Johnny's mind right.

JANE COLLINS BEGAN her testimony immediately after Sally was excused. Angela took her seat at the defense table, feeling drained by her brief exchange with Sally, yet angry at the same time. Angela felt she had undone some of the damage of Sally pointing directly at Johnny, and she had planted the seed of Sally's lie about the blood. Angela had reviewed the crime-scene reports and photographs with Tom and consulted her own notes; the blood had definitely been behind the victim and to his left, away from Sally. She'd harvest that one later.

George Carelli walked Jane methodically through her testimony, from the snatch in front of the school through her recall under hypnosis of the license plate and the receipt by her husband of the first call from the kidnappers. Jane was sad but composed, pretty and convincing. "What did you do with the information about the license plate?" George asked.

"I did nothing. Edward and Johnny were there, along with the therapist, Abigail Grieg."

"You didn't give it to the police?"

"I didn't. I was frightened; we both were."

"But the defendant was there when you remembered the letters and numbers."

"Yes."

"Good. Then came the second phone call."

"The following day."

"Do you recall what was said in detail?"

"Not word-for-word, but the man said we had to drop off the money the next day, then we'd be told where to pick up our daughter. Edward asked for a direct exchange and the man said no, do it his way or we'd be told where to find Sally's body. Then there was a slap and a scream; I'm sure it was Sally."

Carelli looked thoughtfully at the jury. This was the hardest part, because he had to tie Johnny to the crime through the testimony of the parents, but in doing so he was giving the defense an opening; the parents had believed the kidnapping real and had been terrified, and the defense would bring that out. That might cause the jury to reexamine Johnny's motivation and his act, and to doubt the daughter's testimony. "Was the defendant with you and your husband when the call came in?"

"Yes."

"What did he do?"

"He left almost at once. He said he would rescue Sally."

"Did he say how?"

"No. Edward asked him what role he had to play, and Johnny just said 'you won't be going.' "

"Then he left."

"Yes."

"When did you next see him?"

"Not until the beginning of the trial."

Carelli nodded. "Then Sally came home."

"Yes. I was upstairs in bed and Edward came in and woke me,

then rushed outside. A few minutes later they came in together. God, I was so relieved."

"Was Sally relieved?"

"She was—very upset, very angry."

"Angry? Upon being released from her kidnappers?"

"She told us the kidnapping was staged. That her boyfriend, Jeff, had been shot. She was distraught; I didn't think she knew what she was saying and I suppose I didn't even care, I was just so glad she was home and safe."

"Did you think the defendant had effected her release?"

"I didn't think. We called our family doctor, who is a near neighbor, and he came over right away and put Sally to bed with an injection, a sedative. Edward and I were completely exhausted, but we sat up together for a while. We didn't talk; I think he may have had a drink. It was the most frightening three days of my life and suddenly it was over." She looked at Johnny, seated between his lawyers. "If Johnny did save Sally and bring her back to me, I am forever in his debt."

Shit, she had to say that, Carelli thought, but there was nothing for it. He had to get past the rescue and back to the killing fields, but now the defense would make up some of the sympathy it lost yesterday in Sally's direct. George Carelli didn't think Angela Hughes had hurt the girl on cross, but he had a glimmer of worry. Why had Angela brought up the grisly part about the victim's blood? The State's Attorney turned to the defense table. "Your witness."

Judge Kerry spoke up as Tom was getting to his feet. Tom expected this. "It's now eleven-thirty," the judge said. "Will the defense be able to complete its cross-examination before noon?"

"I should think not, Your Honor," Tom said.

"Then perhaps you'd prefer to begin after lunch, not to have an interruption." It wasn't a question. Tom knew that Kerry understood full well where the defense had to go with the parents, and Tom would be better off taking the recess.

"As it pleases the Court," Tom said, stepping back. George rose and came up beside him.

"Court is adjourned. We'll begin again at two o'clock."

J OHNNY SAT WITH Angela and Tom in the interview room. "How did the morning go?" Johnny asked. "The momentum seemed to go back and forth."

"That's the way of trials," Tom said, and bit into a ham and cheese sandwich.

"The defense theory," Angela said, "seems to be that they can wrap this thing around you based on what you told the parents. 'I'll go get her' and 'you won't be going,' even though they can't place you at the scene."

"The mother is clearly sympathetic," Tom said. "The father less so; he thinks he could be culpable for asking you to do it."

"Or asking someone else," Angela said.

"There was no one else," Johnny said simply. "We all know that."

"If what they have shown is all they have, we're in good shape," Tom said. "The cops described a gruesome crime scene, but one sterile of evidence of the intruder. There is no physical evidence to rebut, and the testimony of the girl will fray. Carelli should have kept her more under control, but she doesn't have anything anyway. Do you have any idea why she singled you out?"

He continues to ask questions as if he didn't know I did it, Johnny thought. Is that just method? "What does a Vietnam vet who lives by himself writing books of extreme violence look like to a fifteen-year-old girl? The yacht club crowd does call me Crazy Johnny; I've heard it."

"I'm confident Carelli can't get even close to a conviction with what he has," Tom said, grinning as he bit into a potato chip.

"What about that cop that found Tolliver?" Johnny asked.

"He's off the board," Tom said. "Suspended. There is no way a judge is going to subpoena Tolliver on the basis of the police tape after what Jamal Jones did."

"What if there's another way to tie him in?" Angela asked. "I'll bet Jamal is out there trying to develop a witness, suspended or not."

"Perhaps it were best if Tolliver took a vacation until the end of the trial," Tom said softly.

"I suggested that when he called yesterday. He said he might but didn't say where," Angela said.

"Or when?" Tom asked, frowning.

"I think he meant right away."

"One hopes," Tom said, but he didn't look happy.

M IKE KOLSLOVSKY ENTERED Calley's Tavern across the street from the courthouse. He found George Carelli and Evelyn Pulaski in a booth, and slid in next to Evelyn. A waitress came by and Mike ordered a beer, even though the prosecutors were drinking coffee. "So, how do you think it's going?" Mike asked after a deep pull on his Rolling Rock.

"Shitty, Mike," George said. "Just like I told you guys when you first brought this in. We're creating an impression, a strong one, that Johnny did this and Johnny did that, but the defense always has the last word, and they're going to ask, over and over, where is the proof? The *evidence?* Johnny coulda, woulda and maybe shoulda done this crime, but how can we prove it?"

"I thought the girl was pretty convincing. Her mother certainly was."

"This afternoon Tom Stonewall Fucking Jackson is going to turn her inside out, and she'll help him do it. She *likes* Johnny—shit, everyone, even *you,* Mikey, likes the hump. Edward Collins will swear up and down that Johnny acted alone, because he's afraid to be done for conspiracy or maybe because he's afraid of his angry bitch of a daughter. Hell, the dumb bastard doesn't realize Tom has no interest in him, as many times as I've told him. All Tom needs from fucking Eddy is a bunch of 'I don't remembers' and he's as good as home."

Maybe, Mike thought, waving at Maria for another beer, there is justice. "You're behind on points."

"I think so. But you said you had something for me. I hope it's a life ring."

Mike cleared his throat. "Jamal——"

"Don't talk to me about Jamal."

"Jamal," Mike said doggedly, "has a witness that maybe can place the guy Tolliver at the scene the day before, posing as a gas company inspector. He's checked; there weren't any legitimate inspectors in the area that day, and the witness says this guy went into the murder house after he left her. The witness identified a composite Jamal had made up after he got thrown out of New York."

"Jamal has so tainted that source——," Evelyn began.

"Maybe not irretrievably," George said, leaning forward. "If he has a witness who can ID the guy."

"We could subpoena the guy as a witness," Evelyn said, smiling at Mike. "Once we get him out here, we put him in a lineup and make sure Jamal's new witness can identify him. If we get that far, we put him on the stand. He takes the Fifth Amendment, we immunize him and he has to talk."

"It's very thin," George said. "Let's set it in motion and wait; maybe Stonewall will stumble in his crosses."

"Has he ever?" Evelyn asked.

Maria returned with three burgers. "I believe I'll have a beer with that," George said, smiling slightly. "All around?"

46

"GOOD AFTERNOON, MRS. Collins," Tom said, trying to calm the nervous woman with his gentlest smile. Carelli would have told her he was the enemy, but Tom doubted she believed that.

"Mr. Jackson," Jane replied with a little smile of her own.

"This morning you testified with great exactness about witnessing your daughter's abduction. Your words were 'snatched violently into a van.'" Tom almost never used notes on a cross; it was one of his theatrical strengths. "You also described your desperate call to your husband, and the first and second calls from the kidnappers. Please tell the jury once again how you felt at the snatch, and when the calls came in."

"Terrified, shocked, mortally wounded," Jane said, dabbing her eyes. "I know my husband was frightened as well, but I suspect a mother feels a special pain, a special tearing at the heart."

She's my witness now, Tom thought, struggling to keep triumph out of his expression. "You believed your daughter's kidnapping was entirely genuine?"

"Yes. It was awful."

"You never thought it was a prank?"

"No. God, no."

Tom looked at the jury. Their expressions registered a range of feelings from sympathy to confusion. "Mrs. Collins, is your relationship with your daughter close?"

Jane slumped in her chair. "We were very close when she was little. She's an only child, and my studio is in the house, so we spent a great deal of time together. In the last couple of years, it has been more difficult."

"Difficult?" Gently, Tom thought, don't lose her.

"Sally is growing up, feeling her body change and her mind. It's a difficult time for any kid."

"I know," Tom said. "I remember my son and daughter at Sally's age. Did you argue?"

"Constantly. She became wild. She had always had straight A's at school, but suddenly she lost interest and her grades plummeted. She was very near to suspension from the public high school and hadn't done much better at Westport Country Day. She wanted to run around all the time with new friends, most of which were older and somewhat rougher than we might like. She began to experiment with alcohol, and I think some drugs. My husband and I tried to counsel her, but she pushed us away, often physically."

Tom looked at Sally, seated in the back of the courtroom. Away from Carelli's coaching, she had reverted to what Tom guessed was something closer to her natural demeanor—sullen and detached. Tom looked at the jury and was pleased to find many members following his glance. "Mrs. Collins, is it possible Sally could have cooperated in her own kidnapping?"

Jane dabbed her eyes again. "Yes, I'm afraid it is. She as much as told me so."

George Carelli started to rise. Tom looked at him, a challenge. Carelli shook his head and sat back down. He couldn't attack his own witness no matter how devastating her testimony had become.

"Mrs. Collins," Tom continued, "tell us again what happened when Sally came home."

"She was crazy. She struggled with her father, and she hit me. She screamed at us, accused us of killing her boyfriend. I was afraid of her."

"But you got her under control and called the family physician."

"Not exactly. After she hit me, she fell down on the floor and curled up, sobbing. I was afraid she was having some kind of fit so I called the doctor."

"What did you do after the doctor got her sedated?"

"Just tucked her in and sat with her a while."

"You didn't give her a bath, or help her clean up?"

"No. She was clean enough."

"No blood on her, no tissue?"

Jane frowned. "No. If there had been of course I would have washed it off." Jane looked around Tom at her daughter in the gallery, and Sally looked away.

Tom looked at the jury as their eyes went from mother to daughter and back. The secret of a successful cross is knowing when to quit. "Thank you, Mrs. Collins." He looked up at the judge. "Nothing further, Your Honor."

Judge Kerry looked at the prosecutors. "Redirect, Mr. Carelli?"

George shook his head.

Edward Collins followed his wife to the stand. Carelli led him through his story, with special focus on his first meeting with Johnny, when he asked for money and Johnny said no because he believed the kidnappers would kill the girl if payment was made.

"Mr. Collins, what did you think the defendant intended?"

"I had no idea. He never said."

"Did you encourage him to proceed?"

"I—I don't think so. I kept hoping I could raise the money from him or someone else."

"So you had no foreknowledge of what he intended to do?"

"No."

"Did he tell you about it afterwards?"

"We never spoke afterwards. He was arrested later the same day."

Full of trepidation, George turned to Tom and said, "Your witness."

TOM STOOD AND approached the witness box. In contrast to his gentle manner with Jane, his expression was stern, edged with anger. With Jane he had wanted a mother's fear and despair; from the father he wanted truth and the reversal of lies.

But not the lies Edward thought he was concealing. "Mr. Collins, you had no idea what, if anything, Johnny intended."

"I've just said so."

"Quite. You don't know if he did anything."

"No, but he said—"

"You don't know, and you haven't spoken to him since the rescue."

"That's true," Edward said slowly. He looked cunning as he tried to figure where Tom was going.

"Your daughter just—came home."

"Y-yes."

That takes care of the phone call, Tom said to himself. "And you found her."

"I did. I removed the blindfold and the knot on her wrists and took her into the house."

"Just so. What did she say?"

"That a man had come and taken her away from her friends. Had killed them."

"What did you think?"

"Well, Johnny had left my house a few hours before, and he said he would get Sally—"

"Why didn't you go with him?"

"He wouldn't let me."

"Did he say anything about guns or violence?"

"No."

"Masks? Camouflage uniforms?"

"No."

"What did he say that led you to connect the story told by your distraught daughter of a professional rescue to my client? Anything at all?"

Edward was shrinking in his seat, his eyes darting to the prosecutor and to the jury. "No."

"Mr. Collins, do you know how the police came to suspect my client, and to arrest and charge him the very day your daughter came home?"

"Well, they came out to the house. Apparently Sally called them."

Tom went back to his table and picked up a copy of Jamal's transcript of the Q and A of Edward Collins. "I have here the notes of the lead detective, Jamal Jones of the Bridgeport Police, who, I note for the record, is not in court today." Tom looked at the judge, then took a long moment to look at the State's table, especially at the fidgeting Mike Kolslovsky. "According to Detective Jones's notes that were later typed up as a statement that you signed, you steered the police directly to your friend Johnny Dietrich when they threatened to arrest *you* for the homicides."

Edward looked at Johnny twenty feet away and his eyes danced. Tom had instructed Johnny to stare at Edward throughout his testimony. "I didn't do it. Johnny said he would."

Tom whirled and came right to the railing of the witness box. Edward flinched away. "Johnny said he would do *what?* Kill someone?"

"No, he said he would go get my Sally."

"So because he said he would try to help you, you accused him of murder before the police."

Edward writhed under Tom's increasingly edged tone. "I didn't accuse him; I said he must have gone after Sally."

Tom turned away toward the jury in evident disgust. "Mr. Collins," he said, sweeping the jury with his eyes. "On the morning your daughter returned, did you make any effort at all to talk to Johnny, to find out what he might have done?"

Edward felt the trap close. He hadn't because Johnny had told him when he dropped Sally off, but Edward had already said they hadn't spoken since Johnny left the house. "No."

"No thought of 'thanks' or 'how did it go?' "

Edward started to get a little angry at the strutting lawyer as he jabbed his finger at him from so close to the witness box. But then at last he figured it out. The police weren't about to charge him now, or take his daughter off to jail in Niantic. What did he owe the State? If Johnny did it, let them prove it. "No, I didn't. I guess I was too confused."

Tom shook his head slowly, as in disbelief. "Mr. Collins, your daughter testified that she thought immediately of my client because he was the only person you knew who was capable of a violent act such as the killings for which my client has been charged."

"She did?" Edward was worried again. Carelli, the pompous prick, hadn't anticipated any of this.

"I can have the court reporter read her testimony."

"Well, she did say that to the police."

"Mr. Collins, you are involved in many businesses in this area, are you not?"

"Yes."

"Real estate? Construction? Restaurants, a nightclub?"

"Yes."

"You deal with contractors, vendors, suppliers of all kinds?"

"Yes." Edward saw where Stonewall was heading and looked at the prosecution table for help. None was forthcoming.

"Your restaurants buy meat? Fish? Use linen and cleaning services?"

"Of course."

"Ever hear the name Fat Nicky Ciccone?"

"Objection," Carelli said, rising. "Of what possible relevance?"

Tom approached the bench. "Your Honor, Nico Ciccone controls all linen services in this county. He also has great, ah, influence, shall we say, over wholesale distribution of meat and fish. He is currently under federal indictment for racketeering."

"Overruled. Witness will answer."

"I've heard of him, yes."

"Ever meet him, or any of his associates?"

"Well, the linen—"

"Ever hear of any violence associated with people who were late paying for linen?"

"Well, no one ever is. Late with the linen payments, I mean." Edward smiled thinly.

"Your Honor—" Carelli was still standing.

"Make your point, Mr. Jackson."

"My point is this, Your Honor. The State's case against my client hangs from the thread of the daughter, Sally's, conclusion that Johnny is the only man with a violent past that her father knows. If the witness has had dealings with certain suppliers to his restaurants, as he has reluctantly told us, he knows many violent men, and few of them decorated war veterans."

"Your Honor." Carelli stepped forward. "Defense Counsel is testifying."

"Mr. Collins," the judge said, exasperated. "Did you know any people you dealt with in your businesses that you thought might have been capable of violence?"

"Well, you hear stories—"

"Yea or nay, Mr. Collins," the judge said sternly.

"Yes. Yea."

"There. Are you about finished, Mr. Jackson? It's getting late."

"Only one other question, Your Honor." The judge nodded and Tom turned back to the witness. "When Sally came home, how did she look? Injured, bleeding?"

"She looked fine," Edward said warily. "Just very upset."

"No blood on her?"

"No. I'd have noticed that."

"None at all."

"No."

"Nothing further, Your Honor."

"Redirect, Mr. Carelli?" the judge asked, picking up his gavel. George shook his head. It hurt from the slow movement.

47

ANGELA ESCORTED JOHNNY back to the interview room in the jail. She was finding it hard to hide her elation, but Johnny was subdued. "We had a very good day," she said, punching his shoulder lightly as they sat down side by side. "They're nearly through their case in chief and they have barely proved that a crime was committed."

Johnny shook his head. "They still have three dead boys."

Angela took Johnny's hand. He didn't respond. "You mistook my meaning. Of course a crime was committed, but what did the jury learn today about the proximate cause? Christ, Johnny, what did *you* learn? The mother was terrified; the jury will see that and reject the defense contention that the kidnapping was a misguided prank. The father is covering his ass and nothing more, and Sally's recollection of the scene is obviously tainted by her exaggeration on the issue of blood."

"Still got those three dead boys. Witnesses who can't talk, but perhaps need to be heard before they can rest."

"Johnny, can't you see that Sally set this up? That Edward set *you* up?"

"Angela, please don't think me ungrateful for what you and Tom did today. You were brilliant. I just wish there was some way for me to tell the whole truth and let the jury decide."

Angela stood up, angry despite herself. "I'm going to get coffee. We'll discuss this when Tom comes down."

GEORGE CARELLI LED Evelyn Pulaski and Mike Kolslovsky into his office. He slammed his briefcase down on the conference table and pushed it away from him. "Close the door, Mike," he said. "We need a drink."

Mike closed the office door and took a seat at the table next to Evelyn. The pretty woman looked sad. George took a bottle of Irish Whisky and three not very clean coffee cups from a file cabinet and brought them over to the table. He poured and slid the cups down the smooth surface, then fell into a chair. "So where are we? The mother's a suffering saint with a nasty, spiteful daughter. The father's a scumbag who gave up his pal to save himself from Fat Nicky Ciccone, and the nasty, spiteful daughter has led herself and us into a gaping lie that taints all her testimony."

"We knew this case was difficult," Evelyn said. "You said so."

"Difficult!" George tossed back his drink and poured another. "It's becoming fucking impossible. One of the things every courtroom lawyer learns very early on is that almost every person who ever testifies at a trial is not only likely to lie but also to be revealed as a sleezebag, but these Collins people are an experience unto themselves."

"Plus we have police misconduct," Evelyn said. "Sorry, Mike."

"No, I know it," Mike said. "But maybe Jamal did find the only link between Johnny and the crime."

"I'll see the judge for a certificate this evening. Jackson will have to know about it, of course."

"He wouldn't try to tip the guy," Evelyn asked. "Would he?"

George threw up his hands. "If we don't get his testimony, we might as well do the right thing and dismiss the charges before Stonewall moves for a judgment of acquittal and Judge Kerry grants it with a cheer."

Tᴏᴍ ꜰᴏᴜɴᴅ Jᴏʜɴɴʏ and Angela in the interview room. They were holding hands but let go as he entered. Angela stood up. "Your coffee's cold; I'll get more."

"No, stay. The judge just had me up in chambers with George Carelli. Judge Kerry has issued a certificate under seal to compel Tolliver to appear to testify as a material witness."

"On what grounds?" Angela asked.

"State claims to have a witness that will place Tolliver at the crime scene—in the house, George emphasized—the day before the shootings. Says she recognized his face on an Identikit composite."

"Jamal," Angela whispered.

"George didn't say so, but that's my guess."

"How does a certificate get enforced?" Johnny asked.

"Judge Kerry's certificate says that a criminal prosecution in his court requires the testimony of Tolliver. The certificate is delivered to a judge in New York who will compel Tolliver to a hearing, either by a summons or by having him taken into custody. The judge will then conduct a hearing and determine whether the witness is material and necessary to the proceeding in Connecticut, taking Judge Kerry's certificate as *prima facie* evidence of the facts. The New York judge will doubtless agree with Judge Kerry, and order Tolliver to appear. Carelli argued that because of the seriousness of the charges that *could* be lodged against Tolliver, and because of his long friendship with Johnny, Tolliver may not come here voluntarily. If the New York judge agrees, he can order Tolliver taken into custody and delivered to Judge Kerry's court."

"When will the certificate get delivered?"

"Carelli said as soon as possible. If it were my last shot, I'd find a way to deliver it tonight."

"We can't tell him to hide," Angela said sadly.

"No. Now that the judge has acted, that would be tampering. But we should make sure he is expecting service and has counsel so he can try to have the summons quashed."

Angela made a note. "I'll call him. Tell him be sure to cooperate, bring his lawyer."

"Right," Tom said. "Hopefully he'll realize his best defense is to disappear."

48

"You gotta let me go with you when you pick this guy up," Jamal pleaded. He and Mike were sitting in a bar called Rose's Irish House across the street from Police Headquarters. Mike was waiting for a call on his cell phone from Carelli as soon as he got back to his office with the papers.

"You know I can't, man. Carelli'd have my ass for a football, and if he didn't the judge would."

"Shit, man, I'll ride in the backseat under a blanket. I'll ride in the fucking *trunk.*"

"You got a claim on this guy, I guess. But you know you can't go near him."

"Even to be there for the interrogation, Mike. Hell, I found the damn witness."

Mike's phone buzzed. "Talk to Carelli."

Jamal drained his beer. "Right."

Johnny listened to Tom and Angela prepare for the possibility of Willy Tolliver's testimony. They would have to change their approach completely if Tolliver placed him at the house, and he wondered how they were going to explain to the jury that they had lied to them.

"We didn't lie to them, Johnny," Tom said. "We haven't said anything about what you did or didn't do. We have simply attacked the State's case."

"But if Tolliver is forced to testify, he's going to say 'I got him a weapon and the clothes. I let him off in front of the house, came back when he called on the radio, and picked up him and the girl.' How you gonna square that?"

Angela was up and pacing. "We'll have to go back to your motivation. You were led to believe the girl was in immediate and mortal danger, that there was neither time nor sufficient evidence to bring the police in. You did what you did to help her and her parents. We've already laid the groundwork for that, in case we needed to mount a defense."

Johnny was alarmed. "What do you mean, *in case?*"

"If we'd made it through the State's case without their finding Tolliver, we would have moved for a directed verdict of acquittal, and we'd have gotten it," Tom said calmly. "If the State locates Tolliver and if they can get him to testify as to what you did together, we'll have to defend you based on the facts."

"The facts are I shot three unarmed men."

"Those are daylight facts. There was another set of facts in that darkened house," Tom said. And another set still in the darkness of Johnny's mind, Tom thought grimly. "We're a long way from crippled."

Angela stood and touched Johnny's cheek. "I should get back to the office," she said. "I've got a little more research to do."

"You've already started?" Johnny asked. "You anticipated this?"

"We hoped Tolliver would never appear," Tom said, getting up and patting Johnny on the shoulder. "We may still hope he won't testify, but yes, we anticipated this, and we'll be ready." Tom rapped on the door, the guard came and Johnny was led back to his cell as the lawyers left. Johnny stretched out and closed his eyes. His whole case, so close to victory and release, was back driving him toward prison or worse. He found he didn't feel frightened, or even disappointed. He grinned to himself. It would be nice to see Tolliver again. It would be nice to be reunited with the truth.

Johnny slipped away to sleep. He slid back into the tunnels of the jungle and the basements of Hue, but he was not afraid.

MIKE DROVE INTO New York on I-95 and down the East River Drive to the Criminal Court Building on Centre Street. He presented Judge Kerry's certificate to the clerk of the court and sat outside the courtroom he had been assigned, one of many active round-the-clock. It was past seven o'clock in the evening but the courts were busy as judges conducted business of all kinds. Mike yawned, wishing he'd stopped for coffee before coming in. Carelli had told him to get to the court as fast as he could; Tolliver could get word and flee to avoid testifying against his friend.

Maybe I should have told Jamal to take this to Carelli himself. He wouldn't have. Mike wanted to help Jamal but he didn't want to hurt Johnny. If this Tolliver was really the wheel man, and if he'd entered the murder house posing as a gas inspector, it went a long way to explain how Johnny could have done his in-and-out so smoothly, so untraceably.

"Detective Kolslovsky?" a uniformed bailiff, a pretty young black woman, walked among the benches. "Detective Kolslovsky?"

"Here, ma'am," Mike said, getting stiffly to his feet.

"You're up," she said, and he followed her into the courtroom and all the way forward to the judge's high bench. The judge was a thin black woman with short gray hair and half-glasses. Her nameplate on the face of the bench said Judge Esther Barrow. She peered over the glasses at Mike as he came to a halt before her. "Detective Kolslovsky?"

"Yes, Your Honor. Bridgeport police."

She held up the papers. "As this so states. You have reason to believe the subject might abscond rather than testify?"

"Yes, Your Honor. We believe the witness is in fact an accessory to murder."

"All right. We try to expedite matters before fellow judges, and I'm not inclined to doubt Judge Kerry's conclusion. Address you have is in the Sixth Precinct, do you know where their station house is?"

"I have the address, Your Honor."

She signed a paper and passed the whole stack back to the clerk. "You'll save time if you take this over for me; I have to wait on uniformed officers this time of the evening. It's my order for the witness to appear before me, or if after two A.M. Judge Richmond." She waved him away.

Mike followed the clerk into an alcove behind the bench. The clerk photocopied the papers, affixed a seal to the original of the judge's order, and put them in a large envelope before handing them back to Mike. "That was quick," Mike said.

The clerk smiled. "You were lucky; Judge Barrow likes to put requests from other judges in front. Some of the others would have held this for hours, just to show you how important we are in New Jack City."

Mike drove uptown to Fourteenth Street, then across to the Sixth Precinct station house on West Tenth. Carelli had called the watch commander and the lieutenant had promised cooperation. Mike certainly hoped he would be better received than Jamal had been, but at least he had papers where Jamal had none. Even so, Mike was a little nervous parking in one of the slots in front of the station marked "Police Vehicles Only." He took the "Bridgeport Police" sign off the sun visor and placed it prominently on the dashboard, grabbed his shabby briefcase and went up the stairs.

ISMAEL ANSWERED THE phone in Tolliver's office. "Marines Helping Marines."

"Who's that, Ahmed? Sergeant Manelli at the precinct. I need Tolliver."

"I don't think he's in camp, Sergeant, but let me call his living quarters." Ismael switched to intercom and buzzed Tolliver's Spartan room in the back of the basement. "No answer, Sergeant."

"He coming back tonight?"

"I'm not sure. He's signed out on leave for a week starting seventeen-hundred today. Didn't say where he'd be."

"If he comes back for any reason, ask him to call me before he talks to anyone else."

"Sure thing, Sergeant. What if he doesn't come in?"

"Then I'll see him when he gets back from his vacation. That would be best, Ahmed."

Ismael smiled. "Understood, Sergeant."

Miller looked up from the *New York Post*. "Who was that, Ahmed?"

"The cop, Manelli. Sounds like someone is hunting Staff Sergeant Tolliver again."

"He ain't leaving till tomorrow. I'm taking him to the airport at six."

"Maybe he'd better get out tonight. You know where he is?"

"No, he didn't say," Miller said. "Take a walk around, find him. He looks for lost marines in the parks and doorways on cold nights like this."

Ahmed got up and put on his green winter jacket. "Best he don't come back until he talks to Sergeant Manelli."

"Roger, Ahmed. I'll stay by the phone."

Sᴇʀɢᴇᴀɴᴛ Mᴀɴᴇʟʟɪ ᴘᴜᴛ the phone down. He looked at the Bridgeport detective through the glass wall that separated his office from the squad bay. Why don't these rubes leave Tolliver and his heartsick marines alone? he wondered. He got up and went to the door. The lieutenant said cooperate, but he didn't say how hard. "Detective? Come in, please. Have some coffee."

Mike marched in and took a chair as the sergeant filled two styrofoam cups and placed them on his battered desk. "Black okay? They got sugar and powdered cream outside, but I keep it here, I get ants."

"Black is fine, Sergeant."

Manelli held out his hand. "I'm Ray Manelli."

"Mike Kolslovsky," Mike said, shaking. "I'm here with a court order to appear, a guy in your precinct."

Manelli gave a wintry smile. "I'm glad you recognize our turf."

Mike frowned. "The other guy was just trying a little too hard, is all."

Manelli waved it away. "Shit happens. Can I see your paper?"

Mike handed over the certificate and Judge Barrow's order. Manelli put on half-glasses and began to read. Mike started to burn; the sergeant didn't need to read the certificate, which was quite long and detailed, just recognize the name and address at the top, and the order. Mike was getting stalled and it wouldn't surprise him if the man Tolliver was being warned off as he sat drinking coffee that tasted a week old. Manelli turned a page and read on, serenely. Mike took a peek at his wristwatch and decided to give the sergeant another two minutes.

Cool off, he told himself. Don't be Jamal. If the guy gets away, so what? He hides a week and Johnny walks. Mike had been in court every day and he was convinced that if Johnny had done anything wrong it was because he was set up by the snotty girl and dumped in the shit by her slimy father. Be cool. The sergeant read on, while Mike waited in silence.

After Manelli had read the thing through and looked at parts again, he looked up. Mike held his face expressionless. "You got a room for the night?"

"No, Ray. I'd like to serve the guy immediately; take him to the hearing and back to Bridgeport with me."

"What if we can't find him?"

"We won't if we don't go over there," Mike said evenly.

"We're not really staffed up to serve paper at night."

Mike turned and looked at the squad bay, where men sat reading or drinking coffee and staring at the shift clock. "Come on, Sergeant. All I need is one uniformed officer. You ain't got a free car, I'll drive or we can walk; it's a couple blocks."

"Detective, may I explain something to you? One policeman to another?"

"Sure," Mike said, his anger growing. Patronizing fuck, he thought.

"In this city we got procedures. We got priorities, and in this precinct, we got a lotta crime. Serious crime, Mike; drugs, violence. There are a lot of bad guys out there in the night, and only a few good ones. Willy Tolliver is one of the good ones."

"I got a murder case. The State's Attorney wants this guy's testimony."

"Paper suggests he may be an accessory. That's serious."

"So's my case. Triple homicide."

"Tolliver has done a lot of good in this community. His marines patrol my streets, Mike, they check people out, they watch old ladies going in and out of the subways. Sometimes they're able to fight crime in ways you and I might like to, but can't."

Mike got up and turned around, raising his arms and letting them fall to his thighs with a slap. "The guy's just gotta testify, that's all. Be back in a couple of days."

"What if he doesn't want to go with you?"

"He goes to a hearing, he gets to say. It's all there; you read it. The judge, Judge Barrow, has issued her order for him to appear; it's up to her."

Manelli smiled. "In that case——"

Mike gripped the back of the chair he had been sitting in. "In that case, can I do my job? Please? *Sergeant?*"

Manelli's smile disappeared. "You can't wait till morning? You gotta blow this guy out of his rack for this?"

Mike consulted his watch, then turned it toward the NYPD ball-buster. "It's a quarter to ten, Ray. I thought this was the city that never slept."

Manelli shook his head, and stood up. He straightened his tie and put on his jacket and raincoat. "So I don't have to interrupt serious police work, I'll take you over myself."

"Thank you, Sergeant," Mike said with enough extra courtesy to be mildly offensive.

ANGELA RUBBED HER itchy eyes and turned off her computer at ten. She had been over the defense she and Tom had worked out weeks ago in case Tolliver appeared, and she found no area for improvement. It's still weak, she thought, and placed another call to Tolliver's outreach center. He was out; he might be back and he might not. She left her home and cell phone numbers, locked the office and went out into a chilly rain. Get out of town, Willy Tolliver, she whispered to herself as she unlocked her car. Don't make us take Johnny back into that house of pain.

WILLY TOLLIVER WALKED his new lady home from a SoHo restaurant to her apartment on East Tenth Street. Marguerite Velez-Campo was a psychiatrist who did volunteer work at Marines Helping Marines, and Tolliver had come to like her more than he should. She was in her early thirties, he figured, a Cuban immigrant with skin and hair that indicated some African blood but aquiline features that said white. She was pretty as well as kind, and she had asked him out so many times he finally said yes, and they enjoyed each other's conversation and each other's silence.

Tolliver hadn't come to the business of rescuing marines drowning in their nightmares or their guilt or booze and drugs because he was a saint, he reflected as he followed Marguerite up the stairs to her third-floor loft. He was in the center because he had snakes in his head like all the others, and he needed the center the way an alcoholic who hasn't had a drink in ten years still needed his meetings.

Marguerite unlocked the door. Instead of turning to kiss his cheek as she had done in the past, she reached behind her to grab him by the belt and pulled him into her loft.

MIKE FOLLOWED SERGEANT Manelli down the stairs of the rectory of St. Anne's, thinking of Jamal making the same trip on his way to getting stripped naked and given to the grinning New York cops. Jamal had been wrong but he had been trying to do the job, and Mike reckoned this Tolliver owed Jamal a payback.

Manelli pushed open a door off a smelly corridor and entered a clean hallway that smelled of floor polish. Mike saw that everything gleamed, from the glass wall that gave way to the squared-away bunkroom to the linoleum floor and the old brass fittings on the doors. Manelli knocked on the door marked "Office—Off Limits" and pushed it open. "Hello, Gunny Miller," he said. "This here's Detective Kolslovsky from Bridgeport, Connecticut. Needs to see Willy."

"He hasn't come back, Sergeant," Miller said.

Come *back,* Mike thought. The bastard Manelli did try to warn Tolliver off.

Manelli turned to Kolslovsky and shrugged a "not my fault."

"What do you want to do, Mike?"

"Wait," Mike said stolidly.

"Well, you might, but I can't. Miller, come here, we got to make a deal." He sat on the edge of Tolliver's desk while Miller took the chair behind it. "Miller, this guy's got a court order for Tolliver to appear as a witness in Connecticut. He needs a New York cop to serve it, but I can't wait here, and I can't send a uniform to stay here until Tolliver comes back from his vacation." Manelli winked at Miller knowing Mike would see it. "Mike here wants to wait. If Willy comes back tonight, you call the precinct and I'll send a man over to serve the paper properly. Okay, Mike?"

"Long's Miller, here, and Tolliver when he shows, knows he has to obey the court's order."

Manelli frowned. "He does, Miller. He'll understand I just don't want to park a man here, he might not come back for a week."

Color rose in Miller's pale cheeks. "Staff Sergeant Tolliver obeys the law, Sergeant Manelli, same's we all do in this camp."

"Exactly," Manelli said. "Detective?"

"Okay, I'll wait. Thank you, Sergeant."

Manelli looked at Miller, whose face was clotted with anger. "Lighten up, Miller; this will be all right. Offer Mike some coffee."

WILLY TOLLIVER HAD never encountered a woman like Marguerite Velez-Campo. She had dragged him across her loft to a king-size mattress on a platform raised a few inches above the floor, tearing off or stepping out of her clothes as she went, then throwing him on his back and starting on his, shoes, socks, trousers and underwear gone almost before he could catch his breath. He got his own jacket, tie and shirt off as she hungrily engulfed him in her soft, pulsing mouth. He was nearly gone when suddenly she rose up off the floor and dove onto his chest like a swimmer beginning the hundred-meter freestyle, then rose up and slammed him inside.

This woman hurt you, you resisted, Willy thought as she bucked and moaned above him, silhouetted in the dim light coming in from the street. She hadn't managed to find a light switch on the way in. Willy held himself back, gritting his teeth as she rode him, her long fingernails raking his chest and thighs, and finally she screamed out loud enough to rattle the windows, and collapsed on top of him.

I enjoyed that, Willy thought. I'm also glad I survived it.

Marguerite rolled off him, purring like a cat, and later began to snore. Willy stayed awake, not knowing what to do. He very rarely slept away from the shelter.

Better to stay awake than risk the dreams, he thought.

49

MIKE GOT MILLER talking after a second cup of coffee that, unlike the cop-shop acid, was fresh. Miller wanted to know what it was like being a cop; he'd thought about taking the exam but he wasn't sure he wanted to stay in New York.

"Come out to Bridgeport," Mike said. "There are usually openings."

"I don't know. I'm originally from San Diego. I'd like to go back, but I'd have to find another veterans' program."

"You're a counselor here, right? I mean, like paid staff?"

"Yeah, paid staff, not one of the crazies." Miller grinned. "Mike, we get to be counselors by dealing with our problems, especially the outside problems like drugs and booze and petty crime. Inside, most of us are still troubled and we don't like to be too far from buddies that understand."

"I was over there myself. I never saw anything really awful, even though we were on the line a lot. I guess I was lucky."

"Everybody took it differently," Miller said. "What we've learned is that most of the guys, even guys who were POWs, and what could be worse than that, held it together while they were there, reinforced by their buddies even if no one really talked about it. In other wars, guys trained together in units, went over in those units and came back with the same guys they fought alongside, so even after they got home there were people they could be with that understood. We all got rotated home when our year was up, all by ourselves. That was scary enough, but so many in this country were hostile to the war and blamed the troops. When it came time to deal with the horror, to get it out and get beyond it, we were not only alone but despised."

"I remember," Mike said. "I was already married but she left me after a year, and I went a little nuts. But I come from a huge family of tough Polacks, and my father and my uncles slapped some sense into me and I was okay."

"Family like that keep you out of a place like this. I be happy for you."

I wonder, Mike thought. "Say, Miller, when this case is over, maybe I come here and talk to you guys? You know, nothing formal—"

"Sure, man. The Staff Sergeant always wants friends on the outside, and a lot of our graduates come back when they're feeling low. You'd be welcome."

I wonder, Mike thought, how welcome after I bust their director and throw their benefactor into jail for life.

——

TOLLIVER WAS ALONE in a burning forest. The jungle was shattered, tree trunks blown over or standing, stripped of leaves, branches and even bark. Tolliver ran around huge craters the rain was filling with water even as flames flickered and hissed. Willy kept moving, kept looking. Where had the patrol gone? Where were the lieutenant and the other eighteen men? They'd been dug in for the night, their defensive position set three kilometers south of the broad path through the jungle to be bombed by B-52s flying so high they weren't seen or heard on the ground. Willy had been sent farther south to the river with the Deacon, a new guy, to set up a listening post nearer the river where the VC trails crossed; one going east to Gio Linh and west to Khe Sanh, the other north to the DMZ that separated North Vietnam from South. Willy and the Deacon had listened and looked and had seen nothing, until they heard a sound like rushing wind followed by hundreds of explosions to the north, so close together they sounded like rolling thunder, then the ground began to roll as well and they were forced out of their muddy hole for fear it would collapse in on them.

Trees swayed and shattered, and burst into flame. The Deacon stood up; Willy shouted to him to crawl as he was, but the kid panicked, stood up holding his ears, and a flaming branch a foot thick hit him in the face and tore his head off.

The thunder rolled away west as the Arc Light bombing strike flew on, leaving Willy alone and shivering in the rain. He started north to find the lieutenant and the others.

He found them in the morning, their night defensive position crushed into the mud as if by a giant boot. Mud, trees and body parts were intermixed as if chopped and stirred. Nothing was identifiable as a human being. Willy walked around wringing his hands and sobbing. Either the navigator of the bombers had fucked up or the lieutenant had.

Then Willy saw the lieutenant staring at him from a shattered tree, except it wasn't the LT, just his head, his eyes staring and his tongue drooping obscenely.

Willy screamed as he always did, and woke up as he always did, with the sight of the lieutenant's head etched on the inside of his eyelids and the taste of death in his mouth.

Willy thrashed and screamed again. He didn't know where he was, and someone was grappling with him, holding him down. A light came on and Marguerite slapped him, then he remembered. "Jesus," the woman whispered when Willy's eyes steadied and his breathing lost its harsh rasp. "Did you go back there?"

"Yes." Willy's chest heaved and his body was streaming with sweat. "I'm sorry you had to see that; I'd better go."

"No, stay. I'm a doctor, Willy. I work with your guys, let me work with you."

He got up and went into the tiny bathroom, stood under the cold shower until the shaking stopped, then dried himself and dressed. Marguerite was wearing a thick terry-cloth robe when he came out. "I'm sorry. The dreams. It's why I so seldom stay the night away from the shelter."

"It's all right. Promise you'll call me when you wake up."

"I promise," he said, and hoped he meant it. "Good night, and thank you for caring." Willy kissed her and she held him, then he broke away and let himself out. He walked rapidly west through the darkened city, seeking shelter, seeking comfort.

VIII

WITNESS

50

JOHNNY ROLLED OUT of his dream and sat up in his darkened cell. He felt a strange electric buzz of danger. He listened, the night sounds of the jail were as usual. He heard the footfalls of a guard or a trusty a long way down the corridor. He could make out a wall clock down the hall, just past midnight.

The danger isn't for me, he thought. They're going after Willy Tolliver. He's walking into an ambush, and Johnny could see it, a classic T-shaped setup with a buried mine in the trail for a trigger, det cord in the stream bed that paralleled the trail, and the VC ambush team on the other side. He had to warn Tolliver but he couldn't catch his eye, and his muscles and voice were as frozen as if he were locked in a dream.

Johnny woke up, realizing he had left one dream and gone into another. He stood and stretched to make sure he was really awake this time, and looked and listened again. The clock still read five past twelve, and he still had his sense of foreboding. He stood holding the bars of his cell and listening, but the soft snores and moans told him nothing.

MIKE KOLSLOVSKY YAWNED. He was getting almighty stiff sitting in the little chair by the computer in Staff Sergeant Tolliver's tiny office and he was beginning to wish he had taken Miller's offer of a bunk in the berthing space next door. These men rose and re-tired early, and it was decreasingly likely that Tolliver would come in before morning. If he didn't come in soon, Mike would see what he could do with the Port Authority Police at New York's three air-ports to watch outgoing flights, check the airline computers or what-ever they did. They might catch Tolliver that way; if he left the city by road or rail there was just no way.

TOLLIVER TURNED HIS collar up against the cold rain. The church, with its bright light over the door and another next to the door of the rectory, beckoned like a beacon. Tolliver was still shaky and weak from the dream and all he wanted was to get in his rack in the back of the basement and sleep for a few hours before getting on the plane to Antigua. He had never been to the Caribbean be-fore but he was looking forward to sun and rum and good food, and black people with big smiles who had no knives or guns or wishes to harm anyone.

He hurried through the alley between the church and the rectory and down the stairs to the back door of the basement.

Tolliver took his blazer and slacks off and hung them in his locker. His shoes and socks were as wet as his raincoat, and his shirt smelled of the scared sweat even after his cold shower at Mar-guerite's. He wrapped a towel around his waist and went to the head between the exercise room and the bunkroom. He made as little noise as possible; the place was asleep. He remembered Miller had the watch in the office; Tolliver didn't mind if the men dozed on night duty as long as they were alert to the phones and the buzzer that controlled the door to the rectory hallway. He brushed his teeth and showered quickly. He yawned; he felt completely wrung out and he had to be up in four hours to go to the airport. He dried himself and put on clean marine green shorts and T-shirt, then he heard low voices from the office. Best stick my head in, he thought through the fog of his fatigue. He padded down the polished corridor in bare feet, pushed the door open and saw Miller, Ismael in a wet jacket, and a big white man in a cheap blue suit. "I couldn't find him anywhere," Ismael was saying.

"Find who?" Tolliver asked.

The big white man got slowly to his feet. "Wilson Tolliver?"

"Yes. And you are?"

"Detective Kolslovsky. Mike Kolslovsky, the Bridgeport police. I have a court order to serve on you." Mike held out Judge Barrow's paper.

Tolliver looked at Miller and Ismael, who looked frozen. "You can serve that here?"

"I need a New York cop. Sergeant Manelli said he'd send one over if you came back." *Run*, Mike thought. I won't chase you.

"This is about Johnny Dietrich," Tolliver said.

"Yes."

"All right. Miller, call Sergeant Manelli, tell him what's happening. Then call my lawyer. You don't mind I call my lawyer, do you, Detective?"

"No, I reckon you got that right. I'd like to get back over to the courthouse before two; we'll get a fast audience from the judge who already knows about this."

"I'll get dressed." The Bridgeport cop got up like he was going to follow Tolliver. Tolliver turned and looked at Mike hard. "Before you ask, Detective, yes, there is a back door, and no, I won't be going through it."

Kolslovsky thought about it for a long moment, then nodded slowly and sat back down. "I'll wait here."

"Thank you, Detective."

TOLLIVER SPOKE TO the lawyer, an ex-marine captain named Robby O'Dwyer who had been an infantry officer in 'Nam and gone to law school after he got out. He was a very successful defense attorney who handled high-profile cases, but he always had time for the marines at the center if they got in trouble, which was seldom. "He's right, Willy," O'Dwyer said. "You have to go to the hearing. There isn't much I can do right now, but I'll meet you downtown at Criminal Court. Did you see the judge's name on the court order?"

"Judge Esther Barrow."

"She's tough, an ex-policewoman who went to law school at night, then spent her entire career as a prosecutor. Hates defense attorneys."

"You don't need to get out of bed, Robby. If I have to go I'll just go."

"No, I should be there. You're going to need help with this anyway, even if the judge packs you off to Connecticut tonight."

"Thanks. I'll see you in court, then."

"Yeah, I'll go as soon as I get dressed. Don't worry, and don't volunteer anything."

Tolliver put on clean utilities and packed his blazer, some shirts and ties and his one good pair of civilian slacks, their cuffs still damp from the rain, in a green canvas bag. He went back to the office and found it crowded with his men plus Kolslovsky, Sergeant Manelli and a uniformed officer Tolliver didn't recognize. Tolliver greeted Manelli. "Didn't expect you to come over here yourself, Ray."

"I was just going off-shift. I was kinda hoping I wouldn't see you tonight." He took the court order from Kolslovsky's hand and tapped Tolliver lightly on the chest with it. "Sorry, man, but you're served. I have to deliver you to Judge Barrow's court."

"Let's go." Tolliver was overwhelmed by fatigue and felt nothing.

"Detective, you want to ride with us?" Manelli asked Kolslovsky.

"I'd better follow in my car. If the judge agrees, I'll take the Staff Sergeant with me tonight."

"And they say New York cops are ballbusters," Manelli sneered. "Let's go, then."

R OBBY O'DWYER CAUGHT up with his client and the cops just as they were being called by Judge Barrow's clerk. They filed in and were seated on wooden benches as the judge heard arguments in another matter. O'Dwyer took the judge's order and the Connecticut judge's underlying certificate and began to speed-read. The judge finished the case before her and a skinny Puerto Rican youth with a runny nose was hauled out of court by bailiffs. The boy shouted obscenities in Spanish as he was marched out. The clerk called Kolslovsky's name and Tolliver, Kolslovsky, Sergeant Manelli and Robby O'Dwyer stepped forward. "Detective Kolslovsky," the judge said with a little smile. "Which of these gentlemen is your flight-risk witness?"

"This man, Your Honor," Mike said, placing a hand lightly on Tolliver's bicep.

"If it please the court," O'Dwyer said. "Robby O'Dwyer, appearing for Mr. Tolliver."

The judge nodded. She turned to Manelli and raised an eyebrow.

"Sergeant Manelli, Your Honor, Sixth Precinct, delivering the witness per Your Honor's order."

"Fine. Mr. O'Dwyer, have you read the certificate from Judge Kerry?"

"Just reading it, Your Honor. I was called when Staff Sergeant Tolliver was served, and I'd like to request a continuence so that I may study it and respond."

"Mr. O'Dwyer, you are an eminent defense lawyer. You can see that this is a Connecticut matter. It is the sole responsibility of this court to enforce Judge Kerry's certificate."

"But surely, Your Honor, before my client is removed to Connecticut at great inconvenience to himself, we are entitled to examine the facts, ensure that Mr. Tolliver's testimony is truly needed, and that the summons is founded on probable cause and a connection between Mr. Tolliver and the matter before Judge Kerry."

"If you want to file to quash the summons, Mr. O'Dwyer, you must do so in Connecticut. Now, Mr. Tolliver, do you understand what you have been ordered to do?"

"Go to Connecticut," Tolliver said, biting back a yawn. "Testify at trial."

"Yes. Judge Kerry's certificate says you may be an unwilling witness, and may not appear unless compelled. Do you have anything to say to that?"

"I don't want to go, but I'll obey the law."

"Detective Kolslovsky, when is Mr. Tolliver's presence required?"

"The State's Attorney said bring him in right away, if possible, Your Honor."

"And incarcerate him?"

"I guess. Yes, Your Honor."

"Mr. O'Dwyer?"

"Yes, Your Honor. I—"

"By rights I should honor Judge Kerry's request, and direct Sergeant Manelli to deliver Mr. Tolliver immediately to Judge Kerry's court. Mr. Tolliver, have you had any sleep tonight?"

"No, ma'am. Your Honor."

"Your Honor," O'Dwyer said. "I'll guarantee Mr. Tolliver's attendance upon Judge Kerry. By nine o'clock tomorrow?"

"Today," the judge said. "It's well past midnight."

"Of course, Your Honor."

"What do you say, Detective Kolslovsky? Will you let this man get a good night's sleep if he and his lawyer promise to appear?"

Mike fidgeted. "His lawyer guarantees he'll be there?"

"His lawyer does. He's an officer of this court."

Mike looked at Tolliver, who looked dead on his feet, and at the lawyer. It's my call. Jamal would haul the guy all the way to Bridgeport chained to the bumper of his car. "I'm, er, prepared to be guided by Your Honor."

"Thank you," the judge said. "Mr. O'Dwyer, are you admitted in Connecticut?"

"Yes I am, Your Honor."

"Very well. Make your applications to Judge Kerry at nine o'clock this morning, or as soon thereafter as he may determine." She banged her gavel once and looked over at the clerk. "Next, Latisha?"

51

JOHNNY FOUND ONE of the trusties waiting by his cell when he returned from breakfast at seven-thirty. Johnny found the prison food so awful he barely ate, and he complained of stomach pains and loss of weight. The prison nurse, who visited the detainees once a week, gave him antacid pills. The trusty said, "Put on your suit. Your lawyer's coming by in fifteen minutes."

Johnny nodded. His dream of the hour past midnight haunted him: Tolliver trapped, walking down the trail toward the ambush, never stopping and never seeming to get any farther away. What have I done to Tolliver? he wondered. What have I done to a man who saved my life and many others, and wanted nothing in life but to go on doing so? He changed his clothes and sat on his bunk. The trusty reappeared in ten minutes and took him to the interview room. They no longer handcuffed him before letting him out of the cell; Johnny wondered why that had stopped. He also wondered why he found it so hard to focus. If this ever ends, what damages will be toted up against him? What would be left of Johnny Dietrich?

Angela stood as he was admitted to the interview room. She looked fresh and lovely, out of place in the grimy jail. Johnny had never noticed women's clothes before he met Angela; he suspected he did not only because she was pretty and dressed well, but also because there was so little in Johnny's jail world that evoked any response to beauty. No sun, no leaves, no birds, no sky, no snowy white sails driving his graceful boat through dark swells picked out bright with foam. "Good morning, Angela," he said softly, taking both her hands.

"Johnny. You're not sleeping, are you?"

"Not last night. My stomach hurts me all the time and I dream."

"We thought we'd have had you out of here in a week. We'll request your removal to the hospital for the weekend."

"The cops found Tolliver, didn't they?"

"Yes. He's due in Judge Kerry's court at nine this morning. He's being brought out by his lawyer."

"Then what?"

"Judge Kerry will hold a hearing where Tolliver's counsel will file a motion to quash the summons. Tom will go to the hearing, as will George Carelli. George has laid a pretty strong trail to connect Tolliver with you, and Tom and I believe that if the State's witness identifies Tolliver, he'll have to testify."

"I see."

"I'm sorry, Johnny."

Johnny smiled and sat down, releasing her hands. The room instantly felt colder. "Will Willy's testimony be the last of the prosecution's case?"

"They've listed Abigail Grieg and the psychiatrist who interviewed you. I suspect they'll take Tolliver last."

"Last thing the jury hears."

"Will be Tom's cross-examination, which is really the beginning of the defense."

"What's Tom gonna do?"

"He hasn't said. I don't know." She took his hands on the table-top. "Remember what Tolliver said to me. Keep your faith, Johnny."

Johnny smiled and squeezed her hands. "Semper Fi."

W ILLY T OLLIVER SAT next to Robby O'Dwyer as the lawyer accelerated off the Triboro Bridge into the Bronx, on the way to Connecticut. Robby had invited him to stay at his Park Avenue apartment, make the start easier in the morning, but Tolliver wanted to be at his shelter. If he had another burning return to the killing fields of I Corps, he wanted it to be where he could roll his sweating body in a marine green blanket and moan and whimper his way through by himself. As it was, he had spent a half hour in prayer after Robby dropped him off, then slept quite soundly.

Nevertheless, he felt listless and feverish in the morning when Robby picked him up in his black Mercedes 560 SEL that looked like it had come out of the box that very day. Willy wished he could have slept until noon, until the malaria that shared quarters in his body with the Dream was chased back into the darkness, at least for a while.

"Willy," Robby said as he turned onto the Hutchinson River Parkway. "We're not going to have a lot of time to prepare for this hearing. Can we talk about it?"

Tolliver straightened in his seat. "Sure. Why not?"

"I don't suppose I know you well, Willy, but you seem much less than your positive-thinking self."

"I'm all right, Robby. I had a little malaria attack last night."

"You still dream?"

"Yeah. You?"

"More than I'd like. I went to a shrink for two years, then I got married. Both were good experiences."

Tolliver smiled and tried to relax. "Okay, what's this hearing going to be like?"

"I can file a motion to quash the summons on the grounds that the State's Attorney, who drew up the papers for the judge, hasn't established a causal connection between you and the crime, and you and John Dietrich. For a number of reasons, I'm not inclined to do that."

"What reasons?"

"First, because it probably won't work. Unlike a subpoena that any lawyer can issue, this has already been to the judge and gotten his certificate. The reason for this is so it could be served on you out-of-state, but the effect is that the judge has already decided that the State's Attorney has established the connections and probable cause. Second, because of the foregoing, a motion to quash may be viewed by the judge as obstructionary, and have the effect of pissing him off."

"So we say okay, I go sit down. Then what?"

"I'm guessing something happened very recently, since the other Bridgeport cop came in and rousted you. They have to have something new to connect you to the matter because the judge would never allow the state to use anything that was fruit of the cop's illegal investigation and search. My hunch is they have a witness they just found, and they'll put you in a lineup. If the witness picks you out, he or she will be called to identify you in court, then you go."

"What if I don't get picked out?"

"There's common knowledge among criminals that the best way to avoid being identified in a lineup is to consciously look ordinary. No hard eyes, no aggressive posture, no attitude."

Tolliver chuckled. "Like the way to look your first days in boot camp."

"Exactly. Do nothing to be noticed by the drill instructors. The

State has to play fair in the lineup; put you in with people your approximate height, weight and age. They can't throw you in with five white guys and get an identification that would stand challenge. If the witness doesn't pick you out, we're back in New York for supper."

"Otherwise I go to court. I can take the Fifth Amendment; say nothing, right?"

"If you think you may be the subject of criminal prosecution. You haven't told me what this is all about, maybe you'd better."

Tolliver laid it out, from Johnny's first phone call to throwing the evidence in the Saugatuck River. "Jesus," O'Dwyer said, and was silent as they crossed the border into Connecticut.

ANGELA FOUND TOM in the dingy coffee shop across from the courthouse where, by unwritten agreement, defense lawyers hung out. Cops and prosecutors had the slightly better greasy spoon around the corner. "Tom, I've just left Johnny. He had another bad night and looks terrible."

Tom shrugged. "He's strong. We don't want him to look sleek and happy."

"His stomach pains are bad enough to keep him awake. I think we should try to get him into the hospital, at least let a real doctor look at him, do some tests."

Tom looked up from his papers. "You're assuming this trial is going to go on."

"Won't it? Tolliver is to appear in court this morning."

Tom took his cell phone out of his jacket pocket and laid it on top of his brief. "I just had the most interesting conversation with the famous F. Robert O'Dwyer of New York and every other state where the godly are wrongfully oppressed."

"O'Dwyer? *The* O'Dwyer?"

"Yes, mouthpiece to the rich and famous. You remember how he kept beating his chest about being a marine in that double murder in Los Angeles? Turns out he was a marine, not a lawyer, the combat type. Law school after. He's riding to the rescue as Tolliver's lawyer as we speak."

"What does that do for us? For Johnny?"

Tom waved to a passing waitress and mouthed "Coffee." "Take a seat and I'll tell you."

TOLLIVER AWOKE FROM a shallow sleep. He heard Robby's voice close-by, but indistinct. He shifted in the deep leather seat, sat up rubbing his eyes and running his tongue over sour teeth. Robby was hanging up his car phone. "What was all that about?" Tolliver said as the high-rise buildings of Stamford, Connecticut, moved slowly by in heavy traffic.

"That was your pal Johnny's lawyer. I called him this morning from my apartment and left my numbers with his service. He knows what you just told me; got it from Johnny, who, by the way, wanted you kept out of this. The State does have a witness, a woman who says you entered her house representing yourself as a gas company inspector."

Tolliver nodded. "I told you about that."

"That's their hook. The State is going to ask you one question, you'll take the Fifth, and the State will immediately tell you and the judge that, despite the fact that it could charge and indict you as an accessory to murder before and after the fact, it will not charge you with any crime. The State wants your buddy Johnny bad."

"Fuck the State. I'm not helping them put a noose around Johnny's neck."

"Willy, as your lawyer, I have to tell you the immunity from prosecution is to your great advantage. Besides, you can't refuse it. Once you are granted immunity, the criminal liability is eliminated, and since the Fifth Amendment privilege against self-incrimination is only intended to protect the witness against criminal prosecution, you have no privilege not to testify."

"I *have* to testify? Against Johnny?"

"Yes."

Tolliver shook his head. "Testify *truthfully?*"

"Yes. You'll be immune from prosecution in the matters included, i.e. the murders, lesser offenses like breaking and entering, a gun charge. You won't be immune to prosecution for perjury."

"What if I refuse to say anything?"

"The judge will throw you in jail for contempt."

"For how long?"

"Forever, or until you testify."

"Shit, Robby. I should never have let that cop take me. I don't want to do Johnny; I think he was perfectly justified in believing what he did and doing what he did. I want to help him."

"You can, but not by being a stand-up guy."

"I don't understand. Stand by Johnny is what I want to do and it's the right thing to do."

Robby turned and smiled. "Just like you, Staff Sergeant Tolliver. A marine through and through, 'up the hill, down the hill, through the hill.' "

"What are you suggesting," Tolliver growled, getting angry.

"That you help Johnny while not hurting yourself. Be a stand-up marine and he goes down. Roll over on him and maybe he finds a way out."

"Roll *over* on him?" Tolliver shouted. "On *Johnny?*"

"Yeah, Willy. Be a scumbag."

52

WILLY TOLLIVER STOOD around in the bowels of Police Head-quarters waiting for the lineup to begin. He and the other men had been instructed to change from whatever they were wearing into loose-fitting gray prison uniforms. Willy wondered where they had found the other guys, but it was pretty much as Robby had said, black men, heavy-set and middle-aged like him. Only one other man had a shaved head but another was bald. Six men in all.

The hearing in the judge's court had taken even less than the half hour Robby had predicted. Tolliver had been identified by Detective Kolslovsky as the subject of the judge's certificate, Robby had filed his appearance as Willy's counsel. The State's Attorney requested he be granted an immediate interview with the witness as soon as the lineup was concluded (no mention of what would happen if the witness failed to pick him out; Willy had seen Robby smile at that), and Johnny's lawyer, Tom Jackson, had requested an interview with the witness before his testimony. The State's Attorney objected, and the judge ruled for the State. Again Robby smiled. Tolliver began to feel a little better; Robby gave him confidence in this strange and unfamiliar world of men in black robes and odd phrases Tolliver thought but was by no means sure must be Latin.

Mike Kolslovsky brought Mrs. Perrone down to the basement, to the small hallway separated from the lineup room by one-way glass. The woman was calm; Mike thought fearless. Most people were very nervous before a lineup with a capital felon on the other side of the glass; most asked questions about whether the men in the lineup could see or hear the witness. Mrs. Perrone appeared merely curious, and eager to do her duty. She kept telling Mike how much she liked Jamal, and asking where he was.

The State's Attorney and lawyers for Johnny and Tolliver gathered in the room while Mrs. Perrone was led back outside. The lawyers would view the parade before the witness was brought in; George Carelli was taking no chances on getting his lineup set aside as inadmissible. The three lawyers watched through the glass as the seven black men were brought in, lined up and directed to face front. They were all dressed alike, and indeed looked much alike. Tolliver was second from the right, not the first person a witness would be expected to look at (the left-end position) or in the center. Carelli looked at Tom Jackson and Robert O'Dwyer; both nodded.

A uniformed policewoman joined the witness and Mike Kolslovsky in the anteroom, and the policewoman smiled at Mrs. Perrone. Mike noted that the policewoman was white, and wondered if that was planned; Bridgeport had very few white policewomen since hiring of women had come along at the same time as affirmative action. "Ready for you, ma'am," the policewoman said. Mrs. Perrone nodded, stuck her chin out and marched into the room behind the glass. The lawyers stood off to the side, but in earshot. "Take your time, Mrs. Perrone," the policewoman said as Mike stepped back. "Look at each man in turn."

Mrs. Perrone stepped right up to the glass and studied the seven faces. She opened her shoulder bag and extracted a glasses case. She exchanged the glasses in the case for the ones she was wearing, and looked at the men again. "It's different," she said.

"Mrs. Perrone?" the policewoman said.

"I saw the man that came into my house right up close, with my close-vision glasses, and that's the way I saw the photograph the black detective brought. May I see the photograph again?"

"No," the policewoman said. "You have to look at the men."

"These men are farther away, and even with my distance glasses I can't tell them apart."

Tom Jackson, Robby O'Dwyer and George Carelli looked at one another, each expressionless. Lineups were minefields and they all knew it.

"You can't recognize any of these men as the one who came to your house?" the policewoman prompted.

"I said I can't tell them apart. Can't they come closer?"

The policewoman looked helplessly at the State's Attorney, who was in urgent conversation with the other lawyers. "I want the men to step closer to the glass," Carelli pleaded. "The woman has two different glasses, and these guys are in some middle distance."

"It's the standard lineup, George," Tom Jackson said.

"She said she can't tell them apart," Robby O'Dwyer observed.

"Christ, guys, either you agree to let the men step closer to the glass, or we go back to the judge."

Tom and Robby looked at each other and shrugged. "They step forward, she decides, and that's it," Robby said. "No ID, and I take my client back to New York."

"Yeah," Tom said. "One close look with whatever glasses she wants, and that's it."

Carelli weighed it. The judge might give him more, or he might give him nothing. "Deal."

Mike went out into the corridor and opened the door to the lineup room. He instructed the policeman running the lineup and withdrew. The seven men were instructed to take two steps forward and stop a foot from the glass.

On the other side of the glass, Mrs. Perrone changed her glasses once again, then walked slowly back and forth, studying the faces that were only two or three feet away. All these black fellows look alike, she thought, but would never say such a thing. They all stood so still, where real people smiled or frowned and moved when they talked. She turned to the helpful policewoman who walked beside her. "Second from the right. That's the nice man who checked my range."

"Are you sure, Mrs. Perrone?"

"Yes, sure. Did I pick the wrong one?"

"Just be sure, Mrs. Perrone."

"I am. Can I go now?"

"I think you have to give a short statement, then Detective Kolslovsky will drive you home."

Mike came out of the shadows and took Mrs. Perrone's arm. My, aren't these detectives nice young men, she thought, pleased she had been able to help.

"WE'D BETTER GET back to court," George Carelli said with a grin he couldn't suppress. "We'll have the therapist and the State's psychiatrist, then your man." He marched from the room.

Robby took Tom's arm and pulled him close. "So it goes on. Too bad."

"This case will drown me. A crime that keeps growing like a bloodstain and a client who wants to be a martyr."

"Tolliver is most concerned that you tell your client what he's going to do before he does it."

"I'll prepare him, but not overmuch. He'll have a reason to show disgust, and I want the jury to see that."

"Okay, but tell him right after Tolliver is doing everything he can."

"Done. You coming into court?"

"I'm here; I might as well. You have your work cut out for you."

"Maybe lunch? Maybe we could talk about it?"

Robby frowned. Since the Trial of the Century in Los Angeles, he had sworn he would never share another defense. "I know your reputation; you're a top man."

"Not as famous as you, but to the extent I'm effective, it's because I never fail to listen."

"Lunch, then."

Tom held out his hand and F. Robert O'Dwyer shook it. Tom said, "I'll pick you up as soon as Judge Kerry calls a recess."

53

JUDGE KERRY FINALLY had the jury in the box at ten-thirty, and the State called Abigail Grieg. George Carelli got her name and occupation entered into the record, then stepped back and smiled encouragingly. He really didn't expect much from this witness; might not even have called her if he had been sure Tolliver would be found so quickly and made available. Still, she was a nice-looking woman, very professional, and would, he hoped, shed light on Johnny's mental state and probably reactions to stress. "Ms. Grieg, tell the court and the jury how you came to be involved with this tragedy."

Abby shifted in her seat. She'd never been in court before, and wasn't sure why she was there now. She'd dressed especially carefully in a red wool suit with a high collar, and she'd had her hair cut and styled. She felt as if she was on a stage, and she wondered who was pulling the strings, writing the lines, manipulating the lights. Carelli had brought her in for a short session a week ago, and she had taken an immediate dislike to the man. Evelyn Pulaski spent more time with her and was more sympathetic. *I'm a prosecution witness,* Abby thought, looking at Johnny between his lawyers and sending him a little smile. "Johnny Dietrich called me after the kidnapping. He asked me to help with the victim's family."

"John Dietrich, the defendant."

"Yes."

"What sort of help did he ask for, Ms. Grieg?"

"The girl's mother had seen the actual abduction, but was in shock and remembered little beyond her daughter's cry for help. Johnny wanted me to regress her to see if she could recall useful details."

"Details useful to whom?"

Abby shrugged. "To the police. To anyone wanting to find Sally."

"Did you give these details to the police? Did the defendant?"

"I didn't. I don't know what Johnny did."

George looked at the jury and raised his eyebrows. "So you went to the Collins house in Westport, and you regressed Mrs. Collins? Can you tell us what 'regressed' means?"

"The subject—Mrs. Collins—is first relaxed then induced into a semiconscious state in which she becomes very suggestible. The therapist—me—takes her step by step through the event, tries to pull details out of her memory that are blocked by the emotional content of the trauma."

"You hypnotized her."

"That's not a precise term, but yes."

"And she was able to provide details?"

"Some. Rough descriptions of the kidnappers. A license plate number."

"The defendant took note of the details?"

"I believe he did. So did Mr. Collins."

"But neither passed them on to the police."

"I don't know."

George waved her doubt away. "Did you stay in touch with the family as events went forward?"

"Yes. Mrs. Collins asked me to help her cope. When Sally came home, she asked me to talk to her, because she was very upset and rejected her parents."

"Were you present when the Bridgeport and Westport detectives interviewed the family?"

"Yes. I didn't do anything, I just wanted to protect Sally. She was in a very fragile state, and I didn't want to see her bullied."

"Was she bullied?"

"No. The detectives waited for the father and mother both to be present, and held their questions until all sorts of lawyers were called."

George took another little stroll past the jury. "Ms. Grieg, why would the defendant call you?"

"We're old friends. After my husband died, Johnny helped me get my degree and start my practice."

"Did the defendant ever consult you professionally?"

"Not formally. We talked a lot about Vietnam and what it had done to people."

"People like the defendant?"

"People like my dead husband, Mr. Carelli," Abby said heatedly, leaning forward. "Johnny helped me more than I ever did him."

Carelli paused, showed in his face that he shared her pain as he looked at the jury. "Ms. Grieg, you have told us that the defendant was not your patient, but you knew him well. In your professional opinion, did he suffer from stress-related illness?"

"That was no secret. Johnny went out of his way to help other troubled veterans improve their lives."

"How do men—men with this Post Traumatic Stress Disorder—react to sudden increases in stress?"

"Some have very strong reactions. Some appear to be unaffected by pressure that might break a person who had never experienced PTSD."

"How did the defendant react to the disappearance of Sally Collins?"

"He was very calm. Purposive, controlled, taking charge to help her parents who were incapacitated by their fears."

"Purposive and controlled." Carelli rolled the words off his tongue as he strolled in front of the jury box. "No further questions, Your Honor."

"Mr. Jackson?" the judge said.

Tom rose slowly. "Good morning, Ms. Grieg."

"Good morning, sir."

"Ms. Grieg, I'm wondering why the State called you here."

She smiled. "Me, too."

There was a stirring in the jury box. Tom looked over; they were bored. He turned back to the witness.

"Ms. Grieg, you testified that Johnny never consulted you professionally. Did you nonetheless form an opinion of his overall mental state?" Tom was skating on thin ice here; he was violating the courtroom lawyer's first principal: never ask a witness a question to which the lawyer did not already know the answer. Yet Tom had an instinctive liking for Abby Grieg, and he felt he could trust her. And he needed to build sympathy for his client in advance of Tolliver's testimony, that, however skillfully managed, would be devastating.

"He had a lot of pain," Abby said sadly, "but he dealt with it. Johnny dealt with his pain by helping others."

Tom breathed a little easier. "Was Johnny ever violent?"

"No. Far from it; he was gentle. He *helped* people."

George Carelli got up, Tom thought, reluctantly. "Objection. Counsel is asking questions about matters not testified on direct."

"With respect," Tom insisted. "Your Honor, the State asked the witness if the defendant had consulted her, and she answered: 'not formally, but we talked about Vietnam.' The jury might like to hear what they talked about whether the State followed its own line of inquiry or not."

"I'll allow it," Judge Kerry said.

Tom turned back to the pretty black woman, and tried to ease her own pain with his smile. "Johnny was never violent. How did he feel about children?"

"Very protective. He had a terrible experience in Vietnam with children—"

"Objection," Carelli said. "Hearsay. If the defendant takes the stand he can testify as to his experiences."

"Sustained," Judge Kerry said, making a note.

"Was Johnny protective of children? Within your own experience," Tom said, casting a challenging glance at the State's table.

"He helped me with my son, after my husband died. He helped other families of marines dead or damaged," Abby said hotly, staring at the State's Attorney. "And that was very difficult for Johnny, because he wasn't only damaged himself but also very shy. But he helped kids whenever he could."

"Ms. Grieg, how do you think Johnny *felt* when he learned of Sally Collins's kidnapping?"

Abby shuddered. "He was devastated. Sally is his goddaughter, you know."

Carelli rose again. "Objection, Your Honor. Witness has testified she didn't treat the defendant. This is conjecture."

"My response is the same, Your Honor," Tom Jackson said. "The State raised the conversations between the witness and my client."

"Overruled," Judge Kerry said, glowering at the State's table.

Tom looked over at the jury. "I didn't know Sally was Johnny's goddaughter. What did he say to you?"

"That he feared for her life. Johnny had made some study of statistics; when a kidnapping victim, especially a child, sees her abductors she is rarely returned alive whether the parents pay or not."

"As crime statistics clearly confirm."

"Objection, Your Honor," George said without conviction.

"I'm finished, Your Honor. Thank you, Ms. Grieg."

The judge tapped his gavel as Abby was led out of the courtroom. "I think that will be enough for this morning," he said. "We'll recess for lunch and begin again at two."

Tom found Robby O'Dwyer outside the courtroom after he got away from an aggressive TV reporter from channel 8. He took the famous lawyer's arm and led him down a back passage to an entrance manned by a single guard. "Do you eat Japanese food?" Tom asked when they reached his Mercedes.

"Live on it," Robby said.

Tom telephoned a restaurant called Sakura and asked for a private room, then drove to Westport in silence, sifting the morning's events through his mind, putting everything in order in the context of the case. Robby knew exactly what the other attorney was doing and left him in peace. When they had been led to a small room with a low table and tatami mats, surrendered their shoes, seated themselves and taken their first sips of green tea and sake, Tom spoke.

"We have a confused but sympathetic jury that is about to hear the State's psychiatrist tell them my client is unstable and deeply traumatized. Then they get Tolliver, and suddenly their reluctance to believe this good man killed those men will be swept away."

A Vietnamese waitress entered the room on her knees and placed tekka maki and tempura appetizers on the table and bowed herself out, begging pardon in badly accented Japanese. Robby thanked her in Vietnamese and she giggled. "Have you ever defended a guilty man in a capital case, Tom?" Robby asked.

"I don't think Johnny is guilty, at least not of murder with intent."

"But he did the deed."

"Yes, and I would have preferred the State had never gotten close to a proof than to have to start dealing with Johnny's motivation."

"As well as the conditions of the act." Robby picked up chopsticks, slipped the paper off and rubbed them together. He selected a piece of tekka maki, succulent raw tuna wrapped in rice spiced with hot wasabi and dried seaweed, and popped it into his mouth.

Tom watched him, then selected a deep-fried shrimp. He wasn't sure what he expected from the famous defense lawyer. "To answer you more fully, I've never defended a man who killed someone and felt such remorse. I've gotten a couple of very bad murderers pled down to manslaughter."

"Not an option here."

"No. If the jury believes he did it, they'll have to believe premeditation and intent."

Tom tried the shrimp, cutting the large piece deftly in half with his chopsticks.

"Is Johnny completely sane?"

"As much as any of us. I've asked myself from the very beginning of this case what I would have done if I had been Johnny and received the same information he had."

"And you concluded?"

"I believe I'd have gone to the police."

"Could they have handled it? If the kidnap had been real and enacted by desperate men?"

"Probably not. But these kids weren't pros, and I can't help feeling Johnny should have known that."

"Why?" Robby had reached the same conclusion when Tolliver had told his story, but wanted it confirmed.

"Because Johnny and Willy found the van and the house so quickly. Because the boys let Tolliver in when they could easily have refused—especially if they had been over the house just to check security—well enough to know it had no gas service. Because the house should have been guarded at night, or at least alert."

Robby nodded slowly, sipped his sake. "I tend to agree. But I have questions—questions I ask myself as a defense counsel, questions to help me get inside your client's head. First, you say you'd have called the police. I think I would have as well, but how? Ring up the general number? Call nine-one-one?"

"No, I'd have called the Chief of Detectives, Chief O'Hara."

"Because you know him, and because you are a well-regarded lawyer, he would have responded to you. Did Johnny know any Bridgeport cops?"

"I don't know. I don't know why he would have."

"Second, you were a marine; I was a marine. Tolliver told me he was sure the man he met was armed. Death threats had been made; the clock was ticking fast. If you didn't trust the cops, or believed you couldn't have interested the cops, what would you have done for your goddaughter?"

Tom smiled. He felt a great weight lifted off his heart. " 'Bout what Johnny did."

"Sure you would. Now let's figure out how to make that jury feel as we do."

54

DR. IDA MERRILL took the witness stand as soon as Judge Kerry gaveled the court into session. The afternoon had turned bleak and snow was falling. The courtroom was dim despite its ornate but dirty chandeliers. George Carrelli began by leading the psychiatrist through her qualifications as an expert witness, her degrees, papers she had published especially on Post Traumatic Stress Disorder, her many appearances at trial as an expert. "Dr. Merrill," George Carelli continued, "you examined the defendant at the request of the State, is that correct?"

"I did. I made my report to your office."

"Yes, of course. Please explain to the jury the scope of your examination."

"I was asked to determine whether the defendant was lucid, in sufficient control of his faculties to assist in his own defense, and whether he was in full control of himself and able to commit the offenses charged with criminal responsibility therefore."

"Tell us, please, what you concluded."

"The subject is quite capable of assisting in his own defense, and of understanding his acts."

"He's sane. He's criminally responsible."

"If he did this, yes," Dr. Merrill said acidly.

Carelli realized his mistake. The jury fidgeted, bored and fighting sleep. "Of course, Dr. Merrill. You did not examine the defendant directly about the crime."

"I could not, because the defendant has offered no statement."

"Quite. What did you talk about?"

"Mostly Vietnam. As is the case with so many traumatized veterans, Vietnam remains a central, even defining, event in Johnny Dietrich's life."

"*Traumatized* veterans?"

"Of course. I would categorize Mr. Dietrich as one who had made adjustments in his life to deal with his wounds, which is not to say the wounds themselves do not remain."

"How do you think the defendant would have reacted to the disappearance of Sally Collins?"

"He told me he formed a strong if unspoken bond with children during his duty in Vietnam. He had a particularly horrible experience in the city of Hue, in what turned out to be his last combat mission. He discovered a basement full of children murdered by the retreating enemy; he thought he'd failed them in a personal way. I believe he told me that story to show me exactly how he felt when Sally disappeared; a subject we otherwise couldn't address."

"The defendant felt responsible for Sally?"

"Yes, in a very personal way, because he knew from his experience in Vietnam what the parents could only guess at: that the girl was in mortal danger."

"The defendant would have felt compelled to rescue Sally? Even at risk of his own life?"

"Yes, I believe so. In the world Johnny left behind in Vietnam, exchanging one's own life for another's was a noble act."

No more of this, Carelli thought. He turned to Tom, Angela and Tolliver's lawyer, the hotshot F. Robert O'Dwyer, who had joined them at the defense table. "Your witness."

Tom stood and approached the witness stand. He held his chin in his hand and looked at the witness a bit sideways. She hadn't done any real damage and he was tempted to get rid of her quickly and have Tolliver all afternoon. "Dr. Merrill, you are an acknowledged expert on Post Traumatic Stress Disorder."

"I've written on the subject."

"Does Post Traumatic Stress Disorder lead to insanity?"

She frowned. "Not causally, no. Normally it is a disease that incapacitates its victims; renders them unable to function in society."

"In all cases?"

"No. I didn't mean to imply that. In most cases, patients recover, especially if they get competent help."

"You said Johnny had made adjustments in his life to deal with his wounds. Is Johnny coping, Dr. Merrill?"

"He is, or was. It's impossible to know what a trauma like the kidnapping of a favorite child might do to him."

Favorite child, Tom thought. Thank you. "Might it set him off into some sort of relapse? Some sort of journey in his mind back to the trauma of Vietnam?"

"It's possible."

"Possible *because* he has Post Traumatic Stress Disorder? Or possible for anyone confronting a kidnapping of this kind?"

"You're asking me to speculate."

"You're an expert, Dr. Merrill."

"It's possible that a PTSD sufferer might regress. It's possible anyone close to such a wrenching event might behave in an unpredictable way."

"Anyone close?"

"I said that."

"The victim's mother? Father?"

"Objection!" George Carelli jumped up. "Goes beyond—"

"Sustained. You know better, Mr. Jackson."

"I apologize to the Court. No further questions, Dr. Merrill. Your Honor."

Carelli threw an angry look at the defense table as he rushed back to his witness, who looked bemused. "Dr. Merrill, does the fact that Johnny had traumatic experiences in Vietnam, and in the United States upon his return, predispose him to lapse back into an earlier time, even after his treatment and recovery?"

"It could. It's the nature of the disorder."

"If he saw his earlier failures to protect children in a violent setting, could he see a need for violence in the matter of Sally Collins?"

"He might think that," Dr. Merrill said sharply, leaning forward, her black eyes flashing. "Or he might think just the opposite. Such a conclusion goes way beyond the scope of my examination of the defendant."

George mumbled, "Nothing further," and quick-stepped back to his seat.

"Well done," Robby O'Dwyer whispered. "Now for the main event."

"Yes, finally," Tom Jackson said. "And thank God."

IX

A FRIEND IN NEED

55

MRS. PERRONE COULD not be located. When Mike Kolslovsky
left her at her home, she had promised to stay put and wait for his
call, but she didn't answer. He went to her home, frantically interviewed neighbors. The denizens of Prescott Street saw and heard
nothing, as before, Mike thought sourly. Most likely as always.

Mike called in his lack of success to the State's Attorney, who
duly reported it to the judge, who steamed. George Carelli asked for
a conference with the judge in chambers, as much to buy time as
anything else. Where could a widow who, by her own admission,
rarely left her little house, have disappeared to? Robby O'Dwyer
looked a question at Tom Jackson and got a blank expression in return. "All *right*, gentlemen," Judge Kerry said, looking his apolo-
gies to the jury. "Chambers."

Carelli, Jackson and their assistants followed the judge into his
office. Robby O'Dwyer tagged along, interested in what the angry
judge might do. "Now, Mr. Carelli," the judge said, falling into his
big chair. "You got your witness, complete with high-priced counsel, dragged out from New York under my certificate. You've had
your lineup, by all reports a positive identification, and now at last
we are ready for testimony. You have inexplicably lost sight and
control of your enabling witness, an elderly lady of this city not
likely to flee." The judge was winding himself up and George
dreaded the next few minutes. "So the business of this court, already much delayed, must cease to wait upon your crack inves-

tigative staff's running this enabling witness to earth. Is that what you have to tell me?" The last sentence was a strangled shout.

"Your Honor, I beg the court's pardon; I'd thought Mrs. Perrone was under police escort. But the lineup was properly witnessed and recorded. If opposing counsel will stipulate to the identification, the Court's business may proceed."

Judge Kerry glared at Carelli for half a minute without speaking. "May I presume the State will allow this humble judge to determine what the Court's business is and when it may proceed?" he growled.

"Of course, Your Honor, I didn't mean to imply—"

"Be silent, Mr. Carelli. Does the defense wish to stipulate to the identification? Mr. Jackson?"

"We believe the jury should see that the witness, Mr. Tolliver, is here because he was compelled. The State has agreed to have him identified and immunized in open court." Tom looked over at Robby, who nodded.

"May I take that as a no?" the judge said acidly.

"As much as we'd like to be helpful, Your Honor," Tom began evenly.

"Fine," the judge said, cutting him off. "I'd like to throw this case out, but I'm reluctant to waste the time and inconvenience already taken from those citizens twiddling their thumbs in the jury box. I'll grant a continuance to the State for the purpose of securing the attendance of the witness Perrone until tomorrow morning at nine A.M." Judge Kerry leaned forward, seemed to be gathering his bulk to spring from the chair. "Mr. Carelli, you will not try the Court's patience further on this matter."

Carelli swallowed. "No, Your Honor."

There was a soft knock at the door and the judge's clerk stuck her head it. "Yes, Ermine?" the judge said.

"Detective Kolslovsky, Your Honor. He's located the witness and is bringing her into court."

The judge turned to George Carelli, who was pale but smiling weakly. "Regular Bulldog Drummond, your detective," Kerry said. "Let's get back to work. At least we'll get Perrone out of the way today before she absconds again." The judge allowed himself a bark of laughter in which the defense lawyers joined as George and Evelyn fled.

Mrs. Perrone took the witness stand with great solemnity. Mike had told George and Evelyn that the patrolman detailed belatedly to wait by her house had found the witness as she descended from a taxi after a trip to the beauty parlor. She had, she told Mike, wanted to look her best for him and that nice black detective who spent so much time talking to her.

Vera Perrone dressed with care for her court appearance in a severe black dress she hadn't worn since her husband's funeral five years ago. She had added a collar of fine old lace to give the dress a less somber mien, but it was still serious enough, she believed, for an appearance in a court where murder was being tried. She hoped her hair, carefully shampooed and tinted with silver, didn't look thin. As a girl she had thick black tresses but now she felt she was nearly bald.

She took her seat and was sworn by a woman clerk. The courtroom looked very grand and the judge very impressive in his black robes behind his high bench. Mrs. Perrone wondered why the jurors weren't more appropriately dressed for the occasion.

"Mrs. Perrone? I'm George Carelli, the State's Attorney. We spoke earlier."

"Of course," she said crisply.

"Mrs. Perrone, you're here in court to identify the man who came to your house on October seventeenth and asked to inspect your appliances for a gas leak. Do you understand?"

"Of course I do. I identified him this morning at a lineup."

"You did. Now could you point the man out here in court?"

Mrs. Perrone changed from close glasses to distant and peered around the courtroom. There were many black fellows in the audience, but none had the white coverall of a gas inspector or the gray uniform of the lineup. "I have to see them closer, like I did in my home—like I did in the lineup," she said querulously.

The judge shifted impatiently in his chair. Carelli looked away from him and offered Mrs. Perrone his arm, escorting her quickly down from the witness box and toward the railing that separated the gallery from the prosecution and defense tables. Tolliver was seated in the front row next to the county sheriff, himself a large black man.

Tom tensed his leg muscles, ready to object, but hesitated. The judge clearly intended for Tolliver to testify, and Mrs. Perrone had been sure enough in the lineup. He couldn't be seen to bully the dignified old lady.

"There he is," she said, stopping in front of Tolliver. She smiled at him. "It's nice to see you again."

There was a ripple of laughter from the gallery and smiles in the jury box. The judge stilled his court with a scowl. "Mrs. Perrone," George said softly. "Is this the man who came to your house about the gas?"

"Yes, it is," she said proudly.

George led her back to her chair in the witness box. "Your witness," he said to the defense.

Tom rose halfway to his feet. "No questions, Your Honor."

"Very well," Judge Kerry said. "We seem to be back on track at last. Due to the lateness of the hour, we will begin testimony from the State's *final* witness at ten tomorrow morning." The judge banged his gavel and rose immediately. All in the courtroom rose. Mrs. Perrone alone remained seated, confused. Mike Kolslovsky came over and offered her his arm. "I'll get a car to take you home, ma'am."

George Carelli came over and shook the old woman's hand.

"Thank you so much for doing your duty," he said, already turning away.

Vera Perrone looked at the detective. "You mean, that's *it?*" she said, her chin shaking.

"Yes. Here's Officer Martinez," Mike said, turning Mrs. Perrone over to the policewoman who had helped her through the lineup. "She'll run you home. And thank you." Mike turned and hurried after the State's Attorney.

Vera Perrone shook her head and allowed the policewoman to guide her up the corridor and out of the courtroom.

"I'M GLAD I called you," Tolliver told Robby O'Dwyer as they sat down to dinner at Fagan's Restaurant on the banks of the Housatonic River. "How you been keeping me from sleeping in jail?"

"Simple service of an eminent defense attorney," Robby said lightly, sipping his martini. Willy Tolliver was having a rare beer. "I stand surety for your appearance; you abscond and the judge throws me in jail."

"I see. Well, tomorrow that slick prosecutor gets his shot. I wish to hell I'd taken an earlier flight to the islands."

"If wishes were horses, et cetera. You're here, and you have to play the hand you've been dealt. You have any questions about how you handle this?"

"Tell the truth, the whole truth, and nothing but the truth."

"Right. As your lawyer and an officer of the court, those have to be my instructions."

"But I can interpret. I believe that was your word."

"Be very careful. We know what the State knows, from the trial transcript. We also know, or think we know, what they don't. They know what Johnny told the Collins family, they know what the crime scene looked like the morning after, but of course you never saw the inside of the house after your gas inspection the afternoon before. They know what the girl was able to tell the investigators."

"They don't know that Johnny was at the crime scene, but I have to put him there," Willy said slowly. "They don't know what became of the uniform, mask, gloves and most importantly, the weapon."

"Right, and they don't know, and you don't know, what actually happened inside the house."

"Johnny gonna testify about that? The way he saw it?"

"I doubt it. I sure as hell wouldn't put him on."

"So how's he get off?"

"The State has to prove its case. Without Johnny's testimony it's all conjecture; nobody saw Johnny do anything."

"And I be the chief conjecturer."

"Right. Now let's order," Robby said as a waiter stopped at their table. "Tom told me the poached salmon in puff pastry is excellent, also the Beef Wellington."

"Feel guilty eating like that when Johnny's rotting in his six-by-six cell," Tolliver said sadly.

"I did too, but Tom said he'll bring all of us back here when this is done."

ANGELA BROUGHT JOHNNY two thick sandwiches and a pint of split pea soup from the deli and sat with him in the interview room while he ate. She was pleased to find he had a good appetite away from the stale blandness of jailhouse food. He seemed upbeat, even cheerful on the eve of Tolliver's testimony, unaware despite her briefings and Tom's that Tolliver would have no choice but to place him at the crime scene and fill the biggest hole in the State's case.

Tom came in and sat down. He poured himself coffee from Angela's thermos and topped up her cup and Johnny's. "Just got off the phone with Tolliver's lawyer, Robby O'Dwyer. Nice guy for one so famous."

"Is Willy all right?" Johnny asked.

"He wishes he could stand beside you, even take your place in jail," Tom said carefully. "He's a very good friend. You have to understand he has to tell the truth, and that will be very damaging to the defense we'll have to present when he's done. If he tries to make you look as justified in your actions as we all believe you to be, he digs you in even deeper."

"It's all right. He tells the truth, then I do. The jury can decide."

"Johnny, it's our job to help the jury decide, and the jury wants and expects us to do that. I'm telling you this to prepare you for some of the things Tolliver may say that you won't like. Just keep in mind that he's your friend and biggest booster, and that he's following the lead of two excellent if occasionally devious lawyers."

"We don't have the right to lie."

"No, we don't. Truth, however, is a perception of facts. It's not absolute. We have the right to have the jury see truth as we see it. We have that *right,* Johnny."

Johnny finished his supper in silence. Tom got up and left with a shake of his head. "We believe in you, Johnny," Angela said, taking his hands and squeezing them. "What we do is right."

Johnny seemed a million miles away. He barely nodded when Angela called the guard, kissed his cheek and left.

56

FOR THE FIRST time since Sally Collins's testimony, the spectator seats in Judge Kerry's courtroom were filled before nine o'clock and the press gallery had a full complement of reporters, both print and electronic, although still no cameras. George Carelli had leaked copiously to his flacks at the *Connecticut Post* and the local radio and TV stations that today would be the day that would bust the case wide open for the State and remove a dangerous killer from the community.

Tom Jackson read excerpts from the paper to Robby O'Dwyer as they shared breakfast at the Marriott, where O'Dwyer and Tolliver were staying. "Thing old Knifefighter Carelli does best is manage the press," Tom fumed.

"So what?" Robby said. "This was my case, I'd be spinning too. The jury will read his bombast, even if they don't know he leaked it, and they won't like it. By my reading of the transcript, you've done an outstanding job of making the kidnap victim and her parents look like spoiled brats, and worse, people calling themselves victims who suffered no permanent harm. The working people on that panel will see Johnny more and more as one of them."

"Despite the fact that he killed three boys from more or less working-class families," Tom said sourly.

"I ain't saying it's easy, Tom."

"Your man ready?"

"Sure. Willy would say he 'has his mind right.' "

Tom finished his coffee and covered the check with a twenty-dollar bill. "Let's get on downtown," he said. He left the newspaper behind.

JUDGE KERRY TOOK his seat and looked out across the packed courtroom. This case had filled him with foreboding from its opening arguments. The victims weren't credible, the defendant too hurt-looking. The crime itself was bloody and sensational, but did the shot-up bodies of three men by themselves tell the story? Had the girl been kidnapped and then acquiesced in a "prank"? Had she participated in the crime—the first crime, that the trial had addressed only obliquely—or even designed it? What protection did the court owe the defendant, a man with a past full of troubled children, *murdered* children if the State's psychiatrist's report was accurate? Had he been drawn to the house on Prescott Street like a moth to a flame, or driven there like a lamb to the slaughter? Had he been misled? Had he acted rationally given the threat he perceived to the girl?

Judge Kerry had decided in his own mind that the defendant had indeed shot the three victims—a dangerous thing for a trial judge to assume. Now he wanted, as he was sure the jury wanted, to find out why. He banged his gavel and put on his reading glasses. "Mr. Carelli?"

"Your Honor, the State calls Wilson Tolliver."

Tolliver rose from his seat in the first row of the spectators' gallery and came down into the court. His attorney followed him and took a seat at the defense table as the witness was sworn. Willy felt shabby in his wrinkled slacks and blazer, and still feverish and fatigued.

"Mr. Tolliver," George Carelli said, approaching the witness box. "Please state your name, address and occupation."

Here we go, Kerry thought.

TOLLIVER PINNED THE State's Attorney with his eyes, even though Robby had told him not to. Be the man's adversary, Robby had said, because he has the power to throw you in jail. Then become his friend when he promises he won't. Tolliver answered questions about who he was and where he lived and worked. Carelli paced about, showing his goofy grin to the jury, telling them he was in control. Tolliver waited for the end of the soft questions, but not quite to the end, as Robby had instructed him. "Mr. Tolliver, how long have you known the defendant, Johnny Dietrich?"

Tolliver looked across at the defense table and saw Robby's hands were clasped. His signal. "Upon advice of counsel, I decline to answer on the grounds that it might incriminate me." Tolliver glared at the State's Attorney, then at the jury, and saw several members look away.

They're all afraid of a wild nigger from New York, Tolliver thought. Even the black jurors.

Carelli approached the bench, while looking at the jury with an expression that said he had been wronged. "Your Honor," he said. "The witness has been informed through his counsel and directly that the State of Connecticut will bring no charges related to this matter against him."

"Mr. Tolliver," the judge said, leaning over his high bench to peer down at Willy, "Do you understand that the State has given you immunity from prosecution in all matters relating to the charges against the defendant?"

"It's been explained to me, Your Honor."

"Do you therefore understand that you must answer all questions pertinent to this matter, and answer truthfully?"

"They can't get me for anything related to what happened? To what they say Johnny done?" Tolliver said, following Robby's script for all it was worth, and saying it in street-nigger jive that made several jurors wince.

"That's it. But you must answer fully and truthfully, or you will be held in contempt of this court."

"You throw me in jail." Tolliver grinned at the jury, all but winked at them.

"I can do that. Now, will you testify?"

"Sure. Don't want no damn jail, Your Honor."

George Carelli reapproached the witness. Tolliver thought he looked worried.

IN THE BACK of the courtroom, Jamal Jones looked worried as well. Damned stiff-necked Carelli, he thought, should have asked *me* about his prize witness. Jamal knew what Tolliver could do, and would. Jamal felt free of the case now, and free in his life. He'd all but decided to quit police work and find something where he actually did something useful, something tangible every day.

Despite himself, he was curious to see how far Willy Tolliver carried old Knifefighter George before he dropped him in the shit.

JOHNNY WATCHED TOLLIVER'S opening sparring with the State's Attorney. He was confused; Tolliver seemed almost glad to be testifying. Maybe he is, glad at last to get it off his chest. Johnny nodded to himself. I'll be glad to testify myself, when my turn finally comes.

CARELLI LOOKED THE witness in the eyes. The eyes of black men always disturbed him; they seemed yellowish, filled with anger and latent violence, like a tiger. George was afraid of this man so filled with hostility behind his bland expression, but he held the gaze tight. "Mr. Tolliver," he began carefully, speaking slowly as if to a child. "Tell the court and the jury how you came to enter the house of Mrs. Perrone, who earlier identified you in this court, representing yourself as an inspector for the gas company."

Tolliver grinned broadly. Carrelli waded right in just like Robby had predicted. "I was looking for some boys that had kidnapped a girl. We thought they'd be in that neighborhood because the local cops had found a van, earlier reported stolen, that matched a description of the kidnappers'."

Carelli began to relax, but he couldn't let the man run his mouth. "Just answer the questions as asked, please."

"Want you to get your money's worth," Tolliver said with a grin.

"Just answer, Mr. Tolliver," the judge growled.

"Yes, Your Honor," Tolliver said, still grinning.

"You entered the house at Eleven Prescott Street?"

"Don't recollect the number. Was the place I found the nervous boy and heard the girl arguing in a back room with another man."

"Then what did you do?"

"Drove back to Johnny's. Told him what I seen. Told him the boy had a gun in his waistband."

George saw the jury perk up, finally interested. He couldn't let himself be drawn down the blind alley of a gun that wasn't there. "What did Johnny say?"

"Said we had to get ready to rescue the girl."

"That same night?"

"Yeah. We wasn't really ready, but the parents had received another death threat. Johnny heard it."

"Describe your preparations."

Tolliver shrugged and grinned some more. "I didn't do much; I's just driving and watching out. Johnny got himself all dressed up in cammies and cleaned his weapon."

"What weapon?"

"I don't know. Submachine gun."

"Do you know how he obtained such an illegal weapon?"

Tolliver looked up at the judge as Robby's hands fluttered another sign. "I immune on the gun, too, Your Honor?"

"It's covered by the State's pleading, yes," Kerry said, scowling at Carelli, wondering if they'd immunized the wrong man.

"I got the gun," Tolliver said proudly. "Showed the boy how to use it."

Johnny was flabbergasted but kept his expression merely frozen. Tolliver was making this up as he went along, Johnny thought.

I wanted to tell my story to the jury and let them decide, Johnny thought ruefully. Be careful what you wish for.

Carelli led Tolliver to describe the trip back to Prescott Street in the early hours of the next morning. "I drove him over in my van and dropped him off at the end of the block," Tolliver said amiably, as if describing a normal errand. "Drove away."

"Then what happened?"

"Waited awhile," Tolliver said. No reason to tell this turd about the radios. "Drove back, picked him up at the same spot."

"Just the defendant?"

"Had the girl with him."

"What did he do inside the house?"

"Don't know. Wasn't in there."

"But you know what he planned to do."

"Him planned? Johnny, he don't plan; I had to do the planning."

Carelli knew Tolliver was lying but there was no way to stop him. His whole case hung on the testimony of a man he could neither impeach nor control. "What did you and the defendant plan for him to do?"

"He was supposed to bring the girl out. He did that; we drove her home. We went back to Johnny's house, had some coffee, then I drove back to New York."

"He didn't say what had happened inside the house?"

"No. He was real quiet. What did happen?"

Carelli looked helplessly at the judge. "He said nothing? Didn't mention he shot three men?"

"Objection," Tom Jackson said.

"Your Honor," Carelli pleaded. "I'm entitled to treat this witness as hostile."

"You've asked a borderline question," Judge Kerry said. "The jury should hear the answer."

"Mr. Tolliver, three men were shot inside the house at Eleven Prescott Street. Did the defendant tell you about that or not?"

"Didn't say a word. Just wanted to go to bed, so I left."

Carelli looked at the jury, showing his outrage on his face. Some jurors smirked, others looked confused. George turned back to the witness, who grinned like a clown. "The defendant wore camouflage clothing and carried a submachine gun. Do you know what he did with them?"

"Fool left all that stuff in my van. Lucky I found it before I got back to New York."

Carelli hated to ask the next question, but he had to. "What did you do with the clothing and the weapon?"

"Threw them in a river."

"What river? Where?"

"No idea. Some river with a bridge over it. I never been in Connecticut before, I don't know."

Carelli turned to the jury. He wanted to scream that Tolliver was lying, taking the blame for much of what Johnny had done, burying it under his immunity. He pleaded with the jurors to understand what was happening, what had gone so wrong. He turned away, and walked slowly back to his table. To Tom Jackson he said, "Your witness."

Tom stood, and pretended to consult his notes for a moment before approaching the witness, who sat waiting with the expression of a contented cat. Tom knew that Tolliver was lying, trying to mitigate Johnny's guilt by taking more of the responsibility for the rescue onto himself. Tom wondered how much of what Tolliver was saying had been scripted by his attorney, and how much the witness was simply winging it. Whether he was helping Johnny or not, witnesses going off on their own were dangerous, because they deprived their interrogator of his most valuable asset: foreknowledge of the witness's answer to any question. "Morning, Mr. Tolliver."

"Morning, sir."

"Mr. Tolliver, did you come forward voluntarily to testify at this trial?"

"No, sir. The Bridgeport cops sent a man in to tape my voice for some reason and I ran him off. Then they sent that fellow there"—

Tolliver pointed to Mike Kolslovsky at the state's table—"with some kind of court paper that said I had to come here and that I could be arrested and put in jail if I didn't."

"Yet when you first sat down, you refused to answer, invoking Fifth Amendment privilege."

"I did. I wasn't going to testify against myself since the prosecutor is saying three men were murdered."

"Did the State make any promises to you?"

"Sure did. I answer the questions here and I walk on all the accessory to murder charges."

"But you have to testify against a friend."

"He is my friend, and I hope he forgives me, but I don't got to go to jail for him."

Better leave it, Tom thought. He's done what he came to do, muddy the waters, make the jury think Johnny's responsibility for the crime should at least be shared, and shared by a disloyal friend paid with the State's coin. Tom stepped back and addressed the judge. "Nothing further, Your Honor."

"Redirect, Mr. Carelli?"

"No, Your Honor. The State rests."

"Fine. Mr. Jackson?"

"The Defense will be ready after lunch, Your Honor."

"Excellent. Court is adjourned until two o'clock."

57

"THAT DIDN'T GO at all as I expected," Tom said angrily, slamming his briefcase down on the table in the interview room. "Fucking F. Robert O'Dwyer playing the games that made him famous."

Angela sat down and smiled at Johnny. "The witness came across as rolling over on his friend, and perhaps lying into the bargain."

"I can't believe he said so much," Johnny said bleakly. "Did he have to say all that?"

"Once the State had him at the scene, entering at least two homes under false pretenses, the State had enough to charge him, and thus to immunize him," Tom said. "But his gratuitous remarks about his planning the rescue doesn't make your actions any less premeditated, if that's what he was thinking, and his saying he doesn't know what went on inside the house because you never told him is an obvious lie the jury will remember. You went in and came out with the girl; the men got shot during the same time." Tom got up and began to pace in the tiny room. "The question is what are we to do about it."

"The jurors know what happened in that house," Johnny said. "They've known from the beginning what happened, and now they know I did the shooting. There's nothing left to do but let me tell them why."

"I've told you, Johnny, why doesn't necessarily help. You can't sneak into a darkened house with a weapon no matter how good your intentions."

"If you say that's the law, I'm sure you're right," Johnny said doggedly. "The jury's only remaining decision is how to punish me, and to decide that they have to know why I did what I did."

"No," Tom said gently, sitting down. "I won't put you on the stand to confirm your own guilt. Think of the State's close—the very last thing the jury will hear. The bloody bodies, the young lives cut short by a man with a gun snatching a girl out of an innocent sleepover. No, we'll put Dr. Lewes, the psychiatrist, on to say you suffered a flashback, that you were shooting at shadows nearly thirty years old."

"We agreed at the beginning," Johnny said, his voice growing hard. "I wasn't crazy and I'm not."

"You were set up," Tom said, fighting down his own anger. "Those dumbass kids sucked you into their crazy plot and the threats to the Collinses provided the spark. Those kids—especially the damn girl, who walks away from this without a scratch—were no more innocent victims than a man who walks up to a grizzly bear and kicks it in the balls."

"I want to testify. I have nothing to lose."

"No, it's madness. Let me argue that your disorientation made full understanding of your actions impossible, and therefore premeditation impossible. Get the judge to instruct the jury with an option of murder without intent. Don't forget: this's a death penalty state."

"I could die with a clear conscience."

"Maybe," Angela interjected, "there's another way, a way you both can live with."

Tom got up. "You chat about it. I'll admit I need ideas, but now I've got to go prepare Dr. Lewes."

"I DIDN'T DO any good," Tolliver said angrily as he walked around Bridgeport's trash-choked Main Street near the courthouse.

Robby O'Dwyer, a much shorter man than Tolliver, hurried to keep pace. "Willy, the guy did the shooting. Nothing you could have said changes that, and having you hauled out of the witness box and jailed would have made Johnny look infinitely worse."

"I still feel I let him down. To think all I had to do was to stay the hell out of sight for a few days and he'd be walking free."

"You don't know that. The State's case has been poorly presented, but the elements are there. Johnny was recruited by the parents, he went out and brought the girl back. The kidnappers died. If you hadn't been found, Tom Jackson would have asked the Court for a judgment of acquittal; he thinks he'd have gotten it. I don't. Judges don't like to keep juries sitting through long arguments, then take the decision out of their hands. Tom would have had to mount a defense, and it would have been a mistake, at least in my view, simply to tell the jury the State hasn't proved Johnny was there."

"How would you defend Johnny? If you had to start right now."

"I don't want to second-guess the lawyer who has been working on this since the day of the shooting. It's a very difficult matter because neither the facts nor the law are any help to him."

"Would you put Johnny on the stand?"

"The conventional wisdom among defense lawyers is you never put the defendant on the stand, because on cross-examination the prosecutor can ask questions he has been unable to prove in his own case-in-chief. Hell, the prosecutor could walk right up to Johnny and say, 'Did you shoot those men?' The witness can't lie, can't dissemble. 'Sure, I shot them, with the weapon you never could find, but I can explain.' It can't work."

"There has to be something."

"Yeah, well I'm thinking."

Tolliver took the lawyer's arm. "Now I've testified, can you get me in to see Johnny?"

"I'll have to go through his attorney. We could try to find them now."

"Good. At least I can talk to him, if he'll still talk to me."

DOCTOR LEWES STARED out a dirty window at heavy rain. "I'll testify as to his state of mind when he entered the house, Tom," he said. "I take it you won't be putting him on."

They were meeting in an empty courtroom two doors down from Judge Kerry's. "He wants to testify," Tom said, throwing up his arms. "I can't let him be cross-examined."

"He might be effective. A lot of these post-traumatic stress cases have almost total recall of their illusions. Reality to him when he entered the house was what he saw, even though he knew *at the time* that it was impossible."

"How's that going to do any good?"

"Perhaps, *perhaps,* he could show the jury what he saw. Perhaps they'll see that what he did was appropriate to the time and place he felt he was."

"How's that help? There's no insanity defense in this state, as you well know."

Dr. Lewes took Tom's arm. "Let's discuss that."

Angela explained her concept of defense to Johnny. He liked it, despite the fact that she admitted Tom wouldn't. "It's an outside chance, but it gets you what you said you wanted, a chance to explain."

"Why won't Tom like it?"

"Because it's a cheap theatric. The State will scream and the judge will agree. Tom, or I or both of us, could face sanctions, and the judge will instruct the jury to disregard said cheap theatric."

"I want to do it."

"I'd better go get it, then. Be prepared to have a fight with Tom."

"Ms. Hughes?" A guard stood at the door of the interview room. "Mr. Tolliver and his attorney are out front. Mr. Tolliver wants to come in and see Mr. Dietrich if you'll allow it."

Angela looked at Johnny, who smiled and nodded. "Sure."

George Carelli got out the stained coffee cups and a sealed bottle of whiskey. "Let's see old Stonewall wriggle out of this one," he said, pouring and shoving cups toward Evelyn Pulaski and Mike Kolslovsky.

"The witness was all over the map," Evelyn said, sipping. "You did a hell of a job controlling him."

"Yeah, boss," Mike said. "I'm surprised the guy didn't just confess to doing the killings himself, let Johnny be the wheel man."

"He probably would have if F. Fucking Robert O'Dwyer had let him," George said. "Willy Tolliver was arrogant to the point of taunting. He knew perfectly well what he was doing, and the jury will inevitably compare him to the humble, suffering defendant. As a ploy to confuse the jury, it was brilliant, but nonetheless, the jury got to hear the magic words: Johnny was there, he went in, he came out with the girl. That confirms her story, at least up to her own embellishments. At worst, Tolliver got rid of some of the lesser-included offenses, the gun, disposing of evidence. We still got our three vics and the jury will be reminded of that before we're done."

"Do you think Jackson will put the defendant on the stand?"

Carelli refilled his cup and drank it off. "He's damned either way. Johnny says nothing the jury will conclude what the judge will tell them *not* to conclude: that he's guilty. If he testifies, he has to answer to me on cross, and what's he gonna say?"

"You gonna ask for death?" Mike asked softly.

"No, and I'll say so in my close. No point risking the emergence of a bleeding heart on the jury."

"I want to get some air," Mike said, rising. "I'll catch you in court after lunch."

Carelli nodded. After Mike closed the door behind him, George said, "Mike's still not sure we should have tried this guy."

Evelyn shrugged. "He did what he did. Johnny's style of justice disappeared with Committees of Vigilance and the Ku Klux Klan."

"I have to wonder, though, what set him off inside that house? Those boys wouldn't have offered any resistance if he'd just walked in and grabbed the girl."

"We'll never know."

"Unless he testifies."

TOLLIVER EASED INTO a seat opposite Johnny, who hadn't moved when the guard let the big man in. Tolliver had been searched with offensive thoroughness before they had let him into the jail area, and all his personal articles including his watch had been collected. Johnny looked at him with no expression at all. "Hey, Johnny, man. It's okay you're pissed. I had to say what I did and I tried to, you know, share the blame."

"I don't blame you, Willy," Johnny said tiredly. "I fucked up and that's it."

"I believed the shoot was righteous. I still do."

"When the cops got to that house, they found no weapons."

"Shit, maybe they took whatever the guys had. Cops are always looking for untraceable weapons."

"I doubt the uniforms would lift weapons from a homicide scene, and the two detectives seem pretty straight guys."

"Man, I'm sure the kid I talked to had a piece in his waistband. What else he be reaching for? And you told me the first man up had him an AKS."

"It wasn't found. No weapons were found. Besides, it doesn't matter. I had no right as a private citizen to enter that house or any other, weapons or no, kidnap or no. I should have told the police."

"Bullshit. You had every reason to believe the girl would die long before the cops in this town would have done anything."

Johnny looked up. "We did believe that, didn't we?"

"Sure we did. So'd the girl's parents, you said."

"Yeah. But it won't matter."

"Hell it won't. You tell the jury. You're gonna testify."

"I want to testify. My lawyer doesn't want me to."

"Fuck him. This ain't a thing gnawing on his soul. Ain't his ass gonna rot in jail if you don't get that jury to see what *you* saw, what *you* knew, what *you* did."

"I guess I'll try."

"No. Try, no. You *will*. And when you do, you *will* have your mind right."

A NGELA AND TOM met for lunch at a restaurant called Pjura's a few blocks from the courthouse. Angela explained what she wanted to do, and what Johnny did. She thought Tom would shout her down, question her judgment if not her sanity, but he listened quietly, interrupting only a couple of times with questions as she laid it out. "The judge is gonna shit," he said simply when she finished.

"He will. And Carelli will scream blue murder."

"So how do we explain this to His Honor?"

"The presentation of the evidence? You don't; you insist it was an accident. The evidence itself? It goes against the defense theory that Johnny intended to go in blazing; that he planned to shoot."

"Judge Kerry is too old a dog to buy that."

"What's he going to do? Declare a mistrial? Would Johnny be worse off if he did?"

"All right. How do we work the timing? We have to be perfectly coordinated."

"I have some ideas on that," she said.

J UDGE KERRY TOOK his seat at exactly two o'clock. "Is the Defense ready to proceed?" he asked.

Tom stood at his table. "We are, Your Honor. Defense calls Jamal Jones."

There was a ripple of whispers between Mike Kolslovsky and Evelyn Pulaski, quickly suppressed by George Carelli. Jamal came down from the spectators' gallery, dressed in a double-breasted gray suit, a starched white shirt and a Hermès tie of bright blue silk with a yellow figure. He had been stopped in the hall barely a half hour earlier by Tom Jackson, pulled aside and questioned. Tom had then told him what he would ask and Jamal answered, but he couldn't figure why the defense attorney wanted any of it.

Tom approached the witness box as soon as Jamal was sworn. "Detective Jones, you were the lead investigator in the homicides on Prescott Street last autumn, were you not?"

"I was."

"I hand you a copy of your report of findings at the crime scene, before anything was disturbed. Do you recognize it and your signature?"

Jamal glanced at the report and made to hand it back. Tom held up his hand; no. "This is my report," Jamal said.

"Turn to page two, please, and read down from the paper clip."

Jamal read. " 'Positions of the decedents. Subject number one, a white male identified from wallet contents as Gilbert Herrero of Eleven Prescott Street, Bridgeport. Found next to an upset chair in the living room clutching a street hockey stick. Victim number two, identified as—' "

Tom held up his hand and smiled. "Thank you, Detective. Was this street hockey stick taken into evidence? Marked and numbered?"

Jamal read further down the report. "Bagged and tagged as number thirty-one."

Tom looked up at the jury. Bored, bemused. He turned to Carelli. "Your witness."

George started to rise, then shook his head. Judge Kerry excused Jamal and looked crossly at Tom Jackson. "Defense calls Dr. Frederick Lewes," Tom said quickly.

Dr. Lewes took the stand and was sworn. He was a handsome, dignified man in his late sixties, dressed in a well-cut blue wool suit and an old-fashioned tattersall vest. He had silver hair, blue eyes and an engaging general-purpose smile. He was deeply tanned from frequent visits to his house and sport-fishing boat in the Bahamas.

Tom Jackson led his witness through a recitation of his university degrees, his membership in professional societies, and the accomplishments of a long career. He listed a few of the many cases at which he had been asked to testify. All of this was to establish his qualifications as an expert witness. The jury looked very satisfied.

"Dr. Lewes, did you examine the defendant, Johnny Dietrich?" Tom asked.

"I did, at your request."

"Do you recall why I made that request?"

"Because the State had ordered its own psychiatric examination."

"Quite. Where did your examination take place?"

"In the jail here in Bridgeport. The patient was incarcerated."

"What were your findings?"

"The patient was lucid, calm, truthful and forthcoming. Especially so given the stressful nature of his surroundings and the seriousness of the charges lodged against him."

"Was the patient suffering from stress?"

"Yes. Quite normal under the circumstances."

"Did you discuss any earlier problems Johnny may have had with stress?"

"We did. Johnny told me he had been diagnosed many years ago with Post Traumatic Stress Disorder resulting from trauma he suffered during and after the Vietnam War."

"In your opinion, was that diagnosis correct?"

"Probably yes."

"Can you tell us a little about this disorder?"

"It comes about when a person in subjected to emotional trauma, usually in a situation where it would be impossible or inappropriate for the individual to stop and take stock, try to deal with the problem. Soldiers often suffer from this disorder, so do firemen and emergency workers, air traffic controllers, the like. The bottled-up stress returns to the patient again and again, often in very vivid dreams that disturb sleep, even render it a feared state, adding further to the stress."

"Did you discuss dreams with Johnny?"

"Yes. Like many other sufferers, he has repetitive dreams that are extremely detailed. He can recall all sorts of texture not normally associated with dreaming: smells, tastes, heat and cold, dampness. The feeling in his hands when he touches the victims in his dream."

"Who are the victims in his dreams?"

"Little children. Vietnamese children. Apparently he developed a strong attachment to children when he was serving in Vietnam, and he saw a great many brutally murdered."

Tom took a little stroll by the jury box. They all looked riveted. Dr. Lewes was good; most expert witnesses were pompous and dull. "Dr. Lewes, is it possible that a Post Traumatic Stress Disorder sufferer would mistake his dream for reality?"

"It is, often with tragic consequences. Normally though, when a sufferer receives support and treatment, he learns to accept the dream, even with its horrific message."

"Johnny received treatment, then?"

"Yes, at a VA hospital in New Haven, another in Brooklyn, New York, and finally and most effectively at an outreach program in Manhattan." Tom had told the doctor to run on a bit here, not wanting to alert the jury that Johnny's friend Tolliver, who had just rolled all over him, directed the Manhattan treatment program. "The patient spent nearly four months in the outreach program, and counselors there encouraged him to write. His books brought his conflicts with his past into focus, and made him wealthy as well."

"Johnny's treatment was successful? He's cured?"

"Sadly, PTSD patients are rarely cured, but they learn to deal with the destructive elements of the disorder."

"Destructive elements?"

"Almost always self-destructive. Drugs. Alcohol. Spousal abuse."

"What did Johnny tell you about such behavior?"

Dr. Lewes frowned. "He told me he had severe depression because of a loss of control he experienced as a result of the flashbacks, and that he began to drink heavily to suppress the dreams. It didn't work, of course, except over short periods of alcoholic coma, because the brain, especially the troubled brain, needs to dream. Nonetheless, Johnny continued to drink until he was taken in by the marine outreach program."

"Since then?"

"He doesn't drink. Hasn't drunk in more than twenty years. He copes."

"How would the dreams affect a man in Johnny's state of coping?"

"He dreams, and as I said, recognizes and accepts the dream. He knows he's dreaming, but during a flashback he may feel he is in both past and present. Psychiatrists call it a 'fugue state.' In Johnny's case, Vietnam nearly thirty years ago and here and now."

"I see," Tom said. "But he'd know where he *really* was, place and time?"

"Yes. But he might feel the other experience as kind of a parallel, like watching a movie while sitting in his own living room."

"But he wouldn't enter the movie as an actor? If a character in the dream fired a gun at him, Johnny wouldn't fire back?"

"No more than you'd be likely to shoot out your own television set."

"Thank you, Dr. Lewes," Tom said, stepping back. "Your witness," he said to George Carelli.

The State's Attorney was up at once, bounding forward, rubbing his hands together. "Dr. Lewes, did you reach any conclusion as to the defendant's sanity?"

"I believe the defendant is sane."

"Specifically, was he 'lacking in capacity as a result of mental disease or defect either to appreciate the wrongfulness of his conduct or to conform his conduct to the law'?"

Tom Jackson was quickly on his feet. "Objection, Your Honor. The State is quoting the specifications of 'guilty but not criminally responsible' under the Connecticut statutes. No such plea has been offered."

"I'll rephrase," George said quickly. "In your opinion, Doctor, would this defendant be likely to fail to appreciate the rightness or wrongness of his actions, or be compelled, perhaps by his dreams, to act even though he knew his actions were unlawful and wrong?"

"Objection!" Tom shouted.

"Sustained," Judge Kerry said wearily.

George turned and smiled at Tom. "Nothing further, Your Honor."

Tom stepped forward. "Dr. Lewes, did I, or any member of my office, or the defendant himself, ever suggest to you that he was contemplating a defense of diminished capacity? Of insanity?"

"No, sir," Dr. Lewes said. "You did not."

Tom turned and smiled at George, whose expression was taut. Gotcha, George, Tom thought. It's in the jurors' minds now, and you put it there.

Tom turned back to the judge. "Defense calls John Dietrich."

58

THE JUDGE OFFERED a recess, or an adjournment until the following morning, but Tom said the defendant was ready and eager to tell his story. The judge nodded his assent.

Tom looked up at the high dirty windows of the old courtroom, of the coming gloom of a winter afternoon under leaden sky, gloom that seemed to dim the dusty chandeliers high above. The gathering dusk reflected the attorney's mood.

Johnny came up and was sworn. Tom shook off his doubts and felt charged, alert, but anxious as he approached his witness. He had only put murder defendants on the stand twice in a long career, and both of them had been smooth, pathological liars, not this would-be saint seeking absolution from a jury of his peers. Angela got up and walked out of the courtroom as Tom led Johnny through a few easy questions to loosen him up, but Johnny already seemed loose, even serene. Tom took him through his early involvement in the matter, Edward Collins's unannounced visit and request for a million dollars in ransom. "Did Mr. Collins seem genuinely worried?"

"He did," Johnny said, watching the jury. "He was terrified for his daughter's safety."

"But you didn't lend him the money. Could you have?"

"I had the money; I told him I'd give it to him if that would help, but that crime statistics showed that once the girl had seen her captors, they'd kill her as soon as he paid."

"How did you come upon those statistics?"

"On the Internet. I support the Children's Defense Fund; they compile them."

Tom looked at the jury. Several women nodded; he doubted they had ever heard of such statistics before this trial, but now they'd heard them several times, with no rebuttal. "What did you do then?"

Johnny related his going, with Edward, to the Collins home and the regression by Abby of Mrs. Collins. He talked of Tolliver's coming out from New York with his van and the equipment he needed to rescue the girl. He confirmed Tolliver's story of his entering the house on the pretext of looking for a gas leak, and his discoveries of a youth with a gun who had little knowledge of the house that turned out to have no gas service at all, and the voices down the hall. He related how he had heard the second death threat at the Collins house, and how he had decided to go after the girl that very night.

"Did you consider going to the police?" Tom asked.

"The parents were afraid to, and there didn't seem to be time."

"When you prepared to enter the house, you dressed in camouflage uniform, gloves, a mask. Why? You thought your rescue was justified."

"I didn't want to be seen in a darkened house. The mask and the rest were to prevent my being seen, not recognized."

"Why did you go in armed?" Tom asked delicately. He didn't want to spend time on this question, to raise it again in the minds of jurors, but the defense theory rested heavily on Johnny's intent.

"Willy—Mr. Tolliver—said the man he saw in the house had reached behind himself for a pistol. It seemed reasonable to expect kidnappers to be armed, and if they were, I'd have to oppose them with arms to rescue the girl."

Tom nodded at the jury, signaling them that this was reasonable. "Did you intend to shoot the kidnappers? To punish them for the pain they had caused the girl and her parents?"

"No. I just wanted to take Sally home."

Tom let that sink in. "Why did you shoot?"

Johnny drew himself up. "Because one of the kidnappers came at me with a weapon, a carbine. I saw him bring it up and I fired."

The courtroom erupted, everyone talking at once. Even jurors were getting up and turning this way and that until the judge gaveled the court to order and silence.

"Johnny," Tom said softly. "Let's go back to the time when you first approached the house at Eleven Prescott Street. Take us through it exactly as you saw it."

"Exactly as I saw it?" Johnny was suddenly agitated. Tom had wanted a reaction and hadn't prepared his client for this question.

"Exactly. Paint a picture for us."

ANGELA WAITED IN an empty courtroom, the evidence in its bag on a table beside her. After lunch, she had gone to a Radio Shack on Main Street and purchased a baby monitor. The device consisted of a tiny battery-operated transmitter, now sitting on the defense table, and a receiver on the table in front of her in the empty courtroom. She could hear Johnny. She could hear Tom quite clearly when he faced the table. She could not of course be heard by him as she waited for his signal. It wouldn't be long now.

"WHEN I WENT through the window, I stumbled," Johnny said, his eyes closed as he remembered. "I fell, and suddenly I felt the presence of Vietnam. I seemed to fall down a tunnel, quite a steep one, and very dark. Then the moon came from behind a cloud and I could see the room quite clearly. I had memorized the plan Tolliver had given me of the house, and I started back toward the bedrooms."

Tom held up his hands. "Let's be absolutely clear on this. You felt the presence of Vietnam."

"Yes, memory. I felt the tunnel and smelled it. I even heard distant voices, speaking Vietnamese."

"But you knew Vietnam was a memory. You knew what you were doing and where."

"Of course."

"Then what?"

"Then a man rose up out of a shadow with a carbine."

"A man, or an old memory? A Vietcong soldier?"

"It felt like that, but I knew he couldn't be. But it was an armed man."

"Could you recognize the weapon?"

"Yes. A Russian AKS."

Tom went to the defense table and picked up a newspaper. "May it please the court, I have here a copy of the *Connecticut Post* of last July tenth. There is a front-page article about the seizure of twelve Russian-made AKS and AK 47 carbines at the Marina Village Housing Project in Bridgeport. Could I have this marked as Defense Exhibit A and shown to the jury?"

The judge nodded and made a note. The original newspaper was marked and passed to the jury foreman, Tom gave a copy to the State. "Your honor, I have a couple of slides I'd like to present to show the jury what sort of a weapon the defendant has identified."

"If it will speed things up, Mr. Jackson. It's getting late."

Tom turned on a slide projector on the defense table and aimed it at a white posterboard he had placed on an easel next to the table before the afternoon session began. He turned back to the judge. "May we have the overhead lights down a little?"

The judge nodded to a bailiff in the rear of the court and the lights dimmed. Tom inserted his first slide. There were silhouettes of three weapons. "Johnny can you identify these carbines for the court?"

"The one on the left is an AK 47, a standard Russian infantry weapon. Next to it is an American M-16. On the right, the one with no shoulder stock, is an AKS."

Tom watched as the jurors craned forward. He changed the slide and a blowup of the AKS replaced the three weapons. "This, Johnny?"

"That's what I saw. An AKS."

The door at the rear of the courtroom burst open with a bang. Framed in the bright light from the corridor was a figure advancing rapidly down the aisle, carrying what looked very much like the weapon on the slide high across the body.

A woman screamed, then another. Men shouted and tried to move away from the aisle. A bailiff seated in front of the bench rose and put his hand on his weapon. The judge pounded his gavel, yelled for order and "Lights, damn it!" The bailiff in the rear of the courtroom, who had seen what Angela carried and was not alarmed, turned up the chandeliers to maximum brightness. Angela reached the front of the courtroom and handed the hockey stick, still wrapped in clear plastic, to Tom, who handed it up to the judge. "Defense Exhibit B, Your Honor," Tom said dryly. The judge stared at it in disbelief, his gavel still pounding as if on its own.

X

JUDGMENT

59

GEORGE CARELLI RUSHED to the bench, his face red, his arms flapping as Judge Kerry's pounding gavel finally restored order. Tom Jackson stood aside to let him flap. "Your Honor," George rasped, barely in control. "The State most strenuously objects to this farce. Defense's conduct is improper and designed to engender prejudice, perhaps prejudice severe enough to cause the Court to consider a mistrial."

"You want a *mistrial?*" the judge choked.

"No, but I demand the defense be warned and sanctioned in front of the jury."

"Now stop, Mr. Carelli. Mr. Jackson, don't say a word. I could take this apart in chambers, but I'm more inclined to send the jury out—better yet, send them home for the night."

Carelli fairly jumped up and down. "Your Honor! You can't let them go home with this charade fresh in their minds."

"Nevertheless, that's what I'm going to do. I want to hear from you both as soon as the jury retires." The judge raised his voice. "Bailiff? Show the jury out, please, then clear the courtroom of spectators." The judge bent his head and wrote notes. Carelli, seeing he was being ignored, went back to his table to consult with his junior as uniformed bailiffs cleared the court, once again abuzz with chatter.

Judge Kerry was furious, seething. He prided himself in his ability to control his court, and he had just seen it turned into the center ring of a cheap-ticket circus. Courtroom tricks were the last refuge of desperate attorneys, and as such inexcusable. He completed his notes, took several deep breaths, and reminded himself to be impartial before he flayed Stonewall Jackson's hide from his flesh. "All right, gentlemen, come down. Mr. Carelli, you wished to object?"

"Yes, Your Honor. I object to the introduction of this *toy* into evidence because it's *irrelevant*. I object to the manner in which it was introduced as inflammatory and designed by a desperate defense reduced to conjuring tricks to sway the jury away from the mountain of facts that accuse the defendant."

The judge smiled. "Mr. Jackson?" he said sweetly.

Tom stepped forward, trying to show in face and posture confidence he didn't feel. "Your Honor, we take exception to the State's characterizing of our bringing evidence into court as a conjuring trick. Ms. Hughes went to the police property room at my request, and only just now returned. I was in fact concerned that she would not arrive in time for the exhibit to be entered. As to the item itself, it is a piece collected from the crime scene by the police that they thought significant enough to tag, log and preserve. While repeating that the defense had no ulterior motive in rushing the item into court, only wishing to have it in hand for the Court's inspection, it is apparent from some of the responses in the gallery and most particularly of an experienced, armed bailiff that this item could have appeared to a person in far less light than we had here to have been a weapon much like the one the defendant testified that he saw."

"But, Your Honor," Carelli pleaded, "it's irrelevant. The *person* in question was an *intruder,* a man who had broken into a locked residence armed with a weapon it is illegal for him *even* to *possess!* If he saw a shadow holding a child's toy as an armed man, it was because he was disposed to see him so."

"State makes a point, doesn't it, Mr. Jackson?" the judge said carefully. "Other than to shock the jury, perhaps lead them away from more relevant and more probative evidence, what is the relevance of this"—he picked up the wrapped hockey stick that still lay on the bench—"thing?"

"Your Honor, it goes to the intent of the defendant. Did he intend to harm the occupants of the house? We say not. Did he intend to steal from them? We say not. He intended to rescue the Collins girl from kidnappers he and her parents had very good reason to believe meant to kill her. He thought he saw a weapon he had come to know well in Vietnam, a weapon he associated with the killing of children, and he reacted consistently with the view he took—that a girl was a hostage in that house and in deadly danger."

"Eloquent," Judge Kerry said blandly, allowing himself a little smile. "I'll consider this matter overnight and rule in the morning. I'll consider how to instruct the jury as to this evidence, and whether the defense should be admonished or sanctioned. Then, ladies and gentlemen, we will move to conclude this proceeding before tomorrow sunset."

Carelli opened his mouth to speak, but the judge had already risen, taking his case notes and the hockey stick with him out of court. "Bastard," Carelli hissed at Tom Jackson as he passed.

The lawyers filed out of court, heading for nearby bars. Johnny Dietrich was left where he was in the witness box until one of the bailiffs remembered, came back and took him to his cell.

"H OW MUCH MORE will you ask me?" Johnny asked Tom as he and Angela filed into the interview room and sat.

Tom set his briefcase on the floor and loosened his tie. "Not much. Frankly, that went better than I could have wished, especially since the judge let the jury take it home with them. Just remember to say what you saw and felt; not what you *later* concluded happened."

"What about the cross-examination?" Johnny asked.

"Carelli will be rough. He'll do anything he can to get you to admit you shot those men down in cold blood. He'll press you to describe your actions; more important, your motivation. If he gets to you, the jury will hear *his* voice last as testimony. Your aim should be to look past Carelli's taunts and talk directly to the jury. You're the one they want to hear."

"I'll tell the truth."

"Of course," Tom said, a bit sarcastically. "As you have wished from the beginning. But don't forget truth has many facets, and is more than a collection of answers to my questions, or George Carelli's. The jury is looking at *you*, listening to *you* now; Carelli and I became minor players the moment you began to speak."

"What about closing arguments?"

"We'll deliver a summation, then the State. We'll be eloquent and so will George, but the jury will decide on the basis of what the witnesses said. If you hadn't testified, our close would be important, but now it is not. Juries have a healthy skepticism about lawyers."

"So it's mine to win or lose."

"I'm afraid that's so."

"I'm not afraid."

"Good. Get a good night's rest, and prepare to face a very angry cobra in the morning." Tom got up and lifted the heavy briefcase. "Angela?"

"I'd like to stay and have dinner with Johnny," she said. "Talk a bit. I'll join you in the office before seven to help with the summation."

"Okay. Don't be late; you're not just helping, you're doing half of it." Tom saluted them both and left.

Angela sat heavily and reached for Johnny's hands. "How do you feel?"

"Strange. Tom tells me I have to win my own case, yet I think he sees me headed for the gallows."

"Are you frightened?"

"No. Angela, you look at this as an advocate, as you should. Black and white. I see it differently; I did a great wrong for what I thought was a good reason. I want that jury to decide if the good I meant to do can mitigate the great evil of taking those three lives."

Angela squeezed Johnny's cold hands. "How can I help?"

Johnny smiled. "Do a brilliant close. Make sure I was understood, if I falter."

"You won't falter."

"Thank you for believing. Why do you believe when Tom doesn't?"

"He sees you as a naïve, trusting man led to do a foolish crime. He wishes you would have let him use artifice to fly you from this place."

"Because he thinks I was justified?"

"No, that's not important to Tom. He wants you free. Tom wins his cases and he doesn't want to lose this one, for you or for himself. Besides, he doesn't believe you should be punished for a good, albeit foolish and naïve, act gone wrong."

Johnny brought her hands to his lips and kissed her fingers, slowly. "What do you believe?"

Angela shuddered. "You're the man in the shadows that every woman hopes will be there when she's menaced, frightened as you thought Sally was menaced and frightened. The man who will risk all to save her. You deserve to be free with thanks from a judicial system that does far too little to contain the beasts that stalk all innocents."

Johnny smiled. "What I do or fail to do tomorrow will affect you, too?"

"Of course. God help us both if you don't know that."

"That is what I will tell the jury, if I can. Not Tom's message of excuse, but yours of care."

She pulled him across the table and kissed him deeply. "Do it well."

"Lend me your strength."

"My strength comes from you. Before you I only knew the law."

"Ah." He smiled.

Angela dried her eyes. "What should I get for dinner?"

"I HAVE TO get back to New York," Robby said. "Do you want a ride?"

"Got to see this through," Tolliver said, sipping his ginger ale. The bar at the Marriott was filling up with cold, tired people wet from the snow. "Don't you want to?"

"I have work. So do you."

"I have to see this through," Tolliver insisted.

"Willy, Johnny's gone. At the best, Jackson's stagecraft may get him down to murder two."

"Captain, you know he was a tunnel rat. You know how hard it was for him to go back there in his mind. I never should have let him, girl or no girl."

Robby shifted uneasily and took a large hit from his dark scotch. "I know what you mean."

"Do you? You dealt with 'Nam, shifted through, became a success in the World. Johnny and me, we just get by, trying as hard as we can to make evil give birth to good."

Robby smiled. "You should've been a preacher, Willy."

Willy shrugged. "I've thought about it. I don't think I'm worthy."

"What do you want to do?" Robby said sadly.

"I want to take Johnny back with me. I want to help him heal his soul. I owe him that and so much more."

"I'll stay with you another day. We'll await a miracle together."

"You don't have to. I'll bring him home on a train."

"I'll wait."

60

JUDGE KERRY'S COURT was packed before 9:00 A.M. He declared the court in session, then immediately summoned the lawyers to his chambers. Tom Jackson and George Carelli exchanged looks of false confidence as they gathered their papers and followed their assistants through the door.

Johnny sat alone at the defense table with his thoughts. Everyone is now here in this room, and everything. He had seen the Collins family seated in the gallery when he was brought in, seen their eyes. Sally looked triumphant, Jane sad and Edward looked away, embarrassed. The families of the three dead men took their usual seats away from the Collins family; the women weepy, the men angry. Johnny stared at his hands. When the judge and the lawyers come back, the play will continue. Nothing more will come into this room; it is all here. Truth, lies, love, hatred, death and indifference.

Johnny looked at the jury, seated patiently in the box. Many met his eyes, and he smiled at them. What did they think of him? A murderer, as the State insisted, a rescuer as Tom argued, or a fool as Tom believed?

"ALL RIGHT, GENTLEMEN, ladies," Judge Kerry said, adjusting his reading glasses. "This trial has been a dog's breakfast from the beginning. Criminal trials are messy, but this one far below the norm. Witnesses have lied; that's nothing new, but lied inconsistently. Witnesses have disappeared, albeit later to be found. The jury knows what happened at the scene when the victims lost their lives only through the testimony of a child who may have been a kidnap victim or instead an extortionist. Finally, in place of a murder weapon that would have been helpful, we have a child's hockey stick the defense says *looks* like a weapon the defendant last saw thirty years ago on the other side of the earth. Out of all this *crap* the Court is supposed to fashion justice."

Kerry took off his glasses and rubbed the bridge of his nose. "I'm gonna admit the hockey stick, because Mr. Jackson says it goes to the defendant's intent. I'm not gonna allow any speechifying, Mr. Jackson, that this thing gave any cover to the criminal acts of breaking and entering, or homicide. This stick doesn't erase the illegality of that, nor does it give the defendant any claim to self-defense. Clear?"

Tom cleared his throat. "Yes, Your Honor."

"Fine. I'm not gonna say anything to the jury about Ms. Hughes's melodramatic entry, because I'm sure she is too fine a lawyer to perpetrate such an insult upon this Court." The judge looked hard at Angela and she reddened despite trying very hard not to. "Finally, as to my instructions to the jury, I intend to be as broad as I see fit to spell out what all this nonsense means and what it doesn't. You two"—the judge used both hands to point to Carelli and Jackson—"will examine the witness with care and within the rules. No oratory; you can orate in your summations. Clear?"

"Yes, Your Honor," Carelli and Jackson chorused.

Judge Kerry heaved his bulk out of his chair. "Let's go see if we can find us a glimmer of poor old justice."

JOHNNY TOOK HIS seat in the witness box. The judge peered down at him and reminded him, and the jury, that he was still under oath. Tom Jackson came forward. Johnny looked beyond the lawyer and saw the burning streets of Hue. Oh, God, not now, he thought as automatic-weapons fire crackled in his ears. He felt sweat streaming beneath his shirt and starting on his scalp. He felt his temperature climb as he swallowed and fought for control.

Tom saw the color drain from Johnny's face and his brow become shiny with sweat. Why? he wondered. He's been cool as ice until now. "Morning, Johnny," he said tentatively.

Johnny nodded. His throat felt constricted. The room seemed to dim and strong odors assaulted him. Gunsmoke, blood, decay, feces. He swallowed and blinked and the image of Vietnam began to recede.

"Johnny, tell us what happened after you found the girl."

Johnny shifted in the uncomfortable hard seat. "She was in bed, naked. I found her clothes and tossed them on the bed. She dressed. I tied her wrists and blindfolded her, then took her out to the corner to wait for Willy." Tom had, like Tolliver, decided to avoid mention of the radios; sounded too professional.

"Why did you bind and blindfold her?"

"Because it was apparent from her position in bed with one of the kidnappers that she was a willing participant in the abduction. I didn't know what to make of that but decided she shouldn't see my face, or Willy's."

"Then you took her home."

"Yes. We took her to the gatehouse of her parents' estate, and watched over her until the father came out and got her."

"Then you went home."

"Yes."

"How did you feel?"

"I'd done what had to be done. I'd kept a young girl alive."

Tom turned slowly and faced the State's table. Carelli and Pulaski looked anxious; Mike Kolslovsky looked confused and sad. "Your witness," Tom said.

George Carelli's face registered surprise. "Your Honor, the State requests a brief recess to consider the witness's testimony and our cross."

Judge Kerry scowled. He banged his gavel once. "Thirty minutes, Mr. Carelli."

George Carelli took Evelyn Pulaski by her elbow and all but dragged her out of the buzzing court. Mike Kolslovsky followed. George found an empty hearing room, hustled his assistants in and slammed the door. "Son of a *bitch!*" he shouted as he switched on the lights. "Puts the defendant on and asks him next to nothing. 'I saw a gun'—then his assistant comes running in with a fucking hockey stick, held just-so. 'I blindfolded the girl because she was in cahoots with her kidnappers—no, not in cahoots, in *bed,* for Christ's sake! 'Then I drove her home.' What the fuck do we make of all that?"

"He gave you a fair amount, George. Can't expect him to open up any more than he has to," Evelyn said, opening her notebook and looking at her rough transcript of Johnny Dietrich's testimony. George glared at her.

"What's the problem?" Mike asked. "He's on the stand, under oath. Ask him how the subgun felt kicking in his hands, how their brains looked splashing all over the walls."

"I can't, Mike," George said. "Cross-examination is limited to what the witness has testified on direct. You heard the judge this morning; strict adherence to the rules. I'll bet Stonewall cut his direct short when he heard that."

"Let's see what we have here," Evelyn said. "He admits he entered the house after breaking and forcing a window—well, he almost does. He admits being armed as he went in, and prepared to use the weapon to rescue the girl. He admits shooting at least one of the boys." She flipped a page. "He admits his hallucination and some confusion, and in effect Jackson has admitted for him that the Russian AKS was in fact a child's street hockey stick. He tried to give himself justification for taking a human life where there was none."

George was up and pacing. "We don't want the hallucination," he said. "Don't want the jury thinking he had a touch of madness even though it's not a defense. We don't want the fucking hockey stick— I'd like to take it and shove it up Stonewall's ass after the jury puts this vigilante away, but we don't want the damn thing any more in the jury's mind than it is. We stress the elements of crime here; the breaking and entering, masked and gloved, the weapon, the shooting itself. That's it; do that and sit down." George sat down.

"You might rattle him," Evelyn said.

"Damn it, I intend to."

"Did you notice how pale he got this morning, right after he sat down?" Mike asked. "He looked sick, shining with sweat."

"So he's scared."

"I wonder. His service records indicate a history of malaria. Malaria never goes away, and attacks can be triggered by stress, or fatigue."

"What's your point, Mike?"

"I don't know. I just thought this morning when I looked into his eyes that I finally was there with him in that house."

"What did you see?" Evelyn asked. George threw up his hands.

"Not the house on Prescott Street. The house of pain from his novel. The house in Hue."

"Enough of this metaphysical crap," George said, looking at his watch. "We have to go back to court now. We have to finish this cowboy *now.*"

Not cowboy, Mike thought sadly as he followed the lawyers back to the courtroom. Marine.

61

GEORGE CARELLI APPROACHED the witness box, his hands clasped in front of him. "Well, Mr. Dietrich, we finally get to hear your story."

Johnny said nothing. He felt itching in his brain, whispers. There was an awkward silence, then the judge said, "Ask questions, Mr. Carelli."

George was stung. Jesus, he thought, get on with it! "Mr. Dietrich, you've told us you broke into and entered this locked residence in the middle of the night to rescue a kidnap victim. By what right did you do so? By what right did you enter a dwelling, that could have belonged to anyone in this courtroom"—a quick glance at the jury—"with a loaded military weapon and intent to use it?"

"I didn't know what my rights were. I was thinking only of the girl."

"So you shot a man—a man you didn't know, who could have been anyone in this courtroom. Did you assume you had the right to do that?"

"I was sure he was armed and training his weapon on me."

"So you shot him. Very commendable response in a tunnel in Vietnam, but in a house in Black Rock? A house you had invaded, masked and gloved like a terrorist? You gave yourself the right to break in, sneak in and shoot any innocent householder who got up to defend his family?"

"Mr. Carelli," Johnny said carefully, feeling anger heat his brain another ten degrees. "The house was *not* any house. The house *did* contain the girl who was threatened with death and it *did* contain her kidnappers. You suggest I *could* have entered the house of any of these citizens, but I did not."

"The man you shot was unarmed."

"He looked armed. He was a kidnapper guarding his victim."

George rushed the witness box, looked ready to pounce over the railing. He whirled and addressed the jury. "That, Mr. Dietrich, is a matter for the jury to consider. What did you do next?"

Johnny's world went dark. He was on the floor of the house in Prescott Street, on his knees, the K gun shuddering in his hands. He heard shouting, harsh cries in Vietnamese. He had to wait for the moon before he advanced, then it slipped from behind its cloud. "I advanced," Johnny croaked. Sweat streamed down his face.

"Shooting?" George Carelli bellowed.

"Objection," Tom Jackson said, jumping to his feet. "The State is not entitled to ask questions beyond the scope of the direct examination."

"Approach," Judge Kerry said, beckoning with his fingers. He leaned over and addressed the two lawyers in a quiet but forceful voice. "Strict rules, Mr. Carelli."

"Your Honor, he admits he shot one man; two more were killed, and they didn't even have *hockey sticks!*" George said in a hoarse whisper.

"Your Honor," Tom said very softly. "The State is not entitled to badger the witness to make a case it has not itself been able to make."

"Move back." The lawyers withdrew and the judge looked at the anxious jurors. "Defense counsel's objection is sustained. Move on, Mr. Carelli."

"The children were all in the basement," Johnny said, looking at no one. "I had to get to them before they were slaughtered." He looked at the jury and his eyes focused. "I had to."

"Mr. Dietrich," the judge said, banging his gavel. "You will answer questions put by the State's Attorney, say nothing else."

Johnny snapped his head around. The dream disappeared. He looked up at the judge who looked familiar. He felt and heard a sharp bang inside his head. What did I say?

George walked close to the witness. He could see his distress, his face pale and damp with sweat he wiped on his sleeve, his wildly moving eyes. Should I go on? George wondered. He looked up at the judge, who was also studying the witness. The judge can see him as well as I can, George thought. I must go on. "Mr. Dietrich, you said you 'advanced.' "

"I went on to look for Sally."

He sounds all right, George thought, but this is dangerous ground. "You found her, and took her forcibly from the house."

Johnny didn't hear the question. "It's why men become warriors, to protect the ultimate future of the band, the women and children. Nothing is more vital to the future than children, for they are the seed corn."

Judge Kerry banged his gavel and Johnny flinched, but he continued to look at the jurors' frozen faces. "That's why."

Judge Kerry banged the gavel again. "The witness will be silent. The jury will disregard those statements. Mr. Carelli?"

"Nothing further, Your Honor."

"Redirect, Mr. Jackson?" The judge's tone was clearly meant to discourage.

"No, Your Honor. The Defense rests."

The judge banged the gavel again. "Recess until two P.M." He rose and turned toward the door to his chambers. The court emptied quickly, the press people talking on their cell phones as they pushed out. Johnny was left alone as the state and defense teams huddled separately. The sweat on his body turned cold and he began to shiver, then the world grew dark and he slid from his chair to the floor.

ANGELA FOUND TOM in the hall outside Judge Kerry's chambers. "Where's Johnny?" he whispered.

"Bridgeport Hospital emergency room. I've just come from there."

"What happened? How is he?"

"They're doing tests. He's severely dehydrated and running a high fever. His blood pressure is very low and there is evidence of internal bleeding."

"Is he conscious?"

"In and out. He was delirious in the ambulance, but he knew me."

"Jesus. The judge wants me in chambers. I'm sure he'll consider a mistrial."

"What do you think?"

"I don't know. I'll sound out Carelli. Maybe the State will agree not to retry the case."

"What do you think the jury would do if we gave it to them?"

Tom shook his head. "Convict. I don't know; how will they react to Johnny's strange outbursts? Ironically, it has come out like Johnny always said he wanted: the jury knows he killed those men, and now he's told them why."

"I'd better go back over to the hospital."

"Yes, do. Kerry is going to want to know ASAP when Johnny will be able to return to court. Call me at his clerk's or later on my cell phone."

Angela buttoned her overcoat. "Okay. Good luck."

Tom went into the judge's outer office. Ermine, his matronly black clerk, rose from behind her cluttered desk and opened the door to the judge's private room. "What news?" the judge said without rising from behind his desk. George Carelli sat on the edge of one of the club chairs with Evelyn Pulaski standing behind him.

Tom took the empty club chair. "They're running tests. His blood pressure is very low and internal bleeding is suspected. Angela is on her way back to the hospital; she'll call as soon as his condition is known."

"Mr. Carelli wonders whether Johnny's little sermonettes, and even his collapse, were staged."

Tom reddened. "That's an offensive suggestion. The man is very ill."

"We seemed so close to wrapping this up," Judge Kerry said wistfully. "If the defendant is unable to return to court to assist in his own defense, we may have to declare a mistrial and start again. I should be most unhappy if that were to be the case."

"Defense is not seeking a mistrial," Tom said. Christ, he thought, I want this impossible case behind me. He was ashamed of the notion: his client's life still hung in the balance.

"What says the State?" Kerry asked.

"We'd hate to burden the taxpayers with another trial, Your Honor, but we will pursue this matter to resolution."

"Given what we now know, Mr. Jackson, if a mistrial is declared would the defense consider a plea? To save the taxpayers more expense?"

"I can't possibly contemplate a plea until I'm able to consult with my client, but I'd be inclined to listen."

"Consider that, please, Mr. Carelli."

"Yes, Your Honor."

The judge stood and rubbed his lower back. "Since it's Friday, I'll send the jury home for a long weekend. I'll be here in chambers until five at least, then at the Algonquin Club to listen to the governor talk about tort reform, lastly at home. I'd appreciate hearing from you, Mr. Jackson, as soon as you know the condition and prognosis of your client."

"Yes, Your Honor."

"I'm sure Mr. Carelli would also appreciate being kept informed."

"Please," George said, getting up. "I'll be in my office until who knows when. You have my pager number."

Tom nodded. "I do."

ANGELA FOUND JOHNNY sleeping in a bed in the hospital's intensive care unit. He was hooked up to some sort of monitor and had intravenous tubes in both arms. A pretty young nurse was holding Johnny's wrist, taking his pulse. Angela felt a twinge of jealousy. "How is he?" she said.

The nurse made a note on her chart and turned. "Dr. Sousa will be back in a few minutes. Are you family?"

"I'm his attorney. He's on trial."

"Of course. I've seen the papers. Sit down if you like."

Angela took off her coat and folded it over the back of a chair, then sat. "How is he?" she repeated.

Dr. Sousa, a very dark Indian resident in a dirty lab coat, hurried to the bedside and peered at the monitor. The nurse handed him the chart and left. "I'm Dr. Rajiv Sousa." He didn't offer his hand.

"Angela Hughes, Law Office of Thomas Jackson," she said. "He collapsed at trial."

"So I'm told. He is stable but very weak. He has lost much blood, apparently due to a perforated ulcer in his stomach. He's dehydrated and feverish. We are giving him fluids and nutriments in one arm to help him regain his strength and plasma in the other to build up his blood pressure. His fever spikes are probably related to the intestinal problems, plus he looks to me to be a malaria sufferer. I don't suppose you have any idea where his medical records might be?"

"I don't. I'll try to find out. How long will he be in the hospital?"

Dr. Sousa shrugged. "Overnight for sure, for observation. He's a strong man, his heart and lungs are fine. I'll be able to tell in the morning, I think."

"Can he—speak?"

"Later. He's getting sedatives now to relax the spasms in his stomach and intestines, and drugs to treat the ulcer. I'm confident he will survive long enough for the State of Connecticut to see him off as it sees fit."

"The man is innocent," Angela said hotly, jumping out of the chair.

"Sorry, miss," the doctor said, peering over half-glasses. "Gallows humor goes with this job."

"I'll try to find out where his medical records are," she said. "I'll be back."

62

EVELYN PULASKI ARRIVED at Johnny's bedside shortly after Angela left. The attending nurse looked at her ID and let her into the ICU, but didn't leave the nurses' station with its blinking and beeping monitors. Evelyn took the chair next to Johnny's bed and watched him for a while. How this strange, quiet man had touched our lives, she thought. He has made us look at justice, and at ourselves. At the beginning of the case she had been a fire breather, pushing Carelli to ask for the death penalty. It was a case made in heaven for a liberal crusader like Carelli, and Evelyn was herself a Ted Kennedy–Chris Dodd Democrat. John Dietrich was a little of everything those larger-than-life liberals abhorred. Johnny was guns and violence and Vietnam, mistrustful of government and the police, a willing vigilante. Yet after two weeks of watching the man suffer in silent dignity in court and seeing him now helplessly exhausted and unconscious in a hospital bed with tubes and wires running everywhere, Evelyn found she had no hatred left at all, and no desire whatever to see the man punished.

She wondered if George Carelli might feel the same way.

Angela drove to the office in Westport and called the Marriott, looking for Tolliver. He wasn't in his room so she had him paged in the bar and lounge. After five minutes of listening to canned Christmas music, his rich bass voice startled her. "Ms. Hughes," he said. "How's Johnny?"

"Okay, I guess," she said. "Dehydrated, low blood pressure. Apparently he has a bleeding ulcer."

"Never had that before, even when he was drinking. Damn this trial."

"The doctor who's treating him wants to see his medical records. I've called the Norwalk and Bridgeport hospitals and they found nothing in their own or referring physicians' records. Do you have any idea where he might have been treated?"

"He had a couple of physical exams when he was in rehab with us. I could get those reports, and maybe find his Marine Corps medical file, but it won't happen fast."

"Do you know if he had malaria? The doctor was concerned about his high fever."

"Hell, lady, he was a mud marine in 'Nam; he had malaria. Listen, can I go see him? I could talk to the doctor."

"You'd have to go with me. He's guarded."

"Whenever you're ready," Tolliver said.

"I have to make a few calls. I'll call you from my car when I get close to the Marriott."

"Okay. I'll call my office, get them started on old medical records. I'll be in my room, four-twelve."

"I'll see you in less than an hour." Angela hung up then dialed Tom Jackson's cell phone. She got his recording.

Fuck this, she thought. I'm going back to the hospital.

Johnny awakened slowly. He felt weighted down, paralyzed. He knew the sensation; bad malaria attack. He opened his eyes a crack, then closed them tightly. The glare of the overhead lights was painful. Malaria did that, too. He cracked his eyelids again, looked around. Tubes in his arms. A nurse sitting at a curved console in the middle distance. Beeps and clicks and whirs of instruments and pumps. I'm in a hospital, he thought distantly. He remembered feeling nauseated and faint in the witness box, then nothing. Not surprising, he thought. He'd been shitting and coughing up blood for days. What did I say to the jury? he wondered.

Angela came into his slitted field of vision. She looked lovely in a bright blue woolen overcoat and matching hat that she took off and folded onto a chair. She was wearing the same black suit and creamy silk blouse she had worn in court that morning, so he couldn't have been in the hospital long. She leaned close to his face and stared at him. He ratcheted his eyes a little further open and said, "Angela." It came out a croak.

Angela was startled by Johnny's voice. She sat quickly and touched his hand. "Johnny, how are you?"

"You're beautiful," he said. "More lovely than a sunrise at sea."

She blushed. She felt swollen with love for this damaged man. "How do you feel?"

"Weak. Lightheaded. Malaria."

A shadow blocked the overhead fluorescent lights and Johnny opened his eyes fully. "Why you huggin' your rack in the daytime, Marine?" Willy Tolliver growled.

"Dunno, Staff Sergeant," Johnny said with a wan grin. "I'd shake your hand but they got me tied down."

"You can rest for now. Nurse say you got an ulcer."

"Me? No, Willy. What I got to worry about?"

Tolliver put his big hand on Johnny's brow. "Fever's coming down. Let's be done with this damn trial and get you home."

Johnny looked at Angela. "What did I say to the jury?"

Angela winced. "You said what you wanted. You told them why."

Johnny smiled. "It should be all right, then."

Angela stood up. "I have to find Dr. Sousa. Willy, I'll come back for you."

Johnny watched her go. *I believed I could live in prison,* he thought bleakly. *I'm used to living alone.* Now he wasn't sure he wanted to live anywhere with nothing but his painful memories.

"Woman likes you, boy," Willy said softly, taking the chair Angela had left.

"She's kind to me," Johnny said sadly.

"Dumbass." Willy laughed. *"Kind?"*

Tom Jackson found Judge Kerry at the fund-raiser. The young governor of Connecticut, a terrible speaker, droned on at a distant podium. "Angela's spoken to the doctor," Tom whispered. "Johnny has an ulcer that caused internal bleeding, which in turn caused his blood pressure to drop. He's stable and being treated for his symptoms. He should be able to attend court on Monday if nothing changes."

The judge nodded. "You tell Carelli?"

"Yes."

"You ready to sum up this clusterfuck Monday?"

"Yes, Your Honor."

"Better be good." The judge turned his big head back toward the governor. Tom went back to his own table.

Angela came back to Johnny's bedside with the doctor. Tolliver took him aside and told him what he remembered of Johnny's medical history. Angela took the chair. A little color returned to Johnny's cheeks, spots of red the size of quarters. His eyes were bright with fever. "Do you have attacks of malaria often?" she asked.

"Not anymore. Fatigue brings it on, stress. I'll be very tired tomorrow, then I'll be all right."

"Can we talk about your case? Are you up to that?"

"Sure. We're almost done."

"I hope so. Johnny, you addressed the jury; you told them that the rescue of the girl was your duty, worth your life. That was improper, and the judge may decide that it prejudiced the jury. If he does decide that he could declare a mistrial."

Johnny frowned. "Then what happens?"

"The State could bring the charges again before a new jury. We'd have to do the whole thing all over again."

"I don't want that. I want to finish this; walk free if the jury decides I was justified in my acts, or know my fate if they don't."

"I have to say it doesn't look good."

"You and Tom did what you could. I only wish I could have known you better."

Angela began to cry. She searched in her purse for a tissue. Johnny struggled to raise his hand to touch her tears but his arms were taped to the rails of the bed. "Angela, come here," he said. "Let me kiss the tears away."

She fell on his chest and sobbed. When she looked up his eyes were closed. Dr. Sousa returned and told her she must let the patient rest.

Willy Tolliver took her arm and led her from the hospital.

On MONDAY MORNING, Judge Kerry's court was again packed. Johnny was back at the defense table, dressed in his freshly pressed suit. Angela thought he looked dull-eyed, detached. Tom rose and began his summation before the jury. "You've sat patiently here for more than two weeks. You have heard testimony about a tragedy, the killing of three young men. You'll shortly be asked to deliberate not only about *what* happened to those young men, but *why*.

"In reality, there were two crimes, and one begat the other. A girl was snatched off the street in front of her school, in plain view of her mother. She was taken away and hidden. The kidnappers demanded money of her parents and threatened to kill the girl unless the parents paid an amount of money they didn't have and couldn't raise. The defendant was asked to help, to lend money, and he offered to *give* the money if that would help, but he knew from the mother's description of the abduction that the girl had seen the kidnappers, and *he* knew as *you* now know that in cases where the victim sees the kidnappers, only rarely are such victims seen again by their families *alive.* So Johnny Dietrich pledged to help the girl in the only way he knew, by risking his life to save hers."

Tom stopped his slow pacing and looked at the jurors one by one. He thought they looked thoughtful, even sympathetic. Just before coming into court he had been lectured by the judge in chambers about Johnny's statements of the previous session, but the judge had ruled out a mistrial unless the jury deadlocked. We all want this behind us, Tom thought sadly. Who really speaks for Johnny? "The State, in its closing argument, will tell you that the kidnapping was not real, a teenage prank. But you have heard from the family, the terrified mother and father and the defiant girl. You heard the parents describe their helpless agony, and you heard the girl tell *lies,* the most easily disproved being the one about being covered in her young lover's blood that miraculously disappeared by the time she was taken home. This kidnapping was real to the parents even if the daughter turned it to her own use as a way of extorting money from the parents whose love she rejected." Tom turned and looked at the Collinses in the gallery, Jane crying and clutching Edward's arm, Edward looking pained, and Sally, sitting as far from them as she could on the crowded bench, glaring at Tom across an immeasurable gulf. No more on this, he thought, looking back at the jury. Members were becoming restless. "Johnny Dietrich decided to take the only action he could, and rescue the girl. He should have called the police, but he felt he had no time, and he reasoned, as many of you may have reasoned at various times in your lives in this city, that the police would not act on the very circumstantial evidence he had developed that the girl and her kidnappers were hiding in the house of one of them, at Eleven Prescott Street.

"The State has argued that Johnny broke into the house illegally, and he did. But the State has argued that he was breaking into a house without reason, which he did not. The house he selected did indeed contain the girl and her abductors, and no one else.

"You must ask yourselves what Johnny went into that house to do. Did he go in to steal? We say not, and nothing was taken. Did he go in with a lust to kill? You have heard him say not. He went into that house for one reason and one reason only: to rescue Sally Collins from the kidnappers who had terrorized her parents and told them they would kill their daughter."

Tom paused. The jurors were back on track, concentrating. Tom could see it would be a difficult deliberation for most of them. "Ladies and gentlemen, the first crime, this cruel kidnapping of a young girl almost literally snatched from her mother's arms, set in motion the tragedy that ended in the deaths of three men who committed the first crime. It is your duty to examine the two matters together, and to think of the motivation of the actors in this tragedy. Who did right and who wrong? Who deserves your censure and punishment? Who your thanks? Who are the victims?"

Tom turned away from the jury and looked at Angela and Johnny seated at the defense table. Now the final gamble, he thought. He almost reversed his earlier decision to have Angela conclude the argument, but he nodded to her. Angela had the passion for this sorry case that Tom knew he lacked. Angela would talk about motivation. Tom sat down as Angela walked slowly toward the jury box.

"This trial has been very difficult for all of us," Angela said. "Difficult for Jane and Edward Collins, not knowing what responsibility they may have for the deaths of the three kidnappers, or for Johnny's being placed here, before you, in jeopardy of his life. Difficult for Sally Collins, with her divided loyalties; her friends if so they were, her parents, herself. Difficult for the defendant, who wanted nothing from this but the safe return of a kidnapped girl—his own goddaughter—to her family. Difficult for him as well because he may have made a mistake in that darkened house, seen a weapon that wasn't there—but might have been. He had every reason to believe—from the statements of the kidnappers to the parents—that the kidnappers were violent men bent on violence, and planning the death of their victim. Johnny Dietrich places his fate in your hands, and he does it willingly, because he trusts you to sift through the evidence, to listen to the words of witnesses and see into their hearts.

"Johnny acted out of love. Johnny told you when he testified that he loved children and saw a duty to protect them. He saw much slaughter of children in Vietnam, and that experience drove him to deep despair, a despair that almost killed him. But he recovered, with the help of good friends and his own deeply rooted sense of honor.

"Who accuses Johnny, and what do they want from this Court, from you? The police, the prosecutors are trying to fix blame to balance the tragedy of the loss of three young lives. That's their job. Johnny's old friend testified that Johnny was there, with a weapon and the rest, but don't forget that friend was brought into this court against his will and paid for his testimony with promises that he would never answer the charges that Johnny must answer. Did he say the truth, and only the truth? Remember, the things he said Johnny did are known only to him and Johnny, and Johnny refuses to harm his friend." Angela turned and looked coldly at Willy Tolliver, seated with his lawyer in the first row of the gallery. Sorry, Willy, she thought, but it's what you wanted the jury to remember. She turned back to the jury. "You are asked to judge the guilt or innocence of Johnny Dietrich to the crime of murder, but you must judge not only his actions but his reasons, and his reasons, as the tragedy itself, are rooted in the first crime, the kidnapping of an innocent and her abductors condemning her to death."

Angela turned away and strode back to the defense table and sat. She dabbed her eyes with her fingertips. "Excellent," Tom whispered. Johnny took her hand under the table as George Carelli rose and adjusted the waistcoat of his lucky blue suit.

"Ladies and gentlemen," George began, stalling a bit, trying to digest Tom's and especially Angela's close. He would have expected Judge Kerry to call at least a brief recess, but George's look of entreaty at the judge had been returned with stony indifference. "The defense wants you to believe this is a complicated matter, filled with conflicting currents, emotions, motivations and deception. In fact, as I am sure you will find, it is a simple matter: the defendant, Johnny Dietrich, entered the house at Eleven Prescott Street, in the Black Rock section of your home city of Bridgeport, and *murdered* three young men. He broke into the house, with a submachine gun in his hand, and intent to kill. He did kill. Whatever he may have believed was going on in that house in respect of a kidnapping or any other matter does not excuse his violating the law and the privacy of that house in any way at all. You can't break into my house and I can't break into yours because we might believe a crime was in progress. Even a policeman can't break into your house unless he has a warrant signed by a judge, or unless, under strict rules in rare circumstances, the police officer has probable cause to believe a crime is in progress. In this case, there was no crime in progress, but even if you believe there was, or the defendant so believed, he had no justification *whatsoever* for going in that house, with a weapon, and disposed to kill. He went in and he did kill, as testimony from his accomplice and from his own lips has shown you. These things he did, and you know that, beyond any reasonable doubt." George paused. Two jurors were nodding; others looked confused. Simple and direct, he reminded himself.

"Think how easy this case would have been for the State to present and for you to judge if we had all been in possession of the one hard fact the defense tried repeatedly to tell you wasn't there: John Dietrich's presence at the crime scene. If we had presented Staff Sergeant Tolliver to you at the beginning of the case, right after the police evidence, how much easier would it have been for you to understand what Sally Collins said of her night of terror. Edward Collins told you what he said to the defendant and what came after, but how much clearer would that have been if you already had heard testimony from the defendant's friend and accomplice, that told you that the defendant had gone into that house and returned with the young woman, bound and blindfolded, mere hours before the bloody crime scene was discovered? I ask you in your deliberations to take the events in order, rearrange the puzzle.

"The defense leans heavily on the motivation of the defendant, what he wanted to do and what others wanted him to do. I submit to you that even the loftiest motive, even the saving of an innocent, does not change the facts on which your finding of guilty must be based. But the State is not bitter or vengeful, only seeking after justice, only seeking answers for the families of the victims for their sorrow that can never be assuaged." George looked at the parents and brothers and sisters of the slain boys, prominent in front of the gallery, the women decorously weeping, as he had encouraged. "The defendant himself has led a life touched by tragedy and sorrow. He suffered in Vietnam and from the aftereffects of Vietnam once he returned to this country that did its returning servicemen a great dishonor of indifference. The State demands his conviction because he did these murders, but the State will not seek the death penalty for this troubled man.

"A few final words, and then you can begin what is the most important part of any trial, your deliberations, your decision and your verdict. Remember the pictures of the victims, young men who never even grew old enough to vote, will never love or marry or have children of their own. Remember their grieving families, deprived of the special and irreplaceable joy of their sons. Think of the sanctity of your own homes, and of the safety of your home city, and do what must be done: return a verdict of guilty on each and all counts of murder with intent." George stopped with his hands resting on the rail of the jury box, polling them with his eyes. I think it's right, he thought, keeping his face somber. He turned and walked away without another word.

Judge Kerry let the silence in his courtroom hang for a long moment. It was like a spell: the trial would finally end, and everyone from jurors to bailiffs to reporters and spectators seemed drained and silenced by their participation in it. The judge cleared his throat. "We'll recess for lunch," he said to the jury. "Do not begin your discussions until we return at two, and I give you my instructions. Then you may do your duty." He struck his gavel once and rose, and the people rose with him, and began to talk and shake their heads, shuffle papers and bustle, the spell broken.

XI

VERDICT

63

"DAMN," TOM JACKSON said. "Knifefighter George was good."
Tom sat with Robby O'Dwyer and Willy Tolliver in a famous trattoria called Anacapri in Fairfield. Angela had declined Tom's invitation to join them, rather crossly, he thought, saying she preferred to have sandwiches with Johnny in the interview room at the jail. One way or another, Tom thought, it was finally over.

Robby sipped a huge martini, a signature of Anacapri. "Shit, Tom, he had the facts and the law. The fact that your client was the only good guy in a pool full of sharks and liars didn't change that."

"What would you have done differently?" Tom asked Robby. Tolliver was silent and brooding, his face tight with anger.

"I'm not sure I'd even have taken the case," Robby said. "Carelli said what was; Johnny broke into a locked house and shot it out. On the way, he saved a girl who might or might not have needed saving, or deserved it. Johnny earned a Silver Star for doing that same thing in Hue; here, through Carelli's generous foregoing of the death penalty, he'll get life."

"How come you all giving up so quick?" Tolliver asked angrily. He was drinking a dark bourbon, his first in ten years. "Johnny said his piece. I believed him then and I believe him now."

Robby waved a hand at the pretty dark-haired waitress. "You just can't do what he did, Willy."

"Was okay in 'Nam. You just said so."

"This isn't 'Nam, Willy, you know that. This is the World."

"Maybe that distinction is clearer to the two of you than it has ever been to Johnny and me," Willy said, pushing his chair back and throwing his linen napkin in the center of the table. "I'm going back to the jail."

Robby shrugged as Tolliver stalked out. "Right and wrong never changed for some of our brothers of that war, Tom."

"I can't help but think they may be right, though. This country never brought us home. We, men like you and me, set it aside; were able to spit it out, bad taste and all. Men like Willy and especially Johnny, younger, less educated, less prepared, did all their growing up in the jungles, paddies, and, in Tet and the later battles, the overrun cities and towns. They had to find their way back to self-acceptance with none of the help we had inside us before we ever entered that sad, fucked-up war."

"It's been nearly thirty years, man. We all have to move on." The pretty waitress arrived with *osso buco* for Tom and *linguine alla vongole* for Robby. She carried a third plate, stuffed shells. "Where's the other gentleman?" she asked.

"He had to go. Leave it," Robby said. "We're hungry."

"And another bottle of the Ruffino," Tom said with a smile. The woman smiled brilliantly and left.

"Don't be hard on yourself," Robby said, digging in. "You did very well with next to nothing. Your close was brilliant, especially the counterpoint of Angela; her sad sweetness to your hard logic. It may still work out."

"I wonder. What do you think the judge will do? He's pissed at all of us."

"Hardass, that judge, right?"

"Very."

"He wants his last word, otherwise he would have just given the jury his lesson on the law and let them have at it."

Tom looked at his watch. "Let's enjoy this. We're back in court in an hour and a half."

ANGELA WAS SUMMONED by a guard and had to go out to the entrance of the jail to sign Tolliver in and escort him back to the interview room where Johnny waited, his head in his hands. "Yo, Marine," Tolliver said, sitting down and throwing his beefy arm around the smaller man's shoulders. "Get your damn head up! You ain't never giving up. You got *no* quit in you."

Johnny looked up, furtively wiped his eyes on the sleeve of his orange prison overall. "Never give it up, Staff Sergeant."

Angela retook her seat next to Johnny. She poured soup from a large paper container from the deli across the street that had provided the only food Johnny had been able to enjoy for months, and she with him. "Have some soup, Willy," she said listlessly. "Sandwiches."

"Hey," Willy said, still holding Johnny around his shoulders, "I just left two laughing lawyers eating fine Italian food to come back and watch you two mope? Hoo-*raugh,* Marine!" he all but shouted.

Johnny looked up, and his face colored with anger. "You heard the prosecutor, Willy. I'm going away forever."

Willy shook Johnny by the shoulders, hard. "You be ready to give it up, boy?"

"Willy, for Christ's sake, it's over."

"Isn't. *Isn't,* boy. Even if they gonna hang you, you still got to go back in that court and *face it!*"

Johnny drew himself up, wiped his face. "I do." He looked at Angela, who was suddenly smiling. "I do, Angela."

Willy reached across the table and took Angela's hand away from Johnny's and held it in his huge black paw. "You too, Angela, have to be brave."

Angela smiled. "We have to get our minds right."

"So," Willy Tolliver said. "So it *is.*"

JUDGE KERRY FELT electricity in his courtroom as he took his seat behind the bench. Contrary to the myths of fiction, criminal trials were rarely exciting, mostly just sad, tawdry exercises of little people trying to make their bad acts go away. This trial had genuine conflict, genuine issues of good and evil, and, Judge Kerry would bet, genuine painful struggle to come in the jury deliberations. The trial had also attracted national attention, and the judge wasn't happy about that, especially as he felt obligated by his oath to commit what might later be ruled a reversible error.

The facts cried out for conviction, so did the law, but somehow, after more than two weeks of testimony, after the defendant's outbursts that Judge Kerry had tolerated after the fact because of the Johnny's collapse, after solid summations describing two very different realities, the *answer,* and the illusive *justice,* had not been written clearly across the face of the trial, and the true thing Johnny had done was still not known.

Johnny. The judge looked at the man, his weary face set against his fear. Everyone was calling the man Johnny in his mind; he had transcended "the defendant" and even his whole name, John Dietrich. Who was he and why had he pursued a girl, in his eyes a victim facing certain death, into a darkened private dwelling where, with arms and force of arms, he did kill three men?

Judge Kerry reread the Requests to Charge that the State and Defense had each given him prior to their closing arguments. He would read these to the jury first, along with the usual instructions covering the jury's duty to determine facts, the state's burden of proving every element of each charge beyond a reasonable doubt, the procedures to be followed while deliberating, and various matters of evidence, including what weight they should give or not give to accomplice testimony, the crucial Tolliver statements. George Carelli and Tom Jackson had wrangled at length on this instruction in chambers until the judge had stopped them with a bellow.

Then he would get to the heart of the matter.

He straightened his notes in front of him and looked at the jury. He began his instructions, watching the jurors carefully as he worked through the charges, procedure and law. He watched for signs of inattention or confusion, trying to avoid both.

Connecticut law gave a trial judge wide latitude in going beyond the Requests to Charge and the specifics of law. He could, for example, inform the jury that the Court believed a crime had been committed, and he did so. He could summarize the evidence and comment on the credibility of witnesses, and he did so at length, dwelling on the testimony of Sally Collins and Willy Tolliver. He wondered, as he spoke, if he neared prejudice in favor of the defendant, then he wondered why he felt that way, but he had a nagging feeling that the case as presented and especially the defense had flat *missed something.* He then launched into his summation, his guidance to the jury, his last chance to shape the proceeding that had confused and eluded his normal firm judgment.

"Ladies and gentlemen of the jury, go now and deliberate. Consider all you have seen and heard, and if any of it is unclear, send out a message to me and I will have the record read to you, or the law clarified. Everyone in this court: witnesses, lawyers, even the judge, is done now, and only you can bring this proceeding to a just end.

"You must reach a verdict if you can, and I charge you to try as hard as you can to reason together, to reach a consensus. If the State has not proved the defendant guilty, then you must set him free. If the State has proved guilt beyond a reasonable doubt, then you must find him guilty. But if you should find this man guilty, and I do not make the slightest suggestion that you should, I am giving you an extra charge: you may consider whether he was criminally responsible for his act. There is no defense in this state for insanity; if you find the defendant guilty then guilty he is. But if you so find, and I remind you the Court does not suggest you do so unless the facts so convince you, then you may consider whether he was criminally responsible. The tests for such a finding are simple and specific."

There was a brief commotion at the defense table as the defendant tried to rise. "No!" he whispered loudly. His arms were gripped by his attorneys. He shook off the man and turned to the woman in entreaty. "No, you promised!" he said again, and she shushed him with her fingers to his lips. The judge reached for his gavel and prepared to warn the defendant, but did not as the man quieted, his face twisted with anguish.

The judge took a deep breath and continued. "The tests for determining criminal responsibility are these: did the defendant lack capacity as a result of mental disease or defect to appreciate the wrongfulness of his conduct? Or did he lack capacity to conform his conduct to the law? In other words, did he know what he did was wrong, or, if knowing he did wrong, did he feel compelled by some reason beyond his responsibility that rendered him unable to obey the law? This you may consider in view of the defendant's testimony, but again I must stress, only if you feel the facts of this case compel you to find the defendant proven guilty beyond any reasonable doubt." The judge looked at the jury over his half-glasses, then at the defense table, where the defendant continued to be restrained by the female attorney, lastly at the prosecutor's table, where the two attorneys sat silent and expressionless. "The jury may retire to begin its deliberations," the judge said, rising. "The clerk will show you out."

64

"THE JUDGE CAN do whatever he likes!" Angela insisted, running after Johnny as the bailiffs hustled him back to jail.

"You didn't set that up?" Johnny shouted over his shoulder. "Tom didn't? We all agreed, no insanity!"

"Tom had no more idea the judge would do that than you did," Angela said, wondering if that were true. She slammed the door of the interview room behind her in the face of the startled guard. Johnny was already on the other side of the room, leaning against the cinderblock wall. "We never raised the issue of criminal responsibility," Angela said. "In fact, if you recall, when Carelli pressed Dr. Lewes, Tom specifically got him to say we had not."

Johnny turned, dropped his hands to his sides, his fists balled. He breathed deeply to calm himself; he could see he had frightened Angela. "Then why did the judge bring it up? He all but told the jury they could take it as a middle ground. I don't want to be guilty if I'm not, and shoved into a mental hospital."

"Look, Johnny. Look at me," Angela said, sitting at the table. Johnny's head came slowly up. He looked so helpless Angela felt a hitch in her throat. "If the jury finds you guilty but not criminally responsible, you go to a mental institution for evaluation for ninety days, you exhibit no signs of being dangerous to yourself or others, best result is immediate parole and you're free to leave. Nothing in what you did suggests you would ever do anything like this again."

"I don't want to say I'm insane, Angela. I'm not. I wanted to do a good thing, and I either did or did not. Damn it! I want what the Court promises: judgment!"

Angela felt suffocated by Johnny's rage. "Wait for the verdict. If it's guilty we may appeal; the judge's last charge may be viewed as prejudicial and grounds for reversal. Either way you're not heading for prison."

"For me," he said, sitting opposite and taking her hands, "justice is as important as the sentence."

"CONGRATULATIONS," ROBBY O'DWYER said, catching up with Tom after the two of them had shoved their way through a crowd of reporters with the usual bland remarks about faith in the jury system in its ability to find justice. George Carelli had stayed with the cameras. "Did you tell your client to preach from the witness box or just let it happen?"

"I had no idea he would do that. He had been sad, terribly depressed since the moment of his arrest, but steady, far steadier than I could have been faced with his charges. I don't know what set him off other than his illness; the doctor told Angela that his ulcer had taken weeks to develop at a minimum."

"The jury will clutch at the judge's gift for sure."

"I think so. Oddly enough, Johnny won't be pleased."

"Why not? He just chills out for his evaluation period and he walks."

"He wanted an up or down judgment. He hasn't decided in his own mind if he did good enough to cover the evil."

"Come on, Tom. Who is he, Saint Sebastian? He wants what all criminal defendants want—to walk. Let's not forget he did the shooting."

"He's a strange man. He wants to know what he did."

"Tell him to relax and take the judge's benefice. He wants absolution he can ask a priest."

ANGELA LEFT JOHNNY after two hours of trying to reassure him and went on her second walk of the day to the deli. She wanted to feel good about the very likely verdict the judge had so plainly suggested to the jury, but she wanted to see him truly free, at peace at last with the house of pain. Be realistic, she said to herself. The jury could hardly have freed him, the pictures of three dead men loomed large and overcame all of Tom's art, and even her own small part of the defense. Yet she believed completely in what she had said in her close; Johnny had acted out of love. Could the jury have reached the same conclusion if the judge hadn't given them an easy way out of the hard decision?

Willy Tolliver saw her leave the building and followed her across the street into the deli. "Hey, Angela," he said, catching her as she joined the queue for take out orders. "How's my boy?"

She turned, tried to smile at Willy, failed. "He's pissed. He wanted a clean acquittal, not a trip to the nut house."

Willy frowned. "You reckon that's what'll happen?"

"The judge gave the jury a pretty firm nudge in that direction."

"What do you think?"

"I wanted Johnny to have what he wanted, but I'm afraid we lost the case. He could be free and gone in three months if he behaves; he could travel or relocate, he doesn't need to live here. But that's not what he wants."

Willy shook his head and smiled. "You watch juries for a living. I read people for a living. People I read think they hard to figure, 'cause they always lying, in denial, whatever. How you read that jury panel?"

"When I was delivering my part of the close, I thought they listened. I thought they wanted to believe Johnny did a good thing even if the law says otherwise. But Christ, Willy, he shot those boys, he *did*. When Carelli was through with his close, the faces of the jury closed as well."

"Because they don't like him, that prosecutor," Willy offered. Angela ordered sandwiches, soup and sodas. "You told them what *you* believe; he told them what they *had* to believe. I reckon this trial is about that and nothing more; what did Johnny believe? He took the lives of criminals—and I don't reckon any jury member who ever had a kid or even a dog he loved would buy that baloney about the kidnapping being some teenage prank—to save a girl he believed was both innocent and in deadly peril. That's what you see, and I see, and Johnny saw."

"When you knew Johnny before," Angela said, paying for her purchase and handing Willy the large sack, "did he ever lie to you?"

"Hell, yes. He was a drunk; he'd given up on himself. Of course he lied. He lied to me every day, and to himself, then one day he accepted himself and his sickness, decided to make himself well, and did. In Marine Corps training slogans, he 'improvised, adapted and overcame,' and after that he never again lied to me or himself."

"He's not lying now. He saw a gun in that house."

"I reckon. I thought I saw an armed man, too, don't forget. Johnny and me, we seen guns before. We know you don't get but one split second to react to a gun."

"What do you think the jury will see? Which reality?"

"Judge'd said nothing, straight acquittal. Oh, I know, you don't believe it, maybe Johnny don't, he feels so bad about those boys, but that's what I see. I think maybe the jury believed what the judge said makes it okay to let Johnny go if they want to. I think they'll acquit, and do it today."

They crossed the street and went back down to the jail. Angela signed Tolliver in and they went into the interview room. Tolliver pulled Johnny out of his chair and enfolded him in a bear hug. "You know something I don't, Willy?" Johnny said, grinning, his face losing its look of endless worry in an instant.

"Matter of time, Corporal," Willy said.

65

Tom Jackson sat in the lounge of the Algonquin Club with Robby O'Dwyer. Tom felt acutely depressed and hated to be in a place where people he knew and could not ignore came up to him and made one comment or another about the trial, but the Algonquin was used to lawyers coming over from the nearby superior court and would relay messages promptly. "Why so glum, brother advocate?" Robby said, around a martini.

"I could have done better. I really believed in Johnny."

"He's gonna *walk*, for Christ's sake. Am I the only member of the criminal bar who enjoys winning even if the guy is guilty?"

"I'm happy enough, though a guilty verdict still counts as a loss in my book. You don't know this guy, Robby. He is some strange kind of pure, suffering bastard. He's Vietnam writ large, and I don't want to see him done down, even for ninety days, because a prick like Edward Collins who never served his country in any way except to cheat the IRS has raised up a daughter who hates him almost as much as she hates herself, and led my client into ruin."

"Nice speech." Tom looked up at George Carelli, who stood over their low table looking down. "Almost as good as you were in court."

Tom stiffened but controlled his face. He looked at Robby O'Dwyer, who seemed amused. "I did my best. Your case was masterful," Tom lied, knowing it would piss George off more than if he had rendered the insult he thought the State's case deserved. "Now we wait."

"Surely you can't doubt the outcome. The judge practically wrote the verdict out for the jurors."

"I think Johnny is entitled to a clear acquittal," Tom said smoothly. "Nothing less."

"And I think he deserves fifty thousand volts right through his testicles," George said, his face reddening. "But I'll take him convicted and let the families of the dead boys testify about his sentence."

Tom held the State's Attorney's eyes. Robby chuckled. "Never too late to say 'fuck you' among esteemed colleagues," he said.

"Fuck you," Tom said.

"Fuck you," George all but shouted.

Robby cackled. A uniformed waitress came to the table. "Mr. Jackson, Mr. Carelli, excuse me. Judge Kerry's clerk just called; the jury is coming in."

Tom Jackson signed his drink check and followed the other two lawyers, who were running for the elevators.

Tom GOT INTO the courtroom and took his seat. Carelli and his assistants were in their places. Tom looked around for Angela and Johnny. The judge had not come in, and would not until the lawyers, the defendant and the press had their chance to take their seats.

Robby O'Dwyer sat in the gallery, joined by his client. Tom got up and turned to Tolliver. "Where's Angela and Johnny?"

"Johnny's getting back into his suit," Tolliver said. There was a commotion in the back of the gallery as the parents and siblings of the three slain boys came in, and shortly afterward, the Collins family.

Angela came in with Johnny and the bailiff. "What do you think?" she whispered. "Not even out four hours?"

"Probably means they took the judge's deal," Tom said. "Either hard guilty or acquittal would have taken much longer." Tom looked at Johnny, who looked sad and pale. "How you holding up?" he asked.

"Lightheaded," Johnny said. "Whatever happens, thank you both."

Tom was beginning to hate the way Johnny's unfailing decency made him feel.

"All rise," the judge's round clerk boomed. Judge Kerry swept into the courtroom and took his seat, banging his gavel to command silence. He nodded to the clerk, who went out to fetch the jury from their meeting room.

Tom took a drink of water to ease the parchness in his throat, and immediately felt the need to urinate. He hadn't felt this anxious awaiting a verdict in thirty years. He glanced across at George Carelli, who looked back angrily. Tom was sure George felt the judge had robbed him of a clear conviction, but Tom felt cheated as well. He wondered how Angela felt; she clearly had become attached to the defendant much more than was ever prudent.

The jury filed in, their faces set, determined and somber. None looked at the defendant, a bad sign. The judge cleared his throat after the panel had been seated, and the courtroom fell as silent as a church.

The judge called on the defendant to stand and face the jury. Angela placed her hand on Johnny's elbow as they and Tom rose. The clerk called the jury roll, and asked whether a verdict had been reached. The foreperson, a handsome Hispanic woman, stood and said, yes, the jury had reached a verdict.

The clerk asked, "Announce to the court: is the defendant guilty or not?"

The foreperson cleared her throat, then looked Johnny fully in the eyes. "He is not guilty."

"Not guilty," the clerk said. "So say you all?"

The jurors each stood and confirmed their verdict. The gallery exploded with shouts, cheers and moans until the judge gavelled order. Judge Kerry accepted the verdict, ordered it recorded, and rose. "The defendant is ordered released," he said simply. He banged his gavel once and walked out of court.

Pandemonium resumed.

XII

—

PUNISHMENT

66

THE PARTY IN Carelli's office, arranged as soon as word came up that the jury was coming in, resembled a wake with the State's Attorney as the corpse. People peered at him the way they looked into an open casket, but no one had more than a few words to mumble. Junior staffers took a couple of belts of George's good liquor and slipped away. Mike Kolslovsky sat in a corner with a paper cup of whiskey and kept finding himself grinning, trying to stop when Carelli glared at him. Evelyn Pulaski seemed relieved, but George himself was silent, stunned by the verdict.

Edward Collins came in and shook George's hand. He had a confused, fatuous look on his face, and George moved him along toward the bar. Mario Paglia, the late Jeff's father and a power in the city and county, came in and looked like he wanted to spit in George's face. "What the fuck happened, George?"

"Juries, Mario. No one can predict juries."

"File an appeal. Try the bastard again; get it right."

"Mario, the State can't appeal an acquittal."

"So what about my boy? Does he come back to life?"

"I'm sorry, Mario. We did everything we could."

"Ah," the sad old man said, swiping his hand up and down in a gesture of dismissal. "Forget it, George. Forget everything."

One thing George was sure Paglia intended for him to forget was any thought of becoming lieutenant governor.

Rᴏʙʙʏ O'Dᴡʏᴇʀ ᴀɴᴅ Willy Tolliver rode south on I-95 in Robby's big, silent Mercedes. "You know," Willy said, "right after the judge set the jury off to deliberate, I predicted for Johnny that they'd acquit. I don't know why I felt that."

Robby shrugged. "Maybe it's because you're closer to being what those jurors were than a bunch of hotshot lawyers keeping score of a different game."

"You think the State made its case?"

"Hell, yes. From what I saw myself and read of the trial before we got there, the State proved its case way beyond reasonable doubt. I've seen murderers convicted on far less evidence."

"What do you reckon happened? In that jury room."

"We call it jury nullification. The way the system is supposed to work, the judge lays out the law and tells the jury how to apply it. The jury is supposed to assess the facts. Sometimes juries decide to ignore the judge and the law and apply a standard obvious only to them. Probably there will be interviews with individual jurors over the next few days, and they'll say something like Johnny did what he did but didn't deserve punishment.

"Very often jurors in capital crime cases have to be made to identify with the victims, to fear the defendant might do it to them. George Carelli tried to put that fear into their minds, but Johnny wasn't scary. Johnny was trying to save a life."

"Was there a turning point?"

"Now we know the verdict, which still surprises the hell out of me? I guess Angela's close. 'Johnny did it out of love.' "

"Those two going to be together, I bet."

"Good does come from evil sometimes, Willy."

ANGELA TOOK JOHNNY back to the hospital. He wanted rest and he had no idea what shape his house would be in, and the specialists wanted a couple more days to test and make sure his ulcer was responding to treatment. Angela left at the end of visiting hours; Johnny was already asleep. She wondered how many more days of trial he could have tolerated; she wondered if he would have survived prison.

Angela would use the short time he was in hospital to make sure his house was clean and stocked with food, and to book a vacation for him at the Little Cayman Beach Resort in the Caribbean. She would book the hotel and the scuba diving program for two.

EDWARD COLLINS HOPED the notoriety of the trial might make it easier for him to save his distressed properties and do new deals, but it had the opposite effect. People shied away from him, and eventually a friend, or an ex-friend as it turned out, told him why: he was widely perceived in the community to have set Johnny up, then left him in the lurch. Edward thought this most unfair, but it hastened the slide of his businesses. The banks began foreclosure on the last of his properties, and by June of the following year, Edward had to seek bankruptcy court protection.

Jane Collins discovered that the prolonged anguish of the autumn and winter had given her painting a new urgency, a wild vitality that completely supplanted the conservative, symmetrical pastels of the past. She had a one-woman show at a gallery in Stamford and almost immediately thereafter at a famous gallery on East 57th Street in Manhattan. Paintings she had once given away now sold for tens of thousands of dollars. She was working and happy in her work, but she saw Edward's increasing despair as a distraction. The day he declared bankruptcy she asked him to move out of the house on Beachside Avenue. Fortunately it was in her name. Edward moved to a rented condominium in Fairfield in a building he had built and owned, but was now owned by his ex-bank.

Sally Collins was asked to leave Westport Country Day School because of continuing discipline problems and failing grades. Jane and Edward went to the school together to plead the girl be kept enrolled, Jane most emphatically because she was paying the fees and knew she couldn't control Sally by herself. Sally had refused to speak to her father since the trial.

The school was adamant; Sally had had three suspensions. She was expelled and reentered Staples High School in Westport, where she was promptly suspended for smoking marijuana openly in the school parking lot.

In June, Sally was arrested in Fairfield for offering sex in exchange for crack cocaine to an undercover state police officer. Jane hired Thomas Jackson to defend her at trial, but she was convicted and sentenced to serve eighteen months at Niantic.

GEORGE CARELLI RESIGNED his state post in July and went into private criminal practice. His last act was to arrange the reinstatement of Jamal Jones in the detective bureau. Jamal went back to work, but had no more heart for it. He went to night school to get his teaching certificate. He intended to teach in Bridgeport's hard-pressed public schools. He told Mike he just wanted to help kids.

JOHNNY DIETRICH EMERGED from the hospital, declared well by his doctors but exhausted and disoriented. He was relieved the jury had trusted him and redeemed him, but still unsure of his footing, especially in respect of Angela.

They flew to the Cayman Islands, where they dove every day on Little Cayman's famous towering walls of coral, ate fresh fish and she drank crisp wine and dark rum. He returned very much in love with Angela, and totally confused as to why she seemed to love him in return. He finished *Prometheus,* the novel based on his arrest, incarceration and trial. It was his most successful novel since *House of Pain* and was immediately snapped up for a feature film. He spent a week in New York with Willy Tolliver, then felt the need to return to Angela. Their loving was gentle at first, but became intense beyond either of their previous experience.

Johnny's greatest fear was losing her, yet he saw it coming, because he knew he had to move on, get away from Fairfield and begin a new life where people didn't look sideways at him and whisper behind their hands. He had his big Hans Christian cutter put in the shed at Captain's Cove in Bridgeport, her hull sandblasted and painted, her topsides faired and resprayed, her engine rebuilt. In September he convinced Angela to try cruising with him, and they set out for Newport, Martha's Vineyard and Maine. She loved the heavy, seaworthy boat, the warm windy days and the cool foggy nights.

After they returned to Black Rock, Johnny rigged the self-steering gear, replaced the autopilot and provisioned the boat for an open ocean, single-handed voyage to Antigua in the West Indies with a single stop in Bermuda. He took the sails off and took them to his sailmaker for reinforcement, flushed and filled the freshwater tanks, topped off and stabilized the diesel fuel. He waited through the first cold nights of October, bundled up before the fireplace with Angela. He wanted to ask her to come with him, but he didn't. Tom Jackson had offered her a partnership and she'd said she'd take it. She was sixteen years younger than he was, and she had a life, a good one, a life among men and women. He loved her, but he yearned for the solitude his notoriety had taken from him, that the sea and the distant islands could return.

November came, and early evenings of frost. He closed on the sale of his house and sold his furniture, all except a few favorite items, his computer and his Ford Explorer that he shipped to Antigua. He'd rent something when he got there.

Several members of the old yacht club crowd watched him day-by-day alongside the dock as he adjusted this and tweaked that and filled the boat's capacious lockers with provisions. Some volunteered to sail with him on the delivery, but he sensed they were just as glad to see him off. He wanted the passage to be his alone.

On the sixth of November, the long-range weather forecast cleared of tropical depressions. The tide was right to clear the sound past Block Island, and he'd plotted the Gulf Stream between the U.S. and Bermuda. He topped the tanks again and spent the night aboard tied to the dock, ready to depart before first light to catch the tide. Angela promised to come and see him off; he said it would be awfully early, and almost wished she wouldn't.

He awakened at five A.M. on the seventh, had a ceremonial coffee with the early-departing fishermen and started the motor. He was taking off his dock lines when Angela came down onto the dock, dressed warmly and carrying a brand-new brightly colored sailing bag. He took her in his arms awkwardly around the bag, and kissed her. He felt infinitely sad but had nothing to do for it. "Put the bag aboard," she said.

"What is it?"

"Present."

"Thank you," he said, tossing the bag over the lifelines into the cockpit and climbing over after it. His dock lines were all cast off save one spring he could tend from the boat.

Angela climbed over the lifelines and pushed off. "The bag is my clothes, Captain." She laughed. "The present is us."